Praise for *In High Places*

"Tom Morrisey's best novel to date, *In High Places*, cost me a good night's sleep and a set of chewed-off fingernails. As a young boy's coming-of-age story, it is superb; as a suspense-filled cliffhanger (pardon the pun), it will keep you on the edge of your seat. I found I couldn't put it down until the very last page...."

—Cindy Crosby, faithfulreader.com

"It is rare to find a 'man's man' who knows the human heart, much less one who can write with such a well-balanced combination of sensitivity and adrenaline-charged adventure."

—Athol Dickson, Christy-Award-winning author of *River Rising* and *Winter Haven*

"Beautifully exciting, haunting, and satisfying. Morrisey leaves you hanging by your fingertips."

—Lisa Samson, award-winning author of *The Church Ladies* and *Straight Up*

"Tom Morrisey is a master wordsmith and an expert at weaving gripping stories. If I pick up a book with his name on it, I know I'm going for gold."

—Angela Hunt, author of *Uncharted*

"A great narrative of the hope we have and the journey it takes to find it."

—Alyssa Curry, Christian Book Previews.com

"*In High Places* is not an average coming of age story. It's a story of continued hope and faith made real by the fact that even years later, the narrator continues to struggle with those events..... *In High Places* is my personal pick for best book of the year."

—David White, christianreviewofbooks.com

IN HIGH PLACES

TOM MORRISEY

BETHANY HOUSE PUBLISHERS
Minneapolis, Minnesota

In High Places
Copyright © 2007
Blue Corner Creations, Inc.

Cover design by Studio Gearbox

Scripture quotations are from the King James Version of the Bible.

Published by Bethany House Publishers
11400 Hampshire Avenue South
Bloomington, Minnesota 55438

Bethany House Publishers is a division of
Baker Publishing Group, Grand Rapids, Michigan.

Printed in the United States of America

ISBN   978-0-7642-0467-8

The Library of Congress has cataloged the hardcover edition as follows:

Morrisey, Tom, 1952–
    In high places / Tom Morrisey.
        p.   cm.
    ISBN-13:   978-0-7642-0346-6 (hardcover : alk. paper)
    ISBN-10:   0-7642-0346-0 (hardcover : alk. paper)
    1. Widowers—Fiction. 2. Teenage boys—Fiction. 3. Fathers and sons—Fiction.
4. Loss (Psychology)—Fiction. 5. Rock climbing—Fiction. 6. West Virginia—Fiction.
I. Title.

    PS3613.O776I6   2007
    813'.54—dc22

                                                                    2006038324

For Mary Ann Morrisey:
my mother, my friend and my favorite reader...

And for Char Potts and Jeff Morrisey,
who continue to remind me of the preciousness of family...

And in memory of Thomas J. Morrisey,
still sorely missed after all these years.

For we wrestle not
against flesh and blood, but
against principalities,
against powers,
against the rulers of the
darkness of this world,
against spiritual wickedness
in high places.
    —Ephesians 6:12

And you, my father, there on the sad height,
Curse, bless me now with your fierce tears, I pray.
Do not go gentle into that good night.
Rage, rage against the dying of the light.
    —Dylan Thomas
      "Do Not Go Gentle Into That Good Night"

In any endeavor in which the object is to cheat gravity, prudence—not to mention self-preservation—dictates that provision be made for that statistically inevitable event in which gravity refuses to be cheated. A climbing anchor, whether it be a piece of protection through which the rope passes or a static belay point, provides a necessary element of security, a means of connecting adventurer to firmament, and a way of living to climb another day.

The Eastern Cragman's Guide to Climbing Anchors
(1974)

Friction, opposition, pressure and even gravity are all useful in effecting a hold. Mere willpower is not. An effective handhold or foothold is the product of sound, applied physics and constant and conscientious practice. Form the hold correctly and you will stick, you will progress, you will climb. Form it incorrectly and you will slip and fall. The process is almost brutally Pavlovian.

Rock Climbing Holds and Basics
(1972)

IN HIGH PLACES

Used extensively throughout much of the 19th century and the first half of the 20th, the soft iron piton was extremely malleable and conformed well to irregular fissures, but it was also extremely friable and could crack or deform if not driven with care.

The Eastern Cragman's Guide to Climbing Anchors

ONE

It was not the rock—it was never the rock; it was the air. Air: gusts and threads of it, rustling my hair at the edge of my faded red rugby shirt collar. Air: swaying the thin red climbing rope that dropped beneath me in a single, brief, pendulous loop. Air all around me and above me and behind me, open and empty and unsubstantial, drying the sweat on my dread-paled, beardless face, an entire sea of air, an ocean of it, lying vacantly beneath my jutting, quaking heels.

By fingertips and the thin toes of my shoes, I hung over a deep pool of nothing, a drop one could pass through for an eternity before being swallowed by the bright green, spring-leafed treetops of the Monongahela National Forest.

The Gendarme was an exceptionally airy place, a thirty-foot, twenty-ton, top-heavy block of Tuscarora quartzite, perched tenuously upon the soaring, thin, cloud-feathered notched ridge that joined the twin summits of Seneca Rocks.

From the valley floor, hundreds of feet below, it seemed very nearly insubstantial, a blip in the naked stone skyline, the slightest thin twig of stone. But from its base, it was a gray, orange-lichened obelisk, a tower, soaring high into the stark, blue West Virginia sky.

You didn't step onto the Gendarme; you boarded it, a stretching traverse to the initial foothold, a tentative and overbalanced tiptoe, like stepping into an empty canoe.

Only the Gendarme was built to repel boarders—just fifteen slim degrees of westward tilt separated it from dead vertical. And that very first step left you open and exposed, as hung-out on the rock as one would be after a rope-pitch or two of straight-up conventional climbing.

Still, I felt absolutely ridiculous.

There I was, the sixteen-year-old who'd won four column-inches of praise from the *Toledo Blade* for his junior-varsity football heroics, the cocky kid who'd waltzed up the considerably more challenging Thais face just the afternoon before. I'd climbed much harder routes than this; I'd *styled* much harder routes than this. Yet on this fine, early spring morning, I was clinging to the rock with all the urgency of a terrified primate. My rubber-soled shoes and my two clammy hands were smeared against the climb's rain-worn holds, trying vainly to become one with the rock. I was gripped: frozen into immobility. And I was both of these things less than six feet away from my father.

I could actually turn my head and look him in his calm, brown, crow's-foot-flanked eyes, see the raccoon-in-negative whiteness left there by his sunglasses. Grinning, showing me a row of even, white teeth, he nodded encouragement, his beard brown and blond-streaked and close-trimmed, a bright red bandanna cinched over his hair in the fashion of some time-traveling pirate. Lean and wiry, he clasped the tag end of the rope with all four fingers of his callused and suntanned right hand, ready to lock the belay plate shut and catch me if I slipped so much as an inch.

The Gendarme was a 5.4, a middlingly rated route on the elegantly named Yosemite Decimal System, just three short steps above the Old Ladies' Route that had been my introduction to Seneca Rocks climbing, two long springs and two golden autumns before. Only a 5.4, and only twenty-five feet to the top, but for the way that I felt, it may as well have been twenty-five thousand.

"Take a breath," my father whispered. He *whispered* it, and I heard each word: heard it despite the gusting wind, despite the clinking carabiners on my runner, despite the shrill, distant shrieks of eagles as they rose on towering thermals from the valley floor behind us. "Take a breath and blow it out, shake it off. You're just psyched, a little freaked out, that's all. Come on, Patrick. You can do this."

I could do this.

I knew that he was right. I thought about climbing back at

Whipps Ledges, in Ohio, top-roping the route they called White Pebble. A boulder problem, White Pebble was a bobbing, liquid dance in which the key was to never stop moving. You had to glide up the rock, shifting weight and transferring onto contours so slight that they could be felt, but not quite seen. That was much harder than this; it was graduate-school climbing. But if you fell from White Pebble, it was a four-foot drop onto soft sand, and if you slipped from the Gendarme, well . . .

"Breathe," my father told me again, not whispering now.

I breathed. Closing my eyes, I inhaled slowly, drawing the clean mountain air in through my nose in one long, cooling draught, and then exhaling, my lips pursed. I pictured a candle flame flickering there before my eyes and blew hard enough to move it, but not hard enough to put it out.

I took another breath in exactly the same fashion, the deliberate, yogic breathing that my father had taught me when we'd first gone to the Rocks together, he and my mother and I. Then I did it one more time, and when the breath was all out of me, the exhale squeezed to its dregs, I opened my eyes, and the rock was still there, but the airiness around me was gone.

It was like climbing in a bubble, or a circle of light; like being the escapee in an old-fashioned prison movie, with the searchlight picking out everything within my reach, but blanking all beyond it into nothingness. "The Zone," my father called it, and I was there now, ready to address the task before me.

Legs first. Ignoring the instinct to reach, I stepped up and then stood, straightening my knees until the old handholds were level with my ribs, and only then reaching up for the next.

Moving. I was moving. Moving was good.

I inched up farther, got to a bellying bulge and came to the first bolt, its angled steel hanger in excellent condition. Clipping a carabiner onto my rope, I lifted it to the hanger, slowed, and then stopped.

Its exposure—that overwhelming feeling of airiness on the climb—was not the sole distinguishing feature of the Gendarme.

The ridge that it sat upon wasn't wider than the average city side-walk. And, tilted as it was, narrow at the base and lumpy at the top, the tall block of stone looked absolutely temporary, like a child's building block set on its end, just waiting to topple.

Then there was the icing on the cake, the story that Judd Horton, owner of the general store and gas station down in the village, had told about a moonshiner trying to blast the rock formation off the ridge with dynamite, an act of defiance committed for reasons that became more obscure with each recounting. The story would have been easy to dismiss—most of the "information" that the local people shared about the Rocks took about a ninety-degree departure from reality—except for the fact that the base of the Gendarme, the part that actually sat on the ridge, had cracks running through it that made the Liberty Bell look sound.

Aware that every inch I moved up the rock magnified the stress being placed upon that base—"increased the moment," as my mechanical-engineer father would say—I was hesitant to commit myself by clipping off to the rock. Everybody said that the Gendarme was going to fall someday. It was only a matter of time. And if today was the day, the prospect of going down with it, with the option of leaping clear, was frightening enough. To be forced to ride it into the trees below, fastened to the ancient rock like some berserk and reluctant surfer, sounded all too graphically fatal.

"Go on," my father told me from below. "Clip in. Trust me. You'll feel better."

I moved the carabiner closer. Stopped.

"Patrick," he warned. "You've got twelve feet of rope out. If you don't clip some protection, and you slip, that's a twenty-four foot fall."

Fall to my death or be pulled, I thought. Which sounds better? *The fall. Absolutely, the fall.*

A muted sound, like a small engine turning over but failing to start, drifted up from the belay station.

Laughter. My father was laughing at me. I took a breath, thought about saying something I'd later regret, realized I'd later regret it, and swallowed the comment unspoken.

"Let me guess," he said. "You're worried about the whole climb taking a bomber, am I right?"

The breeze picked up, rocking me. I hesitated.

I nodded.

"And this rock has been sitting here for about what, four hundred million years?" I glanced down and saw my father shaking his head, the red bandanna yawing right, then left, then right again. "But you think that out of all those years, March 28, 1976, is the day it's going to pick to crater? Sport, trust me, it'll never happen. Clip off."

The breeze picked up again. Fifteen feet below, deep within its base, the rock groaned.

"Never mind that. It does that all the time," my father assured me. "Every time I climbed it, at least. Come on, Sport. We've got a long drive ahead of us. Let's top this one off so we can get going, okay? Clip it."

Enough with the "Sport," I thought, but I swallowed that, too. I shook my right hand to coax the blood back into it.

Taking another breath, I thumbed open the gate on the carabiner, clipped it into the bolt hanger, and then flipped the 'biner around so the rope wouldn't open the gate.

"There you go," my father said.

Now I had a reason to climb quickly. I moved up smoothly, keeping three points of contact with the rock at all times, zigzagging slightly across the driveway-wide face as I moved, coming to the next bolt and—in for a penny, in for a pound—clipping off on that, as well. I was beginning to hear noises, the soughing of wind through a nation of distant leaves, a thin susurrus coming from the tree-thick hollow on the far side of the rock. Looking up, I saw why: the summit had come even with my head.

The summit, if you could call it that, was no wider than a dinner plate: tiny and rounded. Eons of thunderstorms had pelted it with their fullest fury, making certain that, at the peak of this pillar of rock, not a single flat plane remained.

But we'd talked about this when I'd proposed the climb over breakfast at the 4U that morning—a short "flash" climb just to get in an hour on the cliffs, and have something to dazzle my mother with when we got back home. I would climb the Gendarme. But even though I'd touched the summit, I hadn't climbed it; not yet, because the climbers who frequented Seneca Rocks had a tradition about the Gendarme.

Just touching the top wasn't enough to complete the climb. Neither was sitting on the bowling-ball-like surface.

You had to stand.

Completely upright.

No hands.

The wind gusted again. If I waited, it would just pick up further.

Not even bothering to clip into the webbing-festooned rappel ring atop the rock, I put both hands on the summit and, like a swimmer raising himself up out of a pool, mantled my way over it.

Glad that we'd stretched before starting, I straightened my arms, brought my right knee up next to my ear, and carefully planted that foot next to my hands. I walked my palms over, set my left foot as flat as the round surface would let me and then, slowly, with both arms out for balance, I stood. Like some tuxedoed maestro finishing his post-performance bow, I straightened up.

Done. The top of the Gendarme was overhung, so I saw no rock, no ledge beneath my summit, just treetops dropping down to a broad, green, wind-brushed valley, far, far beneath my fragile stone perch.

It was like flying.

A patter of applause drifted down from the South Summit, to my left. I looked up and saw some middle-aged folks in flannel shirts—Potomac Appalachian Trail Club members who'd taken any of a dozen or more routes to the rock's true summit. They smiled down at me, gave me thumbs-ups of approval.

Waving back, I bobbled, fought my way back to equilibrium, and felt my face creep red. I looked down at the little five-building village of Mouth of Seneca, at the North Fork wending its way bluely alongside State Route 33, nine hundred feet and then some below. Blue-green mountaintops marched off into the dark, shadowed distance.

"Good climb, Patrick," my father called up. "You styled it. Classy ascent."

"Thanks," I called down. "And, Dad?"

"Yeah?"

"From now on, it's not a summit unless you do this."

Arms out to the side, I drew my right foot up until it rested on my knee, and then stood there, one-legged, crane-fashion.

Fresh applause drifted down from the South Summit.

"Showboat," my father said. He raised his little black Nikkormat one-handed and Kodachromed the moment for posterity.

"That you fellas up there a-climbin' on the Chimbly?" Judd Horton asked. Red-nosed and perennially in need of a shave, he wore his regular uniform of blue jeans, work boots, a once-white T-shirt stretched over his ample belly, and red clip suspenders, the whole outfit topped by a green and yellow John Deere cap. Judd turned the crank that pumped gasoline up into the graduated glass cylinders atop the pumps. His gas pumps, a pair of Texaco antiques, had already been anachronisms for several decades, even back in 1976.

"The Gendarme?" I asked.

"'The John-darm,'" Judd mimicked. "The '*John*-darm.' *Pfft.*"

He spat a viscous brown arc of tobacco that joined the stains of earlier expectorations at the base of the general-store steps. Judd punctuated his sentences with dollops of chewing tobacco, messy mouth-oyster periods at the conclusion of each breath.

"Boy, do you see you any Frenchmen a-walkin' around here? *Pfft.* That there was the Chimbly back before I was borned. That, or the sight to the Gunsight Notch. Or maybe Princess Snowbird, if you want to listen to the Injuns, 'ceptin' there ain't none of them what live 'round here no more. *Pfft.* That there's the Chimbly, and then there's the Old Man, and the Sleeping Bear, and the Rabbit. 'Cept all you city boys have got to come down here and ignore all that wisdom and give 'em your own prissy little names. How would you like it if I was to come up to where you all are from, to Chicago—"

"Toledo."

"Toll-*ee*-doh, Shee-*caw*-go. *Pfft*. Same difference. How'd you like it if I was to come myself up there and started givin' all your-all's streets brand-new names?"

"Well, you get to name it if you were the first to climb it, and—"

"First to climb it? Boy, don't you know nothin'? My granddaddy, my very own flesh and blood, was the very first human being ever to set foot up on top of them ol' rocks. *Pfft*. Why he did it, ain't nobody knows. It's for certain that he didn't never *lose* nothin' up there, but—"

"We filled up yet, Judd?" My father stepped gingerly down the steps, balancing two cold cans of Coke and a grocery bag full of chips and Twinkies.

"Filled up." Judd looked at the gas, still gleaming like gold in the pump's glass cylinder. He shifted his chew to the other cheek, and picked up the hose, walking around to the side of my father's Volkswagen Alpine. "Why, that boy of yours has been standin' here a-talkin' my ear off. Don't you never let him talk at home?"

"Talking his ear off, huh?" My father grinned at me.

"You know me," I told him, nodding. "Absolutely nothing but gab."

I opened the Coke and dropped the pop-top inside, something that would have invited a lecture had my mother been along, but didn't raise so much as an eyebrow from my father. He rested his arms on the VW's big truck-style steering wheel, taking us north on State Highway 28. When I'd been younger, we'd come to Seneca together two, maybe three times a year, usually once in spring and a couple of times in late autumn, because my mother liked the leaves. But now that I could drive, the weekend-warrior excursions had increased to at least once a month, winter included, as long as the forecast didn't call for snow. My father would take us up past the state line, where we'd switch, so the Pennsylvania and Ohio turnpikes—five hours including a stop for burgers and restroom and gas—would be all mine.

"Pretty good weekend, huh?" He looked over at me and smiled. He was wearing his sunglasses, mirrored Ray-Ban Aviators.

"Yeah." I put my stockinged feet up on the VW's rounded metal dash. "I wish Mom could have been here to see the Gendarme."

The little four-cylinder engine in back putted through the following silence, muted by piles of tarps, the tent, two ropes, the rucksacks, and our goose-down jackets and sleeping bags.

"Me, too," my father finally said.

Off to the right, we could see Champe Rocks, stark tan fins of Tuscarora quartzite, the same stone as Seneca, marching halfway up a steep, green hill. We both turned to watch them, running beside us behind the roadside trees. We'd gone there and climbed a few times on holiday weekends, when the big clubs from Cleveland and Pittsburgh brought beginners along and rained loose rock down every pitch at Seneca. Mom had been with us once. I figured I was probably the only teenager in Toledo with a mother who could lead a 5.7 on sight.

We rounded a curve and Champe faded from view.

"Dad."

"Uh-huh?"

"You know, I'm not a little kid anymore."

"Absolutely. Not with the leads you were cranking out this weekend."

"So?"

He turned, the mirrored glasses reflecting twin images of me, of the window and the rolling countryside behind me.

"What?"

"You know," I said. "What about you and Mom?"

"What about us?"

"Dad." I shook my head. "You know what." I wanted to shoot

him a look, but couldn't bring myself to look at him as I said, "I just want to know if things are going to be okay between the two of you. That's all."

My father straightened up gradually and the VW slowed.

"Man." He tapped the big steering wheel twice. "Of all the things that you could worry about when you're sixteen years old, that should so not be one of them." He shook his head. "What have we done, your mother and I?"

He pulled us off onto an overlook and stopped the van.

"We're going to be fine," he told me, slipping the tall, skinny shifter into neutral, letting the engine idle. He turned my way, sunglasses still hiding his eyes. "It's not what you think, Sport. Really. I know she's out of sorts lately, but it's not anything between her and me. Well, not really."

"Then what is it?"

He looked out the window.

"It's the school stuff," he said. "Or not so much the school stuff, per se, as the fact that she's still there now, in school, just finishing her bachelor's, and all the friends she started out with back when she was a freshman are doctors and tenured professors by now. Doing life, instead of school. That's what she's always wanted, you know. She's not one of those people who make a career out of being a student. She wants to write criticism, to teach. But something happened back when we were both undergrads, and only one of us could finish up with college right away, so I did that, so I could get a good job, support us, and she had to wait. Then I had the chance to do night school up at Michigan for my master's, and that meant a pay raise when I finished, so she waited again."

"Me."

"Huh?"

"The thing that happened," I said, the tightness in my temples coming out as a stiffness in my voice. "It was me, wasn't it?"

"Patrick."

Involuntarily, I squinted, my eyes going hot. Hot and damp.

"It was. Don't make up some story. You know it was."

A subtle metamorphosis came over my father. He seemed to stiffen. But he seemed to shrink, as well. And he said nothing.

"So why have me?" My voice was much too loud for a conversation at front-seat distance. "Why? They had abortions back then, didn't they?" The words just ran out of me, like a spill. Like a gush.

My father gazed at me, straightened back up.

"Yeah, they had them." He turned, facing the view. "But you had to go out of state, to New York, to get one, and even then it was kind of shady, you know? And I'll level with you, Sport. I wanted her to get one. Wow. I hate myself for having wanted it, but I did. I mean, I was twenty, she was nineteen, and pretty and young, straight blond hair, and beautiful, and I wanted her to stay that way. Not forever, but for a while longer. I was selfish; I wanted someone for me, not someone for a family. But then she asked me, 'What if this is our only chance?' And you know what? She was right."

I sat there, tossing words back and forth in my head, like loose change, like cards: *I wanted her to get one.*

"And even if she hadn't been," he said, turning back to me and taking off the Ray-Bans, his brown eyes moist. "What are the chances that we'd get anybody halfway near as cool as you the second time around? I mean, most of the guys I work with, they can't even talk to their kids. But you . . .man. Talk about great karma. Patrick, your mother loves you. Loves you like crazy. So do I."

I nodded, my lips tight. As in every case in which I had blown up at my father, my mother, I wanted to call my hot words back. But I couldn't. They were gone, like the distant wind ruffling the treetops.

My father put the glasses back on.

"That's the biggest part of it," he said. "There's a her-me part, as well; you're right there. I'm spending too much time at work. I'm probably spending too much time down here. Not giving her the attention she deserves. Like that patio. I promised it would be ready by what? Easter? And it's not finished yet. Hittin' the rocks instead of layin' the bricks. That doesn't help any. That's for sure."

I drew a breath in through my nose, held it, and let it out slowly, calming myself. Trying not to be obvious about it.

"Next weekend," I finally said.

"Huh?"

"Next weekend. You and me. We'll build her that patio. Have it ready two weeks early."

My father looked at me, eyebrows arched.

"Sport, you're sixteen years old," he said. "Don't you have friends to hang out with?"

"I do." I nodded. "But next weekend, if they want to hang out with me, they're going to be over at our house, laying bricks. Because that's where I'll be. Deal?"

He grinned.

"Okay," he said. "Deal." And we shook on it. "And then, the weekend after next, we'll come back down here. The three of us: you, your mom and I. She can bring her books if she wants to, but she's coming along. I don't want her to just hear about you and the Gendarme. I want her to see it. Agreed?"

"Agreed."

But it never did happen that way. Because we never came back to the Rocks together.

Not the three of us.

Not with my mother.

Formed of hard chrome-molybdenum steel, the Bugaboo style of piton

has long been a standard for extended backcountry routes,

but leaves a permanent scar when removed.

The Eastern Cragman's Guide to Climbing Anchors

TWO

At least we weren't the ones who found her. I've often wondered which one of us it would have damaged worse if we had—my poet-engineer father, or me: his coddled and protected only son.

But that's moot, because it was a neighbor, Dr. Marion, my mother's classical-literature professor, who came home after brunch at Churchill's on Sunday morning, and saw the blue-gray exhaust vapor creeping out from under our closed garage door.

And it was Dr. Marion who had been watching by his window when we pulled into our driveway past nine that Sunday evening.

Our house was a white, two-story Italianate, unremarkable in Toledo's historic Old West End. We hadn't finished wondering about the fact that there wasn't a single light showing anywhere in it when the old professor was there at the curb. First he came to my side and then, when he saw that I was driving, he scuttled around to my father's side and opened the door, tugging him out to the slim, dark lawn of the parkway, whispering urgently. Except that, from half-deaf Dr. Marion, even a whisper was like normal conversation, and I heard every word.

He blurted it out awkwardly, an odd departure for a normally fastidious man, except, of course, there wasn't really a way to tell a person such a thing gracefully. And I was glad that he did it the way he did, raised voice and awkwardness and all, because it spared my father the agony of having to repeat the whole thing to me.

"So you were where, again?"

We were still dressed in what we'd worn for the drive back home: I in my painter's pants and rugby shirt, and my father in his acrylic warm-up pants and one of those Yosemite Mountaineering School *Go climb a rock* T-shirts.

The Toledo police detective wasn't doing much better. A portly black man in his early forties, he was in a shirt and tie, but the shirt had the look of something fished out of a hamper for the late evening call, and the tie, jacket, and trousers all appeared to belong to other outfits. He had a five o'clock shadow, now six hours past its namesake.

"Seneca Rocks," I told him, because my father had fallen mute.

"That's the name of the town, Seneca Rocks?"

"No. The town is Mouth of Seneca."

"'Mouth of . . .'" He looked up from his pad. "What kind of name for a town is *Mouth*?"

"It's where a creek enters a river," my father muttered. "The town sits where Seneca Creek enters the North Fork of the south branch of the Potomac River. So it's at the mouth of the Seneca."

"Humph." The detective made a note. "Learn somethin' new every day. You tell anybody you were going?"

"I told Laurie," my father said. That was my mother's name: Laurie.

"I mean, besides her. For emergencies."

"We were going rock climbing," my father told him. "We figured that if anyone was going to have an emergency, it'd be us."

"Okay. That makes sense. Anybody see you down there?"

"Climbing friends. John Markwell was down this weekend."

"You got a number for this Markwell, Mr. Nolan?"

"No," my father muttered. "I had one for him in Columbus, but that's where he lived five, six years ago."

My father lost his thousand-yard gaze and turned to look at the policeman.

"These questions," he asked the detective, "do they . . . are you saying there was foul play?"

"No, sir. Not at all. But they help rule it out—show I'm being diligent. Doing my job."

"Okay. Sorry."

"Understood, sir. Understood."

"Judd Horton." I turned to the detective as I said it.

"Pardon?"

"Judd Horton will know that we were down there. We stayed in his campground, bought gas from him."

"Got the credit-card receipts?"

"Judd doesn't take plastic," my father said. "That's way too twentieth century for him. But he keeps a notebook, a register of who's paid in the campground. And he'll remember my van. You can get his number from information: Seneca Rocks General Store."

"That'll work," the detective said. "Just a couple more questions, and I'll get out of here and let you people get some sleep."

My father raised his head just enough to peer out from beneath his eyebrows.

"I'm sorry, Mr. Nolan." The detective lifted his hands, dropped them. "I wasn't thinking. But well, we went through here pretty thoroughly when we were here earlier."

"I saw the door," my father muttered.

"Yes, sir. We'll pay for that."

"I didn't mean—"

"No offense taken, sir. Don't mention it. It's just that, well, we looked all over, here, in the car, and in her purse, and we didn't find any sort of note. Did we overlook something? You find anything?"

My father kept his head down. His shoulders shook.

"We didn't see anything," I finally said. I remember feeling funny about that, how I could talk when my father could not. But there was this detachment that had come over me, as if none of what was happening was real. It was like being in a play. "We didn't really look."

"Understood."

"Sir," I asked him. "If you're looking for a note, isn't it possible she didn't do this on purpose? I mean, maybe she just forgot to open the garage door when she started the car, and the exhaust just . . . You know: got to her."

"Son," the detective said, his voice soft, even. "You're a young man. You don't want to be going into all of this. Not at your age."

"No." My father said it quickly. He looked up, his eyes red. "Patrick's old enough. He can know."

"Okay." The detective nodded. He took a long breath. "Carbon monoxide poisoning—that's for sure what happened. The lady had all the signs—cherry-red lips, red moons in her fingernails. Well, something like that takes time. It doesn't get you just like that." He snapped his fingers. "She would have had plenty of time to push a button on the garage door opener. She could even have just gotten out and walked back in the house, through the door, if the opener wasn't working, although it was—we tested it with her remote control. But it would have taken fifteen, twenty minutes, maybe half an hour to get to her. She was sitting with the windows rolled up—"

"But the windows," I interrupted. "Doesn't that prove it wasn't intentional?"

The detective shook his head.

"People doing it, uh, this way they often have the windows up," he said. "Carbon monoxide is odorless, but engine exhaust isn't. Plus, the exhaust stings your throat and eyes, makes you cough. I guess it seems to them that rolling up the windows makes things more tolerable while you . . . uh, you know, while you . . ."

He didn't say "wait." He just stopped talking.

The clock ticked on our living room mantle, next to my parents' wedding picture.

"And then there's the way she was dressed," the detective said.

My father looked up again. "How's that?"

The detective consulted his notebook.

"'Light blue cashmere sweater, pleated gray wool skirt, pearls with matching earrings, flesh-tone hose and patent pumps,'" he read. "And her nails were freshly polished. Hair done. Face done. Did your wife always dress that way, Mr. Nolan?"

My father looked at me vacantly.

"No," I told the policeman. "I've never seen Mom in that skirt except for when she and Dad went to company parties—the AMC Christmas reception, things like that. She usually wears slacks.

Either slacks or jeans, maybe even overalls if she was going to the library. And nail polish? Wow. She hardly ever wears nail polish."

"What did she wear to church?"

"We don't go," my father said.

"Not even Christmas or Easter?"

"Never."

The detective made a note.

"The clothing's another sign, then," he said, not looking at either of us as he spoke. "A thing like this, a lot of folks will dress up for it. They think it makes it better for whoever finds them. And not to judge you in any way, sir, but church folks often go to their pastor when they're feeling overwhelmed. Folks without a church? Well, when things get tough, they sometimes just don't see any other way out."

The clock filled the silence again for a long time, its even ticks echoing off the high ceiling and the polished wooden floor. Finally, the detective cleared his throat.

"Is there somebody you can call to come stay with you?"

"Laurie's and my families are both out East," my father told him.

"Maybe friends or co-workers?"

"Detective, Patrick and I need each other," my father said. He straightened up; it was an effort for him—I could tell. "We're depressed, but not depressed enough to . . . Well, I think I know where you're going with this and, trust me—we'll be fine."

"Okay. I'll be going, then. And, Mr. Nolan?"

"Yes?"

"The cause of death," the detective said, not really looking at either of us. "That'll be up to the medical examiner, of course. But without a note, well, he's not supposed to speculate. So in a case like this, I can pretty much assure you that it will probably just be ruled an accidental death."

My father looked at him, his face blank.

"I just thought I should tell you," the detective said. "That way, there won't be any trouble."

"Trouble?"

"With the insurance, sir."

The sky outside my bedroom window was graying and birds were beginning to sing when I gave up on trying to sleep. I should have been exhausted after the long drive and the even longer night, and I was, but sleep would not come to extinguish my fatigue.

So I got out of bed, pulled on the same painter's pants I'd worn the day before and opened my bedroom door with exaggerated stealth, trying to avoid even the suggestion of sound. I did not suspect for a moment that my father slept. I knew full well that he probably lay on his bed with his mind filled with the same dread, the same images that had flooded mine for the past several hours: my mother closing her eyes and breathing in the essence of death, her body on the cold metal finality of a coroner's table. What would they have done to her in the autopsy? Had they even clothed her after they were done? One cannot sleep with thoughts such as that still fresh in one's mind. One can barely even breathe. But I did not want to see my father while my head was still aching, my eyes dully fevered from lack of sleep.

Walking at the edge of the hall where I knew there were no loose joists to creak, setting each foot down on the outside of the heel and then rolling carefully to the ball of the foot—I had read somewhere that this was how Indians stalked silently—I went downstairs, into the kitchen and then into the small pantry that adjoined it. I stopped at the door at the end of the pantry: the door to the garage.

I stood there for a moment, my hand on the doorknob, and thought how wonderful it would be if, just by wishing it, I could turn back the clock to a time when my mother still lived on the far side of that door. I thought how marvelous it would be if I could rush in, open the door and carry her out, still breathing.

Because I could carry her. I knew that. Just the Christmas before, as she had stood in our big kitchen trying to dress me down for filching cookies off a platter before a holiday party, I had lifted her up in my arms and spun and spun until the two of us had dissolved in laughter.

I thought how much more marvelous still it would have been if I could have talked to her before she had ever stepped into the garage. If I could have listened to her, because we had talked not nearly enough, and I had listened—really listened—even less.

I thought about that, and more. Then I turned the doorknob and stepped into the dark, still garage.

I did not touch the light at first. I just stood there, sensing the empty space all around me. No doubt it was only my imagination, but it seemed to me that I could detect the barest hint of exhaust scent in the air, even though I knew that the police and the fire-and-rescue personnel would have ventilated the place thoroughly.

I went back to the door and flipped the box-mounted light switch, bringing to life the single 60-watt bulb hanging in the center of the garage.

With the light on, the space looked oddly empty. The police had towed my mother's car so they could look at it for . . . well, I wasn't really sure what they were looking for. But my mother had driven the Jeep so rarely that I'd grown accustomed to seeing it parked in there. Removed, it left an emptiness, a gap.

Still, I was drawn into the center of that space, the same way people are drawn to place flowers and crosses at roadsides where their loved ones perished in highway accidents. There is something about death that makes a spot different. There is something that makes it holy.

I stood, then, in that empty space and tried to imagine what it would have been like to leave one's life behind in such a dreary, utilitarian place. Two-car garages were almost unknown in the Old West End; ours had room for just one car, and the Jeep, being newest, had won the right to spend its evenings indoors. About six feet of space adjoined the place allotted for the car, and that was taken up by a walk-behind lawn mower, some bicycles, and various other odds and ends that could be kept outside the house, but still required protection from the elements.

Walking to where the driver's seat would be when the Jeep was parked there, I paused, trying to feel some presence, some last lingering energy. Standing there, looking straight ahead, my gaze fell naturally on a shelf on the back wall and one of the things on it: a small birdhouse. I went to it and took it off the shelf.

As birdhouses go, it was unremarkable: a wren house in plain, unfinished red cedar, the wood slightly silvered after several seasons outdoors. It was on the shelf because my mother never hung it under the garage eave near our back door until after March had ended, after most of the threat of snow and spring storms had passed.

That she ever got occupants for the house—and she did every year—was a wonder to me, because it seemed to me that April was too late to be hanging wren boxes in Toledo. But she did, and then every October she took the house down and put it on this shelf, because the house was precious to her, not because of its pedestrian workmanship, but because the house was a gift: a gift from me.

"When I see it, I think of you," she had told me one time when I'd asked why the birdhouse had not been put up yet. *"So I take care of it, because I always want to see it."*

I turned the house over in my hands. What was it that the police detective had said about ending one's life in such a fashion? *"Something like that takes time."* I wasn't sure how much time, but fifteen or twenty minutes sounded logical. Maybe even longer.

I felt the hole of the birdhouse worn smooth by the countless comings and goings of its seasonal occupants. I looked at the shelf, then back at where the car had been.

Yes. Sitting in the car, sitting behind the driver's wheel, one's gaze would naturally have fallen upon this shelf. Upon the little wooden birdhouse.

"When I see it, I think of you."

And it seemed to me that she must have seen it, might even have stared at it for a quarter of an hour or more while the gases burned her eyes and clawed at her throat. Yet that quarter-hour meditation upon her only son had apparently not been sufficient to convince her to press the garage door opener, leave the car, step out into the fresh spring air, and live.

A small, lapping wave of regret was followed by a huge, churning breaker of anger. Raising the birdhouse head-high, I threw it at the concrete floor as hard as I could, only half hearing the cracking wood over my choking and my sobs. I picked it up and threw it again, my eyes hot with tears, and then did it a third time, breaking it into several splintered pieces.

Now regret rolled onto the shore, and I sank to my knees, gathering the splintered pieces and trying to reassemble them, but the little birdhouse was dashed to kindling, smashed beyond repair. My sobs seemed to emanate from my heart, and I looked to the door that communicated with the house, certain that my father would be there any moment, wondering what all the noise was about, but he did not show and I realized that he must have finally managed to fall asleep.

The trash can sat in the corner, and I lifted the galvanized top carefully and dropped the broken bits of birdhouse inside. Then I took a broom from the garage wall, wiped my running nose on the back of my hand, and set to work, trying to clean up the mess. Trying to set things in order.

THREE

We can stop our lives, but we cannot end them. That duty inevitably
falls to the relatives. And over the next four days, my father and I
attended to details that neither of us wished to contemplate, but
somebody had to take care of.

We didn't even own a cemetery plot. My mother was thirty-five
years old—who'd ever have thought that we would need one? So we
saw to that, plus the uncomfortable duty of selecting a funeral home
in a city where our family had never lost anyone before. And then
there was the business of the casket, the vault, the clothes.

The clothes. The detective had been right—except for an evening gown that she'd worn once to an AMC President's Reception
two autumns earlier, my mother had died wearing the dressiest
clothes in her adult-college-student wardrobe. There'd even been
talk about getting back what she'd been wearing from the coroner's
office and having it dry-cleaned. But in the end, I'd driven to Southwyck, the new mall down by the Turnpike, and bought a dress for
her to wear into eternity. I checked the label on the evening gown,
and bought the second-best one I could find in that size, a cotton
print that looked sunny and summery. The very best one had been
on sale, and somehow, that just hadn't seemed right. So I went with
the runner-up and paid for it with my father's American Express
card, shamelessly forging his signature, knowing he would have
signed for it himself had he been up to that particular errand.

Dr. Marion had positively identified my mother for the police
"at the scene," as they put it, so my father had been spared a trip to
the morgue. And that meant that the first time he or I saw her again
was at the funeral home, in the "family time," an hour before visi-
tation.

The last time we'd laid eyes on her, it had been over dinner the Friday before. We'd had pizza, Domino's carry-out that my father had picked up on the way home from his office at the Jeep plant. All of our gear had been packed into the VW the evening before, and he'd wanted to get going as soon as we could. So it had been a hurried meal. My mother had brought her Norton Anthology with her to the dining room table, and she'd been wearing an old University of Toledo Rockets sweatshirt, and her hair had been up in a messy bun, the way she did it when she put it up one-handed. She'd had on the reading glasses that she'd gotten just the winter before. They made her look quaint, comfortable. And when we finished, we bolted for the back door, my father and I, stooping to kiss her as we passed. Mine hadn't even been a real kiss—only the barest graze against her cheek.

So I wasn't prepared for the way she looked in the casket. She appeared rested. Unharried. The crow's-feet from the squint she'd developed in the months before the glasses were all gone, her temples smooth and soft. And her blond hair was pulled back simply, not a strand out of place, revealing the nape of her neck and the curves of her earlobes. Her lips were pursed and touched in a peach color that suited her, and her cheeks held a blush that looked positively girlish.

I have never had vertigo while climbing, but I had it then, standing before that coffin-length, torchiere-flanked alcove in the funeral home. Because my mother was radiant. Breathtakingly so. And I just hadn't been ready for that.

I'd been to other visitations—for a great-grandmother, a grandfather, an elder great-uncle on my father's side. But all those had been people well into their cotton-haired years, natural to the encapsulating finality of the casket. My mother's wake, on the other hand, was the first, and perhaps the only time, I had ever seen anyone *beautiful* lying in such an awful thing.

The funeral home, uncertain of our spiritual leanings, had placed a kneeler at the casket's open end, and I grabbed it for support, steadying myself until the dizziness passed. My father put his hand on my shoulder, and we stood there for perhaps five minutes before he finally gave me a squeeze with that firm, strong hand and said, "Thanks, Sport. You picked out a really nice dress."

Then they took us into a side room and gave us refreshments—I'd never realized they did that for immediate family—and after that the visitors arrived, my father's family, and my mother's, and legions of people from the university, from American Motors, and from the Old West End preservation societies that my mother had served so faithfully.

People mean well at visitations, but it's painful, nonetheless. They talked about my mother's generosity, not only with contributions to causes, but with her time—how she would stop and listen to anyone, even to the most wild-eyed, militant vegetarian, *Little Red Book*-waving anarchists who frequented the university quad. They talked about her dedication to her studies—how they would see her in the library, absolutely slumped over her books, immune to whispered hellos. There was the department secretary she'd brought soup to, the elderly neighbor she helped out with the shopping. And every time I heard the stories, each sentence was punctuated in my grief-numbed, teenaged mind with not a period, but two words: *never again.*

"And she was such a stitch," one of her classmates told me. "Our Pound professor, Professor Stock? We had his class at seven in the morning—bright and early—and one morning, while he was reading from that book he has coming out this year, Laurie turns my way and she just about falls out of her chair, like she couldn't have stayed awake another minute. She was so convincing! I would have sworn that she was going to hit the floor!"

That hadn't sounded like my mother. She was careful, considerate; I never would have thought she would have it in her to mock. Besides, she liked Professor Stock, and admired his work; we'd even had him over for dinner. And I guess my face must have shown it, because the woman had stopped telling the story, muttered something about, "Guess you would have had to be there," and walked off to find a more appreciative audience.

The funeral was easy by comparison. All we had to do was show up. We held it at the mortuary, as neither my father nor my mother had grown up with a church. Her undergraduate advisor delivered the eulogy, a sad litany of my mother's tremendous but unused potential. One of her classmates read a poem that she had written.

It was the next days, after we'd seen the relatives off to Metcalf Field and up to Metro Airport, outside Detroit, that were the hardest. I stayed home all week from school, and my father's supervisor called and told him to take all the time that he needed. So I heard him in the book-lined study that he and my mother had shared, making phone calls, filing the insurance claim, closing my mother's charge accounts, settling her affairs at school.

And the phone calls we got were just as bad—people asking if they could "do anything," people calling and then not knowing what to say. I tried to take most of those, to spare my father any fresh abrasion to the wound. One was a call from a receptionist at a doctor's office, phoning to verify an appointment. I told her what had happened and she was still stammering as I hung up, and I remember standing there, my hand still on the receiver, thinking that, just a few days before, my mother had been a vital, warm being, with classes and luncheons and doctors' appointments. The house was filled with nothingness: with empty pockets of air, exactly her shape and her size.

But while I could beat my father to the phone—most of the time—he insisted on being John Wayne about wrapping up the loose ends.

"Dad," I told him. "You don't have to do this all in one day."

"I know," he said. "But I'd like it to be over."

"Then let me help. Let me make some of the calls."

He shook his head.

"No, Sport. I've put way too much on your shoulders already."

And he wouldn't be moved from that.

Just before lunch, I was outside the study door when I heard him calling the AMC Jeep dealer up on Central Avenue.

"That's right," he was telling them. "It's in the police impound lot . . . No, not damaged at all. Just like it came off the lot . . . I think eight hundred miles; if it's not that, it won't be much more . . . Uh-huh, like I told you—just like new . . . Yes, I've called them and cleared it for you to pick it up. And could I ask you a favor? When you go through and detail it, could you save anything that you find for me? Personal items, receipts, anything like that? I'll be by next week to pick those up, and you can give me the check at the same time."

He hung up and I heard him turning the pages on the phone book. I knocked on the doorframe.

"Dad?"

He turned.

"Hey, Sport. What's up?"

"Mom's Jeep. Her Wagoneer. You're selling it?"

"Don't worry. I know you'll be needing wheels. We'll find you something."

"No. It's not that. It's just your job."

"What about it?"

"Well . . ." I felt funny, talking to my father about this. "Isn't there a rule or something? That we have to have something new made by American Motors? Because you're a manager?"

"Yeah," my father said, nodding. "AMC, GM, Ford, Chrysler—all the car companies are that way. A new one every two years. But they won't get on my case about this. Not right away, at least. And I just couldn't . . ."

His voice choked.

"I know," I said.

Then we just sat there, silent.

We didn't work on the patio the next weekend. We packed my mother's things. Her clothes. Her books. The files of term papers, some half written. The underwear from her dresser. A little perfume sachet she kept in that drawer, the scent of which seemed to stun my father into frozen silence. There was the envelope that my father had brought home from Northland Jeep, and the manila packet marked PERSONAL EFFECTS that the funeral home had conveyed to us from the medical examiner's office. Both went unopened and uninspected, into a cardboard box, because this was a time of burial, rather than resurrection.

In all it had taken just fourteen sturdy corrugated boxes begged from Collingwood Water to pack up my mother's life. We put a few mothballs into each one, to keep the mice out, and then taped the seams shut and moved them out to the garage. After that, we went to Tony Packo's for a late Saturday dinner, but even Hungarian hot dogs and the Cakewalkin' Jass Band weren't enough to lift the clouds that had settled around us.

I went back to Scott High School the following week, the old brick building suddenly alien to me, because I'd had a mother the last time I'd walked its halls. My teachers were overly solicitous, my classmates mute in my company. I felt like a creature wrapped in cotton, a frail object being passed from hand to hand with exaggerated care.

My father, on the other hand, got out of bed that Monday only long enough to call his office and tell them that he had things to attend to regarding the estate. Then I saw him walk back up the stairs, still in his robe, and the next day he did not leave his bed at all.

When by Thursday he was still unshowered and unshaved, and would have gone unfed had I not baked two TV dinners, I was beginning to wonder who I should call. My aunts and uncles were all in Massachusetts and Vermont, and my grandmother—my father's mother—lived alone and did not travel well.

Then, the following Monday, I awoke early to the smell of bacon, and there he was in the kitchen, dressed in chinos and a sweater, putting breakfast on the table, pouring himself a second cup of coffee.

"Thanks," I said, as he set eggs and hash browns in front of me. My mother had always made do with cereal; it was the first hot breakfast I'd seen in the house since Christmas. I looked at the pants and sweater and asked, "Aren't you going in to Jeep today?"

"Jeep? No, not today," he said. "Maybe in a week or two. I'm going to run the vacuum and straighten up in here a little, make it look less like a bachelor's pad."

And when I got home from school that afternoon, I could see he'd been as good as his word. The house smelled of Murphy's Oil Soap and Lemon Pledge, the parquet floors gleamed, my mother's Oriental rugs had the deep color of a vacuumed nap, and the mantle and windowsills were wiped, not a speck of dust anywhere. There were even clean sheets on my bed, and the clutter on my desk had been set in order.

I looked for him to thank him, but the door to the study was closed and I could hear his voice—not words, but his voice—coming through the oaken door. Talking on the phone. To whom, I wasn't sure, but I didn't really care. All that mattered was that he had come back from the funk that had come over him, and it was good to have him back.

Then the next week was the Easter break. I was home and I'd even asked my father if he felt up for a West Virginia run, but he'd just frowned and said, "Spring break? No. Too many drunks and newbies. We'll get there plenty, later in the year."

So I stayed home, running the lawn mower and trimming the hedges, taking care of those chores without being asked, because it seemed important to do them that way.

And all through the week, we got packages, some small, some nothing but padded envelopes, others large as a suitcase. And I recognized the names: Edelrid, Mammut, E.B., Forrest Mountaineering, CMI, Lowe Alpine Systems, The North Face, Kelty, Chouinard Equipment, Mountain Safety Research, Dolt. Every maker of climbing gear that I'd ever heard of was sending packages to our house. And letters, too. The mailman was leaving number-ten envelopes bundled up with rubber bands, thick bricks of correspondence all addressed to my father.

By the end of that week I was convinced he was about to head off to the Hindu Kush. Then Friday came and he took us for Mexican food to Loma Linda, out on Airport Highway. And over dessert, the mystery was solved.

"I'm quitting Jeep," my father told me as he set his fried ice cream aside.

"GM?" I asked tentatively. General Motors had often been the subject of dinner conversation at our house over the years—they were rumored to pay their engineers more than Ford, Chrysler, or AMC. But going to GM probably meant moving north, to Detroit. That had always stopped any further consideration before.

"No," he said. "Not GM. Not any of them. I called Judd Horton last week."

"You're going to work for Judd Horton?"

My father snorted.

"No!" He laughed again. "But you know that building next to his, only at right angles to it, facing his turnout?"

"Like a shed," I said, picturing it.

"Sort of," my father agreed. "A big shed. He's agreed to lease it to me for a song. Lease with an option to buy."

"To use as. . . ?"

"A climbing shop." He smiled. "I've been going through samples; I have the basic gear selections all worked out."

I felt the ends of my face migrate in opposite directions: eyebrows up, jaw down.

"Listen, Patrick," my father said hurriedly, seeing my reaction. "I know what it's like to be sixteen. I know you'll be able to play varsity next year, and you'll want to be around your friends. So I've talked with Herb Streator, at Jeep—you know his son; he goes to Scott, too. And if you don't want to move down to West Virginia right away, then Herb says—"

"Dad."

". . . that you can stay with him until you've finished high school. Now don't worry about—"

"Dad."

". . . imposing, because, I mean, Herb said it wasn't necessary, but I told him I'd pay your room and board, and give you spending money, and—"

"Dad!" I put my hand on his arm.

"Yes?"

"When?" I asked him.

"When what?"

"When," I asked, "do we move?"

A turn or two of plain white adhesive tape—the type that athletes refer to as "coach's tape"—can protect the knuckles and prevent or delay pain further along the route.

Rock Climbing Holds and Basics

FOUR

"I don't know," I told my father, very nearly shouting so he could hear. "I just can't see the use of stocking double ropes. I mean, Seneca's got roofs, but most people here do pretty direct routes, so rope drag is just not that big an issue, you know? When I think of climbing with two ropes, I think of the Shawangunks."

"True." My father nodded. At least I thought he nodded. All I could really see were the soles of his boots, his foreshortened back, a bit of his bandanna and the bright red climbing rope arcing down into my hands. "But a lot of the guys who come here climb in the 'Gunks, as well."

"Then they can buy their double ropes up in New Paltz. We should carry gear for what we climb, right here. No full lines—pick and choose what's best. Let people come to depend on us having exactly the right gear for our local rock. Besides, that way we're not stuck with something we can't sell."

"So . . ." He glanced over his shoulder at me. "No ice hammers? No axes? No crampons?"

"Ice gear is different," I told him. "People dream with ice gear. They stoke up for their trips out West. We can sell ice gear."

"But they don't dream about the Shawangunks, huh?" My father leaned back and glanced at the next few feet of grayish-tan quartzite. "Okay, I'm going to have to move here. Give me some slack."

"You sure? Your last piece is about ten feet down."

"I'll put in a Stopper right after the crux," he told me. "You ready? I'm moving."

The name of the climb was "Shipley's Shivering Shimmy"—but everybody just called it "Triple S." It had been put up back in 1960, and in an age when most Seneca climbers had been in their twenties or thirties, it had first been free-climbed by a teenager. But it was considered one of the all-time classics at Seneca.

Triple S followed a dihedral, which is to say it ran up the joining seam of a corner, where the Cockscomb, one of the main features visible from the valley floor, intersected at right angles with The Face of a Thousand Pitons. This was a wall full of vertical cracks, where the U.S. Army's 10th Mountain Division, practicing for the invasion of Sicily back in World War II, had left a virtual blacksmith's-shop worth of ironware pounded into the slightly overhung cliff.

But although stepping on or grabbing a piton might have been acceptable to the European climbers of the seventies, it was considered by American rock climbers to be a most severe breach of form, one that blemished the integrity of the climb. And even if it were not, none of the 10th Mountaineering's pins had been left in a position that would be of any help on the crux—the most difficult portion—of Triple S.

The climb was one hundred twenty feet, which made it short enough to be done in a single pitch-one rope length, but long enough to be thought of as *sustained*. And one of the reasons it was considered a classic was because the crux came in just the right place: in the last twenty feet of the climb.

Exactly where my father was.

I was leaning back against our rucksack on the sloping ledge at the bottom of the route, my sit-harness clipped off at the back into a sling around a pine tree. The anchor was designed to keep me from launching heavenward should my father plummet from the route and load the rope. And the rucksack was there because it carried our extra gear—water bottles, sweaters, and rope for rappelling—and because I'd arranged the sweaters and rope inside so it was comfortable behind my back, the rock climber's equivalent of a La-Z-Boy.

Leaning back, I could see my father a hundred feet above me, his legs splayed out like the letter Y, stemming out to both faces of the corner, with the Hexentrics, Stoppers and quick-draws on his rack hanging from his hips like metal-tipped icicles. From the front of the swami belt around his waist, the red rope dropped vertically, passing through a succession of carabiners at the end of sling-lengthened protection placements until it got to the lowest one, where it drooped at an angle over to me and into the smaller hole of the eight-ring I used as a belaying device. As my father tilted his head to peer up the route, I could see the tension in his leg muscles, the royal-blue T-shirt bought one size too large—much neater than his scruffy tan canvas shorts—and the trademark bandanna that he wore to keep the small rocks and grit out of his hair.

Almost automatically, I did what he'd drilled into me from the day of my very first climb. I ran through my options of what to do if he fell and could not continue.

On the bottom half of the route, the primary option was simple—let the rope out slowly and lower him off. But high up, that was no longer an option. The rope wasn't long enough to get him all the way down from up there. So in the case of a disabling fall at this point, I would have to secure the climbing rope, using prussick knots to take the stress off the belay, and then solidly tie off the end with a figure-eight on a bight 'binered into the anchor.

After that, I could free-climb Old Ladies—a beginner's route on which we seldom took a rope, anyhow—establish a single-rope rappel from the top of Triple S, rap down, tie my father off into the end of the rappel line, and then bring him down using a body belay.

So I had options.

It felt good, knowing that.

Because it wasn't a purely academic exercise, planning a rescue. On weekends, Seneca's crags might be crowded with dozens of climbers, but on this weekday afternoon in early May, my father and I were the only two people on the Rocks. That was what allowed us to loudly discuss our inventory strategies across hundred-foot distances—there simply wasn't anyone around to be disturbed by our half-shouted conversation.

But that also meant that, if anything went wrong, we were on our own: strictly on our own.

My father stemmed the dihedral a little more broadly than most of the climbers I'd seen cruxing on Triple S. It seemed to support him more steadily, a foundation based on geometry—the stable, wide triangle formed by his footholds and his fingerlocked hand, his feet back on each wall, so his handholds were forward of his center of gravity, effectively defeating the sheer, overwhelming verticality of the climb. I made a mental note of this and filed it away where I could get to it quickly—I'd be following him up in just a few minutes.

He found another handhold above his first, and gripped it thumb down-most, keeping his elbow high and locking himself in with the opposing power of the two holds. Then he moved his feet up in a pair of fluid hops until his knees rested chest-high, as if he were preparing to spring.

But he didn't spring. He just stood up from the new footholds, put in the Stopper that he'd promised me, added a runner and a carabiner, clipped the rope into it and climbed on past, moving as surely and gracefully as if he had been a workman mounting a ladder. I saw him step right, into the notch at the top of the Cockscomb and, for a few moments, he vanished. Then he reappeared, leaning out against the anchor that he'd tied around the trunk of a pine tree, waving down at me as he shouted, "B'lay off."

I waved back, unclipped the eight-ring, and removed the anchoring system, packing its components into the rucksack. Then I sat down to lace up my shoes.

My shoes: an endless source of amusement to my father.

He did most of his climbing in mountaineering boots, heavy leather boots with thick Vibram soles. They were the sort of boot, as my father had so often pointed out to me, that had been worn by the people who'd put up most of the routes at Seneca in the first place, so he knew the routes could be done in them. And only a few minutes earlier, in just such a pair of old-fashioned boots, he'd made a stroll in the park out of a crux that sent about half its suitors tumbling earthward.

I, on the other hand—or foot, as the case may be—wore EBs. Made of pale red canvas, and looking more like wrestling footwear than climbing gear, these were the latest and greatest in a new genre of rock-climbing specialty tools known as "friction shoes." My EBs were as unlike my father's Vibram-soled clodhoppers as Formula One racing tires are unlike what's used on a tractor. They did not simply provide purchase; they provided grip.

Which made them overkill in my father's estimation. Wearing friction shoes on a route that had not been pioneered with them was, in his words, "Just admitting that you're not as good as the guy who put the route up in the first place."

Not a problem: I could admit that. Wiggling my right foot back and forth in its shoe and tugging on the laces until the tendons stood out in my forearms, I tightened with a vengeance. That was my father's other objection to EBs—or to any friction shoe, for that matter. In order to work well, they had to be purchased at least a full size small, and laced onto one's bare feet with the intensity and vigor of Chinese foot-binding.

I looked up as I strained against the laces and saw my father grinning down from the cliff top.

"Rocket-science stuff like that," he called down, "you probably won't even want a rope, will you?"

"Probably not," I yelled back, tying my left shoe. "But I figure you need the belaying practice"—I gave the laces another toe-numbing tug—"seeing as you're getting to be the age where you start to forget things."

He'd just turned thirty-six the Christmas before.

No comment from the top of the pitch.

I wrapped a couple of turns of adhesive tape around the knuckles of both hands and then stood, shrugging the rucksack onto my shoulders, and fastening the waist belt. Then I draped an empty equipment sling, bandolier style, over my head and right shoulder. That completed the preparations. I walked to the base of the pitch and stood there as my father push-pulled the rope around his waist in a classic hip belay. Seconds later, the rope was tugging upward on my sit harness.

"That's me," I called up. "Climbing."

"Climb away," my father answered.

So I did.

A good rock climb is like a story. It invites you in with just the right blend of the exotic and the familiar, introduces complications, and sustains your interest. Then, earlier than you expected—which is just the right time—it comes to a climax, followed by the briefest bit of resolution, and concludes before you want it to, leaving you asking for more.

Triple S was exactly that sort of climb, and perfect for me. It was well below the limits of what my father could lead, as well as a notch or two lower in difficulty than the most rigorous climb that I could follow, yet it was certainly no Sunday stroll.

Being belayed from above added to my security. Assuming I had tied a secure knot—and my father had taught me no knots that were otherwise—I would fall only far enough to take tension on the rope. That would be mere feet in most cases, or even inches if my father tight-roped me, taking tension as I tackled a difficult move.

It was the procedure he'd developed for furthering my education as a rock climber. He alternated climbs right at the limits of my abilities with climbs well below them—learning situations interspersed with periods of review. Yet all of the climbs I followed him on were well within his abilities as a leader: when I'd been small, I had no sooner learned to read than I had begun thumbing through his climbing magazines, and the frequency with which I saw his name had impressed upon me early that I was the son of an exceptionally gifted climber.

Gauging the climbing to my abilities not only kept things comfortable, it was easier on the rope. A healthy fall—one in which the climber dropped long enough to build up some velocity—put thousands of pounds of strain on one's equipment, and the rope was only designed to hold so many leader falls before it lost most of its ability to stretch under load and absorb energy. But climbing as the second, I was essentially top-roped. I could fall until I was blue in the face without worrying about taxing the rope: the strain it experienced with a belay from above would almost always remain within a few pounds of my modest teenage body weight.

Which was good because, even though we were the wide-eyed

new owners of a climbing shop and could procure such items whole-sale, climbing ropes were expensive, nonetheless. A good one went for better than a hundred dollars, and this was in the days when even a well-paid worker would log twelve hours on the clock to earn such a sum. So having me follow my more experienced father was the most economical way we could climb, as well as being the safest.

Seconding also provided me with a little latitude with which to experiment.

I studied the rock—not just the bit in front of me, but the six feet above, as well, planning my moves. On most climbs, you wanted to plant a foot first, but on Triple S, the first footholds needed opposition from the hands, so I put my right hand in the crack at the dihedral, made a fist, pulled back on it and—glad that I'd taped my knuckles—stepped my feet up, leaning back on my hand and my arm, letting my skeletal system take the weight. The rope at my harness tugged twice as my father took up the slack.

"What do you think," he called down, "about credit cards?"

"Sure," I yelled back. "I'll take one."

"For the shop, you nimrod."

I shrugged, as much as one can shrug while sixty percent of one's weight is on one's right arm, reached my left hand up and said, "We'll ... need to take—ugh—some of them. Bank Americard, American Express, Ma—ugh, little slack—MasterCard. Those three."

"Yeah, but they charge four percent for a processing fee."

"So what?" I joggled left-right, getting my feet up into a higher stem. I was at the first chock now, and I took it out, marveling as I always did that my father's placements came out with just finger pressure. I carried a "nut tool"—actually a modified piece of shelf bracket with a taped-on handle—for fishing out heavily seated place-ments, but I only used that when I climbed with other people. "You make up the fee by the fact that people buy more when they use plastic," I pointed out, grunting as I twisted in my next hand jam. "Especially—ugh, up rope—especially down here. These guys show up with enough cash for gas and beer, and that's about it."

"But look at it this way," my father called down. "A four-percent fee—that's four pennies on the dollar—a buck-four total. But if we went cash-only, we could discount that four percent, make our prices ninety-six percent of what they would have been—that's an eight percent difference."

I mulled this over as I walked my feet up. It seemed to me that he was manipulating the same number twice. But numbers were my father's realm. He was an engineer. He lived in math world.

Or was he just messing with me?

"I don't care if it's ten percent," I finally answered, taking out the next placement up and clipping it onto my gear rack. "You aren't going to get somebody to lay out a hundred bucks to buy a rope he hadn't come in intending to buy if you make him crack his wallet and give you cash. But let him give you a card and you've got a chance at the sale."

Then I climbed in silence for a while, gritting my teeth at the nearly painful pressure of the fist jams, taking out two more chocks, clipping the hardware off my equipment bandolier and putting the flat-sewn nylon web runners over my head and left shoulder. The crux was coming up. I looked it over.

"Give me just a touch of slack," I said. "Don't help me, okay? I want to try something."

"You've got it."

The tugging at my waist belt ceased.

I moved my hands from the crack at the intersection of the two faces, and went to the next crack left, about two feet away. I was off-balance now, so I quickly dug the fingertips of my left hand in as far as I could, which wasn't far—maybe an eighth of an inch. Then I moved my left foot onto the right wall. Now I was *laying back*—the slim handhold and the soles of my feet providing opposition to one another, a tension that kept me in place on the rock.

Moving carefully now, I put my right hand above my left, walked my feet up the Cockscomb wall, and then moved my hands up again. I paused just long enough to glance to my right, taking in the gray expanse of the Cockscomb, a bit of the rock formation called Humphrey's Head (named after a character in the old Joe Palooka comic strip), and then, far across Roy Gap, the vertical natural-stone columns of the Southern Pillar. It was a giddy change of perspective after having spent ten minutes staring at rock less than a foot from my nose.

"What's this?" my father asked. "A five-ten move on a five-eight crux?"

"I've already done it the other way," I grunted, coming up against the stopper my father had put in and taking it out one-handed. I pulled myself back into the dihedral, stemmed the two faces, and swiftly did the last twenty feet, finishing out the climb and stepping into the pine needle-strewn gully where my father was on belay.

"Classy move," he said. "Somebody show that to you?"

"No." I shook my head. "It was improv."

"Very classy."

"Belay off," I told him as I walked past his anchor.

Then the two of us just stood there for a minute, taking in our reward—the view from the top. A smile crept onto my father's face. But it faded almost as soon as it appeared, and I could read that change as easily as I could read a newspaper.

This climb was not a climb like all the others we'd done here. Having finished it, or the one that followed it, or the ones that would follow in the morning, we would not be packing up our things and returning to Toledo. There was no longer anything in Toledo to return to. Nothing to return to, and no one to share the stories with. The person with whom we'd always shared those things was gone now, taken from us with a terrible and staggering finality. She had left behind an empty place as great as the gulf of air that lay beneath our feet.

I could feel a sob rising within me, and knew that my father had to be on the verge of the same thing. I choked it back.

As if someone had signaled us to do so, the two of us turned from the view and swiftly set to work, loose-coiling the rope. We'd rappel down the East Face, and then walk down to the gap. But neither of us had spoken yet, and I felt an overwhelming urge to do so—speak now or be suffocated by the silent ghost that had followed us up the sheer rock.

"The stuff you said about the credit cards," I told him, not looking up as I stowed our gear racks away. "You were just yanking my chain, weren't you?"

"Why would I do that?" my father asked.

I glanced. He was feigning innocence. He was absolutely no good at it at all.

"For the same reason you were yanking my chain about the double ropes," I said. "You want to see if I'm going to be any help to you or a total idiot when it comes to this retail thing."

"Not really." His face colored as he said it. It was his one Achilles' heel; around my mother and me—around me, now—he blushed far too easily. "But I want you to think about this, not just do. It's your shop, too, you know?"

"I know," I told him, looking him in the eyes.

"And I'll need to learn it," I said, nodding at his boots. "After all, anybody who still climbs in things like that? Senility can't be too far away."

I whooped and scrambled down gully to the rappel ledge as a pinecone whistled past my ear.

A placement that cannot possibly hold even a small fall is often referred to as "psychological protection," in that just the sight of one's rope passing through a carabiner is often enough to provide the confidence one needs to make the next move.

The Eastern Cragman's Guide to Climbing Anchors

Hanging by my left hand, I did a slow, controlled one-armed pull-up. Then I lifted a paper-stuffed Kelty rucksack with my free hand, hanging it on the hook I'd just screwed into the rafter.

A stepladder was the one thing we had forgotten to buy as we'd assembled what we'd need to get the shop ready. Then again, given my father's and my natural fluency in all things vertical, a stepladder was a pretty easy thing to do without.

I hand-traversed a few feet over to my left, screwed in another brass coat hook, and my father handed me the last display rucksack. Hanging it up, I straightened it and then dropped softly and nearly silently to the wood-planked floor, bending my legs for the landing. My hands tingled, and I shook them to get the blood back into them.

"Oh, come on," my father teased. "Don't tell me you're burnt already. You were only up there, what? Ten minutes?"

"Eight," I replied, glancing at my watch. "Want me to go back up for another two?"

"Well," Judd Horton said from the open doorway. "Whall" was the way it came out when he said it. The twilight of a West Virginia spring evening showed faintly around him, a dim blue contrast to the incandescent lights burning in our shop. "This ol' place cleans up purty darn good, don't it?"

"I guess it does," my father agreed.

They were right. After we'd hauled out the draft-horse tack, the mouse-eaten feed sacks, the stacks of old newspapers, and the crooked lumber that had cluttered up the large tin-roofed shed, the first thing we'd done was to hire a couple of neighbor ladies to give it a good stem-to-stern scrubbing.

"It saves us the trouble, and it will make us some friends if we give local people some work from time to time," my father had told me. Then, using the same logic, he'd hired an electrician from down the road to put in lights and outlets where we'd need them, and brought in a couple of retired farmers to do the carpentry.

One of the farmers had even scared up an old cast-iron Franklin stove that he'd cleaned, blackened, and then installed for us free of charge, setting it on a square platform of firebrick and venting it through stovepipe that we'd found among the junk we'd cleaned out.

The rest, we'd done ourselves.

Modern display cases would have seemed out of place among the varnished knotty pine paneling and simple flooring that our farmer-carpenters had installed. So my father had made some inquiries and found a hardware store in Elkins that was replacing its counter and display case; the old ones had become ours for the hauling. Halfway through the job of stripping the old finishes off the ancient oak, we'd begun to suspect that perhaps the hardware store had gotten the better end of the deal. But when, half-asphyxiated from the fumes, we'd gotten down to the hardwood and oiled it, it had all seemed worthwhile.

Judd walked all the way in and turned, his ample, T-shirted pot-belly panning slowly like a lighthouse beacon as he took in the varnished split-log benches near the stove, the shelves arranged with a rainbow of neatly coiled and multicolored climbing ropes, the individual climbing shoes on their wall display, the big spools of nylon webbing and Perlon line, the framed and autographed poster of Bill Forrest climbing Redgarden Wall. He nodded at the freestanding racks of printed T-shirts, the North Face anoraks, pile jackets, and mountain parkas. Then he got to the display board behind the sales counter, crammed with metal chocks, tiny RURP pitons, aluminum carabiners and chalk bags, and he scowled.

"You all ain't gonna be sellin' none of that hippie pair-ee-fer-nail-ya, are ya?"

"The hash pipes and hypodermic needles?" My father dead-panned. "No, sir. Those won't get in until late next week."

I still remember the dinosaur-take I did when I heard that. Up until that point, I would have bet good money that my father didn't even know what a hash pipe *was*.

It took Judd a second to realize that he was being had. When he did, he grinned, displaying a row of too-even, store-bought, tobacco-yellowed teeth, and shook my father's hand.

"So tomorrow's the day, huh?" Judd asked.

"That's right," my father said. "Tomorrow's Friday. We probably won't really see more than a couple of people until Saturday morning, but I want to be open and have the lights on when folks come rolling in."

That turned out to be a pretty good idea.

We never did go home that Thursday night, which was not as bad as it sounds. Home was a big, two-story log house, built back in the forties by some Wheeling lawyer as a hunting retreat. It looked Ponderosa-rustic and idyllic, but turned out to be much further in need of renovation than the shop. So my father had found a used Airstream travel trailer and had it hauled out and set up next to "The Lodge" (as we called it) while a slow but meticulous work crew re-chinked the log walls, gave the house a new split-shingle roof, evened warped floors, replaced the windows, re-wired the ground floor and set the place up for gas heat, central air-conditioning, and indoor plumbing.

In the meantime the travel trailer, apparently designed for itin-erant hermits, was turning out to be cramped quarters for two males long accustomed to having a woman pick up after them. Laundry occupied every conceivable surface—the washer and dryer sat in an anteroom of the main house, awaiting plumbing and the LP-gas hookup—and the trailer's kitchen counter had disappeared under a growing mountain of unopened mail and empty TV dinner trays.

The shop, on the other hand, was neat as the proverbial pin, and we spent the night in our sleeping bags, on camping cots in the back room, driving the VW over to the swimming hole on the North Fork at dawn for a brisk and bone-numbingly frigid dip in lieu of a shower the next morning.

By noon our first customers were there: two entire vanloads of Appies—Potomac Appalachian Trail Club members—who were playing hooky from work and didn't leave until they'd purchased three ropes, six pairs of friction shoes, three dozen Hexentrics, yard after yard of webbing and Perlon, and a T-shirt for every man, woman, and child in the bunch.

That group alone would have been enough for the shop to make its numbers for the day, but they were just the start. Almost from the moment he'd first pondered starting the shop, my father had signed himself up for membership in every rock-climbing, mountaineering, and backpacking club he could find within weekend driving distance of Seneca. This had not only made him score after score of new friends; it had also gotten him the members' address roster for each club. Armed with these, he'd purchased a case of Seneca Rocks picture postcards from the same company that supplied Horton's store, and then he'd had a rubber stamp made that said:

OPENING MEMORIAL DAY WEEKEND
THE FIRST ASCENT

Purveyors of the finest in mountaineering and backpacking equipment, with each item carefully selected to complement local conditions. We will be here for you with gear, information and a warm welcome every time you come to the Rocks. 10% off your first purchase with this card. Hope you'll help us get off to a great start. Thanks!

We'd stamped each card, my father had hand-signed each one, and then we'd spent every spare moment addressing them and affixing a small fortune in eleven-cent postage.

Now it seemed they were all being hand-carried back to us. A steady parade of climbers came through our shop all that weekend and for much of the week following, as people tagged vacations onto the long holiday weekend. At night, climbers gathered around the stove, the excess spilling onto the porch as everyone told bald-faced lies about their supposed exploits in Yosemite and the Black Canyon and the Front Range. Some evenings, somebody would bring in a guitar. Some evenings, whoever brought it would even know how to play. It was ten sixteen-hour days of solid and steady work, and I didn't go climbing once during that time, but I learned for the first time that spring that hard work for a business you own yourself is something quite different from labor expended for someone else.

Even Judd Horton was happy. Our mailing campaign had increased visitorship enough to give his store and campground their best Memorial Day week in ten years. He, like us, was just about sold out of T-shirts, and his shelves, like ours, emerged from the busy week gap-toothed with empty spaces.

I remember feeling complacent. The shop had gone from dream to reality; we were no longer dependent on savings, house-sale proceeds, and the insurance payout for our daily bread. It looked to me as if we had turned over a new leaf and everything would soon be all right.

Then again, I was only sixteen that spring—too young to understand how very quickly things can go wrong.

SIX

The trouble began after that first big holiday week, after the hordes of climbers had left and we once again had the Rocks and the shop to ourselves.

We had moved into our log home the week before Memorial Day. Or perhaps it would be more accurate to say that our belongings had moved in. The two of us remained in what my father called our "tin castle"—my father's name for the trailer—as the house's liquid-petroleum gas tank was not yet in service.

Just when the house would be habitable was an open issue. The LP gas tank could not be filled until it was fitted with an over-pressure relief valve, on back order at every supply house in Elkins, and June can still be a cool month in the mountains. While the house had been built to take maximum advantage of its big stone fireplace, with three bedrooms ideally situated to catch the rising heat, stoking a fire was not nearly as convenient as turning the thermostat on the Airstream's tiny furnace. And we would have had to use the trailer to shower, anyhow.

So we remained in our temporary bachelors' quarters, although that did not keep us from arranging the furniture and settling our belongings into the house.

It made it an odd place during the weeks—because it *was* weeks—that we waited for the contractor to add warmth, the sole quality that prevented our house from becoming a home. A sofa and a pair of wingback chairs graced the living room, facing the fireplace with its red cherry mantle. In the dining room, a table far too long for two people stood in the center, surrounded by a sideboard and a china cabinet.

Our winter coats were in the hall closet, and our unused suits were in the bedroom closets, heading rows of similarly idled trousers and hangered dress shirts. Three huge, dyed-in-the-wool, Karastan Oriental rugs—purchased by my mother from Lamson's department store on one of those rare occasions when a Jeep bonus coincided with a sale—covered the freshly laid oak floors in the living room, the dining room, and the master bedroom, giving the rugged old rough-hewn house an air of positive refinement.

Even our beds had been made up, although it had surprised me when my father instructed the movers to put his queen-size bed and cherry dresser into one of the two smaller bedrooms over the living room. The master bedroom, accessible by a short hallway that ran between the other two, held only its rug (too large for either my father's room or mine), my mother's dressing table and chair, and the fourteen brown cardboard boxes in which we'd packed her things.

"I don't need a big old room like that right now," my father had told me when I'd asked. But I could sense the hurt in his voice. When I suggested going through the boxes together, perhaps giving the clothes away to some local families, he'd agreed that it was a good idea in principle.

"But not right now, Sport," he'd added. "I'm just not up to it."

At sixteen, I was old enough to understand exactly how he felt. There was nothing in those cardboard boxes that he needed, nothing that I needed. Yet to give those things up would be to admit that my mother was never, ever coming back to us—that we would never step into a room and find her, refreshed as if back from long travels, her face radiant with thanks for this home that we had prepared for her. To give away the things in the boxes would be to give away, absolutely and forever, even the utterly groundless hope that she would once again be part of our lives.

So the house was filled and furnished, but not occupied. It felt oddly like the preserved homes one sees at historic sites. But my father had an office on the main floor, and he would walk over from the trailer to use it during our off-hours. Even without the LP hookup, doing paper work in the spacious, knotty-pine-paneled office was infinitely preferable to clearing a work space on the Airstream's tiny catchall table.

He headed over there first thing on the Monday morning after Memorial Day week, so I took advantage of his absence to grab a long and leisurely shower.

You had to plan showers in the Airstream. It had one of those RV bathrooms where the whole thing—sink, toilet, medicine cabinet, the works—was also the shower, so you first had to police the area, putting away anything that couldn't get wet. Only then could you turn the water on. And once you did, the bathroom was out of order for anything else until it had been squeegeed and dried. This made showers something of an ordeal (I actually got accustomed to cold-water plunges in the North Fork), but it carried with it the additional advantage of making the bathroom the one place in the little trailer that actually stayed picked up.

Wanting to maximize my investment, I stayed a long time in the little plastic-walled cubicle. My hair was getting shaggy—I was a full month past the point where my mother would have insisted on a cut—so I washed it twice, and then used my father's safety razor and mirror to scrape away the nascent peach fuzz on my chin. I was hoping that frequent shaving would hasten the advent of actual whiskers.

By the time I'd toweled dry and located a clean pair of briefs, nearly an hour had passed, and my father was still at the house. Dressing was a simple matter; if my father wanted to kick back and do a little climbing after we'd straightened the shop up, I'd wear climbing shorts, but if we were running errands in town, I'd need jeans. Uncertain of our plans, I pulled on a pair of Scott High gym shorts and left the trailer, trotting in my bare feet over to the big log lodge.

You could tell that the place was not yet being lived in. As soon as I stepped through the kitchen door, I was aware that it was far too quiet: none of the hum of running appliances or a furnace fan, no mantle clock ticking in the living room. In a place that quiet, it just seemed wrong to be anything but silent, as well. So I walked softly on my bare soles across the kitchen, through the dining room and living room, and into the office.

My father wasn't there.

Just before I would have called out, I heard him. Or rather, I heard his footsteps.

Upstairs. I listened, pinpointing the sound. He was in his bedroom. I wouldn't have been able to tell had the house held the normal noises of habitation. But in that deathly stillness, each step sounded as clearly as a hammer fall on the ceiling over my head.

My father must have gone up just as I'd come in, because I could hear him walking across the floor from the bedroom door, pausing at the left side of the bed before going around it to the right side— my mother's side, back when that bed had stood in our house on Parkwood. He stopped at the bedside for a long while, and the house was silent again except for a creak from the floorboards, right where he'd been standing.

I did not call out, did not make myself known. At first I had merely been curious. But after I had been still for so long, it seemed to me that calling out now would make it obvious I had been spying, or at least listening. I thought about this for a long time, maybe a minute, maybe more, and I had decided I should probably sneak outside and come back in again. But before I could move, the floor creaked again.

Somehow, those two creaks, and the silence in between, made sense. I understood right away that my father had been kneeling.

The footsteps sounded again, across the bedroom floor and out its door. I walked through the living room and dining room to follow them from below, craning my head upward to catch the sounds. My father was walking down the hallway, toward the big master bedroom, vacant except for my mother's dressing table, its chair, and the boxes.

The footsteps were harder to follow now; the Oriental rug muffled their fall. But that larger floor creaked just a little. Moving back into the empty pantry, I could just follow my father as he walked across the floor above and over to the dressing table. There was a brief scrape—the chair being pulled back from the dressing table—and then a muted thump as it was set down next to the wall of boxes. The floorboards creaked again. Was he stepping up onto the chair? It sounded possible. The next thing I heard was a soft thud as one of the heavier boxes was set down on the carpeted floor.

Then the house went silent again, the dead air hollow and still for minutes on end.

Indian-quiet on my bare feet, I padded up the broad wooden staircase to the second floor, made my way down the short hall and paused before the master bedroom door. Guilt ran hot in me. There was no possibility of mistaken perception now; if my father discovered me, he would know I was spying.

But then there was the matter of the door. It was partway open, and inside I could hear my father. At first I thought the sound I heard was laughter—the gasping-for-breath, deep-in-the-throat laugh a person might reserve for a truly tremendous joke. But after a second or two, I understood that the sound was not laughter after all. My father was sobbing.

He was weeping.

In my life, I have had many regrets. There are friendships I wish I had not allowed to fade and words I wish I had not said. But chief among my regrets is that I did not rush into that big, unused room right then, did not wrap my arms around my father and tell him that I loved him, did not assure him that he still had me. Had I been even a year older, I might have. But as it was, I was frozen into inaction, embarrassed at my uncertainty over what to do next.

This was 1976; men embracing men was something that simply did not happen. Not in America. When my father and I embraced, we did so in bear hugs: quick, football-field back crushers that were more a test of endurance than an act of affection. But a bear hug was not what the situation called for, and I had nothing else to offer from my slim repertoire.

So I skulked away, down the short hallway and down the broad stairs, through the quiet mausoleum of a house and out into the fresh mountain morning. I just stood in the sunshine for a while and breathed, already regretting my inaction, and then I went into the trailer to find my jeans, because I knew I would not be climbing that morning.

Twenty minutes later, when my father came in, his tanned, bearded face wore a game smile. But the redness in his eyes gave him away.

"Ready to roll?" he asked.

I grabbed a three-ring binder and headed out to the van, looking for some indication that he wanted to talk, but seeing nothing.

"Looks like it will warm up later," my father said as the VW putted its way down a long two-track. "Sure you want to be in jeans all day? It'll be hot when we get up to the West Face."

"I'm sure." I nodded. I held up the binder. "I've got those essays to do and send back to Scott so they can get the grades in. Thought I'd just wrap that up today, instead of hitting the rocks."

That earned me a long sidelong glance. The part about the essays was true. My chemistry, math and physics teachers had all allowed me to just cram and take a final exam so I could finish my semester early and move to West Virginia. And the coach aced me on my phys-ed class, chuckling as he said, "Climbing every day? Well, I guess you just might stay in shape."

But for social studies and English, I'd been required to write two essays to complete my course requirements: principles of the Monroe Doctrine, and significance of the green light in *The Great Gatsby*, respectively. The Monroe Doctrine was pretty straightforward—all I'd had to do was consult an encyclopedia and my textbook. But even though I'd liked *The Great Gatsby* and considered Nick Carraway a friend, I was having a hard time forcing myself into the role of literary critic. I liked novels, and liked *Gatsby*, even though I'd wished we'd been assigned something more current, something written by what my mother used to call the authors who were "NDY"— Not Dead Yet. But spending time pontificating over the meaning hidden behind each word and phrase? That just seemed to me like time better spent climbing.

Still, the paper needed writing, so I'd made a couple of trips down to Davis-Elkins College and used the library there to scour back issues of literary journals. My notebook was full of words like *hope* and *renewal* and *delusion*.

My father understood I hated that sort of thing. He knew I thought of it as busywork, of no practical value. So I'd been putting off and putting off completing the essays, even though the drop-dead due date was less than two weeks away. For me to suddenly step up and volunteer was several miles out of character.

"Yeah," my father finally said. "You'll probably feel better with those things behind you."

If ever I'd heard an entrée, that was one. All I had to do was say what I'd overheard from the hall outside the master bedroom door. But I couldn't quite muster the courage.

"You were over in the house for quite a while." That was my feeble substitute for what needed to be said.

"We had a good week." My father shrugged. His face looked weary, the crow's-feet more pronounced at the edges of his eyes, his forehead marked from the furrows. "I had a lot of stock to reorder. Good thing most of those folks have 800 numbers. Speaking of which, keep Friday free for me, Sport—I expect the UPS man to drop a ton of stuff on us, and we'll need to have it all squared away by suppertime."

"Sure," I told him. Then, swallowing once, I continued, "I looked for you in your office a while ago. You weren't there."

He worked his lips and took a deep breath, the green mountain pines whizzing past behind him, the air through the open window ruffling his sandy brown hair.

"I went upstairs after I got done," my father finally told me. "Thought I'd look through Laur ... through your mom's, uhm, things, just to see if maybe I could start sorting what we should keep and what we should, you know, give away."

"Make any progress?"

"Not really." He slowly shook his head. "The very first box I got down was full of papers, class notes and term papers, mostly. But this one big, manila file folder was just packed full of notes and letters—and every one was from me. She saved every single thing I'd ever written to her: did you know that? Even if I left a note to let her know I'd run to the store, she saved it. And I could recall writing just about every note, every letter, and I got thinking about then, about her, and, well, it got to me, Sport. I have to admit it. It got to me."

I breathed easier, glad to have that out in the open.

"She really loved you," I told him.

"Yeah. That's what I thought, too."

Thought? As in *used to think?* Or was he talking that way because she was gone?

This time I couldn't ask because, after a pause of ten or fifteen seconds, he was speaking again.

"I'll tell you, Sport," he said. "Just touching things that she had touched, seeing the care of it all, I couldn't avoid . . . I couldn't help but start wondering why again. I mean, all those letters she saved from me. Every single one. If I—if we—meant that much to her, then why did she have to. . . ?"

He shivered despite the sunshine, leaving the thought unfinished, and in that single moment I could swear I saw him age ten years.

"Listen," I told him as we turned off the dirt road onto the pavement of Route 33. "I can go through all that stuff for you. The letters, everything. Let me handle it."

"No." My father shook his head, lips set thin and hard. "Not by yourself. I wouldn't do that to you, Sport. It's way too much."

"It wouldn't be. Not really. I'll just do it fast and get it over with."

"Not by yourself," he repeated firmly. "And fast wouldn't be right, either, Patrick. It's not your stuff. It's not mine. It's your mom's. We owe it to her to be careful."

So we rode in silence the rest of the way to the shop.

As soon as we got there, I started to work, cleaning the floor, and then sweeping off the porch. The long wood-railed porch and the gravel before it were punctuated with cigarette butts and empty Marlboro hard packs. John Wayne and Yul Brynner were both still alive and kicking, and nobody seemed to give lung cancer a second thought.

In fact, it had never crossed our minds to make the shop off-limits to smokers; only health-food stores did that sort of stuff back then, and besides, it would have cut our traffic by half. So I cleaned up all the butts from in front of our place, and then I went over to Judd Horton's store and swept his porch and policed the gravel in front of it, as well. I saw Judd looking my way from the counter, but he turned away as soon as our eyes met, didn't come out, and didn't say anything.

That puzzled me at first. But then I realized that he must have thought that if he acknowledged me he'd have to pay me. That was Judd.

After sweeping, I cleaned the ashes out of the bottom of the Franklin stove—and made a mental note to do that first the next time, and sweep the floor later. Then I swept again, polished the display cases and the shop's single four-paned window with Windex, and scraped the melted nylon off the electric element that my father used for cutting cordage and webbing to order.

Meanwhile, he was tidying up the hardware displays, sorting out the chocks and carabiners that had been returned to their pegs out of order, and rehanging the T-shirts according to style and color and size, the last being the easiest, as "Small" was about all we had left.

Then we broke down the empty cardboard boxes and made as much space available in the tiny stockroom as we could, getting things squared away so we'd be ready to receive our shipments that Friday.

I was out back behind the shop, burning the boxes in a 55-gallon drum, feeding a compact orange cyclone of flames, when my father stepped out. He was in his standard climbing regalia, a worn and nearly threadbare pair of Chouinard Stand-Up Shorts that he refused to throw away out of obstinacy. As if to make amends for the shorts, the T-shirt he wore was brand-new, a red one we'd held back from the rack because the print had smudged. His rucksack sagged with its near emptiness, and it seemed to me that he sagged a little, as well—like a man gone weary after a long, forced march.

"You sure you don't want to get a climb in?" he asked.

"I'm sure."

Which was a complete and utter fabrication; the day had not yet dawned when I would not be ready and willing to climb whatever rock was available. But I'd heard him that morning. Those letters in the boxes had not just gotten to him—they had broken him up, well and truly, and I figured that the last place he needed to be was hanging it all out at the sharp end of a rope.

"I'll just stay here and finish those essays," I told him.

"Well, okay." My father looked at me, pinched his mouth with a thumb and the knuckle of an index finger. "I guess I'll just run up the hill and boulder for a while."

Which was what I'd hoped he would say. Bouldering was how you practiced for rock climbing. You didn't use a rope; you didn't climb up any farther than you would want to fall, so you generally kept your feet within a yard or so of the ground. And for a man who'd just sobbed part of the morning away, bouldering sounded much better to me than climbing. You could boulder distracted and not hurt yourself.

"Have a good one," I told him, quickly shoving another tightly folded box into the steel-drum inferno.

I have never been a good liar, and certainly was not at sixteen. Guilt would dog me unless I did what I said I was going to do. So, since I'd told my father that I was going to stay down and finish my essays, that's what I did.

The Monroe Doctrine was simple: I framed the fifth president's principles, pointed out that Jefferson agreed with him, and tossed in the Cuban missile crisis as a twentieth-century example of the policy in action.

But the critique of *Gatsby* held less gusto for me. Literary criticism has always seemed to me like the sterile dissection of a flower, the careful segmentation of pistil and stamen and petal: when you're finished, you may understand it better, but it won't be beautiful anymore. And besides, it seemed to me that the green light at the end of Daisy's dock, the thing my teacher had harped on all semester, was, when all was said and done, an aid to navigation and nothing more, and I was reluctant to make it something it was not. So I did the assignment briskly and without embellishment, double-checking all my spelling and grammar in hopes that it might creep up from a B-plus to an A, but not really minding if it didn't. It was simply a distasteful job that had to be done, like washing down a dog with tomato juice after an ill-timed encounter with a skunk.

I had a moment myself, then. My mother had been studying to teach college English. My habit had always been to show her my papers before I turned them in, to get an opinion before I committed myself to a grade.

And naturally, I thought of that as I set my pen aside. I thought of that, and I pictured her, reading glasses on, tapping the eraser end of a pencil ever so lightly against her lips as she read my work.

That image was so vibrant, so real, that for the most fleeting fraction of a second, it was as if she were there with me in the little back room of the climbing shop. Then it was over, she was gone—again—and I was left with a pain in my stomach that was as real as if someone had struck me there.

I don't remember my tears, but I do remember wiping my face with my hand and finding my cheeks wet. That had irritated me; I had already decided I needed to be the strong one, needed to step up and carry my father through this the way my mother and he had carried me through . . . well, everything that had happened to me in my sixteen years. I wiped my face and, just as I had done when I'd been tackled hard on the football field, I sucked the pain back inside me and hid it, way down low.

That done, I needed some air, so I headed out to the porch and sat on a bench that had already picked up the first of what would be at least a hundred carved initials. Somebody named CRW had left the world a reminder that he had once graced this spot with his presence.

Judd came out on his porch, as well, having decided, apparently, that sufficient time had passed to allow him to emerge without talk of remuneration for my sweeping services. He gazed up at the Rocks—it was hard not to do so from his porch; they filled up nearly half the sky. Then he bent forward, looked again, and turned my way.

"You ain't up climbin' today?"

Which, admittedly, was a pretty stupid question, what with me sitting there in front of him and all. But to point that out would not go well with Judd. I'd already heard him mention to my father that, in Judd Horton's worldly and wise opinion, kids from up north had a tendency to be "uppity."

I shrugged. "Had to finish some schoolwork."

Judd looked back up at the rock and squinted, which was unusual for Judd. He had a little pair of drugstore half-spectacles that he used for reading, but at a distance, Judd's vision was legendary. Mountain people practically lined up to go hunting with him. He could spot a deer standing in thick brush from half a mile away.

Scowling, he looked back at me a second time.

"Then who is yer daddy up climbin' with?"

"Who?" I leaned forward. There was a huckleberry bush we hadn't cut back yet, growing wild off the east side of our porch, so I couldn't see much of the Rocks.

"Nobody," I told him. "He's by himself."

Judd looked dumbfounded. It was the one and only time in all the years I would know him that I would ever see him speechless.

Looking back at the rock, he scowled again and then asked, "All the way up *there*?"

It's accurate, what people say about having your heart fall. Mine did, and it didn't even bother to stop in the abdomen; it dropped all the way to my knees and quivered a bit. Still, I got to my feet and stepped out onto the turnaround. Sure enough, halfway up the wall beneath the South Summit there was just the suggestion of limbs emanating from a red dot. *Red shirt*, I remembered. My father was wearing a red shirt.

Still scowling, Judd shuffled quickly back into his store, his pot-belly bobbing with urgency. The bell of his cash register sounded, and a moment later he was back, a quarter in his hand.

Judd had a tourist binoculars mounted on the front railing of his porch—one of those coin-operated, weatherproof, twin-lensed monstrosities that look like a cross between a gas mask and a bedpan. He thumbed the quarter into it, initiating a faint whir. Then he stooped and put his eyes to it, twisting the focusing knob.

"My, my, my," he whispered as he peered into the eyepieces. "My, my, my, my, my."

"What?" I asked.

"Yer daddy," Judd muttered. "Boy, he ain't on no rope."

Whenever feasible, avoid placements that force the rope to run through the carabiner at an angle. Such practices produce friction, and the cumulative friction of several such placements can be enough to impede progress.

The Eastern Cragman's Guide to Climbing Anchors

SEVEN

I don't remember climbing the steps to Judd's porch. I'm pretty sure I didn't shove the cantankerous West Virginian out of the way, because that would almost certainly have landed my uppity sixteen-year-old self on my backside. But the next thing I knew, there I was, staring through the shadow-encompassed optics of Judd's tin-plated sightseeing binoculars. The climber was my father, all right. And Judd was right: no rope above him, no rope below. No rope at all.

"Whatever is he thinkin' of?" Judd wondered aloud.

It was an excellent question. The problem was that the only answers I could come up with all had to do with a total loss of one's senses. That was not something I would want to say about my father, particularly not in front of a gossipmonger like Judd. Two pictures flashed through my mind: one of my father straitjacketed in some West Virginian asylum, and the other of me as a ward of the state. Both scared the wits right out of me, so I selfishly kept my peace.

For the most fleeting of moments, I considered trying to snow Judd, trying to say that there was a rope, but we just couldn't see it, that the color was too close to that of the rock behind it. But Judd harbored no humility about his exceptional eyesight. There was no way I was going to convince him that my father was on a rope when he wasn't. Besides, enough climbing ropes had paraded past his general store for Judd to know that there was no such thing as a rock-colored one.

"He's just . . . uh, fourth-classing," I finally said.

"Fourth what-ing?"

"Fourth-classing," I repeated. Was I sweating? "You know how you hear the guys who come through here talking about five-eights and five-nines, and so on?"

"Yeah . . ." Judd dragged the word out, betraying his doubts.

"Well, those are fifth-class climbs—climbs you need a rope on." I warmed to the fabrication, even as I schemed at how to get myself off that porch and up onto the Rocks. "But a fourth-class climb, that's one you climb ropeless."

"Hmmm," Judd rumbled. "I dunno, boy. Seems to me I've seen a heap of fellers take a purty good tumble right about where your daddy's at right now."

"Sure." I nodded, willing myself to sound calm. "But those are newer climbers. My dad's pretty famous as a rock climber, you know. What's fifth-class for a guy like me might only be fourth-class for him."

"I see." Judd's expression proved that he did not.

I tried another look through the binoculars, but the whirring had ceased and the eyepieces had gone black.

"He's probably going to be pretty thirsty after this," I said, deliberately speaking more slowly than usual. The situation was bizarre enough; I didn't want to compound it by doing what every instinct told me to do, and go tearing off the porch. If I wasn't going to make Judd Horton even more suspicious than he already was, I needed to look casual about this. I needed to make it look as if seeing my father one missed handhold away from catastrophe was the most natural thing in the world. So I forced out a smile.

"Can I buy a couple of Cokes from you, Judd?"

I didn't stop to change my shoes. I didn't put on climbing shorts. I did grab a rope and throw it over my head and one shoulder. In blue jeans and my worn Adidas Countrys, I walked, one ice-cold can in each hand, until I was across Route 33 and out of Judd's sight.

Then I dashed at a near run through the deserted NFS campground on Roy Gap Road, bouncing recklessly across the creaking wooden swing bridge across the rushing North Fork. Every once in a while, I would glance up through the trees and see the crimson dot that was my father, inching steadily upward.

Technically, everything I'd told Judd had been the truth. There really was such a thing as fourth-classing, although the phrase was most often pure braggadocio, a deliberate understatement. Climbers talked about fourth-classing a hard route in the same way that Channel swimmers might talk about "going for a dip."

Free soloing. That was the real name for what my father was up to—climbing hard routes without the safeguard of a rope—and you could count on one hand the number of people who did it regularly on hard climbs. There was a yoga-studying bodybuilder from Colorado who was known for it, a college professor from New Hampshire who climbed at Cathedral Rock, a quasi-hippie who hung out at the 'Gunks, and a couple of diehards who literally lived at Camp Four, out in Yosemite. That was about it. And the one thing they all had in common was that everyone else in the sport regarded them as nuts—absolutely, certifiably, and undeniably insane.

Free soloists pointed out that, in fifth-class climbing, the ropes and equipment were only there as safety backups, anyhow. Once you were climbing at a certain grade competently, they argued, the gear became nothing but a hindrance, an added inconvenience that diminished the purity of the climb. So the logical solution, according to their argument, was to eliminate entirely the use of protection.

These claims were fueled by the fact that, of the handful of free soloists then regularly active in America, all were still alive and none had yet suffered a serious or life-threatening accident. But that was just a statistical fluke and everyone—my father included—knew it.

Just a year earlier, moments after completing a hard technical climb on the Diamond, the huge east face of Long's Peak, a good friend of his, one of the top women climbers in the world, had been making her way toward the summit trail over ground that truly was fourth-class—only about a forty-five degree pitch and with handholds like granite buckets—when one of those handholds broke loose as she put her weight on it. She had plummeted the full thousand feet to the Broadway ledge at the top of the Crack of Delight, and then bounced hundreds of feet down the approach rock to the scree field below. People said that the rangers who recovered her body had gone up looking like the summering college kids that they were, and come back looking like shell-shocked combat veterans.

Nor had I lied to Judd about my father's reputation. He really was every bit of a well-known, world-class rock climber. For as long as I could remember, magazines such as *Off Belay*, *Climbing*, and *Summit* had arrived regularly at our house back on Parkwood, and for as long as they had been coming, my father's name had appeared in them. Sometimes the articles were profiles of him; sometimes he was speaking out on route conservation. Mostly they were simply new-route descriptions: he was responsible for dozens. He was humble about it; there were people at Jeep, people with whom my father had worked for years, who didn't even know he was a climber. Yet my father could climb with the best of them, and he often did.

Still, true as those things were, I had lied to Judd Horton. I knew that. And so, I strongly suspect, did Judd.

The trail up Roy Gap was steep and winding. We usually walked it slowly, the better to conserve energy for the climb ahead, but I was moving at a near run. My heart pounded; cold sweat coursed down my back. But that wasn't all from exertion; it had begun the very moment I'd looked through Judd's binoculars.

I was getting close enough to the rock to see relief now. The face my father was climbing looked flat from the valley below, but here, at an angle, I could see that was not true. It headed toward an overhang about five feet deep. I could see him through a gap in the treetops: he was inching nearer to the shelf of rock beneath the summit, and he was dead center beneath it, not angling to either side.

"No." I remember saying that aloud. "Not over. Go around."

That was when I began sprinting. Near the place where the switchbacks ran away from the main trail, there was a little hole, a small depression in a mountain creek where people often set six-packs to cool. I pitched the Cokes into it as I tore past, not caring if they landed in the hole or got carried on downstream by the flow.

Ignoring everything my father had ever taught me about trail conservation, I didn't even bother following the switchbacks. I ran, crawled and climbed straight uphill, pulling at trees for assistance, catching myself when my feet scrabbled in the dead pine needles. In my head, a clock was ticking. When I got a rare clear view of the rock, that clock ticked even faster. My father was right under the overhang now.

There was no way he was going around.

Hot, angry tears coursed down my reddened cheeks. I pushed past trees as I clambered uphill, skinning my palms, barking my knuckles, and cursing the fact that he would place himself at so much risk, that he would bring me down to a place where I knew no one and then try some fool stunt that could orphan me. I angled toward the base of the face he was climbing, sprinted up low, mossy stone terraces, leaping onto knee-high ledges and mantling my way over those that I couldn't jump.

When I broke out of the trees, I was still at the bottom of the jumbled Seneca scree field, but I could see him clearly now, and what I saw stole my breath.

My father was directly under the overhang, his body arched back precariously as he searched for handholds on the hard quartzite roof above him. Beneath his feet, the rock wall dropped away like a huge, lithic curtain, gray with brown lichen, cold and grim. From up close, where he was looked even higher.

He found the holds he was seeking in a narrow crack, worked back even farther, and then lifted his feet, one leg at a time, to find nubbins in opposition to his handholds, deep within the shadow of the roof. Even from nearly two hundred feet below, I could see the strain in his neck, the tendons standing out on his forearms as he reached his left hand back, back, back and worked his fingers onto a hold in a crack at the very lip. The tag ends of the bandanna knotted over his head moved minutely in a gust of wind. And then I very nearly buckled at the knees, because, with a distant but audible scrape, both of my father's feet and his other hand dropped away from their holds, like a wrecking ball, loose and swinging free.

Involuntarily, I shut my eyes, squeezed them, my head drawing into my shoulders as the tension gripped my neck, my lungs frozen in mid-breath. My ears roared. In my mind's eye, I could see him plummeting, falling down the full, sickening length of the lichen-blotched wall. The overhang was high, very high—high enough that it would take five full seconds for him to reach the ground.

Five seconds passed . . . Six . . . Seven . . . Eight . . . There was no sickening thud. No wet-concrete report of the temporary and fragile being dashed against the unyielding and eternal. The wind sighed in the pines behind me, and somewhere a cardinal called. Still holding my breath, I opened my eyes.

He was still up there, the fingers of one hand curled easily over the lip, his body relaxed as he hung by one hand: no rope, no tether, no harness, his only connection to the rock that single handhold. For a moment, I imagined that he was simply hanging on for an instant, taking a moment for the gravity of the situation to fully sink in as he pondered his mistake—pondered it, and then surrendered, and let go.

But it hadn't been a mistake. His legs hung smoothly beneath him; he didn't try to kick and fight his way back onto the holds. His body dangled with just the barest hint of a swing, and he was calm, despite the single handhold.

One long, awful moment passed, and then another.

I couldn't call out to him. I couldn't even breathe. I froze like a small mammal caught in headlights. If I moved, if I so much as clinked rock against rock, I could make a sound that would distract him; I knew that. Swallowing dryly, I kept perfectly still and did the only thing I could do. I watched.

One of my father's legs shook briefly, then the other, then his free right arm, hanging limply from his shoulder. Impossible as it may have seemed, my father was resting, getting the blood moving again in his limbs. It was a lesson he had stressed to me as he'd taught me to climb, the art of staying loose before making a difficult move.

"Don't cling, Sport," he'd told me. *"Don't clench. Remember, muscles tire quickly, but bones don't. Just find a hold that lets you hang by your skeleton and relax and when you get a good, secure hold like that, use it as an opportunity to shake everything out and get the blood moving again."*

So he was resting, but resting also meant that he was tired, nearly exhausted, probably, after all that nonstop climbing, and he was committed now. There was no way to down-climb the roof, no possibility of retreat to the easy 5.6 traverse beneath it. He had to go up. The only way down was through nearly two hundred feet of thin mountain air.

I regretted, right then and there, that my parents had never had a church life, never taken me to the Sunday schools my friends had talked about through grade school. Because what I wanted to do, right then and there, was pray, but I didn't know how.

God, I whispered wordlessly. *I don't know if you're there, God, but if you can hear me, please, please, please don't let my father fall. I'll do anything you want. Just help him. Just get him up top.*

I thought about this, wondered if I'd said enough. It seemed to me that I should be kneeling, but I was afraid I'd make a noise if I tried.

I'm sorry I can't move, I continued. *I hope you'll understand.*

I thought for a moment, wondering if I should add anything else.

"Amen," I whispered aloud.

Head craned back, my father scouted the rock above him. He reached back into the bag at the back of his waist belt and fingered the block of gymnast's chalk he kept there, his movement pensive, almost casual, as if he were pondering his next move in a friendly game of checkers or chess.

Finally he did a pull-up—one-armed, an impressive display of strength after having hung by a single jammed fist for nearly two minutes. He pulled until his shoulder was level with his hand, and then he reached up smoothly, worked his right hand wrist-deep into a crack, and pulled himself up even higher. He brought his left heel up to the side and hooked the edge of the roof, using the three points—two handholds and a tenuous foothold—to lever himself higher on the rock. It was a classic roof-pull, and he worked himself high enough that he could reach up once more with his left hand and grip a nubbin above the converging crack. This gave him the purchase he needed to press higher still and get the toe of his right shoe into the crack, poking it in with his ankle turned inward, and then standing up on it, camming his foot firmly against the crack's sharp, fractured edges.

He didn't slow to shake his left hand awake, although I knew he must have wanted to. He had to be tired, close to the point where his limbs would begin to quake with the effort. Not out of the woods yet.

I repeated the prayer.

Man Overboard. The name of the route he was on came to me all at once. It was one that my father had put up with a climber from Philadelphia three years earlier; my father's second had fallen off just above the roof—thus the name. It had taken a full minute of swinging on the rope for the guy to get back on the wall so he could re-climb the route. Remembering that made me shiver.

In my mind's eye, I could see the route description my father had provided to *A Climber's Guide to Seneca Rocks.* "*Proceed with caution above the overhang,*" he'd written. "*Route is rain-scoured and extremely thin. 5.9a.*"

He was definitely not out of the woods yet.

Alone, small, and starkly exposed, my father put his left foot onto a stance so small as to be invisible from my vantage point. He turned his foot, smearing the sole of his shoe onto the rock for better grip, and then took his other foot out of the crack, moving up onto a similarly minute quartzite nubbin.

His movements were deliberate, very smooth and very fluid, shifting his weight with the heightened control of a climber who knows exactly how much pressure each foothold can bear before the sole of his shoe will simply shear off of it and dump him into the empty air below. The chalk bag went unused now, and I realized he didn't want to put a hand behind his back, didn't want to move even the slightest bit of his center of gravity away from the rock.

There were no more handholds. All he had were pinch-holds and smears: tiny embedded pebbles he could grasp with the very tips of his fingers, or nearly invisible depressions that he could press down into with the palm of his hand. It was like watching a man inch his way up a piece of blank steel plate.

But each move was sure. He didn't back down and try anything twice, didn't hesitate as if pondering the next point on the rock that he would trust with his weight. There was an expression climbers used for someone who could progress so confidently and so relentlessly: "a climbing machine." And that was what I was watching on the thin, featureless rock above the overhang—a resolute climbing machine.

Already my father's head was silhouetted against the startlingly blue West Virginia sky; he was that close to topping off. He moved, one limb at a time, and soon his arms were only visible from the elbows down: the rock was angling inward. Then I couldn't see his arms at all; just his feet, and soon they were blocked, as well. Finally, he vanished altogether. Then his head appeared again and I knew he was standing on top, on a rounded ledge just west of the South Summit. He turned and walked away and, for the first time in nearly a minute, I breathed.

Sinking down onto a boulder at the edge of the scree, I drank in the sweet, soothing relief, that flood of reassurance that comes surging in when something terrible has been narrowly avoided. My heart was pounding like it was trying to beat right through my chest, and my shirt was damp with sweat. I took off the coiled rope and laid it on the boulder beside me.

Then the anger crashed over me. The rage.

I wanted to kill him. I wanted to hit him until I could hit no more, to swing until my fists were numb, to strangle him. It wasn't just the recklessness of what he had done. It was the selfishness, as well. Although we had never discussed the details, and the start-up capital had all been my father's, it was understood that we were partners in the climbing shop, the house, every aspect of the move to West Virginia. My investment had come in the form of my commitment, my willingness to turn my back on what would have been a skyrocketing high-school football career in order to help my father chase his bliss.

Instead, he was doing this. I felt the heat rising in my face and I kicked at the earth, again and again, venting as I contemplated how near I'd just come to being orphaned. Picking up the rope, I made my way up the scree field to the narrow trail next to the rock, and, lips set sternly, began to pick my way south.

For a climber without a rope, there is only one simple descent from the South Summit of Seneca Rocks. True, my father had taken anything but the easy way up, but the climb he'd made had been tasking. I was pretty sure he would look for the simplest way down.

Making my way around the bottom of the Face of a Thousand Pitons, I scrambled up a series of rocky terraces. Sure enough, there were his rucksack and his running shoes, cached up against the rock face on the broad stone shelf that we—like everyone who climbed at Seneca—knew as "Luncheon Ledge."

Tossing my rope down next to the rucksack, I sat down on the broad, sun-warmed ledge. The heat of the day, the warmth of the rock, and my lingering relief slowly quenched my anger. Fatigue seeped in to take its place. The warm rock beckoned, and I leaned back on the rain-smoothed quartzite, rested the back of my head on the rope, blinked twice in the midday sun, and closed my eyes.

The sound of shoes against rock brought me awake again in what seemed like seconds, but proved by my watch to be a good twenty-five minutes.

There's a funny thing about naps. If you sleep for forty-five minutes or longer, you'll be in a funk for the rest of the day. But nod off for anywhere from twenty to thirty minutes, and you'll wake up as refreshed as if you'd just spent a solid eight hours in the comfort of your own bed.

I woke up feeling great. The warm rock had coaxed the tightness out of my back more effectively than the world's most expert masseuse, and I was fresh, awake and alive. Looking up the chimney that leads to the top pitch of Old Ladies, I could see my father coming down: one hand and one foot against the north wall, the other hand and foot against the south. He was facing in, so he could grab the occasional hold on the back of the chimney, and he descended as easily as if he were strolling down a stairway. It wasn't until he got to the bottom that he turned and saw me.

"Hey, Sport." His voice was warm, genial. "Change your mind about doing some climbing?"

He pointed to his feet: EBs—a new pair.

"You were right." He grinned. "These things work great."

He looked just beyond me, at the rope. "Want to run up Conn's East or something?"

I didn't reply. Not right away. I was too awestruck.

Because he was back—the father I'd known before the funeral, the one I'd been climbing with all my life. He stood tall, every hint of slouch gone from his posture. His eyes sparkled, and the crow's-feet looked more like laugh lines. His brow was smooth and unfurrowed, and his smile looked easy and genuine. That old familiar smile.

"No," I finally said, forgetting the lecture I'd sworn to give him. "I . . . uh, just thought you might want a little company for the hike back down."

"That I would." He nodded firmly. "That would be great."

When we got to the bottom of the switchbacks, I went off-trail and walked to the side of the little creek, looking down into the basin.

I was in luck. There, easily visible through the cold, clear water, were the rippled red-and-white forms of two cans. Lying on my belly on the hard stone bank, I reached in, wetting my shirtsleeve, but not caring, as the day was hot. Snagging first one can and then the other, I got back to my feet and handed my father his Coke.

"Hey, Sport—great idea. Thanks."

"I would have brought you a beer. But I don't think Judd would have gone for it."

"This is better." By the look on his face, he meant it.

We both put our pop-tops in the cans this time. My father never littered anywhere around the cliffs. He even carried a Baggie with him so he could clean belay ledges of the cigarette butts and candy wrappers that other climbers left behind.

We sipped our Cokes in silence as we walked. Finally, I glanced over at my father.

"So what was that about?" I asked him.

He looked at me for a long, slow moment.

"You saw?"

I rolled my eyes. "I saw? Judd *Horton* saw. You were on the side of the Rocks that faces the village. He even put a quarter in that telescope of his."

"Oh man . . ." My father shook his head. "I forgot all about old Eagle Eyes."

We walked in silence for nearly a minute. Then he shrugged.

"I started out bouldering, just like I said I was going to," he told me. "And I was, you know, working my way along the base of the cliff, getting used to the new shoes, trying them out on things. Then I got to the bottom of Overboard, and I tried the first two moves? The off-balance ones? Man, the first time I did that route, I must have fallen off that second move six times. Kept landing on my back in the dirt next to my belayer. But today, I pulled them off just as smooth as silk, so I tried the next two, and then the next two, and then the two after that, and the next thing you know, I was all the way up to the belay ledge."

He handed me his can and I stepped behind him, slipping the

two emodies into his rucksack as we walked down the dirt two-track of Roy Gap Road. I knew that the belay ledge on Man Overboard ran all the way over to a 5.5 gully. Not quite a walk-off, but the next best thing to it. There was no reason to go up from there.

"I didn't even think about bailing," my father said, knowing what was on my mind. "This route I mean, I was wired to it, you know? As if I'd been put together to climb it. No doubt. No hesitation. Every move felt just exactly right."

I nodded. That was how he'd looked as he climbed it. I kept my peace, even though he still hadn't gotten to the *why*.

"It was like I can't begin to describe it to you, Patrick," he murmured. "Like seeing the sun come up after a long, dark, winter's night. I mean, the higher I got, the more things started to drop away. Losing your mom, the way she went, the questions that I keep asking myself every single day. The endless stream of 'if-onlys.' It didn't banish them, but it kept pushing them back, further and further and further, until finally there was nothing in my life but that rock. Just the hold I was on, and the one I was going for. Nothing more."

Not even me.

"And finally . . ." He smiled. "When I got to the top? When I stood there? It was like, oh man—there was a phrase they used in my philosophy class, back in college. What was it?

"*Tabula rasa.* That's it. It's Latin, from what's-his-name . . . Locke. Tabula rasa. It means 'a blank slate.' And that's what this climb did for me, Patrick. It wiped the slate clean, if only for the moment."

I looked at him for a long, weighty second.

"And you needed that," I finally said.

"Yes." He looked me in the eye as he said it. "I really did."

We walked in silence until we got to the steps of the footbridge. Turning at the top of them, my father looked down at me, his face warm and gentle.

"I need to apologize to you, Patrick," he said. "What I did up there, I know it had to have scared you. And I regret that. I really do. But I just want to assure you, I was never in any danger. I was totally in control, and I knew that."

"Well, besides, it's not as if you set out to do it. I mean, you were just going to try the first moves, and it developed from there, right?"

"Exactly." He smiled. "Thanks for understanding."

He turned and walked across the bridge, the suspended planks rippling beneath his gate, the white rapids of the North Fork rushing below. I watched him go, and when he got to the other side he turned and smiled again.

I smiled back, but my heart wasn't in it.

Because I was thinking of his rucksack, the one he'd cached at Luncheon Ledge. That was an inconvenient spot to leave something if you meant to just boulder a few spots along the middle cliffs. You'd have to go back up to retrieve your stuff, and then down again to get to the trail.

But it was the perfect place for a climber to leave something if he knew without a doubt that he'd be coming down from the summit.

If he knew that he'd be making a climb.

Wide enough to bridge fissures that are fist-size or wider, the bong is a wide steel
piton, named for the loud sound that it produces as it is being driven.

The Eastern Cragman's Guide to Climbing Anchors

EIGHT

Early the next morning, we jumped into the VW and headed to
Elkins to mail my term papers. Right away, that sounded fishy to
me, because you could put stuff in the mail right at Judd's store, and
as far as an official post office went—one with a flag out front and
FBI most-wanted posters on the wall—the nearest one was in Franklin, only half as far from our place as Elkins.

But my father gave me some story about running a few errands
while we were there and, figuring that he wanted to check again on
the missing valve for the LP tank—the Airstream was really beginning to feel cramped—I went along with the program.

Exactly why we'd gone to Elkins became clear right after the post
office. My father pointed the van up Route 250 and pulled into
Mountaineer Motor Sales. There, sitting at the dealership entrance,
freshly washed and prepped, was a brand-new 1976 Chevrolet Chevette. I no longer recall what Chevrolet called the color, but I still
remember the hue—it was orange. Air Force survival-gear orange.

My father turned to me and nodded at the little car.

"So," he asked, "what do you think of it?"

What did I think? *Why isn't it a Jeep?* That's what I thought.
Technically, we were still using up the months of unused vacation
time my father had accrued with AMC; he wouldn't officially resign
until that was depleted, so we qualified for the employee discount.
But then it hit me: A Jeep would remind him of Toledo. And Toledo
would remind him of my mother.

"Wild color," I finally said, hoping I hadn't been silent for too
long.

"Never have to worry about losing it." He said it as if there
hadn't been a pause in the conversation at all.

"You're thinking of getting that instead of the van?" I asked him. "Will there be enough room?"

"No." He shook his head. "I'm definitely keeping the van. What I meant was, what do you think of this car for you?"

For several long seconds, I was speechless; a pause my father apparently enjoyed, because he smiled.

"A brand-new car? But you're driving this." I waved my hand at the VW in which we sat. "That wouldn't be right."

"This old crate may be getting long in the tooth," my father said, slapping his hand on the big steering wheel. "But we've taken good care of her over the years." That was true. He'd always been meticulous about stopping rust before it could start, and I'd helped him completely rebuild the engine and transaxle two summers earlier.

"And I told you we'd be getting you some wheels after I sold the Jeep," he continued. "The deal I'm getting on that Chevy is about what I'd shell out for something decent, used. Besides, this way, if something goes wrong with the car over the next year, it's GM's problem, not ours. It's got a twelve-month warranty—keeps us from nickel-and-diming ourselves to death. Go on—take a look."

I looked. I liked. One hour later, I was driving the little car home behind my father's van.

"Go gentle on the brakes, and don't run out the gears," he'd told me. "It's not broken in yet."

And I did, because it was new, and it was amazing, and it was mine.

True, as cars went, the Chevette was about as close to a household appliance as one could go. It had a four-cylinder engine that sounded like a sewing machine at speed; a four-on-the-floor transmission that was built for function, not style; a heater for the winter and hand-cranked windows for the summer; and an AM radio that, driving in the mountains where we lived, would only get stations for about thirty seconds at a time. Its sole concession to luxury was the seating, which was cloth-covered, rather than vinyl. But the car was new, with fewer than seven miles on the odometer, and it smelled like a new car, and the rear seat folded down to make room for climbing gear. In fact, I would fold it down as soon as I got home, and it would stay that way until I sold it, the autumn after I got out of college.

And the unexpectedness of the gift had left me absolutely stunned.

Now, looking back on that day, viewing it from the perspective of an adult, it's pretty easy to see that my father was trying to expunge his guilt over the recklessness of the previous day's climb. He was buying absolution, offering an extravagant gift in return for my forgiveness of his outrageous behavior.

And what can I say? I was sixteen. It worked.

By the following Saturday, I had rubbed half a tin of Simonize onto the Chevette and sprayed an entire can of Scotchgard fabric protection into the upholstery. I'd made a second pilgrimage to Elkins the day before so I could stop by the Kmart and purchase a tachometer for the princely sum of $14.99. I mounted it on the steering column, the way I'd seen dragsters set up in magazines. It really was overkill; the Chevette needed a tach about as much as pigs need wings. But it made me happy, and that made my father happy.

Seneca had come into its early summer weather, with blue skies and balmy mornings. We restocked the store early on Friday (I drove in early to straighten up the shop, just to have an excuse to drive) and by late Friday afternoon we were well on the way to hitting our weekend sales goal. Life was good.

We had just opened the shop on Saturday morning when two guys came in who were obviously from the Shawangunks; their torn shorts, faded T-shirts, and bandannas worn, not pirate-style but knotted at four corners, were practically textbook illustrations of the "Vulgarian" style of dress so popular around the New York climbing camps.

"Excuse me, sir," the more clean-cut of the two said to my

father. "But we're, uh, new here. Do you have a guidebook we can look at?"

My father flipped him the shop copies of the *Climber's Guide* and the little waterproof pamphlet-style routes diagram that the Appies had put together. The pair pored over the two publications, buzzed in conversation between themselves, thanked us, and left.

Ten minutes later, they were back.

"Excuse me," the clean-cut one said, "but can you guys tell us, uh, how to get up to the Rocks?"

This broke my father up.

"Tell you what," he said, turning to me as he wiped the corners of his eyes. "Patrick, why don't you take these guys up climbing?"

"Whoa—we can't afford to hire a guide," said the taller of the two, a guy who was trying with very little success to cultivate a goatee.

"Our treat," my father said. "I don't think Patrick wants to be cooped up in the shop on a nice day like this, anyhow. Do you, Sport?"

"But what about the shop?" I asked. "Who spells you for dinner?"

"I can call Yokum's and ask them to run something down to me," my father said. "Or I can just put a note on the door and run up there and get it myself. You've been working a lot—it's high time for a break."

Fifteen minutes later, the necessary introductions having been made, I was leading the two of them down Roy Gap Road. The more clean-cut and genteel one was Paul, a sophomore physics major from SUNY at New Paltz, just a bicycle ride from the Sha-wangunks—the line of cliffs that constituted the most respected rock climbing in New York State. The scruffier, taller one, a dorm mate of Paul's, introduced himself as Mongo, but when I said, "Like in *Blazing Saddles*, right?"—he just looked at me.

Mongo clanked when he walked. While Paul and I carried our gear and our shoes in rucksacks, Mongo had a climbing rope and gear rack crisscrossed over his chest, and his PAs—EB's major competition in the world of friction shoes that year—hanging by the laces from his neck. It was as if he was worried that someone might see him and not know that he was a climber, and we all paid for his image management by having to listen to the incessant *PALANK, PALANK, PALANK* his equipment made as he strode along. I just hoped these guys weren't expecting to spot any wildlife on the approach.

We turned to follow the road along the river and caught our first glimpse of the swing bridge through the trees.

"Okay—so that's how you get across the river," Paul said.

"I told you we wouldn't have to wade it, you moron," Mongo sneered.

I decided that maybe I wouldn't like Mongo.

Two minutes later, after we'd crossed the bridge, Mongo was whining that we were moving too slowly, despite my assurances that it was a long approach, all of it uphill. I increased the pace a little to placate him.

"Is there really a restaurant around here called 'Yokum's'?" Paul asked as we followed the two-track.

"Yeah," I told him. "Restaurant and motel, both."

"Dorky name if you ask me," Mongo muttered. "Sounds like something out of 'Li'l Abner.'"

The probability of my not liking him stepped up a notch or two.

We were passing the National Forest Service sign, the one that warned hikers not to climb unless they were properly trained, when Mongo stopped for a moment.

"'There are no 5.11s,'" he said, reading aloud the graffiti that someone had hand-lettered onto the wooden surface. He turned to Paul. "There, d'you see that? I told you this rock was nothing but a stinkin' kindergarten."

I paused. That hand-lettered comment wasn't a complaint; it was a statement of pride, a philosophical manifesto. While climbers in Yosemite, Joshua Tree, Eldorado Springs Canyon, Cathedral Ledge, and even the Shawangunks had all gone right off the end of the old

Yosemite Decimal System and ranked climbs as 5.11s and even 5.12s, it was tradition at Seneca that the system stopped at 5.10. That was it—no exceptions. So climbs that were much more diffi- cult than the 5.10s found elsewhere were graded "5.10+" at Seneca, or simply referred to as "a hard 5.10." And that bias also extended downward into the ranking system. Good climbers from elsewhere often walked away scratching—or rubbing—their heads after trying a 5.8 or 5.9 at Seneca.

I almost explained that to Mongo.

Almost.

"Man, we wasted our time even comin' here," Mongo muttered before I'd even said a word.

So I kept my mouth shut. I'd decided that I definitely wasn't going to like him.

Mongo was blowing hard by the time we reached the trailhead, but I knew that he'd gripe if I slowed us down, so I decided then and there to go past the switchbacks and take us straight over to the South End.

If you think of the main body of Seneca Rocks as a ship, then the South End would be the bow. Only in this case the bow was about three hundred feet lower than everything else, extending down almost to the bottom of Roy Gap, scree fields falling like a wake from either side. It was the nearest to the road that one could begin a climb at Seneca.

"What grade are you guys climbing?" I asked.

"Anything you can climb," Mongo replied flatly. But Paul quickly added, "We're leading about 5.6 to 5.7, following up to 5.8, maybe 5.9, depending on what kind of 5.9 it is. We've really only climbed at the Trapps."

"I know what you mean," I said, nodding. At the 'Gunks, the seams between the layers of sedimentary rock ran horizontally. At Seneca, they were generally vertical. The two places called for two entirely different styles of climbing. "What say we start out on a 5.7? Right over here's the start of Ye Gods and Little Fishes, and it looks and sounds a whole lot nastier than it actually is."

"You're leading it then," Mongo snapped.

"Sure thing," I told him. "But if I'm leading, will you take my rucksack for me?"

He rolled his eyes and nodded.

I got my shoes, rope, and gear rack out of the nylon-canvas pack. Then, waiting until Mongo was bent over and tying his shoes, I found a rock that hefted out at about six or seven pounds, rolled it up in my wind pants, tucked the rolled parcel into the rucksack, and laid the pack down next to the belay tree.

Five minutes later, we had the rope stacked and ready. Mongo was anchored to a belay tree, and Paul was already tied in to Mongo, ready to follow him as the last member of our team.

I waited. Mongo just sat there.

"Are you on belay?" I asked him.

He looked down at the rope passing through his belay ring.

"Don't I look like I'm on belay?"

He did, but he hadn't told me, "On belay"—he hadn't followed what was pretty much an international safety standard. Deciding that this wasn't the time for a talk on effective climbing communications, I just said, "Climbing."

"Flash or crash," Mongo said, his voice sounding like deliberate half yawn.

There is a highly edifying feeling about being the lead climber on a rope. Following, you always wonder if that tight rope you got at the crux was just to keep you from going too far if you fell off, or if maybe it helped you along, gave you an extra ten pounds or so of boost. But on lead, no such illusions existed. You made upward progress purely on the basis of your own strength and skill.

It was an easy thing to revel in, and I did, liking the warm feeling of the rock under my hands, the honest strain of lifting one's body weight up and past obstacles. I put in a large Hexentric about twenty feet up and opposed it with a stopper on a runner so I wouldn't pull the protection out when I drew the rope up. It was probably unnecessary, but I did it because that was what my father would have done—what he would have done on those occasions when he availed himself of a rope and equipment.

Mongo offered a few observations on the slowness of my progress and added that the route looked far too easy for a climber of his caliber. I ignored him until, a hundred feet and five chock placements later, I reached the belay ledge, where I anchored myself, rigged my eight-ring quickly, pulled most of the slack out of the fifty-meter rope, and called down, "Belay off . . . on belay."

Two minutes later, I heard from far, far below, "Oof! What have you got in this pack, man?"

"Water bottle, lunch and some spare gear," I called down. It was all true; I just didn't mention the rock. "Why? If it's too heavy for you, just leave it there and I'll rap down and pick it up later."

"Naw," Mongo called up. "I can handle it. You got me?"

Mongo talked a better route than he climbed. While he never called out "Tension"—the climber's signal for assistance via the rope—I soon lost count of all the times he shouted, "Up rope." He'd call for me to take in more rope the second it was anything less than cable-taut. I figured he was delivering only about ninety percent of the climbing power, and I was providing the additional ten. But he cleaned the equipment placements without incident, and soon I had him beside me on the ledge.

"You good to bring up Paul, or do you want me to belay him?" I asked.

"I got him," Mongo growled. "Just help me get this stinkin' pack off."

"Sure."

I assisted him as he shed the rucksack, then shifted it over to the other side of me to clip it off on a chock. As I did, I noticed another loose rock lying on the ledge. I picked it up: about five pounds, by the feel of it. Waiting until Mongo was peering down the pitch, I slipped the second rock into the pack, as well.

Paul was not only quieter than Mongo, he was a much better climber. Still, Mongo griped and offered a running critique as he belayed his friend up the pitch. Then he turned to me and asked, "Where's this route end up?"

"A ledge called Broadway," I told him. "It leads both ways around the Rocks, so you can go to the East Face or the West, whatever you want."

"So long as it goes to something better than this," he grumbled. "This ain't nothin' like the 'Gunks."

Yeah, I almost shot back. *It doesn't have a carriage road leading to the bottom of every climb, or a walk-off every fifty feet.*

But I kept my mouth shut.

And not even Mongo could spoil the beauty of the next pitch. Ye Gods is one of those rare climbs with sheer open drops on three sides—like ascending a tower of air. Looking left, I could see the dirt road leading down to the swing bridge, and beyond that, the town and the weathered Appalachian Mountains behind it. To my right was a huge forested valley-like depression—a hollow, or "holler" in local parlance. And behind me, across a seven hundred and fifty-foot gulf of nothingness, the looming gray quartzite of the Southern Pillar rose up from the bottom of Roy Gap, like a stony backbone sticking out from the densely wooded hillside.

Pulling the final overhang, I stepped up to Broadway, anchored to a huge, healthy pine and set up my belay. Twenty minutes later, Mongo and Paul were both there beside me, Mongo complaining bitterly about the pack.

"Well, I'll carry it to wherever we climb next," I said. "Or we can leave it at Luncheon Ledge and grab it on the way down. Speaking of Luncheon Ledge—you guys want some gorp?"

I dug the trail mix out of the rucksack and, while the Shawangunks Two were busily sorting out the gear, took out the two rocks, as well. Paul looked up as I was removing the larger one—I could feel my face burning red, and his whole body shook as he stifled a laugh. Nodding conspiratorially to Paul, I laid the rocks safely away from the edge of Broadway. It occurred to me that, if I climbed with Mongo long enough, I could probably rebuild Seneca Rocks from the ground up.

"What do you want to do next?" I asked as I handed the mix and a water bottle around.

"Something with some teeth to it," Mongo muttered. "At least 5.9. This nursery-school stuff is putting me to sleep."

Paul glanced at his classmate, his eyebrows up in alarm, then looked quickly back at me and said, "Actually, anything at all would be fine, Patrick. This is great. Ye Gods was amazingly cool. We really appreciate your showing us the rock."

And to do more of that, I'd been thinking of Conn's East, a 5.4 route that diagonaled up the eastern face beneath the South Summit and offered tons of exposure, but only the slightest technical challenge.

I was getting tired of Mongo, though, and it was time to shut him up.

"I know just the thing," I told them.

Ten minutes later, having followed Broadway around to the East Face of Seneca, crossing quickly under the novices cringing their way up the second pitch of the Old Ladies' Route, and then up the short rocky "step" dividing Upper Broadway from Lower Broadway, I'd led us to a broad, graveled ledge nearly one hundred fifty feet below, and just north of, the South Peak.

"Here we are," I told the New Yorkers.

Mongo looked up. We were standing right of center beneath a huge detached flake of rock, unrelenting in its verticality. When you looked up, all you saw was rock and sky.

"Where?" he asked.

"It's called 'Thin Man,'" I told him. "My father put it up about three years ago."

"That's not what I mean," Mongo said. "I mean, where's the route?"

"Why, right here." I pointed to a very faint crack that began about thirty feet above where we were standing.

Paul followed my finger.

"Well how do you get to *that*?" His voice actually shook as he asked it.

"It's all nubbins until the crack," I explained. "You're climbing nubbins, and the only place to put protection is between nubbins."

"That's crazy," Paul said.

"That's how it got its name," I told him. "The first guys that tried it told my father to stay away. They said, 'It's too thin, man.'"

Mongo looked up the wall.

"Wait a minute," he said. "What's this rated?"

"It's a 5.9." I shrugged.

It was true. Of course, it was a *Seneca* 5.9, meaning that, anywhere else in the civilized world, it was at least a 5.10, and probably a 5.11. As much as my father disliked underrating routes, he'd decided he had to stay within local guidelines—otherwise you would start to have some 5.10s that were easier than other routes that had already been rated 5.9, and ultimately the rating system would mean nothing.

Mongo looked up the wall again.

"So what do you think?" I asked. "Do you want to lead it or should we go find something easier? You said you wanted something that was at least a 5.9."

I waited. The crux pitch in Thin Man was right in front of us, the very first pitch, practically the very first moves, and you could tell that just by looking at it. I was almost certain that Mongo would refuse to try. That would put him in his place, and after that, we could all walk over about a hundred feet south and climb Conn's East. So I was entirely unprepared for what he said next.

"Sure," he said. "I'll lead it."

My stomach sank. We weren't even wearing helmets, and the protection all the way up to the crack on this climb was purely psychological. If you came off in the first thirty feet, it was a crater, guaranteed.

Still, Mongo and I were both committed—a West Virginian standoff, if you will. Swallowing dryly, I put in a belay anchor at the edge of the ledge and stacked the rope while he rearranged the equipment rack so the small stuff was all easy to find.

"Okay," I said after Mongo was tied on and I was anchored down. "I'm on belay."

Mongo nodded. He looked pale. He put his hand on one nubbin, his foot on another. He stepped up.

He slid off, landing heavily on his feet.

I squelched a smirk. I'd only climbed this route once, following my father, and I remembered that the first move was like a puzzle—you had to stem between nubbins until you were up about four feet, then lay back off a folded seam for another ten. Only after that could you go to conventional, straightforward climbing.

"Take a breath," I told him. "You'll get it."

In about a thousand years.

Mongo shook his hands out, tried the same move, and fell off again.

My conscience got the best of me. At least I had seen this route climbed before I ever tried following on it, and I'd followed it tightly roped from above. Asking Mongo to lead it on sight bordered on outright cruelty.

"Your right foot is on the right place, and so's your right hand," I told him, "but you need to move your left foot over almost a yard. It's a big stem to that tan pebble embedded in the rock. Try it."

Scowling, he did as I told him. He stuck.

"Good," I said. "Now continue to stem. See the bulges about knee level, each side? Those are your footholds. The handholds are just smears for right now."

Legs shaking, Mongo tried the move and slid off again. This time, he landed on his seat.

"You were doing it," I said brightly.

Mongo tried again, but he was pulling at the rock now, trying to muscle it. You couldn't do that on Thin Man—the route called for technique, pure finesse. He fell off before he got to the second move, landing on his back this time.

"Forget this," he muttered, getting to his feet and untying from the rope.

"Sure," I agreed, unclipping from the belay anchor and belay ring. I got to my feet and brushed off the seat of my climbing shorts. "Want to go try something a little easier?"

Not even waiting for his reply, I began packing the gear to move over to Conn's East.

"Wait a minute," Mongo said. "What about you?"

"What about me?" I asked, looking up.

"You picked this. Let's see you lead it."

He glowered at me, gruff and uncouth. My bluff was being called. So it must have been a combination of stupidity and pride that made me say what came next.

"Okay," I told him. "But let's let Paul belay me. It's his turn. He cleaned last time."

Having the more competent of the duo to belay me did little to calm my jitters. Up to the beginning of the crack, there was little a belayer could do to protect me. I wouldn't get a decent protection placement until I reached the crack—*if* I reached the crack. The beginning moves of Thin Man were as difficult as any boulder problem I'd ever attempted. And as for leads, it would certainly be the most difficult 5.9 I'd ever attempted.

After all, on that distant Saturday morning, Thin Man was about to become the *first* 5.9 lead I'd ever attempted.

This was beyond stupid. This was nuts, easily the dumbest thing I'd ever done in my life up to that time and, even though I was only sixteen, that was saying something. I tightened each EB until my toes began to numb, and then I tied in to the red kernmantle rope, forming the knot with the meticulous care of someone who fully expected to need it. Glumly taking in the ten yards of virtually blank rock, I hoped in the back of my mind that it would be someone other than my father who would be sent up with the Stokes litter to fetch me.

I tried to remember how my father had protected this first bit. I knew that he'd made the placement about fifteen feet up. It seemed to me he'd hung one chock and then inverted the other. But I wasn't sure. I wasn't even sure I could get high enough on this route to worry about placing protection. My heart was speeding up just thinking about it. But I couldn't bail on this one. I wouldn't. Not in front of Mongo.

And right then, I knew just what to do.

I breathed.

Closing my eyes, I inhaled slowly, drawing the clean mountain air in through my nose in one long, cooling draught. One, then a second.

"Oh, great," I heard Mongo grumble, as if from some great distance. "Far out. We're climbing with Kwai Chang Caine."

I ignored him and took a third breath, feeling my heart rate drop to a slow but steady rhythm. From somewhere seemingly outside of me, a plan was forming.

I opened my eyes and peered up at the bottom of the crack again, gauging its size. Reaching down, I selected one of the smallest stoppers on my rack. Unclipping it, I turned to Paul.

"On belay," he told me. Wisely, he had several coils of slack between the two of us, loose rope that wouldn't slow me down as I climbed the first few moves.

"Okay," I told him. "Climbing."

I put the cable of the chock between my teeth, the carabiner dangling down against my right cheek, and stepped onto the first slight foothold.

Grabbing a thin seam with my right hand, I pulled to the right on it, stemmed across with my other foot and then, without hesitation, moved up to the two footholds above that, my feet still wide apart, like a long jumper's.

Now I could see it—a seam as slender as the overlapping icing on a cake, just big enough to grip with my fingertips. I did that with both hands and leaned to my left against the tiny fingerholds, switching my feet over to the right and walking them up against barely visible nubbins, keeping pace with myself by going hand-over-hand up the seam.

I was at the spot where my father had placed his chocks the one time I'd followed him here, and I ignored it, climbing past, unwilling to waste my strength on a placement that would be tenuous at best. Reaching up high, I gripped a thin broken flake, only a quarter-inch thick but as reassuring as the rung of a ladder after the miniscule holds of the first few moves. I put both hands on the hold and hopped my feet waist-high to a pair of down-sloping depressions, and used the handhold to lever my body weight in. Then I stood, smoothly moving up to pinch a projecting seam.

I kept moving, keeping my weight in constant oscillation against the holds, never coming to rest long enough to slide off. I saw the bottom of the crack coming and climbed past it, moving up until it was wide enough to accept my fingertips. Then, taking the stopper out of my mouth, I clipped the rope and, in one smooth motion, slid the stopper half its length into the crack and tugged down to set it.

"Showoff," I heard Mongo mutter.

Nothing could have been further from the truth. I wasn't doing this for flash. I was simply climbing quickly in order to get past the hard parts before my strength gave out.

It was a good plan. By staying in motion, I'd arrived amazingly fresh, so I used this. I kept going, fingering and toeing my way up the crack, slowing only long enough to put in another stopper, one size up from the last one, twenty feet farther up the crack. As I left the crack to move back to a series of nubbins that led to the blue sky above, it occurred to me giddily that not only was I leading my first 5.9, but I had placed only two chocks in more than sixty feet of climbing.

Once out of the crack, I placed none at all, working the pencil eraser-size handholds and shallowly dished foot placements with the samba-like grace of a boulder problem, not slowing a bit until I hand-mantled the last move and was standing atop the foot and a half-thick flake, halfway up the East Face of Seneca. With plenty of chocks left to choose from, I built an absolutely bombproof belay anchor, three stoppers in three separate cracks opposed against two cammed hex nuts from below. I clipped into all of them with a pair of carabiners and called down, "Belay off." Then I began pulling up the excess rope until I felt resistance and heard Paul call up, "That's me."

Ten minutes later, Paul appeared over the bellying rock of the upper half of the flake, grinning from ear to ear, a single nylon runner clung over his head and one shoulder. On it were my two chocks. He was wearing my rucksack, too; its bulk told me that the second rope was coiled up in there, and not running down to his dorm mate.

"Where's Mongo?" I asked.

"Said he was too stiff to climb after falling on his back." Paul shrugged.

Sure enough, far down Broadway, I could see a lanky, disheveled figure making his way down the step.

Paul mantled up, clipped off to the anchor I had waiting for him, and handed me his sling, looking with wonder at the two small stoppers that had been my only placements in more than seventy feet of climbing.

"Well," he said. "At least nobody is going to accuse you of stitching your way up this pitch. How many times have you led this, anyhow?"

I looked up at the ninety feet of dimpled wall that lay between us and the skylined summit ridge. Then I looked back at Paul, perched birdlike on the ledge beside me, the landscape dropping, all quartzite and pine trees, behind him.

"Just as soon as we finish this," I told him, "that will make it . . . well, once."

There is this king-of-the-world feeling that comes from climbing something that logic and reason says you should not have been able to climb, particularly after you've done it on the sharp end of the rope. So Paul and I were on cloud nine all the way down Roy Gap Road that afternoon. If someone had tried to enlist us for a summit attempt on Everest, we wouldn't have hesitated for a moment. We would have been game.

"We're camped over at the picnic shelter," Paul told me as we crossed Route 33 to the turnout in front of the shop. "Why don't you join us tonight? We can get up early and hit the Rocks one more time before Mongo and I have to drive back north."

"Sounds good," I told him. "I'll check and see if I'm needed here at the shop. If I'm not, I'll see you tonight."

"Cool."

The shop was dark compared to the sunlit afternoon outside, and my father was ringing up a rucksack for a couple of hikers as I came in. Some of the Seneca regulars were already slouched on the benches around the cold stove, swapping war stories, and a few students from WVU, down with their Rec-Ed class, were going through the T-shirts.

"Hey, Sport," my father said, glancing over the half-glasses he had to wear to read in the darkened environs of the shop. "Have a good climb?"

"Great," I told him, opening the door to the back room and setting my pack inside.

"What'd you climb?" He didn't even look up as he asked it. He just sorted receipts and stuck the most recent one in its place.

"Uhm . . ." I said, stalling, "the South End and then the East Face."

"What on the South End?" he asked. "Skyline Traverse?"

"No—Ye Gods."

"I see." He nodded. "How about on the east side? Conn's East?"

"Uh, no," I muttered. "We did something else."

"I see." He motioned me closer. I moved behind the counter, next to him.

"Harry Priestly was in here earlier," he said, his voice just a shade above a whisper.

Harry was an old friend of my father's, a *National Geographic* photographer who lived in Alexandria. He climbed in boots that looked too small for his body, because he'd lost all of his toes to frostbite on a disastrous K2 expedition.

"Yeah?" I said.

"He said he thought he saw you topping out on Thin Man," my father told me. "Is that right?"

"Yes, sir." I looked down at the counter.

"Leading," my father added. "Is that correct?"

"Yes, sir."

He counted the cash in the till, slid a sheaf of twenties under the coin drawer, and closed the drawer.

"How'd you protect the first thirty feet?" He looked right at me as he asked it.

"I didn't," I told him. "I figured I'd blow up if I stopped to rig something. So I just kept moving until I got to where I could put something solid in the crack."

My father looked me in the eyes for a long moment. Finally he nodded.

"That wasn't really very smart," he asked, "was it?"

A hundred replies came to me at once, any one of which would have wounded him to the quick. So I said nothing.

"Okay." He shrugged, as if reading my thoughts. "Point taken. Just remember, I'm responsible for you. Okay? Try to climb the way you would if I was with you."

"I will," I said. "And I'm sorry."

"For what—leading a 5.9 that would be a stiff 5.10, maybe even a 5.11, anywhere else?" My father chuckled. "Don't be too sorry! How about tomorrow morning? You going up?"

"In the morning," I told him, "if it's okay with you. And don't worry; we're just going to do stuff I can walk. Skyline, maybe Sally's Peril. And I was going to stay with the guys over at the picnic shelter tonight . . . if that's all right with you."

"Sure," he said. "But if anybody breaks out any beer or whacky tobaccy, you'll stay clear, right?"

"Hey," I said. "I've got a season of ball to play come fall—I'm in training."

Judd Horton was a little more vigorous with his interrogation.

"Whatsa matter?" Judd rumbled at me as I signed the spiral-bound notebook that served as the register for Horton's Seneca Acres Campground. "You sass back to your daddy once too often? He kick you out of that big ol' log house of your'un?"

"No." I grinned. "I'm just going climbing with some friends in the morning. And besides, the gas isn't on in the house yet, so we're living in the trailer for the time being."

"You and half of West-by-golly Virginia," Judd barked, chuckling. "'Livin' in the trailer for the time bein'.'"

I fished the campground fee out of my pocket and laid it on Judd's counter: a shiny new Bicentennial quarter with the Revolutionary War drummer on the back of it.

"Thank you kindly," Judd told me, plunking the coin into a pasteboard cigar box on the shelf behind his counter. Then he looked up at me sternly.

"Now, you steer clear of them hippie types over there, you hear me?" He turned sideways and spat into a coffee can on the floor. "The guvament says I can't turn 'em away, but that don't mean I gotta like 'em."

"No hippies," I said, nodding to placate him.

"And anotha thing." Judd glowered at me now. "It's Saturday night. There's gonna be church folk a-comin' in in the mornin'. Don't you go strippin' down in front of them, you hear?"

He-yah is the way he said it.

"Just last month they was all in a dither," Judd told me. "Buncha boys started strippin' down to go climbin' right in front of them church women."

I considered telling Judd that climbing in the nude was not a general practice. But I knew that would just make me "uppity."

"I'll be civil," I promised him.

"You be," he admonished me with a stern nod of his head.

Picking up my rucksack and my stuff-sacked sleeping bag, I headed out into the golden sun of approaching dusk, crossing the highway and the concrete bridge over Seneca Creek, and then turning left down the potholed dirt road that led back into Horton's Seneca Acres.

I'd forgotten about the church people—the "holy rollers," my father called them. They showed up at the picnic shelter every Sunday morning at eight-thirty sharp, which is a little late for climbers, so I'd never seen more than a glimpse of them—lanky farm men in worn, out-of-fashion suits cut too short at the wrists, their Adam's apples perched upon their starched white shirt collars. Their women wore long dresses—not the granny dresses that my mother had once favored, but long calicos with lace collars. I knew that they had a pump organ they brought with them, because we heard it sometimes on the Rocks when the wind was right. But as for what was said there, I hadn't a clue, although my father had cracked jokes about "fire and brimstone."

After a grand entrance under a wooden archway that had seen better days, the dirt road ran into Horton's Seneca Acres, forked, and then petered out in two directions into crabgrass and rye that Judd cropped to ankle height with a gang mower whenever the spirit moved him. Waist-high weeds formed the perimeter, and vans, VW bugs, and a variety of dusty hatchbacks dotted the field in no discernible order, right back to a thicket of holly bushes at the far end.

Many people pitched tents when they camped at Horton's, but the stony ground bent tent pegs, and my father and I had found that, although the ground had been hand-cleared by more than twenty-five years' worth of climbers, it was nearly impossible to select a site that would not leave at least one of its occupants sleeping on a rib-goring hunk of river stone. So, unless we had my mother along (which had always occasioned the use of a motel), we'd long since abandoned tents in favor of the picnic shelter.

Judd had built the open-sided wooden shelter to satisfy the local demand for a place in which to hold family reunions, and it was still used for that on occasion—making it a sort of potluck, alfresco banquet hall. But with its tightly shaked roof and overhanging eaves, it provided perfect shelter from all but the windiest of mountain rainstorms, so climbers got there early on weekend evenings to stake claim to a piece of its worn, rough-planked floor for their sleeping bags.

I did that first thing, putting my ground pad and sleeping bag down right next to the first of the plain wooden benches that Judd kept in the shelter for the church people. I figured that would minimize my chances of getting trod upon by late-night arrivals and any climbers returning from the bars down in Elkins. Then I went looking for the New Yorkers and found them hunkered down next to a little one-burner Peak One stove. A North Face dome tent, so new that it still had its white to-be-removed-by-consumer-only content labels, stood just a few feet away, breathing softly in the light evening breeze.

"Hey, Patrick," Paul said brightly. "We're just heating up some Spaghetti-O's. Want some?"

"Oh—no thanks," I told him. "My dad got chicken from the 4U. I ate before I came." I was glad I had.

"More for us," Mongo muttered.

That was it. Not "good evening." Not "nice lead today." Just, "more for us." It was like talking with a very tall and petulant six-year-old.

Using my half-empty rucksack as an impromptu ground cloth, I sat down next to the two of them and then tried as discreetly as possible to inch away a bit. Before dinner, I had headed down to the swimming hole on the North Fork with a clean towel and a four-ounce bottle of Dr. Bronner's Pure-Castile 18-in-1 peppermint soap. Mongo very obviously had not.

"So what are you guys up for tomorrow?" I asked Paul.

"I dunno." He stirred the billy pot of bland, canned pseudo-spaghetti, lifted the spoon, tasted it, grimaced, and turned the burner up on his stove. "We have to hit the road for New Paltz at about noon. What do you suggest?"

The first thing that came to me was something I did not want to share with Mongo. But I liked Paul, and I wanted him to have the full Seneca experience. So I said it: "Why don't we do something quick, like Marshall's Madness, and then finish up by climbing the Gendarme? It's the signature climb here at Seneca."

Mongo reached into his back pocket, pulled out a new, if bent, copy of *A Climber's Guide to Seneca Rocks*, and checked the page that listed routes alphabetically.

"A 5.8 followed by a 5.4?" He feigned a snore.

"Come on," Paul told him. "We've got a drive—we don't need anything epic tomorrow."

"Easy for you guys to say," Mongo sneered. "You had your 5.9 today."

"You had your chance at it." I said it just like that. No thought involved; it just slipped out.

The look Mongo gave me looked good to melt glass.

"You're right," he said. "I guess I was just too tired out from hauling all those rocks up the first climb."

Blushing—the curse of the Nolan menfold—came far too easily to me back in those days. I hoped the fading light hid it.

Paul looked down intently at his billy pot—I should have known he would have told Mongo. After all, they were dorm mates.

Biting my lip, I shrugged.

"That was pretty immature of me," I told the taller New Yorker. "I shouldn't have done it. I apologize."

"Don't worry," he told me evenly. "I don't get mad. I just get even."

That pretty much set the tone for the rest of the evening. Paul talked about college, about New York, and about the climbing at the 'Gunks. In turn, I told him about Toledo and bouldering at Whipp's Ledges, both of which were immediately judged by Mongo to be "dorky." So after about an hour, I picked up my rucksack and headed back into the picnic shelter, hoping to get to bed right away and get up at first light.

Fat chance.

Maybe it was the fact that I'd gotten accustomed to our secluded travel trailer in the mountains and the muted white noise of its air-conditioner. Maybe it was that, when my father and I camped at the shelter, the crowds had tended to be smaller. Maybe it was Mongo's vague threat about getting even. But whatever it was, it seemed as if I lay awake for hours, hearing every single sound in the camp-ground.

I got as comfortable as possible, pulling off my canvas climbing shorts in the cramped confines of the cocoon-like mummy bag and then stowing them away in my rucksack. Setting the pack under my head for a pillow, I waited in vain for sleep to come as late arrivals slammed car doors and walked across the shelter floor in search of a place to put their sleeping bags. At the far end of the shelter, some-one was trying to light a Coleman lantern as his four companions, all obviously quite drunk, loudly advised him as to what he was doing wrong. Distant laughter floated in from an all-night campfire bull session. And just as I was about to finally drift off, someone walked heavily across the shelter, bumped into one of the corner posts and cursed, drawing a volley of complaints from others trying to get to sleep on the floor.

So it was well after two when I finally drifted off and, while I'd brought no alarm clock, I trusted in the time-honored climber's alarm system—that the first one up from our party would wake the others.

As it turned out, that assumption was only half right.

At times when nothing on the gear sling will fit the opportunity at hand, a placement can often be improvised by stacking two pieces. Quite often, their differences will bridge the gap nicely.

The Eastern Cragman's Guide to Climbing Anchors

NINE

When I woke, it was to the sound of footsteps, a number of people milling in the shelter, and unfamiliar voices addressing one another as "brother" and "sister" in the high drawl of the West-Virginia mountain accent. Opening one eye, I peeked out from under my sleeping-bag hood and saw a long-skirted, gray-haired woman supervising as two black-suited men set up a portable organ at the edge of the shelter. Closer to me, a young man in a shirt and tie was sweeping the shelter floor, taking care to brush the dust and grit away from me and my bag.

I groaned.

The holy rollers; I'd overslept. Sitting up, I looked across the open shelter to the place where Paul and Mongo had pitched their tent. It was gone: nothing there but threadbare ground.

Unzipping the bag a few inches, I reached for my rucksack and touched bare, dusty wood. I peered under the bench next to me and saw only distant, thick-soled brogans.

Sitting with the bag draped around my shoulders, I looked around and finally spotted it: my red rucksack was up under the roof, hanging from the rafter at the far end of the shelter.

Mongo's payback. I should have known. He'd not only convinced Paul to leave me in the shelter while they went climbing, he'd sneaked in before they left and hung my rucksack—my rucksack containing my shorts—thirty feet away from, and nine feet above, where I lay in my sleeping bag.

More Sunday-dressed farmers were arriving by the minute, parking their pickup trucks well shy of the shelter to spare it the dust of the rutted dirt drive. They walked across the dry, tufted grass carefully, as if unused to their suits, their wives all smiles in calico and starched, white lace.

Clearly, if I wanted to make a move to get to the rucksack—if I wanted to get to my *shorts*—I needed to do it sooner, rather than later.

But how? Either I could unzip the bag and bolt across the shelter in my underwear in full view of the church people—thus realizing Judd Horton's worst nightmare—or I could inchworm across the floor in my sleeping bag and then climb into the rafters using arm strength alone. It was something I was fully capable of doing. But it was not something that anyone could do inconspicuously.

"Excuse me, would you like me to get that for you?"

Looking up to see who had spoken, I was momentarily struck dumb.

Peering down on me in my early-morning rumpledness was absolutely the most beautiful girl I'd ever laid eyes on.

She was about my age—I hoped with all my heart that she was about my age—with honey-blond hair tied back in a black velvet ribbon and deep blue eyes. Her voice held just the barest hint of the mountain accent, and had this wonderful liquid quality that made me want to devote a lifetime or two to nothing whatsoever but her care. Like all of the women entering the picnic shelter, she was wearing a dress, but hers was cut from a soft blue denim, rather than calico, worn long enough that all I could see of her legs were her ankles. But even those smooth, tan, sculpted ankles were enough to make me feel weak.

"Are you all right?" Her face was kind, warm, concerned.

"Uh . . . y-yes," I stammered. "And yes, if you could get me my pack, that would be great. But it's up there pretty high. Are you sure you can get it?"

"Not a problem." She turned, looked for a moment, and then called out, "Jimmy!"

Boyfriend, I thought, my heart falling.

But Jimmy turned out to be about nine years old, maybe a small ten. He came running, his black oxford shoes capped with the tan dust of the campground, listened to the girl for a while, grinned, and then, still in his white shirt and tie, clambered up the corner post of the shelter and out onto the rafter. He was no rock climber, but he was obviously no stranger to heights, either.

Jimmy ran to the center of the rafter with the casual air of a circus tightrope walker, dropped astride the timber, and leaned down to unbuckle the pack straps, which had been wrapped around it. When he did, the pack dropped half a foot, almost taking the small boy with it.

"Tell him to be careful," I told the girl. "It's probably full of rocks."

Jimmy hefted the pack, looked back at the corner post, shrugged, and then put on my beat-up nylon rucksack over his immaculate white shirt. He scrambled back to the ground just as gracefully as he'd ascended, dashed across the shelter, and laid the pack next to my sleeping bag as carefully as if it had been a living thing.

"Thanks," I told him.

"You're welcome, sir," he said. It just may have been the first time in my life that anyone other than a fast-food counter attendant had addressed me as "sir."

The girl sat on the bench next to my bag and watched as I opened the rucksack and took out a smooth, bean-shaped river stone, as big as anything I'd put into it the day before, followed by its three larger cousins. I set them aside, and then pulled out my EBs, pouring a double handful of pebbles from each one.

"You're a climber?" she asked.

"Usually I am," I said. "But from the looks of things, not today."

"Your friends ditched you?"

I looked up at the rafter where the pack had been.

"I'm not so certain they were my friends," I told her frankly.

"Then let's you and I be friends." She said it easily, as if it were the most natural thing in the world.

"Uh . . . sure." My voice came out embarrassingly husky.

"I like to bring friends to church," she said brightly. "Will you stay?"

I glanced around at the gawky, thin men in their old-fashioned suits. I listened to the woman warming up on the organ, its pedals being pumped by the ubiquitous Jimmy. His enthusiasm outstripped his sense of rhythm, giving the instrument the sound of a cat being dropped down a long flight of stairs. Then I looked up into those beautiful green eyes. If this girl was a holy roller, then rolling sounded just fine to me.

"Sure," I said, nodding. "You bet."

I found my battered Chouinard Stand-Up Shorts, beat them against the floor, raising a tiny puff of dust, and then pulled them into the sleeping bag with me. Working the shorts down over my feet, I tugged them up. It felt odd, putting my pants on next to this radiantly attractive girl, and she must have known what I was thinking, because she suddenly turned the most beautiful shade of pink and then turned her head.

"I'm Rachel," she told me. She glanced back my way for an instant, extending her hand.

I rubbed my hand on my sleeping bag before taking hers. Her hand was soft and warm, and I was sure my own climbing-callused hand felt like a work glove in those slender, smooth fingers.

"I'm Patrick," I said, feeling my own blush creep into my face at the mere touch of her hand. I didn't want to let go right away, so I kept shaking it and said, "Rachel—that's a beautiful name."

"It's a biblical name." She was facing me again.

"So's Patrick, isn't it?" It seemed like a safe bet at the time; I was pretty sure Saint Patrick had to be somewhere in the Bible.

"No." She shook her head, the fall of hair from her ribbon swaying like a golden, breeze-brushed waterfall. "I don't believe it is."

I buttoned the waistband on my shorts and then unzipped the mummy bag, swinging my legs out onto the wooden floor so I could put on my Countrys. Immediately the lady at the organ arched her eyebrows. A few of the men glanced my way and talked among themselves, and Rachel looked away again.

I looked at my knees. Not only were they the only knees visible in the entire shelter, a good eight inches of sun-reddened thigh showed plainly above them. I liked my climbing shorts just long enough to keep the sit harness from chafing me.

"Uh . . ." I stammered. "It's a little cool this morning, isn't it?"

I dug back into my pack, pulled out my wind pants, and flapped them out in front of me. Another fist-size stone rolled out onto the tan planked floor. Tugging the nylon pants on, I snapped them shut down the sides. My legs immediately began to perspire, but Rachel looked considerably more comfortable.

"You're here with your folks?" I asked as I stuffed my sleeping bag into its sack.

"Just my daddy. Mama's off to Wheeling, helping my cousin with a new baby girl."

Daddy . . . Mama . . . I'd never heard a girl over the age of eight refer to her parents that way. But from Rachel, it didn't sound corny at all. It sounded warm, familiar, and homey—like a fire blazing in the hearth on a brisk autumn morning.

"Which one's your father?" I asked.

"Daddy?" Rachel smiled and nodded toward the front of the shelter. "Why, that's him right there."

I looked up and saw an athletic-looking man in his mid-thirties. His sandy brown hair looked like it had been cut by someone who knew what they were doing, and his suit was not only stylish, it actually fit him well. He had a Bible thumbed open in his left hand, and when he smiled, a perfect row of teeth flashed whitely from his suntanned face.

"Good morning, everyone," he said heartily, "and welcome to Weeping Oak Community Church. We're going to get into the Word of God this morning, but first, let's turn over in our hymnals to page 348, 'When the Roll Is Called Up Yonder,' everybody standing, and everybody singing like you actually intend to be there!"

Around me, twenty or thirty farm families rose to their feet. I stood, as well, but my stomach was headed in the opposite direction.

That's great, Patrick, I told myself as the mountain people all began to sing. *Really peachy. This girl you're falling head over heels for just happens to be the pastor's daughter.*

Not that it made her any less attractive. I looked over at Rachel as we stood and the morning sun was streaming in under the eaves so it hit her blond hair and set it aglow around the edges—what photographers call "key lighting." She smiled as she sang and she was so perfect, so angelic, that I couldn't help but just stare. Rachel was nearly a full head shorter than me, and that just made me like her all the more. Strange, contradictory feelings were awakening in my chest. It was as if I wanted to hold her and prevent anyone from touching her—both at the same time.

Feeling my eyes on her, Rachel half turned, smiled, and moved the worn, red-covered hymnal over toward me so I could see the music. And when I reached out to help her hold the book, our hands touched. That chance, momentary kiss of skin against bare skin was enough to send a shiver all the way down to the soles of my feet.

I didn't sing a note. The memory of my voice cracking two summers earlier had been enough to dissuade me from further public singing. But like any red-blooded American teenager, I could lip-synch with the best of them. So I did that—mouthed the words and stood next to Rachel and hoped against hope that our hands would touch again.

It was wonderful, just hoping for it. We sang another hymn—that is, Rachel sang, and most of the folks around me sang, while I mouthed, "Rock of Ages, cleft for me. Let me hide myself in Thee . . ."

Then that part was over and Rachel's father was complimenting everyone on their "good singing" and asking them to "turn over in your Bibles to Mark 10:17."

Except I didn't have a Bible to "turn over in," so Rachel quickly rectified that, handing me a cloth-covered Bible from a wooden box near the end of the row, and leaving me with the quandary of trying to figure out what "Mark 10:17" meant. Glancing to my right, I saw that most of the folks in the row seemed to be about two-thirds of the way through their Bibles, so I flipped back about that far. But the pages I wound up on were all black print, while theirs seemed to have several patches of red lettering showing. I flipped back and forth until I found a page that seemed to have red lettering in about the right places. Scowling studiously, I silently read the first couple of sentences: *"But I say unto you, That Elijah is come already, and they knew him not, but have done unto him whatsoever they listed. Likewise shall also the Son of man suffer of them."*

I read it again. It looked like English—mostly—but I couldn't make heads or tails of it. I went on to the next sentence: *"The disciples understood that he spake unto them of John the Baptist."*

Spake . . . *Spake?* I was no better off.

Then Rachel's father began reading about a rich young man and Jesus telling him to sell everything he had and to "take up the cross and follow me." That completed my confusion, because there wasn't anything on my pages that said anything like that. But that "take up the cross" part sounded suspiciously like asking to get nailed to one. I figured my parents had probably known what they were doing when they'd decided to stay heathen.

Rachel looked my way, saw where I was in the Bible, smiled, reached over, and flipped me forward about a dozen pages. Now the words matched up, and I mouthed "thank you" as the color mounted in my cheeks.

The pages of Rachel's Bible had the limp, rumpled look of a well-thumbed phone book, but she nodded as her father read, and looked earnestly at the text as if she were seeing it for the very first time. I watched that show of enthusiasm, and wondered if it was a show for the congregation's edification, or if it could possibly—just possibly—be genuine. Then she turned my way and smiled again, and that smile melted me, and I was very glad just to be there.

Besides, if Rachel's object this Sunday morning was to dupe me into attending church so her father—or her congregation, or she— could brainwash me, or use some twisted logic to ensnare me into a cult, or enlist me to some arcane cause, then whoever was behind this was in for a disappointment.

Because all of those things required an attentive listener—an attentive and cooperative and malleable listener. And while I was certainly malleable, I was neither listening nor paying attention to anyone but Rachel.

It was as if the presence of his daughter had heightened certain of my senses—those that registered the sight of her light-haloed hair, the delicate touch of her hands, and the scent of her, a scent that was mostly soap, but not entirely—to the detriment of others, such as hearing.

I would have stayed in that happily poleaxed state forever had the atmosphere of the service not changed. Rachel shifted her posture—head down, contrite—and everyone around us did, as well. Her father was saying, ". . . every head down, every eye closed, no looking around."

Every eye closed . . . Why?

I still hadn't figured out what "holy roller" meant, but—the attractiveness of the pastor's daughter aside—these people were as foreign to me at the time as a roomful of Communists. Letting my guard down that much in a pavilion full of strangers didn't sound like a great idea. But Rachel was doing it, and I was willing to assume oceans of risk in order to stay there, next to her. So I bowed my head and closed my eyes.

"I wonder how many here can say that, if they died today, they'd be going to heaven," Rachel's father said. "If you can say that, please slip your hand up."

Heaven? The question threw me. I wasn't sure there *was* a heaven. I was fairly certain, in fact, that there was not. I was in many ways my father's son, and he took an engineer's view of the world around him: there were things that could be proven mathematically, and there were opinions. He was politely skeptical about beliefs that did not stand up to empirical scrutiny, and just about everything religious fell into that category. So that did not allow for a hereafter. No heaven, no God; nothing beyond the stars but an endless emptiness. I kept my hands folded in front of me.

"Thank you for all those hands, all around the room," Rachel's father said.

All those hands . . . Meaning that many of those around me had a confidence that I did not. I wondered what to think about that. I wondered what my father would think of that.

That they were mountain people—uneducated, simple, easily duped—that's what my father would think.

"And now, I wonder how many people can't say for certain that they would go to heaven, but would like to be able to say that?" Rachel's father paused and let the question sink in. "Raise your hand if you would say that."

Heaven. A place where doubt and apprehension would not be known. A place where fathers would not place their sons in jeopardy.

I wondered if my mother was there. I doubted it—there weren't too many things I was certain about when it came to religion, but I was pretty sure that, even if heaven existed, suicides wouldn't find a place among God's elect.

If God existed at all.

I pictured my mother as she'd been in that casket—pure and calm and beautiful. I thought of her getting into that car, and starting the engine and then waiting. I couldn't see her doing that if my father or I had been home. We would have noticed, would have intervened. So that made it a weak moment, a mistake, and surely if God existed, he . . . or she . . . or it . . . would not punish someone so wonderful for something she'd done in a moment of weakness.

And Rachel. My head had been down and my eyes had been closed, but I was absolutely certain that Rachel's had been one of the hands raised for the first question.

Moving slowly, as if my arm were rusted, I lifted my palm, my forearm, my entire arm.

"Thank you," Rachel's father said. "I see that hand; you can slip it on down."

I see that *hand* ? Singular? Meaning that mine had been the only one raised? My legs were already perspiring from the clammy wind pants. Now the rest of my body joined in. My chest was damp, the small of my back, the recesses beneath my arms, and I could feel tiny drops of perspiration collecting under the sleep-rumpled, uncut hairs of my head.

I opened my eyelids a crack. Rachel's head was still lowered. A floorboard creaked, and I glanced the other way; one of the black-suited farmers was heading my way. Then I saw Rachel's father hold a hand out and shake his head, and the farmer went back to his seat.

My clamminess went up a level. What had that been all about? In retrospect, it seems that I should have been concentrating on what Rachel's father had to say next, but I was not. I sat there in a conflicting stew of thoughts and emotions: just what it was that I was doing there, whether my mother was anywhere other than in a strange Ohio cemetery, the state of my soul if I had one, the nature of God if there was one and—hovering over all the rest of it—the undiminished attraction of the stunningly beautiful blond-haired creature standing next to me.

Then the pump organ began its feline yowl anew, the congregation erupted in song, Rachel was holding the hymnal out toward me, and our hands touched again. I made certain they remained touching, and ninety percent of my being concentrated on the silky kiss of that one square inch of blood-warm flesh, while the other ten percent lip-synched the words to "Blessed Assurance."

Then the service was over and Rachel's father was walking toward us, and she was introducing me to him—my first name only, because that was all she knew, and I was adding, "It's Nolan. Patrick Nolan, Mr. . . . uhm, Pastor . . ."

This coaxed a smile from Rachel's father. Standing near him now, I could see that he was about the same age as my dad.

"Just call me Preacher," he said. "Everybody here does. My wife does. So it's probably best if we don't introduce any variety into the program. You have plans for dinner, Patrick?"

I hesitated just a moment there, because the West Virginian use of the word *dinner* still threw me. In Ohio, that had meant the big meal, at the end of the day—what mountain people called "supper"—but here the word often as not meant "lunch."

But Rachel must have interpreted my pause as polite hesitance, because she reinforced her father's invitation.

"We'd be obliged if you'd come. Some of the church ladies are cooking for us while Mama's away?" She said it that way, the inflection rising at the end, as if it were a question. "And they always make too much. If we end up with one more round of leftovers, there won't be room in the freezer. I'll have to throw something out, and it'd be a shame to waste good food."

"If that's all right with your folks, that is," her father added.

I looked at Rachel's earnest face. The thought of spending more time looking at that face would have been enough to convince me even if I'd already eaten, which I had not.

"My dad's working today," I told them. "He'd be happy to know I was having a home-cooked meal."

"Great!" Rachel's father smiled. "Well, we're in the Travelall, over there. Want to just ride home with us?"

"Thank you, but if you could just draw me a map, I'll be right over, sir." That *sir* didn't come naturally to me back then, but I knew that it was something he would expect. "That way, I can come back later and help my dad, and you won't have to interrupt your Sunday to bring me back."

"You're certain?"

"Yes, sir." It only seemed right.

And besides, I knew that if I didn't get changed out of those wind pants soon, I'd dissolve in a puddle of sweat.

The essence of the double-rope system is that, when drag on the first rope is about to become an issue, the climber begins to protect the route using the second rope. This requires, of course, that the climber know in advance that a second rope will be needed.

Rock Climbing Holds and Basics

TEN

Preacher met me at the door when I got there, and I breathed a little easier when I saw how he was dressed. A suit was the first thing I'd thought of when I'd stopped off at our Lodge-and-Airstream encampment, but I would be going in to the shop after dinner, and I couldn't imagine showing up at The First Ascent in anything dressier than jeans and a sport shirt. Appearing there in a blue serge suit would have been no less outré than walking in wearing chain-mail armor. Besides, after a full weekend of customers, the air in the shop would bear the full and unfettered ambience of Marlboro Country, and I didn't want to burden my father with a dry-cleaning bill.

So jeans and a plaid sport shirt was what I'd changed into. I hoped it would be all right—Rachel had, after all, been wearing a denim skirt at church.

It turned out to be a good guess. Preacher met me wearing jeans and a plaid sport shirt, just the same as me—he laughed about it, in fact. Only he was in a pair of moccasins, rather than the penny loafers, and his belt was a canvas cinch, like what a military person would wear. Subtle differences, but it made his style of dress appear both comfortable and mature, two words that certainly couldn't be applied to me.

Their house was larger and of much more recent construction than what I'd expected—an expansive two-story home made up of cedar shakes and slate on the outside, and pecan paneling and polished oak floors on the inside. The kitchen and baths—two that I could see—were done in quarry tile, and the big living room was dominated by a river-stone fireplace that took up one whole corner. On the other end of the room, sliding glass doors looked out on a half-finished patio, bricks stacked on a pallet off to one side.

"Not what you'd expect on a pastor's salary, huh?" Preacher asked.

"I'm sorry. Was the look on my face that obvious?"

He laughed. "That's the look everybody gets on their face the first time they come here. The folks you saw out at the pavilion built this place for us. And when I say that, I don't just mean that they paid for it, though they mostly did that, too. They *literally* built it— poured the basement, framed the place, cut the shakes and the slate for the outside and put 'em up, even milled the walnut for the paneling and collected the river stones for the fireplace. I tried telling them we really ought to have a church before we go putting up a rectory, but the deacons didn't see it that way. And we *do* meet here when the weather doesn't like Judd Horton's pavilion, so I try to justify it to myself that way. We took three years building this rectory and, God willing, we'll break ground on a church building next spring."

He paused and looked around, as if he were seeing his house for the first time.

"These are good people, Patrick. I know that, to outsiders, they might seem plain or even backward, but they've got wonderful hearts. They're what Jesus called 'the salt of the earth.'"

"'Salt of the earth.'" I'd heard the expression before. "Jesus said that?"

He nodded. "Matthew 5:13."

And I was quiet then, because I didn't have the foggiest idea as to what Matthew 5:13 referred to; for all I knew, it was the name of a band. But if Preacher noticed, he didn't say anything, because Rachel came into the room just then and announced that the church ladies had arrived with dinner.

Rachel. Unlike her father, she had not changed after church, but the soft, indoor lighting had worked a magic that left me pretty much speechless. So I stood there motionless, The Amazing Catatonic Yankee Teenager, and she said, "Hi, Patrick. I'm glad you're here."

She was glad I was there, and I was glad that she was glad, and the two of us were just standing there, being glad, when I realized just how imbecilic I probably appeared, so I untied my tongue long enough to say, "May I help carry anything in?"

And Rachel brightened at that and said that would be nice, so I turned to her father and asked, "Would you excuse me, sir?"—another *sir*, which seemed to me to be laying it on a bit thick, but when in Rome. . . . Then I followed Rachel into the kitchen, separated from the dining room by a counter and some hanging, double-fronted cabinets.

"You can bring everything in through the garage," Rachel told me, showing me an immaculate mudroom and laundry area with a door at its far end. "I think Jimmy is already out there lending a hand."

Jimmy turned out to be the same Jimmy who had made the high-wire rescue of my rucksack at Judd Horton's pavilion. He was in dungarees and a red T-shirt, and he was in the process of gauging how to best lift a roasting pan full of fried chicken off the tailgate of a rusting Dodge station wagon. I picked it up instead—getting a "Thank you, sir" for my troubles—and Jimmy followed me with a foil-covered casserole dish that smelled vaguely Italian and turned out to be spaghetti with meat sauce.

That was the first of three trips we made out to the car. Supervising the operation were two women with gray-streaked hair and the ubiquitous long calico dresses, women who smiled at me with their lips, although eyes kept flicking to the nether regions of my face, reminding me that I was at least two months overdue for a haircut. I was almost at the point where I was going to have to decide between a barber and a ponytail, and one look in the glittering, hawk-sharp eyes of these mountain women was enough to let me know they were anticipating the ponytail and showing me disdain in advance.

But, judgmental or not, if scent was any indication, these women could cook. Under Rachel's direction, Jimmy and I placed the chicken and the spaghetti on the divider counter, buffet style, along with the homemade corn bread, green bean casserole, Jello salad, mixed green salad, potatoes au gratin, chocolate chip cookies and apple pie that had accompanied them on the ride over. I was beginning to feel that Rachel had been right—I was doing them a favor by helping to eat this feast, which was probably not sufficient for an army, but without a doubt would have done justice to a platoon. And one of the mountain ladies said, "My Billy cranked you some ice cream, Preacher. I put it in the freezer," before the two of them departed, chased by the family's effusive thanks.

Then we—the three members-in-residence of the Ransom family and I—were all standing around in the dining room. This made perfect sense to me, because I figured either that Rachel would fill her plate first, because she was the lady, or her father would go first, because he was the pastor. Jimmy wouldn't go first unless they were one of those families on an egalitarian kick, and while I might be expected to go first as the guest, no way was I going to do that without being invited to do so, at least twice.

Then Rachel's father smiled and said, "Let's pray."

Of course: the prayer before meals. I had been to homes that did that, although it had never, to the best of my knowledge, happened in ours. But it made sense that a pastor's family would have a prayer before meals. I figured they probably had prayers for just about everything: brushing teeth, mowing the lawn, starting the car.

So I bowed my head. And then I noticed that Rachel was reaching out to take my hand, which was great, but her father was also holding a hand out to me, and for me, a teenage guy raised in a household where man-hugs were considered shaky ground, this was the upper range of the Richter Scale.

But the three of them were already standing in a crescent, holding hands, waiting for me to close the circle, so I did, simultaneously enchanted by the delicate touch of Rachel's hand and wary at the sandpapery grasp of her father's. I tried to ignore the fact that I was holding hands with a guy—a bad thing—and centered my attention instead on the fact that I was holding hands with Rachel—a very good thing. This proved to be so successful a strategy that I heard not a single word of her father's prayer and hadn't even realized he had finished when Rachel gave my hand a little squeeze and let go.

I was still cherishing that squeeze when Preacher said, "Patrick, you're our guest. Help yourself."

And when I said, "Thank you, sir, but please, ladies first," I saw father and daughter allow the shadow of a grin to pass their faces, both at the same time.

The first course was accompanied by the questions I'd assumed would be asked of me. But they were asked in a gentler manner than I'd expected.

"I see that you and your pappy opened up that new shop in Mouth of Seneca—what about your maw? She move down with you, or she still up North?"

The hardware store owner over in Elkins had been graceless enough to ask me that one weekday, when I'd stopped in to pick up glass cleaner and stove black.

But Preacher didn't do anything like that. He talked instead about how it was great that we had brought a new business to the area, and helped make the valley more attractive to tourists. And then he said how he'd tried a little top-roped climbing when he was on a missions trip to Thailand years before, and how exciting he'd found it, and that got me offering to take him up again, and he'd demurred, but that had opened the door for him to ask me how it was that I had started climbing, so I told him about my parents, and how they'd introduced me to the sport, and then that got me bragging on my mother, and the next thing you know, I was adding, "She, uhm, passed away, earlier this year."

Passed away. I'd already learned to hate the phrase, the overly polite, triangulating sense of it. But I used it just the same. Used it because the only alternative would have been to use the other word.

I saw Rachel look down at her plate, averting her eyes, giving me that privacy. So it was Jimmy, not yet as fully developed in the social skills, who asked, "How'd she die?"

"Car accident," I told him before his father could shoot him a look.

Car accident? Just like that, I said it, my clumsy attempt to make my mother's death something nobler: a mishap, something not her fault. And so, less than six hours after meeting Rachel Ransom and her family, I was already lying to them. I hated that, but I hated it less than becoming the object of their pity.

"After she passed"—that word again—"my father and I decided we'd like a change, something we could do together, and so here we are."

Preacher nodded slowly, as if weighing the wisdom of what he'd just heard.

"And you've already visited our church," he said. "That's great."

Not, *So, Patrick, do you belong to a church?*

"I was going to go climbing this morning, but my friends left without me, and when I woke up, your church was starting. Actually, sir, we've never been a church family, my parents and I."

Another cleaned-up version of the truth, but this one felt okay. Even when he was wearing after-church casual, I couldn't think of a polite way to tell this pastor that I'd put my pants on this morning less than two feet from his daughter.

"Well, I don't believe in coincidence, Patrick," he said, his face open and kind. "I think you slept into our service for a reason, and I hope we'll see you again next Sunday."

Trying to get you into their clutches, Sport.

And then Preacher added, "But first, I hope you'll have another helping of, well, everything. Rachel wasn't kidding about our fridge. We don't have room for another stick of butter in there."

After dinner, Jimmy and Rachel both set about clearing the table, and when Rachel said, "Go ahead and sit with Daddy, Patrick. I'll have these done in no time," I refused, saying, "No, please—let me help you. I need to do something to pay for my supper."

Which was precisely one-third true. The other two-thirds consisted equally of my longing to be in close proximity to Rachel, and my rampant desire to not be left alone with her father.

We washed the plates and glasses first, then Rachel put the leftovers into Tupperware containers and tinfoil pie plates and we washed the dishes they'd come in, first peeling off the pieces of masking tape with "Whitlock" and "Hawkins" and "Harper" written on them and carefully saving them for reapplication once the pieces were washed and dried.

"So, Rachel," I asked as I dried an amber baking dish, "what do you like to do?"

"I sew," she said. "And Mama's teaching me to play the piano, although she is ever so much better than me. She's our usual organist. Mrs. Bartlett, from this morning's service? She was standing in, helping out while Mama's away."

She talked a little more about drawing and watercolors, and school—she and her brother were both homeschooled, and there was talk of building a Christian school with the new church. She told me about church picnics and the work she was doing with a vacation Bible school for the younger kids.

I was only half hearing it. She hadn't answered my question, mostly because I had not really asked it. So I tried again, more directly.

"Do you ever go to movies, or concerts or stuff?"

She cocked her head as she placed the strip of masking tape marked "Hooper" back on the baking dish.

"Do you mean, do I go out on dates?"

"Uhm . . . well, yeah. I guess."

She shook her head.

"Folks in our church don't go to Hollywood movies, Patrick."

That was how she phrased it: *Hollywood movies.*

"Why? Do you think they're . . . what? Sinful?"

"Some people do." She set a dish aside and began replacing the masking-tape label on another. "And in some cases, they're right. But even if they're not—" she glanced at the living room before continuing in a whisper—"I've seen a Hollywood movie . . . or two . . . and they make it seem as if it doesn't matter what you do, that everything will come out perfect in the end, and people see that and then they wonder why their lives don't match that, and it's not that their lives are wrong. It's that the movies have it wrong."

I was still stuck on the part about *they make it seem as if it doesn't matter what you do, that everything will come out perfect in the end.* I could relate. And I didn't like the place that thought was taking me: not while I was talking with such a tremendously nice-looking girl whom I'd so recently met. So I switched gears, asking, "Well, what about music? What's wrong with that?"

Rachel repacked some bowls and a casserole dish into the wicker basket in which they arrived, saying nothing. Then, after a moment, she looked up.

"I don't go out on dates, Patrick. I can't. It's not just what I believe. It's our family. Something like that would make it diffi-cult—for Daddy."

The disappointment must have shown on my face, because she added, "But I suppose I could court."

"Court?"

"When a guy comes calling. So he and a girl can see each other to decide if they're right for one another."

"Right for one another?"

She smiled. "To get married."

Married? It gave *get you into their clutches, Sport* an entirely new meaning.

Still, thick-throated and husky, I found myself asking, "Well, how would a guy ask you out on a . . . How would he *court* you?"

She smiled. "He'd have to ask Daddy's permission."

Then she added, "I think he might say yes. I don't go to public school, and there aren't any boys at all my age in the church, so nobody's asked yet."

Rachel's father was standing near the sliding glass doors, looking out at the unfinished patio, when I joined him.

"Are you building your own?" I asked.

He nodded. "We have a brick mason in our congregation, but I can't see taking him away from a paying job to give my family a place to have a barbecue. So I've been working on it whenever I get a chance."

I'd later learn that, in addition to pastoring a church, Rachel's father taught psychology at Davis-Elkins Junior College, and handled the accounting for a couple of local construction companies.

"I'm still hoping to get this finished by the time Rachel's mother gets back from her sister's," he said. "But I've fallen a bit behind."

I took a deep, but silent, breath.

"I could come help you," I told him.

He continued to look out the sliding glass door at the unfinished patio. "Doesn't your father need you, to help out at the shop?"

"During the day, when we clean and stock. But evenings, during the week, traffic's pretty light—one person can watch it by himself. And we're closed on Mondays."

He kept his gaze directed out the glass door, but even in profile, I could see that he was smiling. "That's a pretty good strategy, Patrick."

"Sir?"

Still looking out at the unfinished patio. "Getting on the good side of the girl's father. I think I was in my twenties before I hit on that approach with Rachel's grandfather."

This large, empty moment passed between us.

"That's part of it, sir," I finally admitted. *That sir thing again.* "I'd like to . . . uh, I'd like to see Rachel. But that's not the only reason I'm offering to help."

I told him about the patio that my father and I had never built for my mother. I still didn't tell him how she really died; I was in too deep on the car-accident story. But I did tell him about my pact with my father, and how we had gotten home just a few hours later and discovered that my mother was gone: that she had been gone even when he and I had discussed our plans on the ride home.

Closure wasn't part of the social vocabulary of 1976, but Rachel's father nodded as I finished.

"Well," he said. "Monday's my day off, too. If you want to come by tomorrow around lunchtime, we'll be here. And I'd welcome the company."

Of course, there is an issue with placing protection so deeply within a crack that it
cannot be seen; the placement could be tenuous, and unable
to withstand the stress of loading.

The Eastern Cragsman's Guide to Climbing Anchors

ELEVEN

"Man, I think you're smoking something strange. People have been trying to finish that route for two years. Read my lips—it ain't gonna happen."

I could hear the voice, a nasal Massachusetts twang, all the way outside the shop, on the long front porch.

My departure from the Ransom household had been delayed while Rachel and her father loaded every ice cube in their household, plus enough leftovers to see my father and me through the rest of the week, into a green-and-tan metal Coleman cooler. That had put me at the shop at sundown—long after the New Yorkers and Ohioans would have departed for home. All that would be left now were the climbers from Pittsburgh and DC—climbers who lived within a couple hours' drive of Seneca and so considered the place their home rock. And as soon as I walked in, I knew what they were talking about, and knew that the debate had probably been going on for an hour or more.

They were talking about "Zardoz."

That was the name of the climb. Or rather, that was the working title because, as I had told Judd Horton, tradition held that whoever made a climb first got to name it and, thus far, no one had climbed the entirety of Zardoz.

Named after a Sean Connery science-fiction movie that had tanked rather spectacularly in 1974—the year the climb had first been attempted—Zardoz had two distinctions that kept it off the radar of all but a handful of Seneca climbers. The first was that the route was on Lower Seneca Rocks, a quartzite formation that stood about sixty yards beneath the main formation, so any climb on it ended not at a summit or a skyline, but at the wooded terminus of the upper Seneca scree field.

Such an anticlimactic ending, in and of itself, would dissuade most newer climbers who didn't consider a climb a climb unless it led to daylight. But Zardoz was rendered even more arcane by virtue of the fact that it was an aid climb.

If you aren't a climber, *aid climbing* takes a little explanation. Contrary to what most people believe, the ropes and hardware that climbers carry are not usually used to help them make the climb. Most times, the equipment is there simply as a safety measure. The chocks, carabiners, and the pitons—the hammer-driven pins that were commonly used up to the 1960s—were all employed simply to redirect the rope and create fulcrum points along the route of the climb. If you take a slip while attempting a climb, and you've placed your protection carefully, your partner should be able to arrest your fall with the rope, the same way one could handle a heavy load with a rope and a pulley.

In aid climbing, though, at least one of the moves on the climb is made with the assistance of equipment.

The definition varies. In Europe, for instance, it was long thought perfectly acceptable for a climber to step on a preexisting piton and claim the climb as a "free"—or unaided—climb. In North America, on the other hand, even a fingerhold created by placing and wedging a pebble in a crack is considered an aid move.

Because of this difference in attitudes, and because Europe has a longer tradition of fixed pitons on established routes, aid climbing in North America had long been thought of as more properly belonging in mountaineering—where the achievement of a summit outweighs the manner in which it is gained—rather than rock climbing.

But Lower Seneca had few of the dihedrals and fist-size cracks that so characterized the upper cliffs. Many of the routes on the lower cliffs had only been done as aid climbs.

When it came to Zardoz, however, even with the use of the most extreme of aid placements—folded bits of chromium steel called "bat hooks" that looped over nubbins of rock, or tiny RURP pitons that were tapped a bare sixteenth or an eighth of an inch into hairline cracks, or miniscule Hexentrics or stoppers threaded onto whispy stainless-steel cable that looked more appropriate for fishing than climbing—there was still a four-foot section of rock on which no aid placement had ever been made. It had been climbed several times up to that point, and at least one enterprising soul had rappelled down to a spot just above that point and then aid-climbed his way back to the top. But that gap persisted, and although a good dozen of the East Coast's best aid climbers had worked on it, no one had done the whole thing from start to finish.

"I'm talking about one bolt. A single, stinking bolt, on a single, stinking climb in a part of Seneca that most climbers will never, ever see." I stepped through the open shop door and the voice became louder. "What could possibly be the harm in that? There are already bolts up on that rock, in case you haven't noticed. There are bolts on the rappel routes. There are even bolts on the Gendarme. It's not as if it would be the first bolt ever put in at Seneca."

"Yes, but it would be the first bolt at Seneca put in purely to finish an aid route—and that's different." The reply had come from a guy standing right near the door as I walked in, a youngish man in his twenties who looked a little like Bob Dylan, and whom I knew by sight, but not by name.

My father glanced up as I entered the shop, and then looked again. I wore jeans only once in a blue moon—climbing shorts and painter's pants were my usual threads. And as for the plaid shirt, the last time I'd worn anything like that had been at Scott High, where the dress code prohibited T-shirts.

"But it wouldn't be the first piece of hardware anybody ever clipped a stirrup to up there." I could see who the speaker was now: it was Phil Tapia, a climber just a couple of years younger than my father. An engineer at the Bureau of Standards, which for some odd reason had managed to employ several generations of world-class rock climbers over the years, Tapia had put up several of Seneca's more difficult free routes in recent years, and virtually all of its extreme aid routes. "I mean, the Face of a Thousand Pitons is called that for a reason, you know? The Army left enough hardware in the Rocks to build a Volkswagen—they were aid-climbing on all of it—and that was better than thirty years ago."

"That's true," my father said. "Of course, they were training to save the world from Hitler, and what you're talking about here is basically drilling rock to connect the dots."

Whoa—touché, Dad!

This drew a bit of a silence, and a couple of the guys there looked as if they wanted to snigger, but they didn't; Tapia was a fairly well-respected guy at Seneca. And besides there wasn't really what you'd call a crowd sitting around the cold stove in the climbing shop—not enough people that a chuckle could pass with anonymity. There were just five or six guys and my father, who was sorting receipts on the counter, and matching them against a cash-register tape.

"But my point is," said Tapia, acting as if his point had been misunderstood, "that it certainly wouldn't be the first permanent piece of hardware left up there."

"But it'd be the first aid-bolt," said a guy sitting in the corner. He had a wisp of beard and was wearing a headband made from a folded bandanna. "It would definitely be the first aid-bolt."

The "bolt" everyone was talking about was an expansion bolt, a piece of hardware developed for bolting factory machinery and whatnot to poured concrete.

Bolts were a throwback in the evolution of climbing hardware. For more than a century, climbers had climbed using pitons—ringed spikes driven by hammer into cracks in the rock face. At first, most of the pitons had been soft iron "pins," which deformed and assumed the shape of the crack, and so were simply left in the rock face.

But shortly after World War II, most climbers made the switch to chromolley pitons. These held their shape as they were driven, and they could be retrieved by the second person on the rope, gen-erally by clipping one end of a short length of chain to the piton, clipping the other end to a rock hammer, and then pounding into thin air to extract the steel pin.

This made rock climbing safer—the steel pitons were considerably less friable than their soft iron cousins—and it also made it more economical, as the same set of pitons could be used over and over.

But the practice had an environmental downside. As chromolley pitons did not deform when hammered, they generally abraded away a thin layer of rock as they were driven in, and then—as it was the custom to loosen a pin by hammering it up and down a few times before extracting it—they removed another, broader, layer as they were pulled. After just one ascent of a route using steel pitons, you could generally spot the raw, worn marks where pitons had been used. After a few dozen ascents, the piton scars often became wide enough to admit a man's hand.

The logical solution was to leave the steel pitons in place. But subsequent climbers, either failing to understand the environmental ethic, or loathe to pass up the opportunity to retrieve a "lost" pin, often pulled the pitons anyhow. And among those pitons that stayed placed, some broke after being constantly re-driven, the standard practice being to give a fixed pin a whack or two with one's hammer to make certain it was really secure. Other placements deteriorated with the weather; after a few seasons, they would be too rusted for either use or retrieval.

The solution to this dilemma came from Wales, where, early in the 1960s, local climbers began threading machine nuts onto lengths of rope or sling. The nuts could be stuck into an old piton hole, used as a protection point, and then retrieved after use simply by tugging on the sling.

It wasn't long before some enterprising soul noticed that machine nuts of various sizes could be used even in cracks that had no piton holes, and it wasn't long after that that first ascents were being done without using a single piton, and "clean climbing" was born.

Soon, equipment manufacturers were responding with nut- and

wedge-shaped aluminum "artificial chockstones," or "chocks," that weighed less than a machine nut and fit a wider variety of crack sizes. It was the dawn of a green new era in rock climbing, an era in which the emphasis was placed on respecting and conserving the rock face, rather than conquering it. But there was one aspect of protection that had not been swept up by this environmental groundswell, and that was bolting.

Bolting was a technique developed for blank sections of rock that lacked cracks for pitons and chocks. To place a bolt, one first drilled a hole into the rock, using a machine-drill bit in an impact socket and a hammer. Then an expansion sleeve was tapped into the hole, and after that, a hanger—a metal ear with a hole for attaching a carabiner—was attached to the rock via a steel bolt screwed into the expansion sleeve with a wrench.

Originally used by rock climbers to create rappel anchors—done properly, a bolted anchor was absolutely bombproof—bolts had also been seized upon first as a means for protecting otherwise unprotectable sections of route, and then for filling in the blank spots between climbable cracks.

Therein hung the dilemma: while clean climbing had been developed to keep the rock face pristine, bolting could only be accomplished by permanently marring it. And once done, the damage caused by bolting was permanent—even if "chopped" with a hammer and a cold chisel, a bolt left a scar on the rock.

"So this bolt," asked the guy who looked like Bob Dylan. "Is it something that could be placed on lead?"

"No," Tapia said. "It'd have to be done on rappel."

A chorus of complaints, every voice except my father's and mine, rose up from around the room. Along with its no-bolting philosophy, Seneca climbing had a strict tradition when it came to pioneering routes: they had to be done from the ground up—no "gardening" or cleaning of lichen and moss from a top-rope, and no pre-placement of protection from a rappel. What Tapia was proposing was a violation of both principles, and the natives were on the verge of an uprising.

"I know, I know," Tapia told the group. "I don't like the idea, either. But if I rap down, I can get away with one bolt. If I try it from bat hooks and stirrups, the highest I can get will still be too low to reach the crack system above. I'd have to place two."

More uproar from around the shop.

"You don't have to place any," said the Dylan-looking guy. "You can leave it, and see if someone eventually comes along who's good enough to pull it off without a drill."

"And who might that be?" Tapia shot back. "You? Anybody here?"

The shop fell quiet again.

Finally the guy with the bandanna headband turned to my father.

"What do you think of all this, Kevin? After all, you're local now. It seems that you should have a say."

My father didn't look up as he continued to reconcile his register tape.

"It's a free country, Phil," he said as he worked. "If you want to bolt the route, the Forest Service won't stop you, and these guys can't and I can't. So it's a moot point. Sounds as if it's up to you, if you ask me."

More silence. Finally, Tapia spoke up.

"I'll give it a week," he said. "If anybody thinks that they can do better, then they should go ahead and do it, because next Sunday morning, if Zardoz hasn't been climbed, I'm going to rap down, bolt it, and then climb it myself."

And with that, it was as if someone had struck the gavel in a courtroom. People glanced at watches, muttered about having to work in the morning, and one by one they filed out. Finally it was just Tapia, my father and me, and Tapia said, "You understand where I'm coming from, don't you, Kevin? I mean, you can see why it has to be done. It will still be the most difficult aid route here at Seneca, bolt or no bolt."

"Understand?" my father asked as he squared the receipts up on the counter and bound them with a rubber band. He looked up. "No. I don't. Personally, I wouldn't bolt it. But like I said, it's a free country, and you can do what you want. Now, you drive carefully on the way home, Phil. It's a long haul back to Washington."

We did not talk about the bolt or Tapia after he had left. My father had always detested rumor and gossip, and he would not talk about a person behind his back. Besides, he had already said what he had to say about the bolt; it was not within him to belabor a point.

But neither of those things prevented him from commenting on how I was dressed.

"What happened?" he asked first. "You run out of clean laundry?"

"No, sir." He about broke his neck looking back at me when I said *sir*. "I met a girl today. Her family asked me to dinner."

"Dinner, huh?" He quirked an eyebrow. "Where'd they take you? Yokum's?"

"No . . ." I caught myself before I said "sir" again. "We went to their house. Up by Weeping Oak."

My father had been banding bills and placing them into a bank bag, and he stopped when I said that.

"A local girl?" He grinned. "Well. Way to go, Patrick. . . . Is she nice?"

"Real nice."

"Interesting?"

"That too."

"Good looking?"

"Oh . . . uh, yeah." I fell silent, thinking about how Rachel looked.

He laughed. "That good, huh? Who are her folks?"

"Her father teaches psychology at the junior college."

He nodded.

"And he's an accountant, too," I added. "He does the books for a couple of the construction companies in the county."

"Psychology and accounting? That's a pretty odd mix."

I shrugged. "He seems like a pretty bright guy."

"Really?" My father placed the last stack of bills in the bag, along with a deposit slip, and zipped it shut. He hefted the bag and looked up at me. "Maybe we can farm our tax work out to him, huh? Leave us more time for the crags?"

He poked me in the ribs and I mustered a smile. It was a skin-deep effort, though. The things I'd said about Preacher were true; he'd mentioned them during dinner. But it was my second half-truth of the day, and a half-truth is still a lie.

And I was not accustomed to lying to my father.

Still, if I did not tell him the important part, the central part, the part about her father being the pastor of a church, it was because so little had been held back between the two of us, my father and I, over the years. And because so little had been held back, I knew what his reaction would be.

Trying to get you into their clutches, Sport.

But it was not his warning that I was dreading.

It was his judgment.

Terse commands and acknowledgements of one or two words—"On belay," or

"climb away" or "up rope"—are sufficient for most climbing situations.

Banter is not required, and the best rope teams are often those who

speak the least while on the rock.

Rock Climbing Holds and Basics

TWELVE

It's not true, what they say. Absence does not really make the heart grow fonder. Mostly, it breeds anxiety. Mostly, it raises doubts.

By the time I woke on Monday, stretching and yawning on the pull-out bed in the Airstream's narrow living room, I was seriously questioning the wisdom of asking Preacher if I could help him with the patio.

It wasn't that my enthusiasm for the project had waned. Certainly I was intrigued by the possibility of seeing Rachel again. And it wasn't that I was in any way sheepish about being seen at the home of a clergyman. I had never been cliquish, never gave that much thought to image.

Besides, who knew me in West Virginia?

But I was far from eager about going back and half-truthing and mealymouthing my way all over again about how my mother had died. And after I got home, when my father asked about my day, I didn't want to lie to him again about Rachel's father—about his profession.

I knew that, among my old friends in Toledo, my concerns would have been seen as strange. I had been the only one I knew who did not habitually hide things from, or blatantly lie to, his parents. Maybe that was because I was an only child, raised in a household in which candor had come as naturally as breathing. Maybe it was because we spent so much time together that I had always viewed my mother and my father as not only my parents, but my best friends.

Then again, I had always assumed that my openness would be reciprocated. My parents' failures in this regard troubled me more than I cared to admit, even to myself. But even in my hurt, I could not find an excuse there. I did not see my own deceit as a *quid pro quo*. I saw it as compounding the problem. My parents were adults with adult issues, and raising me had not, I was sure, been the least of these. I reasoned that their lives were more complicated than anything that I, at sixteen, could ever imagine, although events of late had convinced me that, for this to be true, they would have to be complicated, indeed.

In the end, it was moot, of course. I had told Preacher I would be there, and be there I would. I had given my word and, as off camber as my character may have been at the moment, that particular principle remained none the worse for wear.

Finding the time to help was relatively simple. We swept up as best we could on Sunday nights, and then closed the shop on Mondays. Except for an hour or less of early morning phone time to reorder inventory for the following weekend, my father did not work on Mondays, and neither did I.

Nor were Mondays used for housework, laundry, or similar plebian tasks. Heathen as he was, my father had nonetheless grasped the idea of a Sabbath and followed it to the fullest. We didn't even cook meals on Mondays, usually preferring to go out, although, with the Airstream's tiny refrigerator packed jigsaw-puzzle full of the Ransoms' leftovers, meals would not even require a car ride on this particular day. Bachelors that we were, we breakfasted on fried chicken and saved the spaghetti for lunch. But when I proposed our usual post-lunch excursion—a ride to Church Rocks or Nelsons for a quick one-pitch climb or two, my father had yawned and said, "If it's all the same to you, Sport, I think I'd just as soon soak up some of this sunshine in a lawn chair and veg a while. Okay with you if we climb tomorrow, instead?"

This was an unexpected bonus, and I'd tried to appear as casual as possible as I said, "Well, if it's all right with you, then, I think I'll just run up to Weeping Oak and see that girl I met this weekend."

This got me all of one eyebrow and half of another. "The girl again, huh? This is starting to sound like someone pretty special."

I turned toward the Airstream's window, trying to hide the color rising in my face. "Well, I do have their cooler—probably ought to be getting it back to them."

A smile. "Yeah, you probably should. And if this girl's going to be a recurring theme around here, I suppose we ought to start referring to her by name."

"Oh, sorry. It's Rachel. Rachel Ransom."

It felt good, saying her last name like that. I reasoned that, once he knew her last name, he would be able to inquire about her father, should he feel so inclined, and he would learn that he was a pastor. It felt like less of a sin of omission.

It felt like less of a lie.

The Travelall was missing from the driveway when I got over to the Ransoms' house. This perked me up a bit; I figured that Preacher was late getting back to the house and Rachel and I might have a few minutes alone.

No such luck.

"Hey, Patrick," Preacher greeted me at the door. "You're a man of your word."

"Good to see you again, sir." I glanced behind him into the big living room.

The big *empty* living room.

"We ran Jimmy up to Scout camp at Morgantown early this morning," he said, apparently reading my look. "And Rachel is out soul-winning with one of the ladies from the church."

That sounded as if it needed some acknowledgement, so I nodded.

"Do you know what soul-winning is?" He asked as he waved me in.

"No, sir." This time, I was glad I remembered the *sir*.

"It's where you witness to people, tell them about salvation. They're over in Davis, going door-to-door."

Witness? Salvation? I figured I had to say something, so I asked, "Like salespeople?"

"Yeah." He nodded. "A lot like that."

"Oh," I said. "Cool."

But that wasn't what I was thinking. What I was thinking was, *Weird*.

The day was warm, but I'd figured that, given the looks I'd gotten at church, climbing shorts were not the way to ingratiate myself with Rachel's father. So I'd come over in an old pair of white canvas painter's pants—what I climbed in when it was too cool for shorts. And then, because I wasn't sure of the theological ramifications of T-shirts, I'd topped the painter's pants off with a rugby shirt.

I was perspiring already. The Chevette did not have air-conditioning—I was still two cars away from the first one I would purchase with air. The ride had left the rugby shirt sticking to my back, and we hadn't even begun our work.

Preacher was wearing some old, frayed, olive-green work pants and a faded blue shirt: a pocket T-shirt.

"Have you had lunch?" he asked.

"Yes, sir. I ate at home. Want me to get started on the patio? I mean, if you still have to eat lunch, or have something to do, or something then you can just show me what to do and I can get started."

He laughed. "No—and you're right, Patrick. We've got an agenda today. We'd better get to it."

I don't know. I guess I had been hoping that maybe he would let me help him without him helping me—if that makes sense. Like maybe he could show me what he wanted done and then he could go write a sermon, or something, and leave me alone so he wouldn't ask me about my mom and catch me in the half-lie—all right, the *full* lie—that I'd told him on Sunday. That or ask me about his daughter, which would just plain be embarrassing.

I felt the color rising in my face again and looked across the family room and through the sliding glass doors, at a red-brown cube of round-edged bricks stacked on a rough wooden pallet. The rusted ends of steel bands peeked out from under the pallet skids, and the bricks were staggered, stair-fashion, at the top, where some had already been removed.

"Most people these days make decks," he said as we crossed the room and walked outside. He handed me a pair of canvas work gloves and began to pull on one of his own. "But my wife said that a deck just wouldn't look right with the house. And, of course, she was right."

The brick patio had already been bordered, all the way around, with bricks buried long-way down, so only the ends were exposed, and bricks had been laid at the corner nearest the door, the weathered-looking bricks forming an attractive herringbone pattern. The remainder of the patio had been prepared with fine, off-white sand, worked smooth and level.

Preacher knelt on one knee and began to clear away the leaves and twigs that had blown onto the sand. I joined him as he picked the smooth surface clean. The sand felt damp and I saw a garden hose on the lawn at the edge of the work area, and figured he'd been wetting it down, keeping it packed.

"That's what my mother said, too," I told Preacher as we worked. "Our house in Toledo was old, Victorian, with high ceilings and parquet wood floors, and leaded glass windows. My mom wanted a place where we could sit outside in the summertime, but she wanted to make sure that it would fit. Not just look right, but feel right, too, you know? That's exactly how she put it—'It has to feel right.'"

"It sounds as if your mother had a great sense of aesthetics," Preacher said, and my heart sank.

Fantastic, Patrick. Absolutely fantastic. You didn't want to talk about your mother, so what do you bring up in conversation?

I stayed there on one knee, head bowed, full of dread, waiting for his questions.

But—and the older I get, the wiser this seems to me in retrospect—Preacher didn't ask those questions, at least not right away.

What he did instead was teach me how to build a brick patio. Not *show* me how to build one—he didn't just demonstrate the process—but *teach* me, so I could understand what we were doing, and why.

Preacher told me how he had begun by digging out the ground down to the frost line. Then he had added two layers of stone—crushed stone for the bottom, and then pea gravel to within six inches of ground level. Only then had he added sand, and he had watered the sand, and then packed it with a roller borrowed from one of his congregates.

"I did that part three times," Preacher told me. "I'd let everything dry a while, and then I would add enough sand to bring everything up to level again, and I'd wet it all down and roll it all over again."

"That sounds like a lot of work," I said as we straightened up.

"It was a lot of activity," he agreed, dusting off his knee. "But it wasn't difficult. Wait—maybe I should rephrase that, because my back did complain about all that digging, the next day. But, be that as it may, digging was sort of fun. Laying the bricks is the part that's work—lots of stopping and it's tedious. I really appreciate your coming over to give me a hand, Patrick."

"Thanks," I said, immediately feeling clumsy and awkward because I was thanking him for his thank-you. I felt totally at a loss for social skills at that moment, like some savage raised by wolves. So I covered a little by adding, "I'm glad to be here."

Preacher began shifting bricks from the pallet-load down to the corner where he'd already begun, where the bricks had already been placed. I helped him, and he talked as we worked.

"I took the family to Williamsburg last year for a conference," he said as we piled the bricks. "And there was a man there building a walk just like this, with the same herringbone pattern, and Rachel's mother loved the look of it, so I talked to the man and he showed me how he did it. It's pretty easy, really. Once you've got the sand packed and rolled, all you have to do is keep it wetted down, so it stays packed, and then place your bricks close enough to one another so they won't shift. If you have your border anchored, nothing will move side to side and, other than that, the weight of the bricks keeps everything in place."

"No mortar at all, then?"

"None whatsoever, and thousands of people walk on footpaths built like this in Williamsburg every year, yet the paving lasts for decades."

"Cool." I said it, but then I regretted it. All it could do was remind him of the difference in our ages, get him thinking again like the father of a girl I was interested in.

But what he said was, "Yeah. I agree."

When we had a dozen bricks down where we could reach them, Preacher began setting them in place, fitting them in and tamping them down with the handle of a trowel, sometimes lifting the brick up and re-smoothing the sand beneath it before setting the brick back in place. He had a carpenter's level that he used to check his progress every once in a while, but mostly he worked by feel, trusting when his hands told him the bricks were well seated.

I tried to help him, but soon saw that setting the bricks was a one-man job, so I began to feed the bricks to him instead, bringing them to him from the pallet and making sure he had a supply on hand.

The work went quickly, that way, and we only stopped when we would get to the end of a row, where Preacher would take a pick-like hammer and split a brick to get the triangular piece he needed to fill the gap left between the rows at the end. After he'd done that a couple of times, I split one for him myself, and it fit so well that I began doing that for him regularly, as well. On one swing, I ended up shattering a brick instead of cracking it neatly along a line, but that was because my hands were getting sweaty and the hammer turned in my hand. After that, I wiped my hands on my pants before picking up the hammer, and I didn't ruin any more bricks.

It wasn't really what I would call difficult work. The bricks were heavy, but not exceptionally so. It wasn't as if you needed tremendous strength to handle them. And the work that had already been done pretty much dictated the work that was left to do. So long as we kept the bricks tight against one another, we never had to stop to figure out what to do next or how to make a particular piece fit.

But it was awkward work: lots of bending and stooping, and hardly ever a chance to straighten up.

And then there was the heat. The cool of the mountain spring was long past us. It was summer now, coming on high summer, and the air was still around us and thick with the sound of cicadas, and I soon had rivulets of sweat coursing down my temples and streaming forward, stinging my eyes with the salt as I stooped.

Preacher must have noticed me blinking the sweat away because he asked me, "Aren't you awfully hot in that long-sleeved shirt?"

"Yes, sir, a little I suppose." I straightened up and dragged my forearm across my face, wiping my eyes with my sleeve.

"Well, go ahead and take it off, if you want."

I looked at the house, through the sliding glass doors and into the empty family room.

He laughed. "Don't worry. Rachel's not due back for a couple of hours. And we'll hear her when she pulls into the drive; the driver-side hinges on my old International squeak like a warped screen door. I've been meaning to put some white grease on 'em, but things like this keep getting in the way. Go ahead and take that shirt off, if you're too hot. It's just us guys."

Preacher had misjudged my concern. It wasn't that I was all that modest back in those days. From June to October, if truth be told, I rarely wore a shirt when I was climbing. Weekdays, when no one but my father and I were at the Rocks, we often walked down to the deep pool on the North Fork and skinny-dipped in lieu of a shower back at the Airstream. Give me a fig leaf, and I would have fit right in with Adam and Eve.

That, really, was what was bothering me; if the people in Rachel's church—in Preacher's church—took their modesty so seriously, then what would he think when I pulled off my rugby shirt and displayed the deep, dark, Indian tan underneath?

But as far as I could tell, he thought nothing of it. I pulled my shirt off, he kept placing bricks and tamping them into place with his trowel handle, and I kept bringing him a fresh supply with which to work.

After about an hour, Preacher brought the garden hose over and misted down the sand that had not yet been bricked over. Then, when it was all rewetted and dark, he stepped off to the side, on the lawn, and turned the fine spray on himself.

"Help yourself," he said, laying the hose on the ground and returning to his work.

So I did. First I sprayed myself, and the cold well water—the Ransoms lived, like us, outside of town—was so shocking after the heat of the sun that I gasped. I imagined what it was like to be one of those Swedes who come bursting out of saunas to roll around in the snow; that's what it felt like to me, at least. Then I soaked my sweaty rugby shirt with the hose, wrung it out and draped it over an Adirondack chair to dry.

After that we worked in silence, or pretty much silence, for the next forty-five minutes, and it wasn't as if I was trying to get on the good side of a father whose daughter I was attracted to—even though I was. Nor was it as if we were pals, because we didn't shoot the bull or joke. We just worked. It was as if Preacher had accepted me as a peer, at least a peer within this context, and it was comfortable, working like that. I fell into the rhythm of the labor, and I was surprised when I returned to the nearly empty pallet for more bricks and Preacher finally broke the silence.

"No," he said. "That's good. We've got enough. I'll be finished up here in a second."

"We're quitting?" I asked, surprised.

"No." He laughed, setting two bricks in place. "We're done."

"We are?" I looked at the large square of paving brick in surprise. Preacher laughed again.

"All that's left is this," he said, and as he said it, he reached into a heavy canvas sack and scattered loose sand over the patio. Then he picked up a push broom and swept the sand back and forth over the patio, working the fine sand down into the irregularities between the bricks. "If we did our jobs right, and I'm certain we did, then that's all the maintenance this patio is going to need for years and years to come."

"Cool." *Great, Patrick; you said it again.*

"Very cool," Preacher agreed. And for maybe a minute, we just stood there and admired what we had built.

That's when he asked it.

"So, Patrick, your mom," he said, still looking at the patio, at the new blanket of red-brown bricks where only a low, flat plane of sand had been before. "Has she been gone long?"

My heart sank a little. How can I say this? My grief at the loss of my mother was overshadowed by a deeper, more selfish emotion. I was embarrassed. I didn't want Rachel's father to think of me as the son of a suicide.

I lowered my eyes, joined Preacher in a mute inspection of the patio, of the regular herringbone pattern of the bricks. I exhaled like an old man.

"No, sir," I finally told him. "She . . . uhm, it was just a couple of weeks before Easter."

I risked a sidelong glance. He was still looking at the patio, slowly shaking his head.

"That's rough," he said. Just that: *That's rough.*

He went to the spigot and shut off the flow to the garden hose, squeezed the spray head to let the pressure off, and then he disconnected the hose and began to coil it up. I folded down the top on the bag of sand, picked up his trowel and broom.

"You'll see a couple of dowels for the broom just inside the door of the garage," he told me. "Just put the trowel anywhere on the workbench."

Then: "How's your father taking this?"

I slowed down; my knees were feeling a little shaky. *Has he been talking to Judd Horton?* I turned and glanced back at Preacher; he was still coiling the hose, very matter-of-fact.

"He misses her," I told him. I went into the garage and put away the tools and then, still out of sight, where he couldn't see my face,

I fought to keep my voice steady as I added, "He has good days and bad."

That was honest, wasn't it?

"Yes." Preacher came into the garage and hung the hose on a wheel bolted to the wall. "Yes. I imagine he does."

I swiped at my face with both hands, nose to ears, trying to make it look like I was brushing away a sheen of sweat. Not trusting my voice, I nodded, and he let me walk out of the garage ahead of him.

"If he wants to talk with anybody about things, you let him know that I'm available, all right?"

I waited for a hand to land upon my shoulder, that firm, adult-to-adolescent reinforcement. *Got it, son?* It didn't come.

"I . . . I don't think he'd be too crazy about talking with a minister, sir." I turned and faced him as I said that. It only seemed right.

Preacher nodded.

"Understood. Well, we'll leave that up to your judgment, okay?" He held out his hand.

I shook it. "All right."

There was the sound of an engine on the far side of the garage. It stopped, and then there was a squeak, followed by the *thunk* of a car door closing.

"That'll be Rachel," Preacher said.

I released his hand and fetched my shirt from the back of the Adirondack chair.

A piton may be bridged lengthwise across a wider crack and tied off with a length of
webbing. In such a case, although the piton may still appear to be a piton,
it is actually being employed as a chock.

The Eastern Cragman's Guide to Climbing Anchors

THIRTEEN

When I got home, it was late afternoon, the shadows of the tall pines reaching like outstretched fingers across the slate roof of the old log house. My father's VW was there, and with the windows of the Chevette down, I could hear the sporadic *thuck* of an axe even before I killed the ignition. I followed the sound and found him on the far side of the house: shirt off, chest glistening with sweat. He was using a tree stump as a block, and there was a pile of cut wood to his right, and an even larger pile of split wood to his left.

"Hey, Sport." He shot me a smile and swung the axe, cleaving a bread loaf–size chunk of wood in two with a single stroke.

"I didn't know you had work to be done around here." Flustered, I went into the woodshed—the place was old enough to have one—and looked around for something with which to help him. The only other axe had a head that looked loose enough to be lethal, but I found a wedge and a sledge that looked serviceable, so I brought those outside.

"I didn't have work when you left this morning," my father told me. He swung the axe with a stifled grunt. "But a man stopped by with a truckload of oak, and he wasn't asking much for it, and I figured we might as well put this warm weather to work drying some firewood. As much time as they're taking to get that valve for the LP tank, who knows? We might need it. Besides, the furnace needs electricity to run, as well, and you know the old wires up in these hills. The power goes out if the wind blows the right way."

That was right. We lost power at the shop and the Airstream, both, just about every time there was a thunderstorm. We kept a battery lantern in the trailer, and several oil lamps at the shop.

Yet I knew better. I knew that wasn't really why my father had purchased all that firewood. I knew that the truck that had shown up had probably seen better days: sagging on its springs, and with a list to its bed. And I knew that its driver had probably been down on his luck, maybe an old man past his prime and too old for hiring, or a young man who looked as if he might have a family. I would have laid money on it; my father had, beyond the shadow of a doubt, bought the wood out of compassion, rather than need. And now, having acquired his truckload of wood, he was splitting it to justify the purchase.

But either way, it was work and, planned or not, I was feeling guilty for leaving him to do it all alone while I was away, socializing. Rachel and I had enjoyed an iced tea out on the newly finished patio after her father and I had completed his work. Truth be told, we'd enjoyed more than one, and I wondered how long my father had been here, swinging an axe in the heat by himself.

I stripped off my own shirt and joined him, and for the next hour the only sounds that passed between us were the solid *thuck* of his axe and the clink and creak of my wedge driving the larger pieces into yawning, reluctant halves. When we'd finished, we had wood piled as high as I could reach, and I fetched an old iron-wheeled barrow out of the woodshed and we shuttled the firewood into it and stacked it all the way to the rafters, alternating the layers, log cabin-style, to let air circulate around the newly split logs. By the time we had finished, the sun had set behind the hills on the west side of the hollow, and wispy clouds were turning pink and golden in the darkening sky.

"There," my father said when we had put the last of it away and squirted WD-40 onto the tools. "Even if that valve comes in tomorrow, we've got a good, solid week's worth of backup heat in there for this winter. And if we want a roaring fire Christmas Eve, well we've got it."

We started toward the trailer and then he stopped walking, looking at the house.

"What?"

"Oh, I was just thinking about Christmas." He shook his head. "This will be a great place at Christmas, Sport."

And the look in his eyes was so hollow that I shivered, despite the warmth of the evening.

Opposing one chock placement with another is an oftentimes-reliable means of keeping protection in place. The opposing chock does nothing in the event of a fall, but comes into play when rope movement threatens to move the primary placement in the opposite direction.

The Eastern Cragsman's Guide to Climbing Anchors

FOURTEEN

Years later, when I witnessed my first solar eclipse, I would instantly think of my father's fluctuations of spirit during that summer of 1976.

Or at least I would think so during the first half of the eclipse—that steadily creeping shadow that ate the warmth, devoured the light and turned high noon into a dimmed, spectral shadow of itself. At the moment of totality, there was only the fringe suggestion of brilliance, but the inner part, the core, was icy black. Empty.

That was my father as the West Virginia weekdays deprived him of the bustle and distraction of a shop full of customers. Once the shop floor had been swept, the inventory accounted for and orders placed for future goods, once the place had been readied for the next flight of business that was still several days away, he was alone with nothing but his thoughts—his doubts and his yearnings—and those thoughts were not his friends.

That is, at least, what I see now in the finely etched vision of hindsight. Did I see it then? I'd like to think I didn't—that sixteen was too young for inference, that I'd not yet developed the ear and the eye for such things. And sometimes, when I tell this story—on the rare occasions when I do tell this story—I grant myself that small bit of grace. But the fact of the matter is that I was sixteen, newly infatuated, absorbed in a girl and trying to get on with my life, and unwilling to follow my father into his darkness. I thought I was ready to get on.

I was selfish.

And that is probably why, that Thursday morning, when my father had not uttered two successive sentences in more than forty-eight hours, when he had gone into the house "to use the study" but I had seen the light come on in the big master bedroom window, and when his appetite had dwindled to bare forkfuls—when all of these signs had been there, and he asked me to drive my Chevette into Elkins to attend to a laundry list of errands obviously contrived to occupy me for the better part of the day . . . I had gone. I had gone and accepted at face value his story that he was going to head up to the shop, make space for some inventory that was arriving in the morning, and then go up and run some trails to burn off a little steam.

There was one way that the eclipse metaphor broke down when it came to my father's moods. Eclipses wax and wane. When my father's black moods went away, they disintegrated, the occluding disk vanishing like a well-shot clay pigeon, light rendering the darkness conspicuous by its absence.

And that, of course, is what I found when I got back to the shop, the five-hundred-mile checkup having been completed on the Chevette, the cargo space beneath its hatchback packed with paper goods and laundry detergent and a dozen other things that we could easily have gone another week without. My father met me as I popped the hatch, helped me carry in the shop's share of the shopping, told me about the idea he'd had for a climbing hardware museum, to be mounted on the shop's only vacant vertical surface—the door leading into the back room—and asked me if I was ready to go to Yokum's for dinner, because Thursday nights were chicken nights, and he was famished.

In the vernacular of a later epoch, I didn't ask, and he didn't tell. I went to Yokum's with him, glad to have my father back, and I tried not to think of what event it must have been that could have wreaked such a visible change. I would find out soon enough, the next day.

The UPS man came at noon the next day, a Friday. The UPS visits were always a little like Christmas; we knew what we had ordered, but this was in the days before personal computers and online status checks, so we never quite knew what we were going to receive, or when. My father tried to project our needs two or three weeks out, and we were adapting as we learned what sold, but it was our first year; we were still pretty new at this.

This particular Friday brought us some ropes and rucksacks that we were expecting. It also brought us five boxes of chocks, carabiners, rappel rings and other hardware, and that took us some time to check in and get stocked. We were still doing that at three in the afternoon, when Phil Tapia stormed in through the open front door.

"What's the deal with Zardoz?" He nearly shouted the question at my father, who raised a hand and went on counting a box of carabiners, checking them off against an invoice.

"What about Zardoz?" I asked.

Tapia looked at me as if he was wondering where I had come from.

"There's chalk all the way up it."

I felt as if a giant hand had reached out and given me a firm shove in the chest. I didn't move—I don't think I moved—but I felt as if I had staggered nonetheless.

Tapia turned back to my father. "What'd somebody do—toprope it?"

My father held his hand up again, counted out three more carabiners, marked a number off the invoice, and then looked up at Tapia.

"Well, good afternoon, Phil." My father smiled, two rows of even, white teeth, and came around the counter, right hand out. "What'd you do, play hooky on the Bureau for the day?"

Tapia looked at my father's outstretched hand as if not certain what to do with it. Then he blinked, shook hands, and said, "I had a sick day coming, so I took it to get up here before the . . . For the love of Mike—what's going on with Zardoz, Kevin?"

My father reduced his grin to a half smile. "I'm afraid it's not called 'Zardoz' any longer, Phil."

In the silence that followed, I heard a truck shifting down as it came down Route 33, the highway that ran next to Seneca Creek. It came to a stop at the T and turned north, toward Petersburg.

"It's been climbed," Tapia replied flatly.

"It has."

Tapia shook his head. "I looked at every inch of that route, Kevin. There's not a bolt on it. Nobody's hung a stirrup on that blank section."

My father's smile faded to a thin line. He raised his eyebrows a bit. "That's because it wasn't done on aid, Phil."

No truck this time. Just the wind, rustling the leaves in the trees to the side of the shop, and somewhere the sound of birds.

Tapia almost pushed past my father to get to the counter. I knew what he was after—my father kept a route book there, a plain pasteboard-bound accountant's record with pale green pages on which anyone who'd put up a new route could record the details. Tapia got to the tall gray book and opened it to the most recent entry.

Setting down the rope I'd been pricing, I stepped behind him and read over his shoulder:

Thunderbolt and Lightfoot

That was the new name of the climb. It was the name of another movie that came out in 1974, the same year as *Zardoz*.

So, I realized, was *Death Wish*.

The description went on:

> **Lower Seneca Rocks. Very hard, exceedingly thin 5.10+. Follows the line of the uncompleted Zardoz aid route. Climb increasingly thin face, topping out at the lower edge of the Upper Seneca scree field. Protection opportunities are thin throughout, and nonexistent for much of the upper third. First ascent: June 17, 1976, by . . .**

"'Anonymous?'" Tapia turned around and looked past me, eyes wide, at my father. "Oh, come on, Kevin—some guy waltzes in here and says he topped out on, says he *freed* Zardoz, and you just accept the claim even though he won't sign his name? Do you even know who wrote this entry?"

"I do," my father said.

Tapia stepped around me.

"Then who is it?"

"Anonymous. He doesn't want his name known, and that's cool with me. No rule that says you have to sign the route, as long as you climbed it."

"Well who was the second?"

"No second."

"He self-belayed?"

"He free-soloed."

Tapia had his back to me, but I'm guessing he rolled his eyes.

"And you're buying this? I can't believe what I'm hearing, Kevin. Someone's put you on. They rapped down the route, spotted it with chalk marks, and then came in here and claimed to have bagged it."

My father shook his head.

"Not how it worked, Phil. He got it fair and square."

More bird sounds.

"And how are you so sure?"

My father shrugged.

"I was up there yesterday. I saw the whole thing. Free solo, bottom to top."

He began collecting the carabiners and returning them to their shipping box. I could hear the *clink clink clink* as he stacked them atop one another.

"You saw it." Tapia said it straight, a statement, but there was still a question in there somewhere.

My father nodded. "With my own eyes. And trust me, Phil. I know this guy."

So did I. Maybe a little too well. I'd known it before I'd even seen the route book, but I was certain once I'd seen the first word.

The description was in my father's handwriting.

A blind hold—a hold that cannot be seen by the climber—can still be used with confidence if it is thoroughly explored first by touch.

Rock Climbing Holds and Basics

Codependence was a term that had not yet entered my vocabulary at sixteen, but I knew that I had to do something. My father had just completed—without a rope—the most technically demanding route at Seneca in those days. That he had rated it a difficult 5.10 was more of a nod to Seneca tradition than it was to accuracy. Over the next two years, scores of young tigers would make the pilgrimage to have a go at Thunderbolt and Lightfoot, and there would be several broken ankles, a couple of fractured femurs, and at least one broken collarbone before the route saw its second ascent. The joke in those days was that at least the trail to the base of the climb widened and improved, thanks to the near constant foot traffic with the Stokes litter.

But any nascent humor was lost on me. The talk around the shop, into the evening on Friday and through the day on Saturday, was all about how someone had poached the climb out from under Tapia and robbed him of the chance to place his bolt. Had it simply been a free ascent on an uncompleted aid route, it would have made news. That it had been done without a rope was enough to ensure that the shop traffic would talk of nothing else. By midday on Saturday, *Summit, Off Belay* and *Mountain* magazines had all gotten wind of it—or at least their East Coast stringers had. And my father gave them all the same story he had given Tapia on Friday: that the person who'd made the climb wanted to remain anonymous, but the climb had most definitely been made because he—my father—had witnessed it. Most of the magazines had follow-up questions, and I heard my father answering them as I sold carabiners and webbing to a steady stream of traffic: yes, the climber was a Seneca regular; yes, he was one of the small group of people who regularly climbed in the upper ratings; no, he had not rappelled down and rehearsed the crux beforehand; and—a pause here as he thought this one over—the entire climb had taken only about five or six minutes, putting the ascent in the category that was referred to in those days as a "blitz."

Looking back on it, what amazes me now is that no one—not a single one of the people who called that Saturday, nor the dozens upon dozens that streamed into our shop—thought to ask my father if *he* had been that anonymous climber. Partly it was the innocence of a time when things such as Watergate had been special-edition news, and not just a callous expectation. But mostly it was because, for my father, the song and dance about anonymity and him being a witness—both of which, technically, were true—was as deep into the wilds of prevarication as he had ever gone with his friends and acquaintances. The outright lie, such as claiming that he had only intended to boulder when he topped out on Man Overboard, seemed to be something that he exclusively reserved for me.

I remember wondering, as I explained the difference between PAs and EBs to a kid from Georgetown who obviously was not going to break out his wallet and buy either one, exactly what my father would have said if someone, particularly someone from the magazines, had asked the question. Free-soloing had never been in my father's nature, and it would have prompted the obvious follow-up question: *Why?*

Perhaps if someone had, it would have been cathartic, could have startled my father out of that tightening cycle he had so recently entered. In hindsight, I often wonder why I did not do it myself, didn't say, in front of witnesses, "Dad—uhm, isn't that your handwriting?"

But I didn't. In fact, I became his willing accomplice, telling those who asked that I had been out running errands when the climb was made, and that, as far as I knew, my father was the only witness. And even saying those things felt like ashes and dust in my mouth. Misdirection, covering for my father—those were new skills for me that summer.

To remedy that would involve more misdirection. Oddly

enough, I didn't see that as a contradiction. Part of that was reciprocity, and part of it was the fact that I had nowhere else to turn.

I went to church.

Preacher's sermon that Sunday was . . . Well, I'll be honest—I have no idea what Preacher spoke on that following morning. That it was not wages-of-sin or turn-or-burn is fairly certain; Preacher favored the loving aspects of God, a trait that would, I would later discover, place him in a vanguard yet to be caught up with by his evangelical brethren.

I remember what Rachel looked like that Sunday: the sea-blue of her eyes; the way her blond hair formed a soft, luminous frame to her face; the faint scent of soap, as wonderful to me as any perfume; the lingering touch of her slender hand; and the slender swell of her body beneath her dress. I remember all of those things, remember them as clearly as if it was yesterday, because . . . well, because I do, and not even the demons gripping my father could have caused me to overlook them.

And I do remember that Preacher had a pattern to his services. He would conclude the message, then he would ask the congregation to join him in prayer, and then the organ would start up and everyone would stand and sing a recessional hymn.

This time, though, I must have missed Preacher's change of timbre as he concluded, missed the hush throughout the open-air pavilion and the bowing of heads all around me as he prayed. The next thing I knew, everyone was standing, and I was still looking at Rachel in what I hoped was a sidelong glance, but it wasn't, because she looked right at me, a question written there in her eyes, and then she opened her hymnal and she began to sing.

"Patrick, what is it?"

We were walking across the dusty ground of Judd Horton's campground. The sun was warm on my back and it shadowed her face, making it hard to read her expression.

"It?" I felt badly, being rude like that. I didn't know what else to say.

"You were looking my way all through the service."

"Well, Rachel, you're . . . you're a very nice-looking girl."

The sun hit her face then, and I could see that she was blushing.

I swallowed, felt the shirt collar against the base of my throat. Trying to blend in, I'd gone so far as to put on a dress shirt—pale blue, purchased for my mother's funeral, together with one of the two neckties I owned, fashioned after two or three attempts into a reasonable facsimile of a full Windsor knot.

"I . . ." My voice cracked then, and I took a breath before trying again. "I need to talk to you."

"We're talking." We had stopped walking by now, and her eyes searched mine—left, then right, then left again.

"Not . . ." People were walking in groups to the old cars and pickup trucks parked across the rutted earthen drive from the picnic pavilion. They passed so close that I could smell the hair tonic on the men, hear the women talking to one another about roasts in the oven and visitors coming for dinner.

"Not here." I finally got the words out.

Rachel nodded at the people passing and smiled as someone said her name. Then she looked straight into my eyes and searched there for a moment.

"All right." She finally said. "I'm helping Daddy for the rest of the day. And tomorrow we're driving over to the old folks' home in Petersburg, to volunteer. Can it be Tuesday?"

I thought about this and nodded, once.

"Do you know the cliff up by the church on Acker's Hollow?" She didn't whisper it—just said it in a normal voice, like we were having a normal conversation, talking about the weather.

"Church Rock." I nodded. My father and I had climbed there several times.

"Meet me there Tuesday at—" she looked up for a moment,

thinking—"at noon. Can you do that?"

I nodded again.

"And Patrick?" Her eyes met mine. "Don't tell anybody I'm doing this. The folks here wouldn't approve of my coming alone."

SIXTEEN

I got to Church Rock just a few minutes after eleven. "Going out to do a little bouldering"—that's the story I'd told my father. And to my great relief he had not offered to come along.

To my even greater relief, he'd had no plans to go climbing on his own. He was going in to the shop. There was a manufacturer's rep stopping by from Company Three; we were kicking around the idea of carrying mountaineering skis during the off-season.

I parked my Chevette on a curve in the gravel road at the base of the rock. Below me, at the bottom of the curve, the small one-room church appeared newly painted, so white it almost hurt to look at it in the midday sun. The church was by itself under a hill covered with spruce, and the grass around it was neatly trimmed and smooth, no worn spots and no tire tracks.

That made me wonder if the place was even being used anymore. And if it wasn't, I wondered who was taking care of it, and why. Then the story I'd told my father came back to me again, so I opened the hatchback on the Chevette, sat on the back bumper and pulled on my EBs.

The face of Church Rock was split by a couple of vertical cracks—the obvious routes—and I ignored them. I found a blank-looking section in between, concave and overhanging, a chess problem in quartzite and gravity.

After five or six attempts, I'd gotten about eight feet off the ground and was fooling with a little lip of an overhang, experimenting with a heel hook, not really trying to pull it, just playing with it, working on technique, when I heard the sound of a big V8 engine lumbering up the hollow.

I looked over my shoulder. It was the Ransoms' Travelall, a familiar bell of blond hair behind the wheel.

Rachel.

I let my legs fall beneath me, swung free of the rock, and dropped to the ground, crouching to absorb the force of the landing. I stood, wiping my damp palms against my pant legs, hoping I did not look as gritty as I felt, as Rachel got out of the old truck, smiling as she looked up at the rock and then back at me.

"Patrick Nolan! You scared me half to death; I thought you'd fallen."

Skeered was the way it came out, the high mountain accent surfacing for a moment in her fright.

"I'm sorry. I didn't mean to startle you."

Next to me now, the day seemed to brighten a bit. Rachel turned and looked up at the rock again.

"Goodness. You were climbing on nothing, weren't you?"

The day seemed brighter still.

I shook my head. "It just looks like nothing. If you look close, you can find holds. Maybe not anything you can really latch onto, but enough to stay on."

She looked at the rock face and shook her head. "That's amazing. I can't imagine . . ."

"I could teach you."

She turned to me, head cocked. "You could do that?"

"Sure. For the first move, here, you just use these nubbins for balance while you move your feet up onto these sloping seams, see?" I demonstrated the move. "Then you keep enough inside pressure on the left nubbin to keep you in place while you move the right hand higher . . . like this."

I completed the move and then hopped down, landing almost noiselessly on the sand at the base of the rock.

"There. Now you try."

"Now?" Rachel glanced around as if anticipating an audience.

"No time like the present."

She blushed, just a little. I loved that.

"Okay." Rachel placed her hands on the rock where mine had been and put her left foot on the hold I'd shown her. She moved her right foot and toppled backward; I caught her and kept her upright as she landed, and her back was firm and warm beneath the thin cotton of her blouse. I did my best to think distant thoughts.

"You okay?"

She turned. My hands fell away from her. "I'm fine," she said. "I just stepped on the hem of my skirt."

"Probably not the best wardrobe for rock climbing."

"Probably not." She looked down at the skirt, one side of her mouth puckered in a half scowl. Glancing around one more time, she grabbed the fabric of her skirt on either side about halfway down, lifted it and tucked it into its own waistband, and then tried the first moves on the boulder problem again.

I raised my hands as she made the first move, then the second. Slowly, she moved up. Now my hands were poised just a fraction of an inch from her waist . . . now they were at the small of her back . . . now they were . . . lower. I felt warm.

Rachel glanced down.

"Patrick Nolan! Are you staring at my legs?"

Was I staring at her legs? Of course I was staring at her legs. In fact, I was beyond staring; I was *gaping* at her legs.

I can't explain that. Or rather I can, but it takes some doing. I mean, the majorettes that pom-pomed their way in front of the Scott High marching band in practically every parade I'd ever watched, female gymnasts on TV, the girls on just about any beach I'd ever visited, even the vacationing co-eds on the midway at Cedar Point—they'd all exhibited considerably more flesh than Rachel was baring on this rock climb. But you have to view it in context. After all, she was the pastor's daughter, and there was this whole forbidden-fruit factor, this unapproachability—and besides, I'd never seen more of her legs than her ankle.

"You *are* staring at my legs, aren't you?" Rachel was down-climbing now, and doing an amazingly good job of it. She got to the ground, turned, and looked at me, arms akimbo.

"Well," I said, "they're so . . ."

"So . . . ?"

I glanced down. "They're so . . . tan."

Rachel adjusted her skirt, untucking it and letting it drop back to its full length. Her blond hair hid her face as she did so, and when she looked up, brushing her hair back, she raised her chin a bit and said, "I lay out in the sun sometimes when nobody else is home."

"In a swimsuit, you mean?"

She glanced down. "In a two-piece . . . My aunt—my daddy's sister—got it for me when I was visiting with her last year."

When she looked up, her face was almost ashen. "Patrick—you can't tell anybody about that suit."

"Why? What's wrong with a swimsuit? It's not like you were tanning naked."

Her ashen face changed to a blush. "That's not what everybody would say. There's a place in Exodus where it says that showing the thigh is the same thing as being naked."

Showing the thigh? I thought back to the first time I'd met her, when I'd gotten out of my sleeping bag in front of her entire church wearing my climbing shorts. Yikes.

"So that means what? Nobody in your church goes swimming?"

"We do, at church camp. But the ladies swim separate from the men. And we wear culottes, the kind that look like skirts, you know? That's because Deuteronomy 22:5 says 'a woman shall not wear that which pertaineth to a man.'"

I barely heard the second part. That's because I was trying to imagine how awkward it would have to feel to go swimming in culottes. I mean, my father and I were so used to skinny-dipping in the North Fork when no one else was around that I considered even swim trunks to be a major pain. *Culottes?*

"So . . ." I dropped my gaze. I didn't think I could look her right in the eyes at that moment. "This Exodus and Dude—"

"Deuteronomy."

"Yeah. That. That's in the Bible, right?"

Even with my gaze fixed on her shoulder, I could see that she was nodding.

"And you buy it?"

"You mean, do I honor it?"

"Honor it, believe it . . ."

"Those aren't necessarily the same thing." She walked a couple of steps to a low boulder at the base of the cliff, brushed it with her hand and sat. She patted the rock and I sat beside her. "I mean, three verses after that part about 'pertaineth to a man,' the Bible says you shouldn't build a house without a parapet, and Daddy says he doesn't see many homes going up with railings around the rooftops these days."

I grinned then, and it occurred to me that my gaze was still dropped. She might think I was staring at her chest. With good reason. So I looked up. "All right. So you think it's all bull . . . All, uh, bunk."

She shook her head. "The way I look at it, it's like a prescription."

"A prescription?"

She nodded—two nods. "Let's say you're sick and the doctor prescribes penicillin, and you take it and you get well. The prescription could even save your life."

"Okay."

"But if somebody else picks that prescription up and gets it filled? And they're allergic to penicillin? The same thing that saved your life could *kill* them."

She looked at me, eyebrows raised, and I bobbed my head to show I was following her.

"Daddy says that, whenever you read something in the Bible, the first thing you have to ask is who was it written for, and what were they going through at the time? In lots of cases, God's establishing rules to complement situations that no longer exist . . . that haven't existed for centuries."

I scratched an ear and looked at her sideways. "Then why is it still in there?"

"To show that God loves us. That he has always loved us and offered us his guidance."

Glancing down at her long skirt, I asked, "And so, you dress this way because. . . ?"

Rachel closed her eyes, pushed her long, blond hair back with both hands, and reopened her eyes. "Not everybody in the church sees Scripture the same way that Daddy does . . . that I do. There are folks who take a more word-for-word view, and this just isn't a big enough issue for me to alienate them."

"So you dress this way . . . for them?"

She sighed. "You must think I'm a hypocrite."

Well, yes.

I said nothing.

Rachel sighed. "It's biblical, Patrick. Not dressing this way, but dressing this way so others in my church don't become upset. I mean, churches have dealt with this sort of issue for thousands of years, and when Paul wrote his first letter to the church at Corinth, he instructed them to behave in ways that would not offend their weaker brothers and sisters in Christ. The idea is that they can't grow unless they listen, so I bend to their opinions to help them continue to listen."

At the time, I thought Corinth was a town in Tennessee or Georgia, one of the two. As for Paul, I was without a clue, although I figured he had to be a friend of her father's. But I got the general picture. And yes, it struck me as weird.

"These people you dress this way for," I asked her, "do you think they'd do the same for you?"

Rachel rolled her lips in just a little, wetting them. She closed her eyes, and when she reopened them I was surprised at how blue they were.

"I think," Rachel said, her voice not a whisper, but soft, "that Jesus would do the same. For them, for me. For anyone."

The grin crept onto my face of its own volition. "And how about sunbathing in a two-piece? Is that something Jesus would do, too?"

I regretted that instantly. Rachel's face flushed so red that she had to turn away for a moment. But when she looked back, she was composed.

"I think," she said, "that Jesus made the sun. It's his gift to us. *One* of his gifts to us."

What she did next surprised me. She took my right hand and squeezed it. And then she said, "So . . . you wanted to talk?"

I blinked, lost there for a moment; it took a couple of seconds for her question to sink in, and when it did, the day darkened a little. Somehow, with the bouldering, and seeing Rachel, and seizing that very satisfying opportunity to look at her legs, and having what had seemed at the time to me to be a relatively meaningless theological discussion, I'd managed to push my concerns out of my mind for a moment. But that was over now. I looked down at her hand in mine, and I squeezed it back. It was amazing, just how comforting, how satisfying that simple action was, even given the gravity of what I had to say. I cleared my throat.

She still held my hand in hers, and now she covered it with her other hand, which only served to further muddy the waters. I wanted nothing more than to sit with my hand in hers forever, but maybe there was some nascent portion of the gospel message alive in me even then: dying to self, concern for others. Gently as I could, I worked my hand free and collected my thoughts, taking a deep breath of spruce-touched air. Down at the roadside, the Travelall's engine was ticking as it cooled.

"What I'm going to tell you now," I said. "It's just between us. It has to stay here. Okay?"

She quirked an eyebrow. "Gee, Patrick. What did you do? Kill somebody?"

"Maybe. But it stays between us. Right?"

Rachel studied my face.

"Okay," she finally said. "Between us."

Where to start? I took a deep breath. "I told you my mother died a few months ago."

Rachel sat up. "Oh, Patrick . . ." Her voice was just a thread. "You didn't kill your mama . . . Did you?"

"Please. Just listen. I told you that she died in . . ."

Her head bobbed slowly. "In a highway accident."

I shook my head. "In her car, yes. But not in a highway accident."

Then it all came tumbling out: What my father had told me on the drive back to Ohio. Dr. Marion. The police. The move to West Virginia. The shop. The house. How I'd heard my father weeping in the room with the boxes.

I told her about finding him on Man Overboard. About Tapia's plan to bolt Zardoz. About the anonymous route-book entry.

When I'd told her everything, I felt empty. Empty, and unburdened, in a hollow sort of way, and exhausted, all at the same time. But there was also this tremendous sense of relief, of knowing that I didn't have to keep it all to myself anymore.

I felt clean. I felt limp—I couldn't have stood right then if my life depended on it. There was just this great big well of . . . everything rising within me. I closed my eyes to hold back the tears, and felt Rachel's arms around my shoulder, pulling me to her, burying my face in the nape of her neck, veiling my hurt with her hair.

Just five minutes earlier, having her arms around me would have led to an entirely new set of emotions. But in this space, it just led to submersion. I didn't hug her back. I just let her do what she was doing, holding me and rocking me ever so slowly, and for a long time we sat there, wrapped in that soothing moment. Gradually it dawned on me that the most amazing, most naturally sensuous girl I'd ever met was holding me like a child. I extracted myself with as much grace as I could, which wasn't much. Then I turned away from her until I was sure my eyes were dry.

When finally I could once again face her, Rachel's eyes were wide with concern.

"Patrick," she whispered. "This is serious. This is your daddy we're talking about here. You've got to do something. You have to tell somebody."

"Who? The police? He's not breaking any laws. And if I get . . ."

I don't know, social workers and whatnot involved, they'll think he's not fit as a father."

"Well? Is he?"

I thought about that for a long moment, and we were so still that a jay landed not two feet from where we sat and looked at us with one eye, head cocked. I cleared my throat and the bird flew away.

"He's hurting, Rachel. He goes upstairs in the house, and he goes through her things, and he gets buried by the memories. Then he does these climbs just to . . . to clear out the garbage. He's not suicidal, not trying to harm himself. He's just carrying too much, and he thinks the climbing helps . . . takes it away for a while."

"But, trying or not, he could still die, couldn't he?"

I nodded.

"Then what are you going to do?"

I looked up at the sky and it was a rich, heavy blue, the air as clear as crystal.

"Can you come with me?" I asked. I didn't look at her as I asked that. I kept gazing at the sky. "To our house?"

Rachel didn't answer right away, so I looked her in the eyes. Those blue eyes.

She blinked. "Now?"

I nodded.

Her face sobered, her lips thin. "Just the two of us?"

Alone in our house with Rachel. What a tousled hairball of emotions *that* thought raised. I pushed aside all but the one that mattered, and nodded again.

"I promised my father I wouldn't go through my mother's things by myself," I told her. "He thinks it's too much for one person alone, and . . . Well, I promised, and I won't go back on my word to him. But if you're with me, then I'm not alone. I'm keeping my word."

She looked at me, silent.

"There isn't anyone else, Rachel. I haven't told anybody else. I can't."

She stood, took a breath, put her hand out to me.

"All right," she said. "Let's go."

The clothes were easy. The boxes were marked; we didn't even open them. I just carried them downstairs to the drive and loaded them into the cavernous back end of the Travelall.

"Maybe your mom can use some of this," I said as Rachel helped me shift the boxes, making room for them all. "Or some of the ladies in your church."

"No." She shook her head. "What if we do that, and then your daddy goes to the store someday? And there's a lady there wearing one of your mama's blouses? Or carrying her purse? That could start him hurting all over again. We'll take this up to Wheeling, when my mama's done helping with the baby—leave it with the ladies in the church up there."

We returned to the big upstairs bedroom. It was close, and you could smell the cardboard boxes in the still, dusty air, so I opened the windows, and the curtains filled and fluttered softly as the breeze came in.

I found the big envelope my father had mentioned—the one with the notes and letters—and, out of deference to him, I just set it aside. We went through the school things next: textbooks and three-ring binders and exam blue books and mimeographed hand-outs of reading lists and course requirements. I very nearly took some of the reference books down to the office: the dictionary and the thesaurus and *Bartlett's Familiar Quotations*. Then, worried that even the sight of those covers would retrigger my father's remorse, I packed it all up again—the school things and the notes from my father, and everything—and Rachel helped me work it up through the trapdoor in the bedroom closet ceiling. I climbed up behind it, coughing at the dust I raised from the sill, and put the box away in the attic, setting it behind a tarnished mirror left by the house's previous owners. It was hot work, up under the thick, rough under-side of the roof, and I would have taken my shirt off, but I knew that would have made Rachel uncomfortable; she was already uncomfortable with just the two of us being there. So I was sweating by the time I lowered myself back into the closet, and I lifted my shirt away from me, cooling myself. I saw Rachel looking my way as I did that, and she blushed. I hated it when I did that, but loved it on Rachel. All of a sudden I wanted to hold her, but the damp shirt stopped me, and I knew that was probably best.

The bedroom was looking empty now. Just one box left: it, and my mother's vanity, and the big Oriental carpet on the floor. I wondered about the vanity; we couldn't just take that away, not without talking to my father first. Then I wondered if it mattered. We could take everything away, every single possession that my mother had ever owned, had ever touched, and there would still be me, wouldn't there? And wouldn't that be enough? Wasn't I a walking, breathing reminder to my father—a daily token of all that he had lost?

"What's in this one?" Rachel had moved the last cardboard box out into the center of the big burgundy rug. Unlike the others, it was not labeled with Magic Marker. I remembered why.

"Those are her things," I said. And then, realizing how stupid that sounded—every single one of the boxes we'd handled so far had been filled with my mother's things—I added, "What she had in her car and her . . . I mean, the stuff she had in her purse when she . . ."

I fell silent.

"Okay." Rachel sat on the rug, her hand atop the box. "Do you want me to open it?"

"That's all right. I can do it; I have my knife."

I sank down, cross-legged, next to Rachel on the rug, and cut the gator-tape holding the flaps of the box, the blade of my Swiss Army knife stuttering through the nylon threads in the tape. Setting the knife aside, I lifted the flaps. We leaned forward, looked inside.

On top was a large paper bag. White with red printing—CENTRAL AVENUE AMC/JEEP and GENUINE AMC PARTS—it was stapled shut, the top tented. I opened it.

Jumper cables. Safety flares. A can of Instant Seal-N-Air—a product for fixing flats. Evidence of my father trying to take care of my mother even when he couldn't be there with her.

Under that we found a Lucas County road map, three pencils missing their points, a cellophane-wrapped lemon air freshener, shaped like an American flag, from a local car wash. There were three months' worth of credit-card receipts from gas stations, which wasn't all that many, because my mother had ridden her bicycle to the university or even walked, when the weather was nice. A pair of sunglasses—Foster Grants, because she lost sunglasses all the time and refused to buy anything expensive—seven bronze hairpins, a hairbrush still holding strands of her honey-colored hair.

I set the brush aside with two hands and looked at the rest of it: the little colored rubber bands she used to pull back her hair, a pencil-type tire-pressure gauge—my father again—two cassette tapes of Dylan Thomas reading his poems, a quarter, six dimes, and five nickels. That and half a pack of CareFree sugarless gum was all there was. I set the bag behind us on the rug and returned to the box.

Eighteen rubber-banded packets of mail were next: all of the mail that had arrived at our house on Parkwood, addressed to my mother, during the three weeks following her death. After that point, I'd gotten to the mailbox first and sorted through things myself, but my father had bundled together absolutely everything with my mother's name on it, as if he were saving it for her to read later.

I slipped the rubber bands off and went through the envelopes. Most of it—almost all of it—was junk mail: credit-card offers and sales circulars, shopping coupons, subscription renewal notices from *National Geographic* and *Reader's Digest*, a ticket offer for the spring concert series at the Toledo Museum of Art and a schedule for the free summer band concert series at the zoo, a circular hawking season tickets to the Toledo Mudhens minor-league baseball home games, something from Greenpeace about saving whales and harp seals, and preprinted invitations to Bicentennial planning dinners, Bicentennial barbecues, Bicentennial picnics.

There were only a few envelopes that weren't junk mail: Easter cards from old classmates and relatives who must have mailed them early, a typewriter-addressed envelope from the Medical College of

Ohio, her spring tuition statement from the University of Toledo, a postcard from a cousin vacationing in Grand Canyon National Park, and a letter stamped *Spring Banquet Information* from the UT Honors Program, which had accepted her as a member the previous autumn.

I got to my feet and put all the personal mail on the vanity, and then I came back and sat cross-legged again next to Rachel, the short pile of the rug giving way underneath me like close-cropped grass.

I took another look in the box. Paper clips. Pennies. A half-crumpled book of first-class stamps. Colored lint. Dust.

"That's it," I said. "That's all of it. We're done."

Rachel was quiet then, and the curtain on the open window lifted and then fell, as if the air itself was leaving. I turned and looked at her and she pulled her hair back with both hands, the skin of her neck moist.

I leaned back on my hands, the rug soft beneath them. I thought about the room that we were in. Nearly empty as it was, even lacking as it did a bed, the fact remained that, in the plan of this house, it was still a bedroom. Just thinking that made my throat thick, and I swallowed.

At the sound, Rachel turned my way, and I saw her cheeks redden. She patted her skirted knees, twice, with both hands.

"Let me get rid of this," she said, rising to her knees and reaching for the box. "I'll just take it—" She stopped. "There's something in here."

I got to my knees beside her—a pair of communicants, peering into a tilted cardboard box.

There *was* something in there: a very small brown book, partly covered by the lifted flap of the box bottom. The box tilted in Rachel's hands and the book slid out farther. Gilt print. Block letters. The right half of a title:

EW
AMENT
ND
LMS

"A Bible?" I asked.

"It's a Workman's Bible," Rachel said. She took it out, opened it up.

The pages looked crisp. New. I stared at the twin columns of fly-type script. "Why would my mother have bought a Bible?"

"She didn't." Rachel opened the little book to the title page where, under a subtitle ("Authorized, or King James Version") there were smaller block letters: GIDEONS INTERNATIONAL.

"She got it from a hotel?" I didn't like where this was going.

"No. No, no, no, no." Rachel closed the book and tapped on the cover. "The ones they leave in hotels are the whole Bible—sixty-six books. This just has the New Testament, Psalms and Proverbs. Twenty-nine books. My uncle—my daddy's cousin—he's a Gideon."

"A missionary?"

"No. Gideons aren't preachers. They're businesspeople. Like a club. They meet to pray together once a week, and they spend free time spreading the Word."

"About. . . ?"

"Pardon?"

"'The word.' What word?"

"Of God." She tapped on the cover again. "These little testaments: the covers are color-coded. The ones they give to public-school students, high school and the like? They're red. White means it was given to a nurse. The military testaments are green. But this one, the brown one? It's a Workman's Bible."

I opened my hands, palms up.

"The other testaments, the other colors, are supplied to a Gideon," Rachel explained. "But the Workman's Bible is special. It's one that each man buys with his own money—just a few copies, usually, as many as he thinks he can use each month. They generally only give a Workman's Bible away when they find somebody who's serious. What Daddy calls a 'seeker.' Either that or a convert."

"A convert . . ."

"To Christianity. Like . . ." And here she paused and riffled through the business-card-size pages to the back, slowing in the last few, stopping after a moment. She took in a sharp nibble of breath, rolled the tips of her lips inward, and touched one perfect knuckle to her mouth. She looked at me and her eyes were welling, and then she showed me the page, a single paragraph of type, followed by a signature, a date, and a second signature and the handwritten notation: WITNESS.

I did not recognize the second signature, the witness's signature, but the first was one I had seen all of my life, on permission slips for camp and Scouts, on checks for class trips, on the bottoms of my report cards when I carried them back to school. There it was, in the same familiar, careful, feminine hand: *Laurie Cynthia Nolan.*

"Like your mama, Patrick." Rachel's voice was broken, a half-choked whisper, as she placed the small, brown book in my hand. "Like your mama."

Beginners are taught to always have three points in contact with the rock, but this basic imperative often goes by the board on extremely advanced climbs. Be that as it may, the climber should know that anytime he trusts his full weight to a single hold, he is taking a chance, and the odds are against him.

Rock Climbing Holds and Basics

SEVENTEEN

Preacher driving, the Travelall rolled down 28 into Mouth of Seneca, big, deep-treaded truck tires thrumming on the crowned asphalt, lights on against the dusk that came so early to the hollows, even at the height of summer. When we pulled into the turnoff in front of the shop, it was already in deep shadow, but the West Face of Seneca and the Southern Pillar were still in full sun, the golden light painting the rock with amber and sharp, black shadows. A single blue-shirted climber was topping off on Thais, and just to his right there was a group of three at the top of the regular rappel route, their fourth in mid-abseil beneath them, a distant brown dot of a spider, dropping on the breadth of a thread into deep, leafy darkness below.

The door to the shop stood open, so I stepped in first, Preacher following me and, after him, Rachel. My father was alone, perched on a stool behind the counter, a copy of *Mountain* magazine open on the glass top at his elbow, a big cellophane bag of cheese corn lying next to it, the bag top rolled to stand open, its contents half gone. He stood as we entered, taking off his half-moon reading glasses and setting them atop his magazine, wiping his hands against the white-threaded thighs of his jeans.

"Dad, this is Pastor Ransom from Weeping Oak Community Church, and this is his daughter, my—" I looked her way and felt my face redden—"my friend, Rachel."

"Kevin Nolan." My father extended his deeply suntanned right hand.

"Jim," Preacher told him as they shook. The two men released hands and my father nodded at Rachel, and then my way, and then back at Rachel. That done, he turned his attention to her father, a stranger to the shop, but not at all out of place in his plaid shirt and khaki work pants.

"So." My father glanced at me again. "What's up?"

"We have news, Kevin," Preacher told him. "Good news. Can we sit?"

My father nodded and stepped around the counter, holding out a hand toward the two split-log benches that made an L, with the cold stove as their corner. We settled, Rachel and Preacher on one bench, and my father and me on the other.

"Patrick and Rachel were over to your place earlier this afternoon," Preacher began, and as he said that, my father glanced at me, eyebrows raised, and I shook my head, a quick, small, left-right shake. He nodded once and turned back to Preacher.

"I know," Preacher said. "And I wouldn't want to see them make a habit of that, either. But Patrick said he had promised you that he would not sort through your wife's belongings alone . . ."

A second glance, briefly, no eyebrow this time.

". . . And he felt that he could honor that promise by having Rachel with him. I hope, Kevin, that these young people did not overstep their bounds. But that's what they did today, and they found this."

He reached into his shirt pocket and took out the little brown Workman's Bible. He handed it to my father.

"Let me explain what that is," Preacher said.

"I know what it is."

That stunned all three of us—Preacher, Rachel and me—into a brief and rapt silence.

"It's some literature that Laurie picked up from some koo . . . from some person out at the university," my father said. He turned to me. "You know what she was like. She was always so concerned about hurting people's feelings . . . people she didn't know. She'd talk to anyone."

He raised his eyebrows as he said that, and I had to nod. It was true.

Preacher reached for the little Bible. "But you need to look at the back—at what she signed."

My father kept the book in his hands. "I know what she signed, Reverend. She showed it to me the Friday that . . . the last day that we . . ."

But his voice remained flat as he spoke, which is probably why Preacher asked, "And what did you think about that, Kevin?"

My father shifted his eyes—just his eyes—to look my way. Then he tapped the book against his free hand.

"She wanted to talk about it when we were getting ready to go." He looked my way again. "You were up in your room, getting your things."

He took a breath, leaned back and set his shoulders. I hadn't seen this gesture that often with him, but I had seen it often enough to recognize it: *Getting ready to fire the broadside.* I almost said something. Almost. Then he glanced at Rachel and his head bowed ever so slightly.

"Listen," he told Preacher. "I know you people have your beliefs. And I respect that. But Laurie and I, we . . . well, we're not the sort of people who . . ."

He set his lips hard, glanced at Rachel again. "It just seemed very out of character for her. And I told her so."

Preacher gave me a lesson then. His face didn't harden. He didn't get all didactic. He seemed to warm. He leaned forward and said, "Because the two of you are educated people, you mean."

Two slow nods from my father.

"Mr. Nolan," Rachel half-whispered. "My daddy got his divinity degree from Princeton Theological Seminary. His people—the people in his church—scraped for years to raise the money to help send him there."

"That's enough, Rachel," Preacher told her.

"In another year, he's going to have a master's degree," Rachel continued.

"Rachel."

She kept her head high. "I just wanted him to know that

we're . . . we're not ignorant people."

I waited for my father to apologize, to say something concilia-tory, something gracious. He did not.

"Kevin." Preacher leaned forward, his hand on his knees. His face was earnest, his voice soft. "Do you know where your Laurie is? Right now?"

My father looked up.

"My wife is dead, Reverend." His voice sounded dead as he said it.

Preacher smiled, shaking his head.

"She is not." He touched the book once. "If you know what she signed, then you know what decision she made, Kevin. And my daughter's right. We are not ignorant people, and neither is your wife. She made a good choice. She's alive. She's with him right now—with God."

My father's lips began moving then, but no sound worked its way out. He covered it with his free hand, and squeezed his eyes shut, tears beading at the corners. He shook his head, tap-tap-tapping the book against his thigh. And then finally he said a single word. Said it twice.

"No," he told us. "No."

Preacher looked at me, and I lifted my shoulders, so he leaned toward my father and rested an open hand on the thin-denimed crown of his knee.

"We're certain of it, Kevin," he said, but then my father pushed his hand off of his knee. Not a harsh movement, but not tenuous at all.

"Certain?" He looked at the three of us in turn, lingered a moment on me and then turned back to Preacher, the tears trailing down his dark, tanned cheeks. "Of what? That there's this God that loved my wife like a parent loves his child, and so he does what? Lets her march out to the garage one Sunday and *kill herself*?"

"Kevin, I don't know—"

"No. You don't know. *I* don't know. But one thing I am certain of, Reverend Ransom, is this: The kind of parent that would stand by and let his child do that—that would let her leave her own child without a mother—is no fit parent. Not by any stretch of the imagination. I don't see a loving God in that picture, Pastor. I don't see a God there at all."

Preacher took a deep breath. His lips tightened and I could see tears there in his eyes, as well.

"Are you really willing to say that, Kevin? Are you really ready to make that your stand?" He nodded toward me. "Your family's stand?"

My father's face reddened. "If there is a God? And this is the way he does his business? Then yes. I'll make my stand right now. I don't want any part of that."

"Kevin . . ."

My father closed the little book and put it firmly in Preacher's hand. "It was good to meet you, Reverend. Thank you for taking the trouble to come here."

"Kevin . . ."

"Dad . . ." I added.

My father stood. "Patrick, go sweep up the stockroom, will you? Pastor, Rachel . . ." It was the first time he'd said her name. He nodded toward the door. "I'm afraid it's getting late. We need to close up. Good night."

Every climb has its crux, and that crux is, more often than not, composed of a single committed move. Hesitation before making such a move is natural, but when the attempt is made, it must be made with the full expectation of success. Anything less is only asking to fail. Visualization precedes realization.

Rock Climbing Holds and Basics

EIGHTEEN

It goes without saying that the drive home was less than comfortable. I'd left the Chevette in the driveway, back at home, at The Lodge. Rachel and I had ridden to the Ransoms' in her Travelall. So after the stockroom had been swept, and then re-swept, and then re-swept once again, there was nothing left for me to do but to ride home in the VW with my father. We were six miles from the shop, two miles from the house, when finally he looked my way.

"What were you thinking."

He said it just that way, a statement, rather than a question, his inflection letting me know that I was not expected to respond. So I didn't, and we went the rest of the way in silence, the weight of those four words growing heavier with each passing minute.

We'd had to ride home together. We had to live together, in the elbow-to-elbow confines of the Airstream no less, because the valve had come in, but the man who needed to install it was away, in Florida, at a bass-fishing tournament, and it had to be installed by him or the warranty would be no good. We still took our cold plunges in the North Fork together after work, but they became mechanical, silent affairs—a moment of camaraderie reduced to an act of hygiene.

At the shop, we had to work together, and he had to speak to me, to tell me what he wanted done. But that was all he did: "Patrick, that window could use a washing." And, "Break those boxes down and carry them out back, would you, Patrick?"

Patrick. The name was like a brick, heavy and hard on my shoulder.

Call me "Sport," I wanted to tell him. But I didn't. I washed the windows and broke down the boxes and tried to stay out of his way. The weather was warm, the air thick with the drone of an early hatch of cicadas. A couple of Europeans stopped by in the afternoon, and my father opened up a guidebook and spoke with them, a long conversation in state-university German, a language I did not understand.

By the time we closed the shop at five, no more than a few dozen words had passed between my father and me, and these were far from conversations, my contributions having been limited to two words, and two words only: "Yes, sir."

"I've got a meeting with the tourism board tonight," he told me as he walked to his VW.

It wasn't the sort of thing I would normally want to attend, but it twisted the knife, hearing him say it like that, not the slightest hint of invitation in his voice. In the spring, we had been partners; I apparently was an employee, now, and an unpaid employee at that.

I drove home by myself in my Chevette, the little orange car just another reminder of a time, now past, when I hadn't been a disappointment to my father. I thought about Toledo as I drove, the first hint of homesickness I'd felt since we'd moved to West Virginia. If I'd stayed at Scott High, I would have been starting summer football practice in less than a month: long afternoons sweating in full pads and a helmet, feet wet and blistering in the hot leather shoes, stomach queasy from too many salt tablets, and the thing with my father had me so miserable that I actually missed it.

If. If. *If.* I curled my lips in as I drove, felt the sun-chapped skin there against my teeth. If my mother hadn't died, I could go home to her right now. I could go home to her and do something nice: wash her car, or weed around her flower beds, or vacuum the rugs. And then she would make me lemonade the way she always made it, the chunks of lemon hanging heavy under the ice in the water-beaded glass, and she would put her hand on my head, that gesture she had that was half tousle, half caress, and when my father came home she would brag me up to him, "Guess what this young gentleman did without even being asked?" And then it would be right between us again.

But it couldn't happen that way. Not ever again. And as I drove it didn't seem as if anything could ever be right again at all.

By the time I turned into the gravel lane leading back to our house, my misery was turning to anger: anger at my mother for being dead, at my father for not being hopeful, at myself for my stupid, sheep-dumb optimism, at God for not being vigilant, not taking care of his children.

I tried to be angry with Rachel, but I could not. Rachel had only done what she had felt was right, a notion that did not surprise me. As far as I could see, Rachel had always done what she felt to be right, would always do the thing that would make her most pleasing to her God. I thought about what it would be like to have a wife like that, a beautiful, loving wife without a selfish bone in her body. It would be comforting, I thought. It would be secure. She would be the kind of wife one would want to come home to: the kind who would never step out into the garage and kill herself while her only child was away with his father, having fun.

That brought tears to my eyes, a reaction that made me hot with self-disdain. My father had never told me that men don't cry, so maybe it was something I had picked up from movies, from TV, from my friends. But I had clung to that sentiment ever since my mother's death. I had not broken down and wept at the wake, I had not shed a tear at the funeral, and I swore to a God I mistrusted that I would not, under any condition, weep now.

I stepped out of the car into air that was thick and still, not a whisper of breeze, not even in the tops of the Logan pines that marched away, up the hillside behind our house. There was no insect sound here in this hollow, no sound of any sort, and the solitude felt like a wall.

I wanted a friend, but the closest thing I had to a friend in the entire state of West Virginia was Rachel. I thought about that. Then I remembered it was Wednesday. Wednesday evening, and Weeping Oak Community met on Wednesday evenings.

Stripping off my cutoffs and T-shirt right there in the gravel turnaround at the end of our drive, I tossed my clothes back into the car. Then I trotted into the Airstream in my skivvies and went through the laundry baskets we were using instead of chests of drawers, and I started looking—looking for something I could wear to church.

"'. . . of ages, cleft for me, let me hide myself in thee.'"

Windows down on the Chevette, creeping along in first gear to avoid raising dust on the ancient two-track leading back into Judd Horton's campground, I could hear them singing before I even caught sight of the pavilion.

Late. I was late. Although, truth be told, I was not; I'd actually had no idea what time Wednesday evening church started, and had simply guessed that it would be six-thirty or seven.

I glanced at my watch, a self-winding Timex my parents had given me for Christmas two years earlier. It was twenty of seven.

Parking at the end of a long row of ancient F–100 pickups, rusting Chevy wagons, and listing Oldsmobiles, I got out, closed the door as quietly as I could, and was relieved when the pump organ started up again and three dozen voices started in on "Bringing in the Sheaves" in two different keys. With the congregation's noses buried in their hymnals, I hoped that I might be able to slip into a seat unnoticed.

Sure enough, just about everyone was holding open their own copies of variably faded, red-leather books as I approached the pavilion from the side. And rather than Sunday-best, they were in everyday clothes, the men mostly attired, as was I, in jeans and a short-sleeved shirt, a few of them in dungarees. My running shoes— and my hair—were the only things that would make me stand out. And the women were in the usual long skirts, some topped by blouses and some by work shirts. A few wore knitted shawls over their shoulders, despite the stifling heat.

I was perhaps thirty feet away when the congregation turned as one and looked my way, because the hymn, of course, was an old one, one that most of the people there had probably memorized in childhood, making the songbooks nothing but pro forma. Even Preacher turned and looked at me, although he smiled broadly when he did, which did wonders for my embarrassment.

Rachel was there at her usual seat, up front, and she smiled, as well, then bent low to say something to her brother, who ducked under the bench and scurried away, reappearing moments later in a gaggle of other little boys three rows back, all of them standing on the bench with hymnals in their hands, and all of them staring, like their parents, at me as I approached.

Rachel waved and pointed to the space vacated by her brother. Under the scrutiny of seventy-two somber eyes, I joined her, drawn as certainly as a hooked bass to the angler's hand.

Rachel was dressed that Wednesday evening in a manner more West Coast than West Virginian—still in a skirt, as always, but a gypsy skirt this time, topped by a peasant blouse of unbleached gauze that looked fresh and new, despite the lingering heat. Her feet were shod in sandals, open sandals that showed off the turn of her ankles, and her pink-polished toes, two details that seemed both secret and exciting. She handed me a hymnal as I joined her, and when she did, her bare forearm brushed mine, a downy kiss that forced me to stifle a shiver. I forgot my father's coolness and his distance, forgot the tension at the shop and the calculated wall of silence that most certainly awaited me at home. The congregation sat, Rachel sat, and I sat with her, remembering the smooth tanness of her legs and waiting for her to brush against me again. Before us, not ten feet away, her father stood up dressed in sage green slacks and a short-sleeved shirt, plain shoes, no tie, his worn Bible lying open upon his hand.

Now, given what I am about to tell you, the urgencies of story suggest that I should relate here the details of Preacher's message; the point-by-point, carefully constructed progression of his logic; the support plucked from ancient, foundational Scripture; the illustrations, vivid and apropos. The right thing would be to repeat for you here his message, the Spirit-inspired apologetic, the seamlessly mortised construction of his argument.

I cannot. Gypsy skirt . . . Peasant blouse . . . Naked ankles . . . Pink-painted toes . . . The easy blond fall of Rachel's hair . . . The soft, forbidden warmness of her forearm . . . That is all that I can remember. Not that I have forgotten. For . . . I don't know—quite a while—those are the only things I noticed at all.

Time compressed, and half an hour later, I was aware of Rachel bowing her head, slender hands folded on the Bible in her lap, lips moving minutely, whispering. Or not whispering, because whispering implies at least the hint of a murmur, a susurrus, and she was making no sound whatsoever.

The invitation.

That, I'd learned, was what they called it. "The invitation"—a moment of reflection and decision that formed a participatory interlude, a bridge between the message and the end of the service.

Rachel's head turned, a shimmering curtain of blond hair moving aside as her blue eyes met mine. They stayed there for the briefest of instants, then she glanced in the direction of her father, closing them again. Taking the hint, I closed my eyes as well and focused my sightless attention on Preacher, on the warm, smooth baritone of his voice.

"'For God so loved the world,'" Preacher was saying. "'For God so loved the world . . .' We all know that Bible verse, we know it so well and learned it so long ago that we tend to move ahead, to step right on to 'that he gave his only begotten son.' We want to get to the giving, want it so much that we skip right past what we've already been given . . . the love of the God who created it."

Hellfire. Damnation. This was not those things. Squinting my eyes shut, I leaned forward, my right fist clasped within my left hand, my forearms on my knees. Preacher was only half right—I had never before heard of the verse—but his was a gentle voice in an ungentle time, and he had my full attention.

"Friends," Preacher said, "God did love the world and he does love the world: this world. He made it a garden and filled it with perfect things. That was where we were meant to dwell forever, where we are meant to dwell forever, because God's book talks about a new heaven and a new earth. And the only thing that prevents it from being that right now is sin, and sin is the only thing that can possibly separate us from the loving, eternal God who created us."

"Aye-men," a man muttered behind me.

"That sin has a price," Preacher said, his voice soothing, almost hypnotically low. "But we—you and I—don't have the means with which to pay it. Scripture says that the best we have to offer is as filthy rags. Only one being has ever had the sort of payment that our heavenly Father understands, and that's Jesus."

"A-men," went the voice behind me again. And then, "That's right."

Preacher did not respond. Nor did he seem the slightest bit disconcerted by the fact that one of his congregants was talking back during the message. He just kept going, moving along into his next point.

"But God has so much respect for us that he would not dream of forcing us into his company. His gift—the gift of the life's blood of his own son—is something we have to accept."

"Preach it," went the voice behind me. I silently wished he'd shut up.

He did. He fell silent. Preacher fell silent, as well. He paused for so long that I was almost ready to raise my head when he continued, "Now, with every head bowed and every eye closed, how many here can tell me that they can remember a time and a place when they accepted that gift? Just slip your hand up and down if you can say that."

I kept my hands together. In the stillness that followed, I heard the distant burble of a motorcycle coming down the long grade of Route 33.

"Thank you for those hands," Preacher said. "Hands all over this place. But there are some here who could not raise a hand when I asked that, and I admire that honesty. So if you were one of those who could not raise a hand just now, let me ask you a different question. How many here would like to accept that gift this evening?

How many would like to get eternity taken care of today?"

A hand closed upon my wrist—small, warm, clutching it almost fiercely. I sneaked a peek at Rachel, and she was gripping my wrist so tightly that a tendon was standing up, ridgelike, in that perfect, slender forearm of hers. Her head was still bowed, and her lips still moved noiselessly.

The evening was warm, my skin damp because the long jeans and the sport shirt were more than I was accustomed to wearing. And that was the first thing I thought of: that the wrist Rachel was gripping was damp. But if she noticed it, she gave no sign. She kept her hand clamped there.

"If you would say that is you," Preacher said. "If you would like to accept Jesus Christ as your Savior, then God's book says that now is the day of salvation. If that's you, raise your hand right now."

Rachel squeezed my wrist more tightly, squeezed it so hard that, had it not been her hand, her touch, it most certainly would have hurt. She squeezed, then relaxed her grip completely and squeezed again.

I risked another look. Rachel was nodding now as she whispered, and I could hear what she was saying this time, the same thing over and over again, "Please, Lord Jesus; please, Lord Jesus; please . . ."

She squeezed hard one last time.

I bit my lip.

I raised my hand.

A "bucket" is just what it sounds like: a handhold so ample that it will accommodate the thumb and all four fingers, and so deep that it can be well and truly gripped. Climbers love buckets; provided that the rock from which it is formed is solid and sturdy, it is all but impossible to fall from one.

Rock Climbing Holds and Basics

NINETEEN

The next thing I knew, Rachel had released my wrist. I opened my eyes and there was Preacher standing before me, both hands out, palms up, waving his fingers: *stand up*.

I glanced from Preacher to Rachel, and then back to Preacher again.

Stand up?

I'd hoped what I'd just done was private, a closeted decision to be witnessed by God, with Preacher, and—of course—Rachel as onlookers. But *stand up?* I was sitting in the front row. If I stood, I'd be standing in front of everyone.

I looked at Rachel again. She was looking back at me, face red, smiling, her blue eyes moist with tears. She nodded, rolled her lips in just a bit, smiled anew and nodded again.

I stood up, and Preacher took me by the elbow and led me away from the still-silent congregation, taking me to the front of the pavilion, where he bent close to me.

"I'm proud of you, Patrick," he told me. "It takes a man to make the decision you just made. But I want to make sure that you know what you're doing. Do you?"

Did I? We were facing each other, with the congregation at our sides—his right, my left. I glanced at the church members for a moment. They were still seated with their heads bowed, all except Rachel. Rachel had slipped out of her seat and was kneeling in her gauze skirt on the worn wooden planking of the pavilion, her hands clasped in front of her, eyes closed, tears rolling down those perfect cheeks. She looked like a supplicant angel; all she lacked was a pair of wings. She wanted me to do this. Nothing could have been more obvious. And in that moment, I would have done anything she wanted: rob banks, leave the country, take a desk job, for crying out loud. Anything at all.

I closed my eyes, and when I opened them once again, I was looking back into Preacher's kind eyes. I nodded. One nod.

"Well, then," he said softly. "Amen."

He turned and faced his congregation, his arm around my shoulder.

"Look up here for a moment, please." His voice was as mellow as old hickory. The congregation's heads came up, three dozen pale suns rising. The women blinked behind frameless glasses. The men stared back impassively, all eyebrows and Adam's apples.

"I believe some of you know Patrick Nolan," Preacher said, squeezing my shoulder. "And you may know that Patrick and his daddy moved here from Ohio. And you may know that Patrick's mama passed on early this spring."

The women's faces seemed to soften at that, but the men remained frozen, somber—hollow statues.

"But what you don't know is that, yesterday, Patrick learned some good news," Preacher said. "He found out that his mama did not pass away. She made a decision before that happened. She went home to be with the Lord."

"Amen!" The word erupted in a dozen male voices, and now the men seemed unfrozen, looking at me with what could have been the distant cousins of smiles.

"But the good news doesn't stop there," Preacher said. "Patrick just told me that he's made that same decision."

More shouts, and the amen-er who'd been sitting behind me, a little farmer a foot too short for his baritone voice, scuttled forward, pumped my hand once, and then scurried back to his seat. As I watched him go, I saw Rachel rising to her feet, her tear-streaked face lifted as she mouthed silent words to the rafters.

"In the New Testament, a decision such as this was almost always accompanied by a public sign, and Patrick has made that sign today by stepping forward and proclaiming his faith before you all.

But there is a traditional sign, as well, one made time and time again by the saints of the Gospel and one made by Jesus himself." Preacher looked at me and smiled. "Patrick, would you like to be baptized?"

Baptized? I'd only been to one baptism in my life, the infant daughter of one of my father's co-workers. I'd had my learner's permit then, and I'd driven my mother to Southwyck Center mall so she could pick out a christening gift: a tiny cut-crystal teddy bear.

The baptism itself I remembered as a knot of people in an alcove of a church. They'd poured a small silver saucer of water over the back of the baby's head, and thumbed a drop of oil to her forehead. I wasn't sure what they did for older people, but I remembered kids showing up at Scott High with crosses smudged onto their foreheads in ash. I figured it had to be something like that. After all, how could you possibly pick up a grown person to pour water on his forehead?

I looked at Rachel, and she was smiling and nodding. I turned to her father.

"Sure," I said.

That, I figured, would be the cue for someone to step up with a little chalice of water. That or a tiny vial of oil, like the little glass perfume samplers that my mother used to pick up at Lamson's.

But it didn't work that way.

Preacher took me gently by the elbow and began guiding me out of the pavilion and onto the sunburnt grass. I turned to ask him where we were going, and I saw that the entire congregation—the American-Gothic-thin men, their bun-haired women, and even the dungareed children—was following us, Rachel at their head.

We were headed for the loose semicircle of parked cars and pickup trucks. *Maybe we're going to drive somewhere else—maybe we're all going over to Preacher's house?* That hinted of privacy. It seemed like a great idea.

But no: that wasn't it. We walked right through the cars, the congregation threading through them like a stream coursing around the boulders of a rapid. We turned just a little and aimed for a break in the trees, a break that framed the tan sand gully of a footpath.

And that was when I understood that we were headed for the creek.

I knew about the creek—Seneca Creek—because my father and I had camped at Judd's campground many times before we moved to West Virginia, and while we'd always gotten our cooking water from an iron-handled water pump across the highway at the state park, we—like virtually all of the campground tenants—had always found the creek more convenient for getting water for dishes, or for washing up, or even for taking a quick, brisk, predawn plunge in lieu of a morning shower.

Maybe nobody remembered to bring a bottle of water?

We stepped up, over and down the gully and came to the pebble-strewn bank of the creek.

"Go ahead and take your shoes off, Patrick," Preacher whispered. "No use ruining a good pair of shoes." And with that, he bent down and began to unlace his oxfords.

Take my shoes off? I looked down. The creek bank was mostly pebbles: smooth, water-polished pebbles. But there was a little sand and dirt mixed in, and it would get muddy if it got water dripped on it, so I figured that was what Preacher was up to. Maybe he wanted to step off, ankle-deep into the water, and splash a little on my head there, where it wouldn't make things slippery for the older folks in his congregation.

Fair enough. I bent down and unlaced my Adidas Countrys, slipping them off and then doing as Preacher was doing: rolling my socks and slipping them into my shoes. Buying socks for me had been one of the things that my mother had done, so that hadn't happened in a while, and those were the last pair of white athletic socks I owned that were completely without holes. I was glad of that as the congregation spilled and spread out three-deep along the bank, watching us.

Still bent over, I began to cuff up my blue jeans, but stopped when I saw that Preacher was doing no such thing.

All right. Maybe we aren't going in that far. The water right next to the bank was only a few inches deep and sometimes less than that, riffled in places by the pebbles beneath. *Or maybe we aren't supposed to show that much skin.* I still remembered what Rachel had told me about swimming in culottes, and while a bare calf and ankle didn't seem like much to me, I knew that Weeping Oak Community Church marched to a completely different drum. And maybe they had a point; I couldn't deny that Rachel's legs—her *ankles*, for pete's sake—had wreaked some pretty substantial damage on my ability to articulate. While I couldn't fathom my ankles having a similar effect on anybody—to my eyes, they looked like oversize chicken necks wrapped in tan leather—I assumed they applied the same standard to everyone. What my father called a "level playing field."

I straightened up and Preacher put his arm around me once again, his hand on my shoulder.

"In the eighth chapter of Acts," he said, "the disciple Philip witnesses to the treasurer of Candace, the queen of Ethiopia, and after Philip has led him to the Lord, the treasurer says, 'Here is water. What is to hinder me from being baptized?' To which Philip replies, 'If thou believest with all thy heart, thou mayest.' And the Ethiopian replies, as Patrick, here, has replied, 'I believe that Jesus Christ is the Son of God.'"

Had I said that? I couldn't remember saying *anything* like that. But it wouldn't have been polite to contradict Preacher, so I just glanced at the crowd standing on the creek bank, and looked for Rachel.

She wasn't there.

That hardly seemed possible. She'd been weeping with joy over me just a few minutes earlier, hadn't she? How could she not be there? Why would I do this if she *wasn't* there?

"Come on, Patrick." Preacher squeezed my shoulder and turned us around, our backs to the congregation. We stepped into the water, cold on my bare feet, and then we took another step, and another. I felt the water swirl in and under the bottoms of my jeans, but if Preacher didn't mind getting his slacks wet, I certainly wasn't about to complain about a pair of Levi's; sure, I would have to wash them when I got home, but I wanted to wash them, anyhow—they were still too stiff, too new.

Preacher and I stepped out farther. The water rose up to my knees. We were headed toward a part of the creek my father called "the trout hole," a place where the water was better than waist deep.

What the . . .

The water crept up my thigh as I walked, and then it rose higher still and I gasped, and Preacher chuckled and said, "Yes, sir. One thing's for sure: you'll never forget a cold-water baptism."

I was walking as carefully as I could. The river stones were slick and viscous beneath the bare soles of my feet. It was like walking on a bed of ice cubes.

Finally, when the water was up to my ribs, we stopped walking and Preacher turned to face his church members on the bank. He had a white handkerchief in his right hand and it was still dry—he had apparently been carrying it in his hand, up and out of the water, ever since we'd left the bank.

"There's a story in Luke that most of you all know by heart," he said. "It's the story of the prodigal son—the son who leaves home with half the family fortune, loses it all, and then comes home begging for his father to take him in as a hired hand. But his daddy doesn't do that. He welcomes that boy home with glory and honor. He throws a banquet, and when people ask why, he says, 'My son, who was dead, is alive.'"

From up on the bank, the little farmer answered with a baritone "Amen." I looked that direction. Still no sign of Rachel.

"Patrick here," Preacher said, "was dead. Just as all are dead who have not claimed Christ Jesus as Savior. But he's not dead any longer."

Another "Amen" and a shout or two from shore.

"And it is as a sign of that change that we do what we do now . . ."

Then Preacher's voice dropped to a whisper as he told me, "You know, Patrick, the Bible assures us that when finally we close our eyes at the end of this life, the next face we see when we open them again will be that of the Lord. But there'll be another one there for you, son—your mama. She lives forever with Jesus. The same way you will live forever with him as he reigns."

I looked at him, the question forming on my lips. But before I could ask it, he had clamped the handkerchief over my nose and was pushing me back, my body pivoting at his hand, at the small of my back.

"Buried in the likeness of His death," Preacher said, full-voiced, and the trees seemed to fall on either side of me as he leaned me back. It was water, then trees, then treetops, and then sky, nothing but blue sky, a West Virginia window to the heavens. Then the water received me, wrapped up and around me and closed over my face like liquid glass, as those two words of Preacher's echoed over and over again in my head . . .

"She lives . . ."

She lives. Not an angel. Not a ghost. My mother, fully the person that she was when I last saw her, but eternal now. Not gone, but trans-formed. Completed.

Perfected.

I suppose that I should have been uncomfortable in that airless moment under the water, Preacher's handkerchiefed palm over my mouth and nose, but I was not. My eyes were still open, looking up through a shimmering oval of sky-blue ever-light, gazing up into that eternity as I thought about the possibility that I had been given what I'd never thought feasible: an alternate ending. A finality that wasn't catastrophic and dreadful. A reprieve. A coda.

A second chance.

Then Preacher shifted his hand on my back and lifted me, and as I came up out of the water, gasping, I was glad my face was wet, because the water hid my tears.

"Raised in the likeness of His life," Preacher shouted, and suddenly it was as if something heavy had been lifted away from me. Lifted away and tossed an impossible distance, and the lightness it left behind it made me laugh out loud. And when I looked at the applauding creek bank, there was Rachel, standing in the midst of her church members, a thick, white, terry-cloth towel in either hand.

The leader places protection as he climbs, and the last man on the rope is responsible

for removing it: a practice known as "cleaning the climb." Ideally,

the process leaves no evidence of the rope team's passing.

Rock Climbing Holds and Basics

I drove home sitting on one of those towels, grateful that Preacher had insisted on my taking it because, even with a full can of Scotch-gard sprayed into it, the Chevette's cloth upholstery was no match for a saturated pair of Levi's. Two miles from the house, I pulled to the side, checked to make sure there were no approaching head-lamps, slid low in the seat, took off my wet clothes, underwear and all, and pulled on the shorts and T-shirt that I'd had on when I'd left the shop.

I felt my hair, which was now definitely on the long side: it was still a little damp, but only barely.

"Okay," I remember saying aloud. Things were as in order as I was going to make them. I was reasonably sure that I had restored my appearance to the point that my father wouldn't ask any ques-tions about what had gone on earlier in the evening.

That proved to be an unnecessary precaution. When I pulled into our drive, both the house and the Airstream were dark, my father's meeting obviously either running long or gone on to include a late dinner.

The uninstalled gas valve not only prevented us from using the house's furnace, it kept us from using the water heater, as well. But I figured that if I could wash my face and brush my teeth with Dr. Bronner's when we went camping, then it would probably work in the washing machine, even if all we had was cold water. And the dryer was electric, so it would work whether we had a working LP gas tank or not.

That seemed like a plan. I bundled up my soggy clothes and, stopping first in the Airstream to pick up more dirty laundry and the 16-ounce bottle of soap, I went into The Lodge where the laundry area sat in an alcove off the kitchen.

It still felt like trespass, being in that house. The quiet seemed unnatural, and I was glad for the rush and splash of water when I turned and pulled the knob on the washer. I shot in a squirt of soap, then a second squirt for good measure. Then I loaded in the clothes. They were all dark clothes, all except the underwear, which I didn't worry about, because, after all, who sees underwear? It was my mother who had first told me about the wash-darks-with-darks principle, and as I thought about that, the room seemed to dim a bit, the renovated walls waning dingy and tired despite their fresh coat of high-gloss, off-white paint.

That got me thinking. My mother's clothes were, after all, gone from the house now—taken to the Ransoms', sorted, and probably on their way to Wheeling, or Charlestown, or the grateful young backs of far-flung missionary wives. I'd even disposed of the jumper cables and road flares that my father had given my mother; they were tucked in the back of Rachel's Travelall. And I couldn't imagine my father squirreling up through the tiny trapdoor into the attic, especially now, in the heat of midsummer. So that was all settled. Settled at a cost, but settled.

What else? There was my mother's vanity. But no. My great-grandmother, whom I'd never met, had given that vanity to my father the Christmas he'd turned sixteen. The story was one of our family legends.

"For your future bride," she'd told him. *"Whomever she may turn out to be."* And my father had accepted it because he knew that the old lady was given to eccentricities. He'd accepted it, then put it away in the basement—his parents' basement, because he was only my age at the time.

And then, when he and my mother had gotten engaged, he'd remembered the strange gift, gotten it out, polished it, and presented it to her on their wedding day. My mother had fallen in love with it: it and the story behind it, both.

Would the vanity remind my father of my mother? Without a

doubt, it would—every time he saw it. But to give it away would be unconscionable, especially with relations between the two of us as strained as they were. Even hiding it was out of the question. It would have to be left where it was.

But the mail . . . I'd left the last of my mother's mail sitting there, on the vanity, walked away and left it after Rachel found the little brown Bible.

And that I could do something about.

The washer stopped agitating, clicked, and gurgled as it discharged water, readying itself for the rinse cycle. I stepped into the dark kitchen and put my face close to the window, hands around my eyes, scrutinizing the drive and the trees to either side.

The leaves were dark, shadowed clumps, unsilvered by approaching headlights. Slipping off my shoes, I crossed through the silent dining room and padded up the stairs.

I had never before been upstairs in the big house after dark. The bedroom doors were all shut, an attempt to keep the entire second story from growing over warm during hot summer days, and it was dark—darkness so complete that it made you think you could see holes in it, deeper voids within the blackness.

My right hand brushed the light switch, one of those old-fashioned two-button switches that we'd not yet replaced there, on the second floor of the house. But I did not press it. Even a sliver of light in the upper story would bring my father upstairs if he saw it as he was driving in. And I didn't want the conversation that would certainly ensue if he found me going through any of my mother's belongings again, even her old, unopened mail.

Trailing my fingers along the wall, I passed my parents' room—my father's room—then the room we were planning to use as a guest room, right across the hall from my room: the room with my dresser, my nightstand, and a bed I hadn't slept in for nearly three months. After I'd passed the second door, I slowed, and three steps later my outstretched left hand touched it: the door to the big room. The door at the end of the hall.

I turned the knob, opened it. My mother's vanity sat in a dim, slanted block of gray-blue moonlight, like a prop on an otherwise empty stage, waiting for its actress to make her entry. On the vanity top, to the right of the mirror, exactly in the place where my mother had always rested her silver-handled hairbrush, sat the stack of envelopes, as tidy as any stack of assorted-size envelopes could be. They seemed to glow in the thin, blue light.

I crossed the room, my footfalls absolutely silent on the densely napped Oriental rug. There was a momentary start when I caught my own vague, shadowed reflection in the mirror: an edgy spike of alarm, dissolving with recognition into sheepish humility. Picking up the envelopes, re-squaring them with a soft tap against the vanity top, I transferred them with my left hand and returned to the door, pausing there to take one last look at the empty vanity in its faint, blue patch of light.

The washer was chugging steadily, agitating its way through the rinse cycle, as I walked through the kitchen. The sound got louder as I returned to the laundry room. I put the envelopes on top of the dryer, sorting them out on the white metal surface.

The postcard from my mother's cousin read: *Sure is a long way to go, just to see a big hole in the ground. Just kidding—it's beautiful. See you soon. —Sue*

I turned it over. It showed five people on mules, heading down a trail into the Grand Canyon. All the riders wore bright colors and ball caps, except for the lead rider, who wore khakis and a cowboy hat: the wrangler, I supposed.

See you soon. She had; the cousin had come to the funeral. Biting my lip, I set the postcard off to the side, message side down.

The Easter cards were from people I'd heard mentioned on rare occasions, but never had actually met. Maybe some of them had come to the funeral. That or the viewing. Both days had been well attended, mostly by people I was meeting for the first time: colleagues of my father, or my mother's teachers and classmates. They'd moved in separate circles—I'd never thought about that before, but they had. I wondered if that had somehow factored into what had happened.

The cards were all several months old. So either their senders knew about my mother, or if they didn't, I didn't want to tell them. And certainly my father didn't need to. I set the greeting cards on top of the postcard.

The tuition statement and the invitation to the honors-program banquet were easy; my mother's passing had been the tragedy of the semester for the university, an honor usually reserved for post-sporting-event car wrecks. Everyone had heard about it: no loose ends to tie up there.

I added the university envelopes to the pile, wondering when I'd become such a cynic.

That left one letter. Number-ten envelope, business size. Type-written address, looking very official. From the Medical College of Ohio, on Arlington Drive, in Toledo.

Back home. What used to be home.

I picked the envelope up, hefted it. There was more than one sheet of paper within. I tapped it against the dryer top.

The washer stopped agitating, clicked, fell silent as a stone for perhaps a full minute, and then began to empty: a mechanical whir and the hollow gurgle of rushing water.

I didn't want to open the envelope because I was afraid it contained dreadful news. Yet I did want to open the envelope because I *hoped* it contained dreadful news. *Dear Mrs. Nolan: We regret to inform you that you are in the early stages of an illness of the most grave and painful sort and, all things considered, you may wish to wait until your family is out of the house and then dress yourself in your very best clothes and go out to the garage and quietly end it all. . . .*

My face burned at the thought. But the shame could not hide the truth: that if my mother had killed herself because she had a terminal illness, it would somehow be better than if she had done it because she could not face another day as my father's wife. As my mother.

And perhaps if my father knew that, in dying, my mother had

avoided a death equally certain, but infinitely more painful, he would no longer feel inclined to escape from it through dangerous acts that, sooner rather than later, would mean his death, as well.

I hefted the envelope again.

The washer clicked, rumbled, and started its spin cycle.

I opened the envelope.

There was no letter inside, only forms: one pink, one green, two white. The colored pages were filled out, the lines completed with the smudged gray-blue lettering of carbon copies. The white ones were still blank.

I looked at the blank ones first; it seemed like less of an intrusion. One was an outpatient admission form to Medical College Hospital. It asked what I assumed were the standard questions: name, address, Social Security number, family doctor, and insurance information—lots of space for insurance information.

The other was a combination consent form for diagnostic procedures and an authorization for the release of medical records.

Outpatient admission? Diagnostic procedures? I'd been admitted as an outpatient at MCO a year earlier, when I overextended my knee at football practice. That had been more or less like a visit to a slightly better-equipped doctor's office. We'd only gone there because Dr. Conant, our family doctor, didn't have his own X-ray machine.

So those forms didn't seem like anything serious. *Certainly not something worth . . .* I shook the thought away and, still feeling as if I were prying, looked at the other two forms.

One was an appointment slip for Medical College Hospital's Diagnostic Imaging Unit—the same place I'd been with my knee. Only my mother wasn't scheduled for an X-ray. She was scheduled for a CAT scan.

I'd heard of CAT scans. While I wasn't quite sure what they were, I knew that a friend of mine had gone in for one after the driver's-ed car got rear-ended at a stoplight. He'd said it had consisted of a lot of holding still for long periods of time and not much else—*"pretty boring, really"* was how he'd described it. That still sounded pretty run-of-the-mill.

The other form was another appointment slip for later on in the same day. This one was for an EKG, and that got my attention. I knew EKG stood for *electrocardiogram* and *cardio* meant it had something to do with the heart. *Had my mother had some sort of heart disease?* But if it was serious, wouldn't she have been admitted into intensive care, rather than coming in as an outpatient?

There was an additional instruction in smudged carbon-copy type at the bottom of the EKG order:

"Attending physician to perform carotid sinus massage during course of EKG. Patient has history of transient syncope with focal neurological signs. EKG required to confirm tentative diagnosis of Weiss-Baker syndrome (carotid sinus hypersensitivity)."

Under that was an illegible scrawl above a typed name, J. Singh, MD. And there was a date: 3/24/76.

The Wednesday before my mother's death.

I reread the entire paragraph three times. The only medical term there that even remotely made sense to me was *sinus*. It was there in the first line: "sinus massage." So what did that mean—that the doctor was going to rub her nose? And then there was the phrase, "sinus hypersensitivity."

That pretty much cinched it for me; it sounded as if my mother had been seeing a doctor about her allergies.

A dead end. I added the forms and the medical-college envelope to the small stack of paper on top of the washer. The washer clicked and the spin cycle came to an end, the white machine falling eerily silent.

I loaded everything into the electric dryer, closed the door, set the dryer on Gentle, because my mother had always dried everything on Gentle, and pushed the Start button. The dryer started its own regular beat, subtle in contrast to the noise of the washing machine. I gathered up the paper and envelopes and put out the light.

We had a burning barrel at the house, same as at the shop: a 55-gallon drum with the top removed, three V-shaped holes punched into the steel just above the base, to provide a draft. Dropping the old mail into the barrel, I almost turned to go back into the house to get the farmer's matches, but decided against it. The small pile of paper hardly warranted a fire, and besides, if my father drove in and saw smoke, he'd wonder why I was burning trash so late at night. I'd done my job; I'd removed the mail from the house, gotten rid of it where my father wouldn't find it. There wasn't an envelope left in the house or the trailer with my mother's name on it—no written reminders to trigger my father's remorse.

I went into the Airstream, unrolled the old square-bottomed Boy Scout sleeping bag that I'd been using in the trailer to avoid having to make a bed, and put it on the built-in sofa in the living area, my pillow in its cotton case the only conventional piece of bedding that I used in our temporary living quarters. Taking off my climbing shorts in the dark, I got into the bag and pulled the zipper most of the way up, wrapping the loose top under my shoulder because it felt more snug that way, more comforting.

I'd just settled like this when white headlamp beams traced squares across the curtains just above me. Then the *putt putt putt* of the VW's little four cylinder engine became audible, grew in volume as my father came up the drive. The lights and the engine sound both ceased at the same time, and I heard the medium metallic *thunk* of the door closing. Then the screen door opened on the Airstream, and I squeezed my eyes shut, buried my forehead in the flannel of the old sleeping bag.

"Patrick?" My father's voice sounded neutral, a little tired. "You still awake?"

Sport. Call me "Sport" and I'll be awake. Talk to me like before, and I'll stay up and I'll listen to you all night.

I heard his footsteps moving toward the bedroom at the far end of the trailer, and I risked a peek. He hadn't turned on a light, so there wasn't much to see, but I could smell cigarette smoke, and my father didn't smoke and never had, so that was a pretty good sign that the meeting had moved to a restaurant.

I heard his shoes fall to the floor, one and then the other, then there was a silence of perhaps half a minute, and after that the small squeak of the thin box spring under the double bed in the back of the trailer.

I thought of all that had happened since I'd last seen him, of all the news I had to share but couldn't share: not with him, and not right now, and maybe never. I thought of the invitation, of me raising my hand, going forward, of the cold water in the creek, of Preacher's words.

"My son, who was dead, is alive."

Was dead.

Is alive.

"Just as all are dead who have not claimed Christ Jesus as their Savior."

I thought of my father lying still, silent, hands folded on his chest, on the small, square bed at the back of the Airstream.

"Your mama. She lives." I pictured my mother vibrant, still young, never growing old. I thought of her as Preacher thought of her, as Rachel did, as she was to every member of their church—of my church.

Alive.

But not to my father.

So my mother was dead in my father's eyes, and if what Preacher had told me was true, my father was dead in my mother's eyes. I examined that thought, turning it like the Mobius strip that it was. And then, squeezing my eyes shut again, I took a deep breath, and drifted by fits and starts into troubled sleep—the shallow, restless slumber of an orphan.

TWENTY-ONE

On Thursday, the first day of July, I got to the shop late. My father was already there; he had approached the coming Bicentennial weekend with the meticulous planning of a general anticipating a siege, and he'd come in early to check and inventory a shipment of T-shirts because, romance aside, T-shirts were where better than half of our margin came from on the shop. You could sell a climber shoes once a year, and a rope every two years. But T-shirts? As long as you got fresh designs, you could sell him a T-shirt every time he walked into the shop.

"There you are!" He boomed the greeting as I walked into the shop, and just like that, I was alert. That was how our lives had become—anytime my father sounded happy, or content, I became suspicious. But then I saw that he was not alone. There were two other people in the shop: a man whose white hair and beard were at odds with his power-lifter physique, and a redheaded woman who looked to be in her thirties, which seemed ancient to me back in the day, although, even to my sixteen-year-old eyes, she was obviously very pretty.

"Patrick, I'd like you to meet Klaus van Leijenhorst."

"Really?" I perked up. "Wow, I've read all about you. You're, like, a legend."

It was no exaggeration. *Summit, Off Belay, Climbing, Mountain* . . . Klaus van Leijenhorst's name appeared in those magazines with even greater frequency than my father's. But while my father had been strictly a North American rock climber, Klaus got around. Patagonia, Chamonix, Thailand—he'd put up hard routes on literally every single continent, including Antarctica. And he was a friend of Yvonne Chouinard's; you saw his picture in the Chouinard Equipment catalogue all the time.

"In my own mind!" Klaus laughed. I'd expected him to sound Bavarian, maybe Austrian. But his accent was pure South Boston—that *pahk the cah* way of speaking they had that echoed of John F. Kennedy. "And you should talk. Harry Priestly tells me he saw you lead Thin Man on what? A paper clip and a wad of chewing gum for protection?"

"It was two stoppers." I liked him. "And I would have put in more, but I was too scared to slow down."

The big man's laugh sounded sufficient to shake the building down. "Spoken like a true rock-jock! Patrick, this is my fiancée, Nancy."

I shook her hand and she arched her eyebrows at my father. "You didn't tell me he was handsome! Wow, Klaus, you'd better keep me under lock and key. And look! He blushes!" She got up on tiptoe and kissed me on my cheek: my flushed and burning cheek.

Klaus laughed again. "Don't mind her, Patrick. Hit 'er with a bucket of ice water and she calms right down."

"So," I asked, desperate for a change of subject, "you guys heading up this morning?"

Klaus nodded. "South End. I'd like to be up and down by three. Radio says they're expecting thunderstorms later on. Then clear for the weekend, though." He shrugged at my father. "You ready for the Mongolian hoards?"

"Ready as I'll ever be. Hey, show Patrick that new gear sling they're bringing out."

Klaus opened the rucksack at his feet and pulled out a bright blue nylon bandolier that was positively dripping with shiny aluminum chocks and carabiners. Lots of climbers knotted a web sling and carried it over their head and one shoulder so they could have ready access to their gear, but this was the same idea taken to the next level: a curved lamb's-wool shoulder pad, and gear loops stitched onto the webbing so the gear stayed distributed, rather than clumping all together.

"I've never been much of a sling guy." Klaus put the gear sling on and modeled it for us. "Too much climbing with the Brits. Got used to carrying all my junk on a swami belt, y'know? But this is pretty well-thought-out, and it fits really snug: doesn't move around on you." He took it off. "Here. Try it."

I put it on, bandolier-style. Klaus was right; the fit was somewhat snug, even on me, and I was built much more slightly than he was. But I could see how that would have its advantages on a thin climb, where you wouldn't want things swinging out behind you and messing up your center of gravity.

"Nice," I told him, handing it back.

"Well . . ." Klaus squinted at the window, checking the sky. "We'd better run. I thought we'd do something fairly quick, maybe get some shots of this sling for the catalogue." He cocked his head at my father. "What time you closing up tonight?"

"Five," my father said. "I'm guessing most people will leave after work and get in late, so the invasion won't begin until tomorrow."

"That Italian place still there up in Elkins?"

"Last I checked."

"Great." Klaus shrugged the heavy rucksack onto his broad shoulders. "What say we pick you guys up here at five and run on up there and get a bite? My treat."

"You're on."

We all shook hands and Nancy looked at me and then smiled at my father again.

"Lock and key." She laughed. "I'm telling you guys: lock and key!"

Almost as soon as the two of them had left the shop, my father had visibly cooled, become less talkative. *An act,* I thought. *He was putting on a front.*

That bothered me. I wondered how many times in recent weeks he had put on the same front for me.

The two of us worked quietly during the day. At noon, I went over to Judd's and bought two Cokes, a loaf of bread, and a packet of pimento loaf, and we made sandwiches and ate while we stocked shelves and broke down boxes. By one o'clock the sky was cloudy.

By two, it was darkening visibly. And forty-five minutes later, we heard the first rumble of distant thunder.

"Hope those guys get down before that weather rolls in," my father muttered. It was the first thing he'd said since lunch.

"No joke." Lightning was the bane of rock climbers. When an electrical storm closed in, what you were climbing on was generally the tallest thing around. And lightning, like rock climbers, tended to follow cracks.

We turned the lights on a few minutes later. It was getting that dark. A lady stopped in and asked us to put up a flyer for a Lion's Club Fourth-of-July picnic in Petersburg, and we did, and then she thanked us and left, saying, "I'd better get on up the road afore this-all cuts loose."

The thunder got closer and then, during a moment of eerie quiet, the front door flew open and there was Nancy, climbing helmet askew, face dirty and flushed, the knees worn away on her climbing pants.

"I . . . need help." She spoke in gasps, winded. "It's Klaus. Kevin . . . he fell. He's not moving."

Designed to work in hairline cracks, the RURP (Realized Ultimate Reality Piton) may
seem laughingly insubstantial in the hand. But when it is all that stands
between you and a fall to the scree field, it can be a godsend.

The Eastern Cragman's Guide to Climbing Anchors

TWENTY-TWO

Mummy-shaped, constructed of brazed aluminum tubing and chicken wire, the Stokes litter had been a fixture on the front wall of our climbing shop since the first day we'd opened: before it, in fact. There was that, and underneath it was a rescue locker, a long chest—used as a porch seat most of the time—that contained four coils of twisted Goldline climbing rope, a collection of old, Army-surplus steel carabiners, and long padlock-hasp-like carabiner brakes that could be used to slow the descent of a heavy object. That locker, despite its name, was never locked; all that secured it was a thin bit of cable and a Forest Service lead seal, and it was taken as a matter of honor that no one would ever open it unless the gear was needed in an emergency.

This was an emergency, but we left the rescue locker unopened. My father and I both kept fully stocked rucksacks in the back room of the shop, and it had taken us all of ten seconds to grab those, two ropes apiece, and snag the Stokes litter off the wall at a dead run. We tore across Route 33 and toward the Rocks, Nancy sprinting behind us.

We should have been spent by the time we got there, carrying all that gear and handling the long, awkward litter between the two of us. But we weren't. I imagined that the long months of climbing must have conditioned us.

Still, I was barely breathing hard, and even in the gloom of the approaching storm, the colors of the trees, the rocks, my father's shirt all looked super bright: bright, but in soft focus. It wasn't just the conditioning, I decided. It was the adrenaline; it dilated the pupils in something I would later learn is called a "parasympathetic response."

We got to the place on Roy Gap Trail where you turn to go up to the South End, and we stepped back, south, so we could see over the tops of the trees that crowded the narrow two-track. My father craned his head back, peered up, and muttered, "Aw, nuts . . ." I stepped beside him.

Nuts, indeed.

Klaus was dangling, spider-like, beneath the overhang on the third pitch of Ecstasy, a stiff 5.7 route that ran parallel to a sister climb, Agony. His legs, arms, and head all hung limp and lifeless, his abdomen—where the sit harness was tied—the highest point on his body.

"Klaus!" My father made a megaphone of his hands and called his name again.

Nothing. The only movement was the dead weight of the climber's body, revolving slowly in the lifting wind.

My father went silent and peered up at the rock beneath Klaus. He was doing, I imagined, the same thing I was—looking at what was keeping the climber from falling.

It appeared as though Nancy had kept her head. She'd secured her end of the rope with a five-point anchor, and while we couldn't see much—it was a good hundred and twenty feet above us—it looked secure. She'd also lowered him as much as the rope would allow, which was not much. It looked as though he had already cleared the overhang and had clipped off on a fixed bolt about twenty feet from the top of the route before he had fallen. A rope was dangling from the upper belay ledge, where Nancy must have done a single-rope rappel. There was no rope on the lower pitch; she had obviously down-climbed it, which was impressive, because while the first pitch of Ecstasy is deceptively easy, no route is easy to down-climb when you're freaked out and a storm is closing in.

White lightning strobe-lighted the rock. Fifteen seconds later, its thunder reached and rolled around us. The wind began blowing in earnest, and the leaves of the trees showed their pale undersides.

"Okay," my father shouted in my ear, over the wind. "We're not gonna get him up over that overhang. Not with just two guys, and not in the time we have. We need to get above him and lower him off."

I nodded as Nancy caught up with us. She bent over, hands on her knees, and gasped and retched. Any adrenaline in her system had all been used up. My father had pulled a big, military-surplus walkie-talkie from his rucksack and was shouting into it, talking between bursts of lightning-induced static with the Petersburg ranger station. I heard the words "ambulance," "fire," and "rescue." Then he turned to me.

"You got your radio?"

I nodded. "In my pack."

My father handed his walkie-talkie to Nancy and yelled over the wind, "You push the button to talk. But stay off it until we call you. We need you to stay here and spot. All right?"

She nodded. Weakly.

" 'Kay." My father picked up the litter. "Let's go."

That wasn't the first time I'd been on the trail to Luncheon Ledge as a thunderstorm rolled in. But it was the first time I'd been going *up* as a storm rolled in, and that seemed wrong. It seemed beyond wrong—it felt insane.

But I understood my father's worry. An unconscious climber? Particularly one who remained unconscious nearly an hour after a fall? That was emergency enough. And so was an approaching electrical storm. But to make matters worse, Klaus had fallen above an overhang, and that meant that his climbing rope, the rope that was now holding his full, swaying body weight, had to pass over the lip of the overhanging rock—twice. And while climbing ropes are made to resist abrasion, they are not made to resist it indefinitely.

At Luncheon Ledge, we took turns holding each other by the belt of our climbing harnesses while we leaned out and looked down the dizzying length of the route. But we could not see Klaus and we could not see his rope—the top part of the pitch was too overhung.

Still, we knew where the route topped off, so my father started building an anchor, wrapping webbing around a boulder-like knob, while I put two runners and two carabiners well up on the trunk of a foot-thick pine, creating a high fulcrum that could help keep the rope from rubbing too much on the rock as we lowered the litter. By the time I'd gotten done with that, large, fat drops of rain were beginning to fall. And when I looked up, there was my father, fastening a locking carabiner on his sit harness and knotting two ropes together.

"What're you doing?" I shouted over the wind.

"Getting ready to rap down."

I shook my head. "I'll go. I'm smaller than you. You're stronger than I am. If we need to belay a climber and a litter, we'll need all the help we can get."

He scowled.

"I can't belay you and lower the litter at the same time," he shouted as lightning flashed. This time, the thunder was only six seconds behind.

"I won't need a belay. I'll be on rappel."

More lightning. More wind.

"We gotta go," I yelled.

My father got his radio out of his pack, keyed the mike, and said, "Nancy, it's Kevin. Is he moving yet?"

I didn't hear her response, but I didn't need to. My father shook his head. Then he nodded.

We clipped four three-foot runners to the locking carabiners on the litter, bundling the free ends together in another locking carabiner, which we clipped onto a bight knotted at the end of the rope. I passed our joined ropes around a tree and hurled the free ends well out into space, hoping they would not tangle as they fell. Then I threaded an eight-ring onto the doubled ropes, clipped that into my harness, grabbed the Stokes litter in my left hand and the rappel rope in my right, and walked back, to the rounded ledge at the top of the cliff.

"You be careful," my father shouted.

"You know it," I yelled back, and with that, I stepped off into space.

There is a positively otherworldly aspect to rappelling. You are leaning out, far out, away from the rock, only making contact with your feet. Gravity appears to work sideways. It is thrilling in a way— there are, in fact, some adrenaline junkies who do nothing but rappel—but it is also frightening, because it is one of those few areas of mountaineering in which the climber's fate rests solely with the quality and security of his equipment.

I knew this. My father knew this. From the time I'd first ventured onto the Rocks with him, he had drummed into me the statistic that ninety percent of all climbing fatalities take place during the descent, and that accidents on rappel accounted for the overwhelming majority of that statistic. Like most extraordinary climbers, he strongly disliked rappels, using them only when absolutely necessary, preferring to down-climb whenever the option presented itself.

But in this case, time was of the essence, and one can hardly down-climb while guiding a Stokes litter. So rappelling was the only way to go.

I went carefully, not the bounding, gliding rappel that one sees in war movies, but a careful, steady, backward walk down the rock face. Dark, quarter-size wet spots bloomed and polka-dotted the rock around me, and the rain on my climbing helmet beat a steady and building tap. Lightning split the sky and this time the thunder followed before I'd finished flinching. I continued my descent, the Stokes litter dropping steadily beside me.

The top pitch of Ecstasy angles to the right a bit at the end, so when I came even with the bolt upon which Klaus had fallen, it was actually several feet off to my left.

The rain was beating on me steadily now, the rappel ropes a wet, singing chord that stretched up into a dropping wall of gray. I stopped rappelling and was almost pulled sideways by the Stokes litter, but my father must have seen the slack in the rope, because he took it back up until the rope was taut again, and held it there.

The wind picked up enormously, hitting the rock prow of the South End straight on, coming one moment from the left, the next from the right. It was like being caught in a revolving door, with people pushing at it from both directions. The Stokes litter ripped out of my left hand, whirled out into space and swung back. I jumped to the right and it bashed into the rock where I'd been standing just a second before, as more lightning shattered the clouds above me. The rain was falling steadily now, the jagged bolts of lightning were falling like a hail of bright arrows, and the thunder seemed nearly continuous.

I'd had the foresight to keep my running shoes on for the trip down—friction shoes in the wet can be like ice skates. But even the broad-soled Adidas Countrys were having trouble keeping purchase with the rock. I brought them up, farther, so I could lean straight out and look down.

Klaus dangled below me and to my left. I could only see part of him at any time, but he was turning in the wind, and that let me see all of him in progression: his head and arm, then the other arm, then one leg, then the other. His helmet was knocked askew and there was drying blood running from a cut by his left ear. But there wasn't much blood, and his face looked ruddy, not ashen, and that was good.

Then the lightning flashed again, and my attention was drawn by something—I wasn't sure what—about his rope. Another bolt of lightning followed, and this time I saw it: the rope was blue, bright blue along its entire length, except for the place where it passed over the lip of the overhang, and there it changed color.

It was white.

White. The core of a kernmantle rope is snow white. If I could see it, that could mean only one thing: at least part of the Perlon sheath was missing—worn away.

More wind buffeted us, and Klaus's body swung as it turned. It was impossible to hear anything but wind and thunder at that point, but it seemed to me that I could hear the rasping of the hard, quartzite stone, chewing into the soft interior of his rope. The litter ripped from my hands again, smacked my helmet as well as the rock this time, and made me see stars.

It was time to do something, and the first thing I had to do was get that Stokes litter secured so it wouldn't kill me. A thumb-size crack ran down the rock face right in front of me, intersected a couple of feet farther down by a half-inch crack traveling in from the right.

I rappelled down a little more, wrapped the rappel ropes around my right leg, and then squeezed them between my feet.

This kept me from dropping farther, but it robbed me of my broad, stable stance on the rock, and the wind immediately slammed me sideways, pushing the breath out of me. Groaning, I reached down to the small gear sling on my sit harness, unclipped a pair of Hexentrics, and slotted them into the cracks, tugging until I was sure they were bombproof. I clipped the litter off to these, and then I tugged once on the rope that belayed it. The rope went slack and I unclipped it from the litter's suspension. Then I tugged five times in a row, the rope bouncing up in a series of staccato jigs and disappearing into the ceiling of rain.

I still needed to get to Klaus, but he was suspended in space, five feet under the overhang and at least as many off to my left. I had one chock left on my harness and, just above where his rope was fraying at the edge of the overhang, there was a crack. I grabbed my rappel ropes in my right hand, unwrapped them from around my legs, and began to walk sideways—left, then right—until I was slowly swinging like a pendulum back and forth on the rock face.

On the forth swing, I grabbed the crack, held it with the toe of a running shoe long enough to slip the chock in, and then clipped the runner off to my rappel ropes, just above the eight-ring.

My rappel was now redirected. It would run down at an angle, to the chock, and from there it would drop straight down—straight to Klaus.

I could see the fray in his rope now. It was nearly two-thirds of the way through. I rappelled farther downward, past the overhang, into dangling space, and soon was bumping into Klaus as the wind brought us together.

My gear was nearly gone, so I retrieved runners and a selection of chocks from his gear sling and clipped them onto my harness. My first thought had been to just clip his harness off to mine, but I thought better of it; he'd be almost impossible to handle that way, and we were still better than three hundred feet above the ground.

Lightning flashed, the thunder simultaneous with it now. I needed to do something—fast. Then it hit me. I pulled up the tag ends of my rappel line, tied them one-handed into a double bight, and clipped them off to the locking carabiner on Klaus's harness.

A short sigh puffed out of my wet lips. Things were a little bit better. Klaus could still fall. He could fall a good thirty feet, but he couldn't fall to the ground. And one immediate concern was that, if he did fall, the pressure he'd put on my rope would keep me from rappelling any farther. We'd both be stuck.

So my next challenge was to come up with a more permanent solution, and to do that, I had to get onto the rock.

I rappelled on down, the loop of rope shortening beneath me as I went, until I was about eight feet below Klaus. Then, like a kid in a playground, I began to swing: in, then out, then in again, each time going a bit farther, until I could sink my free hand into a crack in the wall.

I released the rappel rope. It was still threaded into my eight-ring, and I was still on it, although I would slide if I fell. But the crack here felt pretty secure, so I climbed it, wet running shoes and all, until I'd gotten to the back of the overhang.

Here, the crack continued on out, and I began to put hardware into it, its satellite fractures, and the cracks running adjacent to it. When I had five pieces in, I clipped them all off to one locking carabiner. To that, I attached not one but a pair of five-foot nylon web runners. And to the other end of those runners, I clipped a single carabiner, and then there was just one thing left to do.

I had to clip off to Klaus.

I down-climbed a bit, leaned out, almost touched him, and then the wind picked up, pivoted me on my single handhold and foothold, and swung me away. I tried it again, pivoted again. Pivoted a third time.

Thunder rang the valley like a gong. My foothold was slipping. My hand was getting tired. I knew what I had to do, and I hated it.

Transferring the carabiner and its runner to my teeth, I reached down with my free hand. I undid the locking carabiner that secured me to the rappel rope, opened the gate, and let it drop free.

Instantly, I stopped pivoting. But now there were only two things between me and the scree field, a great, yawning, vertical football field below—the fingertips of one hand and the toe of one shoe.

Groaning with fright, I leaned out, timed the swing of Klaus's body, and lurched out with the carabiner when he was at his closest. The gate rang shut with a snap and his mass swung back against my arm.

And that was when his rope snapped, and he dropped.

Three fingers of my right hand were still within that carabiner as I closed it. That was the bad news, because it pulled me from my two holds as he fell. But that was the good news, too, because those three fingers closed upon that carabiner with every last milligram of adrenaline in my body, closed on it, and grabbed it like a handle, and there I was, my wrist bent around Klaus's waist, my fingers on the carabiner, hanging by one hand.

There was this brief moment of extraordinary clarity, where it seemed that I could see everything all around me, three hundred and sixty degrees of vision, all at once. Five red lights were flashing in the distance down by the swing bridge. There were people, people in uniforms—police blue, and firefighter yellow, and Forest Service green—hurrying up Roy Gap Trail. I could see Nancy down below me in the rain, the walkie-talkie to her mouth and ear. I knew that I was surrounded by people.

And I knew that none of them, not one of them, could save me. *Save me.*

Savior.

I closed my eyes. *God, help me.*

And just like that, it hit me—what to do.

A person cannot climb a piece of nylon webbing. You just can't do it. It's too slippery. Pulled tight, with the weight of two bodies on it, it is even more so. Wet, it is slickness compounded. Swinging and lurching up, I could reach with my free hand above the carabiner and grab the runner, but I could not climb it.

But I could climb Klaus. I pulled and got both elbows on the big man's bobbing, pitching abdomen. I could mantle on him, like a swimmer clambering out of a rubber-walled pool. I did this, and he said, "Oomph . . ." and groaned—the first indication that I'd had so far that he was still alive.

I swung a foot around, gained soft purchase against his armpit, pushed, and pulled myself into a sitting position right up against the runner that was holding him. I clipped another runner to my harness, clipped it off to the same locking carabiner that was holding Klaus up, and with that single action took the prospect of dying out of my immediate future.

I was still charged with adrenaline, and wanted to use that while I could. So I unclipped the tag ends of the rappel rope, let them drop, pulled my feet up so I was squatting on Klaus's beltline—more oomphing and groaning from the unconscious climber—stood, hand-jammed my way along the crack back to the rear seam, and then built myself an anchor that could hold up a dropping Sherman tank.

I'm not sure how long it took for the rappel line to stop moving again. I know that the rescue squads had gotten up the trail and gathered next to Nancy, and I know that the thunder diminished enough that I could hear squawking snatches from their radios from time to time.

Then the rappel ropes danced some more, and I saw one of my father's feet, and then the Stokes litter was being passed to me under the overhang, and I saw that it had a rope we hadn't brought with us tied into it—a twisted Goldline static rope—and I understood that the rescue teams had daisy-chained some ropes together so they could belay the litter from above while we rappelled with Klaus between us.

Little by little, my father lowered himself to join us—I saw first his legs, then his waist, then his torso. Then, finally, his face came into view, and it shocked me, because it was a face that I had never seen before, a face absolutely ashen with fear and dread.

And that's when I understood who Nancy had been talking to on the radio after my fall.

He didn't say anything about it. That was the worst part. He just told me what to do as we tied Klaus into the Stokes litter, rigged our rappel anchors and made our way down.

Then, once we were on the ground, he couldn't say anything about it and my father—well, it just wasn't what he did. We were involved in other issues: handing Klaus over to the paramedics, telling them what we knew about his injuries.

So it was later, much later, after we had bundled the slowly reviving Klaus into the ambulance, after Nancy had assured us that they would be fine and she would call us in the morning, and after we had given our final debriefing to the forest ranger, that we were walking back to the shop and our benighted VW, and I finally broke the silence and said, "Listen, Dad, I . . ."

But he shook his head and held his hand up, and the message was clear. *Not now.*

So we rode home in silence and I wondered, *Then when?*

"Stitching" a route—placing protection points too close together—is a common mistake made by climbers just learning to lead. But the error at the opposite extreme—ignoring potential protection placements to the point that an overly long run-out results—can be far more costly.

The Eastern Cragman's Guide to Climbing Anchors

TWENTY-THREE

The next day was Friday, July 2. The beginning of the Bicentennial weekend: the start of our busiest period of the year. For businesses such as ours, which depended on a tourist trade—even a specialty tourist trade—it was probably the beginning of the busiest four-day weekend of the century.

So I shouldn't have been surprised when my father was up ahead of me—awake, and dressed, and very nearly ready to step out the door. But I *was* surprised when I glanced at my Pocket Ben alarm clock and saw that it was not yet five in the morning.

"Hang on," I said as my feet hit the floor. "I'll come with you."

"Shake a leg, then. We still have stock to set out. Last night sort of threw us off schedule."

My face reddened. I could feel it.

"Listen," I began. "About last night—"

"Later, Patrick. Get dressed, if you're coming with. I've got to get moving."

So I dressed, and I got in the VW—it made sense to take just one vehicle into the shop and leave more room for the customers to park, and besides, I was hoping I could try and clear things up between us on the way in. But that didn't happen. Driving time from our place to the shop was twelve minutes, and my father spent the entire interval running over the to-do list, laying out his strategy for getting everything set in order by our opening time, which he'd moved up to seven o'clock from our usual weekend opening time of eight—technically it was a weekday, on which we would sometimes not even open until noon—in order to take care of those early risers who'd gotten up at sunrise only to discover that they'd left behind a climbing harness, or a rope.

It was a very shrewd move on his part. A few climbers were already hanging out on our porch when we got to the shop. We both set to work, hanging up the last few boxes of hardware, and packing the T-shirt rack so tightly that shirts billowed from either end, and when we opened the front door at six-forty-five, a dozen climbers streamed through, rapidly buying gymnast's chalk, carabiners, ropes, and at least two pairs of climbing shoes, so they could join the steady trickle of people already heading up toward the Rocks.

It remained like that all day. I never got the chance to talk with him about the night before. There was neither the privacy nor the opportunity. If we weren't helping people try shoes or telling packs of newbies how to get up to Roy Gap Trail, we were setting the stock back in place or sweeping and picking up the trash that is almost inevitable when a small space gets the foot traffic of Grand Central Station.

We didn't even stop to run and get meals. Lunch and dinner were both brought to us by friends, climbing buddies of my father's who had stopped in to see how we were doing.

Still, throughout the hectic day, I kept hoping for a window of opportunity, for the chance to get my father aside and tell him that I was sorry, and that I didn't want to worry him, and I wouldn't do anything like that again. But as the day went on and then day turned into night, it became apparent that no such window was going to appear.

It was ten o'clock when my father finally shooed the last browsers out of the shop. Ten o'clock, and then we spent another half hour picking things up and straightening, and sweeping, and after that I set all the stock back in order by size while my father did the books and got the bank deposit ready. By the time we got in the VW to drive home, it was nearly midnight.

And then—wouldn't you know it?

I fell asleep on the way home.

Fixed protection—pitons or bolts placed or left by previous parties—can be extremely
useful if it is still sound. And encountering a "pin" right where
one is needed can come as a pleasant surprise.

The Eastern Cragman's Guide to Climbing Anchors

TWENTY-FOUR

Yokum's was already packed when we got there at six the next morning. There was a line waiting, but Ruth, one of the owners, saw us and knew we had a shop to open so, despite my father's assurances that we would be happy to wait our turn, she shooed us to the first open table, setting his coffee and my orange juice in front of us without even being asked.

My father had always had this remarkable ability to thrive on four hours of sleep a night, when need be—the result, he said, of working eight-hour days, then going to his MBA classes, and then getting up early the next day to study before work. I had not inherited that particular gene, and so had fallen back asleep on the ride in. That left fences that still needed mending between us, and while he had not mentioned the rescue and how it had gone since that single comment on Thursday night, I was feeling guilt, remorse and, yes, selfishness over what I had done. I'd taken risks that could have left my father all alone, and I knew that, and I knew firsthand the sort of damage that possibility could cause. For me to condemn his risk-taking and practice my own? It seemed inexcuseable. What I'd done could have killed me and left Klaus still in peril. So as soon as Ruth's daughter had taken our order and left the table, I started in. "Listen. About Thursday night . . ."

"It was Thursday night," my father said. He smiled. "And this is Saturday morning, and what's done is done, and life goes on, you know? You're a brave guy, Patrick. A father might regret many things in his life, but having a courageous kid is not one of them. You know how I felt then, and I'm sure you'll take that into account in the future. And if anything, I need to apologize to you for getting all hot when all you did was what I've always hoped you'd do: you analyzed the situation, you saw what needed to be done, you assessed the risk and then you acted. And that's pretty rare."

"But I was wrong to do that."

"I'll bet Klaus doesn't think so." He smiled as a pair of climbers stopped by our table to say hello. "And while I can understand your feeling that way, I'd say that there are some times when right and wrong really only emerge after the outcome. And you had a good outcome." He said hello to two more visitors. "Besides, what it all comes down to, Patrick, is that it is water over the dam. So let's forget about it."

I nodded my agreement. But it wasn't lost on me that he still called me "Patrick"—what he chose to call me when there was distance between us. So there was water over the dam. But there was water behind it, as well.

By the time our food came, my father was talking about what we could do with the business in the years to come. He'd been speaking with some equipment reps, and they thought that his specialized approach to gear—selling what was just right for an area—could be expanded to include other East Coast climbing areas and maybe, if we enlisted the help of respected guides, every major climbing area in the country. He was considering going into catalogue sales, hiring help for the shop to allow the two of us to concentrate on expansion, maybe putting a second shop in down near the New River Gorge.

As he spoke, I realized that overwork had the same effect on him that fourth-classing did. It blocked the pain. And I wondered what would happen to him when this long weekend came to a close and we were back to long weekdays with empty hours. I wondered if he realized that, and perhaps that was why he was trying to keep us busy. And I had just thought that when I saw my father smile a full-toothed smile and I felt a hand fall heavily on my shoulder, and a Boston baritone boomed, "I understand I have to rewrite my will and leave everything to this guy."

It was Klaus, his head bandaged, Nancy at his side. My father laughed and said, "Don't get your hopes up, Patrick. All this character has to his name is a stack of bar tabs a mile high." Then, "Let me get you two some chairs."

They joined us, Klaus ordering a couple of coffees from Ruth's daughter and pocketing our check with a look that showed he would brook no arguments. He told us that the X-rays showed no fractures, just a contusion, and he was preparing to go back to Washington and self-medicate with Glenlivit. As we spoke, the conversation came around to why he had fallen and Klaus raised a hand in mock exasperation.

"Doctors," he muttered. "I think I need to find me a one-armed physician, so he can't answer questions with, 'On the one hand . . .'"

My father grinned.

"But essentially what he told me," Klaus continued, "is that I'm probably getting too old for this stuff."

My father shook his head. "That's bull. You're in great shape."

Nancy cut in. "And that's not what he said at all, Klaus."

"Well, it's part of it." Klaus brushed a hand back roughly through his thick, white hair. "And the new sling's part of it. Maybe."

"The gear sling?" my father asked.

Klaus nodded. "The guy who was looking after me was some kid, just out of medical school, and he said that it might be some condition that he'd never actually seen, but he'd read about it. Called, uh . . ."

"Weiss-Baker syndrome," Nancy said.

Klaus glanced at her incredulously. "How do you remember that stuff?"

"I remember important things. And if it's about you, it's important."

The two of them were quiet for a second, Klaus glancing at Nancy while Ruth came by and freshened everyone's coffee. The sound of a dozen different conversations in the background came flooding in and then, as Klaus stirred his coffee, he said, "Yeah.

That's it. Weiss-Baker syndrome. And the doc had a layman's name for it, as well: 'Tight collar syndrome.'"

"Tight collar syndrome?" my father asked.

"Yeah," Klaus said. "Certain people—not everybody—you put pressure on their neck, where the carotid artery is, it sends the heart racing. They get light-headed and then pass out. They call it that because, with some people, just wearing a tight collar and glancing to the side, like to check a clock, is enough to black 'em out."

"I've never heard of that," my father said.

"No reason you would. The doc said it mostly shows up in old far—" he glanced my way—"in old guys like me. Over fifty, and I guess the muscle mass starts to thin out or something. Makes you more susceptible. The doc gave me the name and number of a neurologist to contact up in Beantown. They need to do some testing to diagnose it positively. But it's nothing life threatening, and even if I do have it . . . hey, it's just one more reason to never wear a necktie."

My father laughed and Klaus turned to me. "As for you, Pat"— I hated having my name shortened to that single, non-gender-specific syllable, but was willing to tolerate it from someone as famous as Klaus—"I am not forgetting what you did. Consider me your godfather after the fact. You need anything, you tell me."

"I didn't do that much. All I did was rap down and clip you off."

"Spoken like a true hero," Nancy said as she stroked my cheek softly with the back of her hand, which should have sent me blushing crimson, but didn't because my mind was wandering. Part of what Klaus said had reminded me of . . . something. I just couldn't put my hand on exactly what.

It was late afternoon when it finally hit me. Some big group from Cleveland came in and bought up all the extra-larges we had set out of our most popular T-shirt design, so I was back in the stockroom, getting a fresh stack, when I remembered where I had heard of "Weiss-Baker syndrome" before: it was in the papers that the medical college had sent to my mother. The ones I'd thought had something to do with allergies. The ones I'd tossed into the barrel outside.

The Hexentric, a type of artificial chockstone developed by Chouinard Equipment, is unique in that it is asymmetrical, so placements can often be made even in situations in which the piece does not at first appear to fit.

The Eastern Cragman's Guide to Climbing Anchors

TWENTY-FIVE

My mother had always been a very private person. She did her best to never spring hanging issues or unresolved questions on either my father or me. We'd only learned that she had applied to enter the honors program at the University of Toledo after she had been accepted. The one time she thought she had become pregnant again, we heard about it at the dinner table after it had turned out not to be so.

Maybe I inherited that gene from her. Or perhaps I didn't want to tell my father about going through my mother's mail—or to meet the skepticism with which I was certain he would come armed—until I was more certain of things. But for whatever reason, I kept what I had remembered to myself, and that made it a very long day at the shop. Busy or not, the hours seemed to drag.

It also made the minutes drag once we had gotten home and I waited for him to retire to the little bedroom at the far end of the Airstream. He'd wanted to talk about our day, and why wouldn't he? Sales had exceeded our wildest expectations. So I did my best to act enthusiastic, and then yawned, glanced at the clock and stretched.

"Yeah," he'd said. "Big day tomorrow, too. We'd better turn in."

I waited while he disappeared into the bedroom, and waited again for the light to go out. Then, once I was pretty sure he had settled, I got the flashlight from where we kept it, on the ledge above the small kitchen table, and opened the trailer's screen door as stealthily as a minute hand, inched outside, pushed the door silently shut behind me, and padded in my bare feet to the burning barrel.

Cupping my hands around the flashlight lens, I risked a light and prayed that my father had not gotten up early one morning to burn trash, that I would not be greeted with nothing but charred cardboard and flaky gray ash.

The flashlight picked out colors: white, yellow and green, and I allowed myself a sigh of relief. The papers from Medical College of Ohio were lying right on top, and I pulled them out, got out the order for the EKG, and, still hooding the flashlight with my hand, read once more the note at the bottom: *". . . EKG required to confirm tentative diagnosis of Weiss-Baker syndrome (carotid sinus hypersensitivity)."*

I still didn't get the "sinus" part, but the name of the condition matched what Klaus and Nancy had been talking about—Weiss-Baker syndrome. I remembered what Klaus had said: *"Certain people, you put pressure on their neck, it sends the heart racing. Just wearing a tight collar and glancing to the side, like to check a clock, is enough to black 'em out."*

To black 'em out.

Could my mother have suddenly lost consciousness in the car? Was there even the ghost of a possibility that her death had been not a suicide, but an accident?

There was this long, disorienting movement, as if I were suddenly too tall. But doubt came chasing after it. My mother had been wearing a soft, V-necked, cashmere sweater when she had died: there was nothing tight about its collar. Properly speaking, it hadn't even *had* a collar. And then there was the other thing Klaus had mentioned: the part about the condition mostly showing up in men, rather than women. Men in their fifties, at that.

My mother had been thirty-six years old.

"Patrick?"

I turned, shoving the papers into my shorts pocket. My father was backlit in the entrance of the Airstream, peering out into the night.

"What are you up to?" he asked.

"A . . . r-raccoon," I stammered. "There was a raccoon . . . trying to get into the trash."

He laughed. "Losing battle, guy. If they want in, they'll get in. Leave it. We'll pick things up in the morning."

TWENTY-SIX

Sunday was the big day—the Fourth of July, 1976. The Bicentennial. It went without saying that my father and I rode in to the shop together, and got there early, even though there wasn't a lot of tidying to be done: we'd taken care of most of it the night before. But I still got out the bottle of Windex and cleaned the glass countertop and the window behind it.

As I did that, I checked my back pocket and made sure the papers from the Medical College of Ohio were still in there. I'd thought about showing them to my father on the way in, but then, in the broad light of day, that had seemed like a bad idea. The questions still outnumbered the answers, and I didn't want to let him know I'd been snooping in my mother's mail until I had all the answers that were available to be had.

But how to get those answers—that was a real conundrum. In July 1976, the Internet was still pretty much an idea being kicked around by academics. I'd certainly never heard of it, nor had anyone I knew. Microsoft was a little start-up company, only one year old, Apple Computer had only come into existence the previous April, and Google would not be founded for another twenty-two years, so nobody had ever even *heard* of a search engine.

In 1976, if I was going to learn any more about this mysterious Weiss-Baker syndrome, I was going to need a library, and not just any old library—not even a university library—was going to do. I needed a library that subscribed to medical literature—a medical library. To get to one of those was going to take some traveling. Some real traveling. And as long as I was contemplating a long trip . . .

I made sure my father was still in back and checked the papers a second time: *J. Singh, MD.* Her doctor. Certainly J. Singh, MD would have a better handle on all of this. But I doubted that any doctor was going to talk with a total stranger on the phone about one of his patients; even back then, patient confidentiality was taken pretty seriously. But maybe if I spoke to this doctor face-to-face . . .

I returned the papers to my pocket and studied the Lowe's Alpine calendar we had tacked to the wall behind the cash register. It was the Fourth, the next day would be the fifth, and I figured that my mother's doctor would be off on the fifth as well. Most people were using vacation days to extend their Bicentennial holiday weekend. But the sixth would probably be a workday.

I glanced out the window at Seneca Rocks and swallowed hard. Was I really thinking of sneaking off, and crossing three states without my father's knowledge, on the slight chance that my mother's doctor just *might* be able to shed some light on her death? I thought about it, and it seemed to me like one of those foam-core signs that shopping-mall stores dangle on a thread from the ceiling, the kind that turn in the breeze from the air-conditioning with SALE on one side and HANDBAGS on the other. Only the sign in my mind's eye had ONLY HOPE on one side and REALLY STUPID IDEA on the other.

"I think you should go." My father's voice startled me, and I jumped.

"Pardon?" I hoped I did not look as rattled as I felt.

"You're right." My father nodded at the calendar. "It's Sunday. You ought to go to church, see your girl."

What a convoluted hairball of guilt, thoughts and emotions *that* set in motion.

"Ch-church?" I finally stammered out. "I thought you didn't think much of that church."

He curled his lips in and huffed through his nose. "You got me there. I don't think much of churches in general. But that one . . . well, the minister's heart seems to be in the right place. And it's not right that I should be living your life for you."

My heart regained a semblance of normal rhythm.

"Dad, it's the Fourth of July. It's going to be a zoo here today."

"Not this morning. Tonight? When they begin to head out? Maybe. People'll be buying their souvenir T-shirts and replacing whatever they trashed or lost up on the Rocks this weekend. But I think yesterday was our rush. We'll have steady business until noon, sure, but nothing I can't handle myself.

"Besides"—he glanced away from me, out at the Rocks—"that Rachel is a looker. And she's got spunk. Reminds me of your mom." He shot me a grin. "You'd better pay some attention to her before some local yokel waltzes in and steals her out from under your nose."

"You sure you'll be okay here by yourself?"

"I'll be fine."

I slipped my hands in my back pockets. The medical papers felt smooth and warm beneath my fingertips. "Well, okay, then. I'll go."

"Good decision."

And the scary thing was, I *had* made a decision.

The line of climbers leaving to walk up to the Rocks looked like a straggling, ragtag army as I made my way over to the campground. Luckily, all my climbing shorts were in the laundry and neither my father nor I had had the time to run a load of wash for several days, so despite the warmth of the July day, I was in white painter's pants and a First Ascent T-shirt—nowhere near my Sunday best, but both were clean and well within Weeping Oak Community Church standards of propriety.

Preacher greeted me like he'd fully expected to see me, and I took advantage of my rough dress, offering to carry and set up the organ and lug the boxes of Bibles from the listing Ford pickup truck that had brought them. Rachel was nowhere to be seen, and I tried to mask my disappointment at that. But then she drove up in the Travelall, opened the back, and started tugging a big green Coleman cooler from it. I ran over to help her.

The Coleman cooler was just the start of it. The entire back end of the big proto-SUV was packed with wicker hampers, Eskimo jugs, and tall stacks of styrofoam cups.

"Wow. What's all this?"

"Picnic." She grinned. "Church tradition. Actually a church tradition that Daddy just invented last week. We'll just have a short service today, and then a picnic afterward. You can fix a plate later on and take it to your daddy when we set this all out."

The brevity of that morning's service was a blessing. My mind was on the papers in my pocket, on what I was planning to do.

"Patrick?"

I looked up, startled. The final hymn had ended and some of the men were carrying long trestle tables onto the platform. Rachel was looking at me, her head tilted just a touch to her right.

"Well, you were a million miles away there for a moment, weren't you?"

I helped her carry a couple of hampers to the tables and set the contents out.

"Busy weekend?" she asked. "Thinking about the shop?"

"No." I shook my head. "The shop's fine. You know my father: Captain Organization. He set everything up weeks ago, and it's running like a well-oiled machine."

She laughed, and then she sobered again and said, "I heard there was an accident of some sort up on the Rocks last week. Is that what's got you so quiet?"

"Sort of." Glancing left and then right to make sure we were not being overheard, I told her about finding the papers. Then I described Klaus's accident—minimizing my role in the rescue because I knew that she would focus on that—and explained what he had told my father and me at Yokum's.

I showed her the papers. "You see? It's the same condition that made Klaus pass out."

Rachel read the papers. "And you haven't shown this to your daddy?"

I shook my head.

Her face became dead set. Earnest. "Patrick, you've got to. Your mama's death . . . it might not have been . . ."

I shook my head. "I know where you're going, but not yet. My father—" I took a deep breath—"my father's an engineer. In his heart, I mean. And to an engineer, there's no such thing as a shade of gray. A thing either is, or it is not. He doesn't put a lot of stock in 'maybe.' And what I've got here is one great big maybe. I mean, I'm not even sure what I'm talking about—all I have is some second-hand information that I got from Klaus. That's pretty shaky. And I need to make it un-shaky."

"How are you going to do that?"

I checked a second time to make sure we weren't being over-heard.

"Monday is usually our day off," I told her. "Except tomorrow, it won't be, because it's the long weekend. And my father doesn't want to close us up on Tuesday, instead, because that's not how we regularly do it, and people that took their vacations along with the holiday might be expecting us to be open. But he will open up late, about one in the afternoon or so. And he'll probably sleep in on Tuesday; he does that every once in a while, to charge back up. So that gives me some time to work with, there. I figure there's a chance that this doctor will be in on Tuesday, first day back after the long holiday weekend, and I'm going to go see him."

I paused there, because the plan seemed much more real, now that I had spoken about it.

Rachel drew in a breath. "In Ohio?"

I nodded.

"By yourself?"

I nodded again.

She smiled as a lady set a casserole down on the table, then she turned back to me, her face serious. "When are you going?"

I rubbed my chin. "We'll be open late tomorrow night. Until eight, at least. And then we'll want to straighten and whatnot so we won't have to face that the next day. It'll probably be close to midnight before my father falls asleep. But as soon as he does, I'm leaving. If I drive all night, I can be at the medical college first thing Tuesday."

Rachel was quiet for a moment and then she took my hand.

"Patrick, you need to come by the house and see me before you go."

"It'll be late, Rachel. Really late."

"I understand. But you need to do it. Something like this? We need to pray before you go." She lifted her eyebrows and leaned my way. "Will you come? Promise?"

I nodded. "I promise."

"Good." She bobbed her head. "Now, let's get you some chicken and fix a big plate for that daddy of yours."

Gear should be arranged on the sling by type and by size, and carried in such a
fashion that it can be sorted through by touch, if necessary.
A good climb begins with good preparation.
The Eastern Cragman's Guide to Climbing Anchors

TWENTY-SEVEN

I woke up to an unusual sound—the shower running in the Airstream's little convertible bathroom. Then I thought about it for a moment and it made sense. It was Monday, the final day of the big Bicentennial weekend, and the swimming hole on the North Fork was probably going to be crowded with early risers among the tourists. No skinny-dipping for my father and me that day.

The shower had just started; I was pretty sure of that. So while it ran, and to the through-the-wall accompaniment of my father singing old Beatles tunes only slightly off-key, I rolled up my sleeping bag, stuffed a change of clothes into an old gym bag, and retrieved a Mason jar full of change from the shelf where I'd been keeping it. In one of the kitchen drawers, there was $280 in twenties—although I had never drawn a salary from the shop, my father had this habit of handing me money anytime I was heading over to see Rachel, and since her family didn't go to movies, and we usually ate at her house, I'd never had the opportunity to spend most of it. Root beers and sundaes just didn't cost all that much.

I took everything out to the Chevette and put it in back, tucked away among the climbing gear and the paperbacks that had taken up residence there.

The noise of the shower cut off as I came back inside. Two minutes later, the door opened and there was my father, wearing his faded Stand-Up shorts, his damp hair sticking up every which way.

"Hey, Sport." He smiled. "Grab yourself a shower. We'll drive in together, in the VW again. If you can be ready in five minutes, I'll take us to Yokum's for breakfast. We're gonna need a good one. Big day ahead, y'know?"

"I'll be ready in five," I promised him.

And I wondered what had happened to make me a "Sport" again.

Work that day was a blur. So much traffic came through the door that I wondered if the wooden threshold wouldn't wear out from the tramping to and fro of all those feet. We never really had anything that could be called a conversation, but my father's state of mind seemed lighter again, reinforcing my theory that work left little room for his dark moods. That was okay on a busy day, but the next day was Tuesday, and the big holiday weekend would be over.

We took turns running to Yokum's for the meals—I went and got BLTs for lunch, and then I tended the shop alone for half an hour at five while my father made a fried-chicken run. By eight, the last of the climbers who were hitting the road had done so, and my father just bundled the receipts and the cash-drawer contents up and stuck them in the old safe in the back room.

"The accounting will just have to wait for tomorrow," he told me. "This day's been long enough. This *weekend's* been long enough."

We got back to the trailer at nine, and I was glad he was too tired to notice that my sleeping bag was missing from the Airstream sofa. My father went to bed, and I shut off the lights and lay down on the sofa. For a few minutes there, I actually nodded off. Then, when the distant sound of his breathing had become regular, I got up, crept out, shut the trailer door quietly behind me, and walked away into the starry night.

Our drive ran downhill from the house to the highway, and I was glad of that as I opened the driver-side door and, one hand on the wheel, pushed the little Chevette away from the trailer. Fifty feet from the state road, I jumped in and let inertia carry me out onto the asphalt. I let the car roll down the long grade until I was a quarter mile from our place. Then I switched the ignition on, popped the clutch to start the engine, pulled on the headlights, and drove the ten minutes to the Ransoms'.

When I got to the road in front of their house, everything was dark, so I shut off both the engine and the lights and rolled into the drive with no sound other than the gravel crunching beneath my tires. As I did that, a figure emerged from the house's long front porch.

Rachel.

And she was carrying a duffel bag.

She got in and passed the duffel back, between the seats.

"You're coming with?"

"Uh-huh."

"And do I get any say in this?"

"Huh-uh."

Even in the darkness, the set of her chin was apparent. The Ransoms' sodium-vapor yard light was reflected in her eyes, and she gazed back at me, unblinking.

"Rachel," I said, "this is a bad idea. Scratch that: it's a terrible idea."

She shook her head. "Letting you go by yourself would be worse."

"But I thought you said that you wanted me to stop by so you could pray."

She nodded. "I'll pray while you drive."

I sighed, ran my fingers back through my hair, let my hands plop back into my lap. "Rachel. Come on. Get out of the car."

She shook her head again. "I will not. You've been working all day, and you're going to need to be spelled. Now," she whorled a finger in the air between us, "you'd better get a-goin'."

I looked at the darkened house.

"Daddy and Jimmy went to Washington with the church right after the picnic yesterday. Fireworks on the Mall. And then they were planning on going to the Smithsonian and that new air-and-space museum today. They won't be back until tomorrow."

She whorled her finger again and I shook my head, sighed, and started the engine. I pulled on the lights, and we backed out onto the county road. As we drove off, I could see Rachel's head bowed, and hear her sibilant whispering.

Praying.

Just like she'd said.

Placements should be practiced at ground level until they become second nature. A climber needs confidence in his protection. Two pitches up on an overhanging route is no place for self-doubt.

The Eastern Cragman's Guide to Climbing Anchors

TWENTY-EIGHT

I woke up not knowing where I was. There was a coiled climbing rope under my head; that much I knew. I had slept using a rope as a pillow often enough to recognize the feel of one. Then I tried to sit up and bumped my head on the glass of the Chevette's rear hatch.

Rachel must have heard the thump, because she asked if I was okay.

"Yeah." I rubbed my forehead, opened my eyes and then squinted at brilliant blue sky rushing by overhead. I was angled across the load area and the folded rear seat of the Chevette—the car was too small to lie lengthwise—and my head was toward the rear of the vehicle. I could rise just enough to see the tops of telephone poles, but that was it. Beneath me, the pitch of the tires humming told me that we were still on the highway. I squinted again at the sky: full daylight. "What time is it?"

"Just a couple minutes past seven. We just passed the exit for someplace called 'Sandusky.'"

Sandusky. Several times a year, our family had driven to Cedar Point, an amusement park near Sandusky. It was only about an hour east of Toledo. And if it was coming up on seven, then . . .

"Rachel!" I began crabbing around to get my head nearer to the front of the car. "I thought you were just going to let me sleep for a few hours."

"I did," she said. "And then I let you sleep for just a few hours more."

"Like maybe six?"

"You were tired. And I got a nap yesterday before you came, because I knew we'd be driving all night. And besides, Patrick Nolan, you have got the cutest little snore."

I scratched my head and tried to wake up. I didn't know about the snore, but she was right about my being tired. Twice on the way up through Pennsylvania, I'd caught myself nodding off. The second time, Rachel had asked me, "Are you okay?" And though I'd assured her I was, she didn't have to offer twice when we got up to the turnpike. I gave her the wheel at the first service plaza.

Speaking of which . . .

"If we just passed Sandusky—" I tried to see out the windshield, but I wasn't turned around far enough to do that yet—"there should be a service plaza coming up, shouldn't there?"

"Blue Heron Service Plaza, one mile—that's what the sign says. Want a pit stop?"

"Please."

This was back in the day when the turnpike service plazas had real sit-down restaurants in them, rather than the food courts they have today. So, after I had attended to the most pressing needs and thrown some cold water on my face, I bought us breakfast at a booth that had a view of the 18-wheelers roaring by on the four-lane.

"You know," I told Rachel, "this seemed like a pretty good idea back in West Virginia. But now? Well, we're both going to be in hot water when we get home, and I was ready for it. But I shouldn't have pulled you in with me."

"You didn't pull me in. I volunteered. As a matter of fact, I insisted."

"I could have refused your help."

"And then driven off the road in the middle of the night? How would that have made me feel?"

I finished the last of my breakfast: pigs in a blanket. My mother had ordered me pigs in a blanket on the first road trip I could ever remember taking.

"This is crazy," I said, "I don't even know if this doctor is going to be at the medical college today. I mean, I'm pretty sure they run a 12-month academic year—the big deal about MCO has always been that they have this accelerated program. But even doctors take vacations sometime. And let's say he *is* there, who's to say he'll have time to see us?"

"I think he will," Rachel told me. "I have faith that he will. But before he does, we have to do one thing."

"Pray again?" I asked.

"No." She fished the car keys out of her skirt pocket. "First we have to get there."

While either side of a double fisherman's knot will slip when pulled,
together they form a snug and immovable union.

Rock Climbing Holds and Basics

TWENTY-NINE

"Dr. Singh? Is he faculty, a fellow, or an intern?"

I rubbed the bird's-eye maple of the counter and wondered if I
looked even half as raunchy as I felt. Sleeping in the back of the
Chevette had left me anything but fresh. Rachel, on the other hand,
had ducked into the ground-floor ladies' room of the administration
building at the Medical College of Ohio, and emerged five minutes
later, unrumpled and even smelling good. Those were two character-
istics that I was pretty certain did not apply to me.

I turned back to the person who'd asked the question, a young
woman with thick, black-rimmed glasses.

"Uhm. I don't know."

She pushed her glasses higher on the bridge of her nose, waiting.
She didn't look that much older than Rachel or me. *Summer job,* I
figured. I dug the papers out of my jeans pocket and laid them on
the counter between us.

If the soot smudges on the paper bothered her, the receptionist
didn't show it.

"This appointment was for quite some time ago," she said.
"They'll have to reschedule you."

Then, before I could set her straight about whose appointment
it was, she'd consulted a phone book the size of a small magazine and
written an office number on the bottom of the appointment slip.

"Dr. Singh is in the Health Science Building," she told me. She
pulled a map from a bound pad of them and slid it across the
counter to me. "You can get to it from here without going outdoors—just follow the corridor on the south end of the building."

I'd expected a small room with a desk and a couple of chairs; Dr.
Singh's office turned out to be more of a suite, or rather a small

clinic of sorts. You entered into a waiting room with a dozen chairs and, right across from the door was an open window staffed by a large, unsmiling woman in a nurse's uniform.

"Good morning," I told her. "Would the doctor be—"

"You need to sign in, sugar," she told me, tapping a clipboard on the window ledge.

"Actually, I just wanted to see—"

"Uh-uh-uh." She shook her head. "We aren't gonna go inventing something new at this stage in the game, honey. You come in here, you sign in. And print your name, okay? I left my decoding ring at home."

She folded her arms and I signed my name while she looked over my shoulder at Rachel.

"You two together?"

"Yes, ma'am," Rachel said.

The nurse chuckled. "That his idea of a date? Take a pretty little thing like you to a doctor's office? Sweetheart, you make him take you to a restaurant when you leave here. You make him take you to a movie."

"No, ma'am, we're—"

"I know. I know. Just runnin' your errands. Understood. But I'm telling you, sweetness, don't let 'em get all cheap on you when you're datin'. 'Cause I'm gonna be the first to tell you, their pocketbooks don't open up any wider once you marry 'em. You understand? I know he does—just look at how his face reds up when I say that." She took the clipboard back from me and said, "All right, then, Mr. . . . Patrick Nolan. You take this pretty girl over there and have a seat, and we'll call you."

"But I—"

"We'll call you. Understand?"

I understood. We were on the big nurse's turf. So Rachel and I retreated to a corner of the waiting room. *Once you marry them? Where had she gotten *that* from? I was still wondering about it when the nurse called, "Patrick?"

"Ma'am?"

"Don't talk to me from way over there, sugar. I might be gettin' ready to say somethin' embarrassin' about you medically. Now you come on over here."

I returned to the window.

"This your first visit here, honey? I'm not findin' you in the file."

"Yes, ma'am." That was all I said. I'd learned by that point not to offer unsolicited explanations.

"I'm not findin' you in the appointment book either. Your doctor's office make it for you?"

"No, ma'am. I don't have an appointment."

"No appointment?" The smile dropped from her face like a glacier calving. "Well, I can see about makin' one for you. You got your referral slip?"

"Ma'am?"

"Your referral slip? From the doctor who sent you here?"

"Oh." I took a little breath. This was going to take an explanation, solicited or not. "No, ma'am. I wasn't referred by anybody. I just wanted to see Dr. Singh—"

"Uh, uh . . . uh!" She folded her arms and shook her head. "This ain't Burger King, honey. You don't just walk in. This here's a *specialist's* office. You got to be referred."

"But I just wanted to talk to the doctor about—"

She shook her head again and leaned forward. "No, sir. You don't talk to the doctor about nothin' without a referral and an appointment. You want to say, 'Good mornin', Dr. Singh,' you go see your doctor and get a referral and we set you up. You want to stand in his doorway and wave hello, you get a referral slip and come make an appointment. You understand?"

"But wait a minute. I just—"

Now she was practically leaning through the window. "I don't *got* no minute to wait. We got sick people here that took the time to do things right and got their referrals, and I got all I can do to take care of them. Now, either you understand, or I can call campus security and have them explain it to you."

Security. I pictured myself trying to explain why two teenagers were hundreds of miles from home, trying to barge into a doctor's office.

"All right." I turned to see Rachel standing next to me. "We'd better go."

"Get you a referral," the nurse repeated. "We'll get you in. I'll see to that myself. But we need to follow procedures, y'know."

"Thank you, ma'am," Rachel said.

"Don't mention it, sugar."

And just like that, we were back outside, in the hallway.

The wide corridor, very nearly deserted when we'd entered the office, was now crowded with people in blue lab coats, walking purposefully—the change between classes, I assumed. Most were in their twenties, but some looked twice that, and the occasional head-gear—yarmulkes, turbans, and even a few of those squat round caps that African Muslims wore at the United Nations—gave the crowd a positively international air.

"Well . . ." I studied my campus map. "I suppose we can try the library and see what we can look up. I doubt they'll give us the boot unless we try to check something out."

Rachel snagged the sleeve of my shirt and tugged.

"What's Dr. Singh's first name?" Her voice sounded urgent.

"Huh? Name?" I looked at the papers I'd brought from home. "I don't know. There's just an initial . . ."

"Is it 'J'?"

"Huh?" It seemed as if everyone in the corridor was talking at once. I could barely hear her.

"'J,'" she repeated, speaking right into my ear now. "Like Jatin-dar?"

"Like what?"

Now Rachel was pulling me along in the flow of people walking down the hall.

"That man just ahead of us—the one in the white turban—he

was wearing a name badge that said *Jatindar Singh*." Then, raising her voice, Rachel called out, "Excuse me? Dr. Singh?"

The man in the turban slowed, and then stopped walking.

He turned to face us.

Strictly speaking, some handholds are not holds at all, but simply constrictions.
Jamming—placing a fist above the narrow spot in a crack—can provide a hold from
which the climber's entire bodyweight can easily depend.

Rock Climbing Holds and Basics

THIRTY

Dr. Singh was tall, his turban accompanied by a full beard, two items that I would later learn are common to all traditional Indian men with the surname of Singh. His eyeglasses had the oversize lenses so popular back then, the glass of the lenses slightly dark, over a face that seemed browned as much by time outdoors as it was by ancestry. A watch, gold and very expensive looking, peeked from under the left sleeve of his rounds coat and, unlike the young men and women accompanying him, he did not wear a stethoscope.

He said something to his companions and they walked on without him. I remembered my manners right about then and crossed the ten feet between us, Rachel at my side.

"Dr. Singh, I'm Patrick Nolan. This is my . . . friend, Rachel. Rachel Ransom."

"Jatindar Singh." He had surgeon's hands, strong looking, with long black hair on the back of them, the edge of his palm soft in my rock-climber's grip. "But then, you already . . ." He paused, smiled, tilted his head—and his turban—to my right. "I'm sorry. How do we . . . ?"

"You don't know us, Dr. Singh," Rachel said. The doctor's smile faded a bit, and Rachel added, "But we drove all night to see you."

"All night?" He squinted behind the tinted lenses, and his eyebrows jumped above the frames: a single, tiny jump. "Whatever for?"

"It's about my mother, Doctor." I remembered hearing somewhere that some doctors could get peevish if you didn't call them "Doctor," rather than "sir."

He straightened up, then.

"Your mother? She is a patient? Of mine?"

I hesitated, then nodded.

"And your mother—does she know that you are here? That you are speaking with me about her?"

I didn't answer him. I wanted to, but I couldn't. The words just crumbled in my throat.

"I'm very, very sorry," the doctor told me. "But it would not be proper at all for—"

"She's dead, sir." It was Rachel: the first time—and the only time—I ever heard her interrupt anyone, let alone a complete stranger.

"I beg your pardon?" This time, his eyebrows rose and stayed there.

"Patrick's mother, sir." If this doctor took offense at "sir," he did not show it. "She's dead."

He looked my way. "Yes? This is true?"

I nodded, my words still deserting me. For several seconds, none of us said anything. Then Rachel spoke up again.

"Is there somewhere that we can go, sir? To talk? We're . . . we're not upset or anything. But if you could give us just five minutes, it would make all the difference in the world."

Dr. Singh glanced at his watch and said, "*Engh . . .*" in that descending, half-hummed manner that people only adopt if they have spent considerable time in Britain. He glanced back, over his shoulder, looked at us and pursed his lips. At least I think he pursed his lips—I saw the beard move. Then he looked once again at his watch.

"Are the two of you in much of a rush?" He directed the question at Rachel.

She glanced my way and I shook my head. Then, uncertain what her look had meant, I nodded.

Rachel leaned forward an inch or two, raised an eyebrow of her own. She must have seen something in my eyes that told her she was on her own, because she looked up and smiled at the doctor.

"No, sir," she told him. "You take your time. We've got all day."

"Smashing!" He actually said that. It remains, to this day, the only time I've heard someone actually say it in everyday conversation, but the way he said it was quite natural, as if things like that just rolled right off his tongue at regular intervals.

Dr. Singh consulted his watch a third time.

"Come along with me," he told us. "I've one thing to do as we go, but we shan't be long at all."

Shan't?

We followed him down a long, broad corridor, up a hallway to the side, and through what appeared to be a large coat closet. At the door at the far end of that room, he paused, held a finger to his lips and said, "Give me but a moment, would you please?"

"We'd be happy to," Rachel told him. He opened the door and we had a glimpse of a large lecture hall mostly filled with people in the light blue lab coats, light glinting off the shiny silver bits of stethoscopes here and there. The door shushed closed behind him and we heard his amplified voice, only the accent coming through the walls, none of the actual words. He spoke for a few minutes, then there was the faint sound of applause—the tempered susurrus of polite acknowledgment. Thirty seconds later, the door opened, and there was Dr. Singh. The metallic *thunk* of a slide projector sounded behind him, then we got the briefest glimpse of a dark-haired woman at a lectern, her stern voice saying, "Palliation aside, there has to date been no valid clinical measure . . ." Then Dr. Singh was back with us, the door clicked shut behind him, and he glanced at his watch.

"Right," he said. "That will hold things for the next forty minutes. You said you have been driving all night; have you had your breakfast?"

"Yes, sir." Rachel, it seemed, had figured out that the questions regarding my mother had left me unable to speak—or at very least unable to speak and retain any semblance of composure. "We stopped at one of the service plazas? Out on the turnpike?"

If Dr. Singh was trying to disguise his opinion of service-plaza cuisine, he was doing a poor job. He wrinkled his nose, then smiled.

"Then I suppose we may as well retire to my study. Shall we? It is only just down this hall."

We went in through a side door that bypassed the reception area entirely. Dr. Singh's "study" was the size of a generous studio apartment, with an aircraft-carrier-like desk, a conference table that could seat eight, walls hung with abstract paintings that had the bumps and crags of original artwork, and a leather sofa and two armchairs arranged around a coffee table in a conversation nook. That was where he motioned us, taking one of the armchairs for himself as Rachel and I settled to our own separate cushions on the sofa.

"So . . ." The doctor took a small leather notebook from his breast pocket and held a gold Cross fountain pen poised above it. "Let us start with your mother's full name and address."

Rachel looked my way, eyebrows arched, and I finally found my voice, giving the doctor my mother's name and our Parkwood address. He looked up at the last part and I added, "We moved to West Virginia after she . . . passed."

"I see." He made a note on the pad, stood, walked to the door, and opened it, saying, "Charlene, would you be so good as to bring me this file?"

The doctor came back and sat and for a good minute or more, none of us said anything. Then the door opened, and I saw Rachel's face blanche a little as she looked past me.

I turned and saw why: it was the large, round nurse who had given us the boot from his reception area just fifteen minutes earlier. But either she had dismal short-term memory, or she was a consummate actor, because she did not look our way or react to us at all. She simply handed a folder to the doctor, who smiled his thanks, and then she left the way she'd come in. There was no "hmpff," no "Well, I'll be." The only sound was that of the doctor, leafing through the few pages in the file.

His face clouded.

"This does not seem to be—" he turned back in the file and slowly reread a page—"a life-threatening condition."

He looked at me over the tops of his glasses. "May I ask how your mother died?"

I swallowed, tried to find words, and Rachel came to my rescue again. "The man next door found her, sir. She was sitting in her car with the engine running. In the garage, sir. The door was closed."

"Goodness gracious." The doctor's turban bobbed as he said it, the British accent slipping into pure, unadulterated Hindi for those two words. "Had she been depressed?"

Another look from Rachel.

"Not . . . not more than most people," I told him. "She was taking longer than she wanted to finish school. I guess that, uhm . . ." I searched for words, not wanting to say *bummed her out* to a doctor. "I guess it made her . . . uh, she didn't feel she was . . . succeeding."

The doctor pursed his lips, the thick beard seeming to dimple and then expand as he did it.

"Well." He closed the file, slipped his notebook back into his breast pocket, and shrugged. "I am very, very sorry, but it seems to me that—"

"No!" They—the doctor and Rachel, both—jumped a little at the sharpness of my voice. *Get a grip, Patrick.* I took a breath and, trying to speak evenly, rationally, told him about the police, about the lack of a note, about Klaus and his accident and what he had told us about Weiss-Baker syndrome. I dug the papers, sooty from the burning barrel, out of my jeans pocket and handed them to the doctor.

He studied the papers, looked at the file, looked at the papers again. Then he looked up.

"Your mother—she did not have these procedures?"

I opened my mouth to speak, but my throat closed up again.

"Patrick's mama," Rachel said, bailing me out again, "she passed away, before the appointment."

"I see." He took the gold Cross pen from his pocket and tapped it against the file. Then he looked at me. The look was kind, and I could understand my mother coming to this doctor. She had been

picky about things like that, insisting that her gynecologist, the ther-
apists who'd worked on my knee, and even our dentists be people
who were not only professional and competent, but wise, and kind,
as well.

"What do you need from me?" he asked.

"Her condition . . ." I told him. For reasons unbeknownst to
me, I no longer had trouble speaking. "Could it have contributed?"

"To her death, you mean?"

"Yes, Doctor. To her death."

Dr. Singh looked at his notes, tapped them again with his gold
pen.

"Tell me," he finally said. "The car your mother was in, was it
new?"

"The Jeep? Yes. It was brand-new. We'd only had it for a few
months."

"And your mother—she wore her seat belt regularly?"

I laughed, forgetting for the moment that we were talking about
my mother's death. "She wouldn't even back out of the driveway
unless everyone was buckled up."

"I see. And this car was new, so it would have a shoulder belt.
Did her last car have a shoulder belt?"

"No." I shook my head. "She used to drive the VW—an old
VW Alpine van that my father drives now. And it's ancient: almost
twenty years old. He had it in college. It only has lap belts: the old
kind that you lift up on to release—they look as if they're out of an
airplane or something."

He made a little sound, as if he was sucking on his teeth. "You
would not happen to know if the radio was on when she was found,
would you?"

"The radio?" I shook my head. "The police didn't say. But the
car had a tape player. She listened to tapes all the time. Not music.
She hardly ever listened to music when she drove. She had tapes of
writers, writers reading their work."

"Dylan Thomas!" It was Rachel, and the doctor and I both
turned her way. "It was in her things." She looked at me, her eyes

bright. "The envelope that you and I went through—the things that were left in her car. One was a cassette tape of Dylan Thomas reading 'A Child's Christmas in Wales.' I remember what it was, because my momma and I read it last December. In school."

"Aha." Behind the tinted glasses, Dr. Singh closed his eyes. He nodded. "Well. That is certainly a . . . Yes. I have seen such a thing in my practice before. Only the last time there was not a . . ."

He opened his eyes and looked at me. "If your mother was afflicted with carotid sinus hypersensitivity—Weiss-Baker—increased pressure from the shoulder belt could have triggered a syncopic episode, a fainting spell. Normally these episodes are very, very brief, only a few seconds or so. The person loses consciousness, and then, when they fall over, the change of orientation in the inner ear reawakens them. That or simply the impact of falling. But if the pressure is continuous, and the seat belt keeps the person upright? Keeps them from collapsing? Goodness. Then I do not think that they would awaken so quickly. No—not at all. They would remain unconscious for five minutes, ten . . . who knows? Half an hour, perhaps more, if the pressure continues to stimulate the carotid sinus. Certainly long enough for one to be overcome by carbon monoxide poisoning."

"Praise God," I heard Rachel whisper.

And I had to agree. An elephant. That's the image that came to me: an elephant, taking its foot off my chest. Then, just as quickly, I felt the elephant's foot return.

"But is that what you think happened, Doctor?"

The doctor tapped the file with his pen again.

"I must admit that this is most unusual," he said. "Your mother was still a young woman, and carotid sinus hypersensitivity sufferers tend, predominantly, to be older men. Still, it is not exclusively linked to gender and age, and some people have a congenital predisposition toward the condition. So this would certainly be a possibility." He checked his notes again. "I see that your mother's general practitioner charted tachycardia—an elevated heart rate—upon carotid sinus massage . . . when her neck was pressed. That is certainly an indicator. And given the circumstances—the new car and the seat belts and all? Yes, I would tend to believe that this was quite likely the case with your mother."

I would tend to believe . . . The elephant continued to press away.

"Could. . . ?" Even as I framed the question, I had this disquieting image of a cemetery, a front-end loader, exhuming my mother's grave. "Is there a way that we could prove this? For certain?"

"With an autopsy, you mean."

A sterile lab. Opening the casket, months and months after the fact. I hated that image. But I hated the thought of my father's torment even more.

"Yes," I said.

The doctor sucked his teeth again. Then he shook his head. "I am afraid that would not be possible. Had your mother had these tests, then yes, a positive diagnosis would have been a very simple matter. But for CSH to be diagnosed, the subject would have to be viable . . . alive."

Black or white. No shades of gray. I could feel my shoulders sag.

Rachel moved forward, to the edge of her chair.

"Sir," she said, "do you think that you could write us a note, explaining what you just said?"

"A note?"

"Yes, sir."

"In writing."

"Yes, sir."

Dr. Singh looked at me. "Is there a problem with the insurance? Is that what this is about?"

I wondered how much I should tell him about my father.

Not much.

"Patrick is hoping we can come back with something to . . . console his daddy," Rachel said. "Something to let him know that it was an accident. That his mama didn't . . . Well, that she wasn't trying to . . . to leave the two of them."

Dr. Singh touched the pen to his lips. He looked at me, then at Rachel, then at me again.

"But I could not be definitive. I do not have the data, the test results. It would simply be conjecture, and nothing more. Nothing that could be used for evidence. To go beyond that would not be ethical."

"All we're asking for," Rachel said, "is a note from you, explaining what you think."

The doctor exhaled, a long, slow exhale through his nose, his lips tight. He looked my way again, and then he nodded.

"All right," he told us, picking up the small, rectangular microphone of his Dictaphone. "I can do that."

Checking sling knots, recutting and refusing the tag ends of ropes and working carabiner gates to examine them for play may not be the most glamorous part of climbing, but it is part of it nonetheless: a necessity that precedes the activity.

Rock Climbing Holds and Basics

THIRTY-ONE

We didn't say much once we'd gotten back into the car, mostly because I wasn't saying much. The doctor's letter was safe, tucked up under Rachel's sun visor, and I glanced its way as we headed back down the business-thick section of Reynolds Road, driving toward the Ohio Turnpike. I hadn't gotten what I'd come for. Not quite. Nor, though, had I come away empty-handed.

A small sound, a sniffing, pulled me out of my thoughts. It was Rachel, her face turned away from me, so I could see nothing but the thick fall of her long, blond hair. But I didn't need to see her face to know what the sound was.

Reaching out, touching her, seemed wrong. So I drove, cursed myself wordlessly for my selfishness in bringing her along on this, and watched the commercial signage at the side of the road until I saw what I was looking for.

As the car slowed and we turned into a pancake-shop parking lot, Rachel lifted her head. I still could not see her face, but her voice sounded strained as she asked, "What are we stopping for?"

I reached behind her seat and retrieved the Mason jar I'd set there the day before. I handed it to her, and she turned it in her hand as she looked at it; quarters, nickels, and dimes tumbled inside the green-blue glass.

I pointed to the sign at the entrance: PHONE HERE.

"Your father's probably worried sick," I told her. "You'd better call home."

She hefted the jar, nodded, and without a word left the car and walked into the restaurant. I saw her go to the phone—one of those white, wall-mounted consoles with the outline of a telephone receiver drilled into its sides, and a little shelf underneath for the cable-tethered phone book.

Standing outside, leaning against the car and allowing her some privacy, I watched as she pressed the keys on the phone, deposited coins, and then spoke, nodding several times as her conversation lasted for the space of perhaps three minutes. Then she hung up, but she did not leave the phone right away. Her head was down and her left hand was cupped over her right. I wondered about that for a moment, but then I understood it; she was praying.

Smiling bravely, she handed me the jar as she walked up to the car.

"Your turn," she said. And when I accepted the jar but stayed where I was, she added, "We came here for your daddy, Patrick. And you know he's worried about you right now, wondering if you're all right. Now, you set his mind at ease. Just call him and let him know you'll be home directly."

So I did that. I was secretly relieved when, behind my father's curt and businesslike "First Ascent," I could hear voices laughing and joking.

He had customers. It wouldn't be easy for him to lose his cool over the phone if he had customers in the shop.

So he spoke in a civil sort of code, instead. "You all right?" was about as emotional as he got. He did say, "I got some phone calls this morning, and I'm guessing you're not alone," so I told him he was right—that Rachel was with me and she had already phoned her father. Then I heard my father say, his voice half-muffled, "Be right with you," and I knew that some of the customers were looking for attention, so I took advantage of that. Without giving him time to ask me where I was, I told him that I would be home by that evening, and explain everything then.

And with that, I walked back out to the car where Rachel was waiting, leaning in the sun with her back against the little orange Chevette. She smiled at me, and I smiled back, and I set the Mason jar on the roof of the car and leaned toward her. But just before our faces met, she turned and lowered her head, not quickly, but not slowly either, and my kiss landed on the soft part in her hair.

"I love you, Rachel." It felt stupid, saying that after being denied a kiss, but I couldn't help it. Those four words had been waiting in my throat ever since I'd hung up the phone, and there was no way they would not find voice. And besides, some hopeful and dimwitted part of me was waiting for an *I love you, too, Patrick*.

But it would keep waiting.

"We'd best get on the road," she told me, her head still lowered. "Your daddy and mine are going to be counting the minutes."

There have been more than a few occasions in recent years in which parties claim to have ascended a route on which they stopped short, or claim to have freed a route on which they actually took a point of aid. In such cases, no one is the victor. In discussing one's accomplishments, telling the truth, even if it means admitting defeat, is infinitely preferable to being found out later as a fraud.

Rock Climbing Holds and Basics

THIRTY-TWO

The thunderstorms began shortly after we crossed the state line, at Wheeling. Low clouds had been forming all day, throughout the journey east, and they finally opened, with rain and lightning both, as we turned off I–70 and began driving south.

It was proof of Rachel's fatigue that she fell asleep as we turned off the Interstate, and stayed asleep, despite the artillery-report crashes sounding directly over our heads and echoing from hillside to hillside. At times I had to slow the little car to less than forty-five miles per hour just to see where I was going. The wiper blades were semaphoring at top speed, but rain still streaked and warped the view through the windshield. And the bridges we crossed showed us that the creeks and rivers were up, their water turned tan by the fresh runoff, branches and even whole trunks of trees borne along in the high water.

Still, the storm had all but let up as we turned east and followed Route 33 back to Mouth of Seneca. Back home.

We had stopped for lunch on the Ohio Turnpike—my idea, rather than Rachel's. I had been in no hurry to get to the inquisition that I fully expected and richly deserved. But while my central emotion was a sort of dread, Rachel's was more one of sadness.

It was just that: sadness, not remorse. I was absolutely certain that all the things she had done over the last day and night were things that she would gladly do again, should the circumstances arise. But in doing so, she had hurt those who loved her, and knowing that obviously wounded her to the quick.

So she'd eaten little and said less during our lunch stop. I got the message: she was ready to be home and ease their minds.

And that was why, as I slowed to make the turn onto the county road that led to her house, I was surprised to see her sit straight up, look at me, and ask, "What are you doing?"

"Do. . . ? I'm taking you home."

"No!" She brought her voice back under control. "No. We have to go see your daddy first."

"Rachel, your father is going to be frantic with worry."

"For no good reason unless we see your daddy and make him understand what we learned on this trip."

She put her hand on mine, atop the shifter.

"Please, Patrick. We've done so much today. The two of us: you and I. Let's finish it. Let's see it all the way through. Together. Okay?"

At any other time, that touch of her hand would have been electric, exciting. This time, it just made me want to spend the rest of my life with her. To grow old with her.

Seneca Creek was very nearly overflowing its banks as we neared the town. Here and there, freshly broken tree limbs lay in the ditch and on the shoulder of the road, and the pavement was still glistening, still wet. It was raining no longer, but the clouds remained, dark and low enough that the top of the Rocks was obscured. As we drove past the houses on the outskirts of the little town, their windows yawned darkly back at us.

"No lights," I muttered.

"The power's out," Rachel said. "From the storm."

We came to the T and we both saw it: the Ransoms' International Travelall, parked in front of the climbing shop.

Judd Horton's store windows were dark, as well, but that didn't mean Judd had closed up for the night. His gas pumps were hand-cranked, as was his cash register. He usually stayed open until eight on the weeknights after a holiday, and I assumed that he would tonight, too—if nothing else, to sell lantern batteries to those who'd been caught short.

I remembered what my father had once said: *"There are three methods of high-speed communication around Seneca—telephone, telegraph, and tell Judd Horton."* And I figured that, if I pulled up in front of the shop, our fathers would see us through the open front door and come out, and I didn't care for what Judd might see in the moments that followed. So I drove past the turnout in front of the shop and took the drive beyond, the one that would lead me to the smaller graveled area behind, the one that we used for deliveries.

Careful to park where Rachel would not have to step out into a puddle, I stopped the engine, went around to her side of the little orange car, and opened her door. She took my hand as she got out, and I squeezed hers softly. She squeezed back.

"I love you, Rachel," I told her again, although this time I made no move to hold her.

With her free hand, she stroked my cheek, just once, and looked me in the eyes, her face a picture of composure, of contentment, of peace.

"I know," she said. Then she squeezed my hand again, released it, and we went inside, through the back door of the shop.

The back room of the climbing shop contained two Army cots, an ancient, condenser-crowned refrigerator, a wooden table with a two-burner Coleman camp stove sitting on it, and a single metal shelving unit that was mostly used for storing our stock of extra T-shirts and friction boots. That was it. The rest of the floor space, which was not much, was open area that we used for taking deliveries. We didn't keep climbing gear in the back room, because there wasn't room; everything was out front, on the shelves. Crossing that little room seemed to take forever.

I opened the door into the front part of the shop for Rachel, heard Preacher Ransom say, "Baby . . ." Then Rachel rushed forward, into her father's arms.

My father was standing next to them, but he did not hold his arms out to me. He did not even offer me his hand. He just stood there with the same look on his face that he'd had as he'd inspected the VW's engine, the weekend before we pulled it out and replaced it with a rebuild.

Because the valley lost power so often, we had three oil lamps in the shop: one on a shelf behind the counter, and two on wall fixtures in the corner, to either side of the wood stove. All three of those were lit, and they provided a light that was not light, illumination that was quaint and funereal, both at the same time. They gave our faces shadows that moved slightly with the dancing of the little flames, and softened our features so ours looked like faces remembered, rather than faces seen.

"I missed you," Preacher told his daughter.

Cheek still pressed against his chest, she said, "I'm sorry, Daddy. I missed you, too."

She leaned back and looked up into his eyes, her own eyes wet with tears.

Wiping them away with his fingers, Preacher asked quietly, "Are you all right?"

Rachel nodded twice, quickly.

"Well," my father said. It was the first word he'd spoken since we'd entered the shop. "I suppose we'd better talk."

"I suppose we'd better," I agreed, and we all walked back to the corner where the stove was—the same place we'd sat on Rachel's and Preacher's first visit to the shop.

When we got there, Rachel did a curious thing. Rather than sitting next to her father, as she had before, or next to me—as some part of me still wished that she would—she took a seat on the bench next to my father, leaving me to sit on the facing bench, next to Preacher. It was curious, but it was also, I quickly realized, brilliant. It removed both possible we-they connotations from the seating arrangements, and it eased, however slightly, the tension in our group.

But if my father was disarmed, he did not show it. I had the feeling he'd assembled some sort of mental outline of the questions he meant to ask, and he was determined to trot them all out in short order.

"So," he began, "where were you two?"

"Toledo," I said. But that was all I got out.

"Toledo?" He leaned forward. "You mean to say you left the *state?*"

"Well, we had to, because we—"

"Where," he asked, "did you sleep last night?"

"In the car."

"You slept in the car?"

"Together?" Preacher added. Then they were both talking, both at the same time.

Slowly, with measured movements, Rachel got to her feet, walked over to me, took both of my hands in hers and gently pulled me to my feet. Then, as we were standing toe-to-toe, she reached up, pulled my face down toward hers, and softly, gently, sweetly, slowly, she kissed me.

In that instant, I knew what schizophrenia feels like. Part of me was shocked: my father was right there. *Her* father was right there. But part of me was delighted, because it was not a peck on the lips. It was a *kiss*.

Her lips tasted of peppermint and her hair, so near on both sides, was lightly scented with vanilla and coconut. As we kissed, her hands moved to the small of my back and pulled me nearer, and I wanted to reciprocate, but again—our fathers were right there. So I left my own arms at my sides: awkward, gangly.

And Rachel's father and mine finally noticed what was happening, because they stopped talking. Then they spoke again.

My father said, "What the—?"

And Preacher said, "Rachel Christine Ransom!"

But Rachel paid them no mind. She finished her kiss and just held me, nuzzling my lips, my face, with hers. She got up on tiptoe, and in a voice so small that even I could barely hear it, she whispered in my ear, "I love you, too, Patrick. I will *always* love you."

Then her hands slid away from my back and we turned to face our astonished fathers.

"Daddy," Rachel said. "That was the first time I have ever—

ever—kissed Patrick. In fact, that was the first time that I ever kissed a boy. And if you want, I will promise you, I will swear to you right now that I will never kiss a boy again until I am standing at the altar, and you'll be there to see that one, too."

"Uh . . ." Preacher fumbled. "I don't think . . ."

But Rachel had already turned and was looking at my father.

"Mr. Nolan," she said, "I know what's probably going through your mind now, but I want you to know that Patrick has never been anything but a perfect gentleman with me, and you have every right to be proud of him."

She glanced at her father. "Patrick didn't want me to go with him to Ohio. I made him take me. He was tired"—*tarred* was how it came out, because Rachel was obviously mostly spent herself, and the West Virginian accent was creeping back into her voice—"and I couldn't bear the thought that he might fall asleep on the highway and hurt himself. And besides, I knew what he was doing, and I wanted to help him."

She looked at my father again. "And he was doing it for you, Mr. Nolan. Doing it because he loves you, and he doesn't want you to be sad, and he wanted to make things better."

She took a step back, so she could look at both of our fathers at once.

"Now," she said, her voice growing weaker, as if the declarations had cost her. "Would you please, please, please, please, *please* stop asking all your questions and let Patrick tell you where we went, and why?"

My father nodded. We sat, in the same places, and I began talking.

I told them about sorting through my mother's old mail and finding the doctor's appointment. I told them how I remembered the name of the condition, Weiss-Baker syndrome, over breakfast when Klaus had told us about his experience at the hospital.

I showed my father the papers I'd rescued from the burning barrel. Then I described how I'd decided to go find some answers for myself, how I'd stopped at the Ransoms' before I left.

"And, Preacher," I added, "I've got to tell you—I didn't argue much when Rachel insisted on coming. I didn't argue at all. That was selfish of me. I could have just driven off and left her standing there, in your drive. But I didn't, because I welcomed her help. It was good to have her with. It was . . . it was great."

He nodded.

I described our visit with Dr. Singh, and what he had told us.

"And after that," I concluded, "we came home. But the doctor gave me this to give to you."

I pulled the envelope out of my back pocket, unfolded it, and handed it to my father. He looked at the Medical College of Ohio return address, then he slit the top with his thumb, took the letter out, and read it silently.

He sighed, put his arm around Rachel, hugged her, and muttered, "You two are a couple of brave kids." Then he handed the letter to Preacher who read it, nodded, said, "Well. Praise God," and handed it back.

My father read the entire letter through one more time.

"This is good to know," he said. "And I'm glad you . . ." He swallowed. "Thanks, Sport. Thank you, Rachel." He kept his head down, as if reading again.

I could tell that he was not.

He shook his head.

"What is it, Kevin?" Preacher asked.

"Oh, it's just . . ." My father tapped the letter on his knee. "There are a lot of 'I thinks' and 'possiblys' and 'probablys' in this letter. It's not very conclusive."

My heart fell.

Preacher held his hand out, took the letter, and read it again.

"You're right," he said. "It's not. This doctor sounds like a careful man, and it's clear that, in cases such as this, it's impossible to be conclusive. But it's hopeful, wouldn't you agree?"

My father nodded. Once, then twice. Slowly.

"Well," Preacher said, handing back the letter, "sometimes hope is all we have. And I'll tell you something, Kevin . . ."

My father looked up.

"Sometimes," Preacher said, answering his look, "hope is enough."

The principal virtue of the locking carabiner is that the knurled knob holds the gate secure; it will not release unless you want it to release.

The Eastern Cragman's Guide to Climbing Anchors

Our fathers may not have condoned what we had done, but they understood it. Our community was another matter.

In a way, despite my misgivings, the trip to Ohio had succeeded, because my father's mood swings seemed to subside and he never again risked another dangerous solo climb. Or at least he never risked one that I was aware of.

But in another fashion that trip had cost us—Rachel and me—and cost us dearly. What I'd told Rachel back in Toledo turned out to be true. She had sacrificed her reputation by insisting on accompanying me.

Nothing was said openly, of course. Preacher's position within the church and the valley had assured us at least that level of discretion. Still, everyone from Elkins, to Franklin, to Petersburg knew that Rachel Ransom had not only gone missing for twenty-four hours after the Fourth of July, she had gone missing with me, and I was not just some boy. I was an outsider. I was from up north. And I was a climber—an activity regarded with great suspicion by the local people, who saw it as both frivolous and dangerous, and were probably right on both accounts.

That added up to three strikes against me, and while Rachel never insisted on our public separation, I did. Being seen alone with her, or even sitting with her in church, would do nothing but shovel fodder to the gossips. And I would not, could not, hurt her anew.

So we did not go out together. On Sundays and Wednesdays, I saw her in church, but I kept my distance. We lived in different school districts, and when I started my junior year at Franklin that fall, there were dances and proms, but I did not attend any of them, because Rachel's family did not dance, so I did not dance.

Throughout the school years and the summers that followed, I restricted our contact to calling on Rachel's family after church. Again, it was my doing. While we were oftentimes out of earshot of her father and her mother on a Sunday afternoon, we were never out of sight, and if anyone else was visiting the family then, I stayed away. This was decades before programs such as The Silver Ring Thing began to appear on the horizon, but, by common accord, we did not hold hands, we did not touch, and that fleeting, chaste moment in the climbing shop remained the one and only time that we ever kissed.

It was—I can admit it now—almost physically painful. At least it was for me. But it was the only way to restore to Rachel some semblance of the deference and the honor that she deserved.

It went that way through the rest of high school. I was just ending my sophomore year at WVU when things began to change.

It was my doing. The months between the academic year were really the only time I had to see Rachel on anything approaching a regular basis, yet when one of my father's friends contacted us to see if I would be interested in a summer job as a climbing guide at Yosemite, I agreed to go immediately.

It was one of the few times that my father ever questioned one of my decisions.

"Are you sure about this, Sport?" He'd asked me.

And I gave him some story about temptation, about how difficult it was for me, having Rachel right there, but knowing that, if I so much as took her to a movie in Elkins, that if I even walked with her and held her hand—that if I did any of those things, after having once absconded with her across a state line—her reputation would be ruined.

My father seemed to accept this, even though he understood that, because of Rachel, I had all but stopped noticing other girls. I didn't date, didn't go to mixers, didn't even chat with girls between classes at the Student Union when I was away at school. Monks on mountaintops had more of a social life than I did.

Still, I have to wonder what I was really thinking back then. Was

I taking the moral high road, or was I secretly hoping that something would transpire that would shift things, change them, give both of us a life that was more normal—more like the lives of the people our age all around us?

If you'd asked me that at two different times back then, I might have given you two different answers. And if you asked me that at two different times today, who knows? I still might.

Bottom line: I went to California. I went, and I came back with glorious memories of waking up after hanging bivouacs on the Nose Route of El Capitan, of doing long, glorious, zero-gravity-like running pendulums on Half Dome, of all-night bull sessions around a fire at Camp Four. And while it is true that many of those bull sessions involved mixed company, I retained a distance, the Rachel-light still burning there in the back of my mind. I was high-fidelity and low-resolution, both at the same time.

I returned home with all of those memories, and I returned home to a Rachel who'd grown, if only a little, away from me.

Of course, I had all but told her to do so. And of course, I took her distance as reason to instill a bit more distance of my own. By the time I left to go back to WVU that year, by the time she left for her own junior year at Oral Roberts—her first school year away from home, because she had finished her freshman and sophomore years as a commuter at Davis Elkins—we were still friends, and even close friends. But the closeness was going away, lifting like low morning clouds from a West Virginia hillside.

This was 1980. The phone companies had introduced calling cards by then—not the prepays that they have today, but the kind that billed calls to a home number. And my father, that aging and benign lothario-by-proxy, gave me one with instructions to call home at least once a month, and to call Rachel at least once a week—more often if I so desired.

"Live a little," he'd told me. "The mail-order business that we added is doing better than I'd ever thought. May as well put some of that dough to use for a good purpose, like making sure I'll have grandkids some day."

There was no way to tell him that Rachel and I had probably already passed that station. So I went off to Morgantown, and made my phone calls to Virginia, often calling on a Friday night or a Saturday, just to see if Rachel was in her dorm room. And she almost always was.

It happened during that year's home leave: Christmas break. It was Christmas Eve. Preacher had held an evening service, and we were gathered at the Ransoms' for dinner. My father was even there. He had missed the service, of course, claiming that he had some last-minute mail-orders to attend to, an excuse that was lame for any number of reasons, not the least of which was that he and I had had a blow-up the afternoon before. But he had accepted Preacher's invitation, and he would not have dreamed of backing out. Through all his highs and lows of spirit, my father remained that—a man of principle.

So the families were gathered. It would have been a propitious time to formally start the courtship Rachel had spoken of better than four years earlier. It would have, for that matter, been the perfect time for me to step into Preacher's study with him and ask if he would bless the enterprise if I asked Rachel to marry me. We all knew one another well enough, and my father had a successful business in which I was part owner. I could have offered Preacher's daughter a secure future and a home from which she could still visit her mother every single day if she so desired.

But I pursued neither courtship nor Rachel's hand, and that was the source of the discord between me and my father. As Rachel and I sat in a corner of the family room, crystal cups of eggnog in our hands, I'd told her that I'd learned through friends of my father's— through Klaus and Nancy, to be specific—that there was an opening on an expedition to K2 in the spring. Klaus had urged me to go. A couple of equipment companies had offered to sponsor me if I wanted to do it, and I'd decided to accept their offer.

I could tell by the look in her eyes that this was not what she had been expecting, or hoping, to hear.

"You're leaving school?"

"Have to," I told her. "There's just a brief climbing window, twice a year, and both times fall at least partially during the school year. We'll want to summit no later than the middle of June."

I launched into optimistic patter—how I would be going to Washington early to walk my passport application through the State Department's passport agency there, how I had already sent in my measurements for the high-altitude double-boots, the down suit, the rest of my gear. I spoke of the winter training climbs that had been planned for the Alps, how I would be leaving to do those in mid-January. I told her everything as if I expected her to be enthused. And she listened to it all.

Then she said, "Patrick, I know about K2."

I had figured that she would. Climbing was important to me, so Rachel, whose sum total of climbing experience had taken place on that long-ago summer morning at Church Rock, read climbing magazines.

"It's the second highest mountain in the world," she'd said, her voice strained, on the edge of something. "Only Everest is higher. But K2 is tougher, isn't it? People die there, Patrick. Don't they? Lots and lots of people?"

It was true. The Karakoram claimed a significantly greater percentage of lives than the Himalaya as a whole, and K2 was a climber's mountain. It had challenges that made Everest look like a scramble.

"I'll be okay," I told her.

"You don't know that." She had tears in her eyes as she'd said that: she—my first love, the only love I'd ever known. "It's just . . . I don't know, Patrick. Is this what we are going to do from now on? Am I going to wait while you go off to places you might not come back from? I mean—I know that this is who you are, has always been who you are. But . . ."

Her eyes were welling as she looked at me, took both of my hands in hers, held them.

"I've tried to wait, Patrick," she'd told me. "I have. I want to. But I'm not as good at it as I'd like to be. I'm running out of 'wait.'"

She looked me square in the eyes. There it was. My turn.

"Then don't," I'd told her. "Then don't."

Two words. That was all it took to establish me as ignoble, self-ish, an ingrate. And even before I'd said them, as I'd felt them rising, coming up from the soles of my feet, some part of me had wanted to squelch them, but it could not overpower the stubborn and inde-pendent runt of my ego, my pride. Nor could it prevail in its wish to call them back once they'd been said. I'd spoken them, and they had lain there, two stillborn angels resting in the air between us.

I will not even attempt to apologize for the cad I'd grown into then, in the winter of my twentieth year. And if that makes me seem loathsome, I understand.

I was.

Perhaps I still am.

I will say this, though: among the spiritual gifts my Rachel had demonstrated, even at that tender age—along with her pure love, her kindness, her empathy, her selfless generosity and her ability to teach without seeming didactic—she had one gift more.

She was, as it turned out, a prophet.

Easily tied, even with one hand, the clove hitch provides a relatively strong anchor
when pulled snug, but can be loosened and slid to a new position
on the rope as the need arises.

The Eastern Cragman's Guide to Climbing Anchors

THIRTY-FOUR

"People die there, Patrick. Don't they? Lots of people?"

That's what Rachel had said. And she was right. They did die
there. They died there that spring.

For the first three weeks, everything seemed to have gone almost
too well. The weather was glorious. Our progress was ahead of
schedule. Two of our climbers had been returned to Base Camp with
symptoms of altitude sickness, but there were twelve on our team,
and having better than eighty percent of our climbers on the mountain and functioning was a better outcome than any of us had
hoped for.

As the youngest member of the team, I had the least experience
on snow and ice, but I was in excellent condition—I'd just finished
my second year of playing junior-varsity ball for the Mountaineers—
and I was easily the best all-around climber on the team. Moreover,
I turned out to be naturally resistant to altitude sickness. Even in the
"Death Zone" above 25,000 feet—that area in which human beings
simply cannot survive for more than a few days—I was able to sleep,
albeit fitfully, and my appetite continued unabated.

Still, it was sheer chance that put me on the summit team. One
of the senior climbers from Italy and I had just established a high
camp with two of our Balti porters. Our orders called for us to overnight there and head back first thing in the morning. But then Base
Camp radioed with a weather report; a front was moving in and was
expected to linger for days, perhaps as long as a week. Maybe more.
They gave us the okay to make a summit bid in the morning, if we
so desired. It would be an "insurance" bid: a long shot, but a way to
possibly get on top and guarantee the expedition's success.

We agreed that no one would be forced to go. The Italian had not summited in his last three expeditions, and was hungry for a change. The younger porter smelled a bonus if he got us up top and satisfied our sponsors. The older porter was fatigued and felt he would hold us up, so he elected to head down in the morning. We'd fixed rope all the way to the camp, so the return trip would not be excessively dangerous, not even alone.

And me? I was twenty years old and I'd had a sniff of glory. There was no way I was turning back.

We left camp an hour before sunrise, taking turns on the lead, so there was always somebody fresh up front, chopping steps, placing ice screws, and pushing through the snow on the few sections of route that were sloped gently enough to hold snow.

I can perfectly remember that last sunrise on K2. The sun hit the summit and turned it a perfect rose gold, and there was a wind up top, strong enough to send a plume of gold-pink spindrift off into the deep, blue sky. In the early light, it looked like a tongue of ethereal, heavenly flame.

The other two were on oxygen, but I was climbing without it, trying to conserve my supply for the final push to the summit. Finally, about thirty minutes after sunrise, the climbing had become vertical enough, and the top looked reachable enough, that I felt it was time to turn my cylinder on. To secure myself while I got to it, I sank my ice axe up to the hilt and threw a hitch around it, creating an impromptu anchor.

I'm still not certain what happened next. Perhaps something up top loosened in the growing morning light. Perhaps it was the wind, now blowing spindrift around us, as well.

I do know that I saw it before I heard it—just the ghost of a movement, of something plummeting, at the edge of my vision. Had I not removed my goggles to put on the oxygen mask, I doubt I would have seen even that.

I did call out. I distinctly remember that. But I'd just put the mask on; it's doubtful that anyone heard me. So next, I fell on the broad head of my ice axe, trying to sink the shaft down, into the soft ice beneath me, driving it downward every centimeter that I could.

What I saw after that, I saw sideways, then, but even at that unusual angle, it did not seem that severe. It was not an avalanche by any means—the slope we were on was far too steep to hold snow in any quantity. But there was ice falling, and there was rock falling: less than a dozen pieces of each, none of them larger than a football.

Some of that hit the Italian, pivoting him backward, off the front points of his crampons. And then, just as the rope between him and the porter was coming taut, a rock hit the rope, struck it precisely at a point where it was crossing an exposed rib of granite, and cut it as cleanly as a pair of shears.

The porter went next, struck by ice, not rock, and yanked from his stance by the momentary tug of the rope. I pushed with all my might on the ice axe, trying to will myself to become heavier, dreading what I knew was coming next.

The ice axe ripped out from under me and I clung to it, wrenching the head point downmost, driving it into the skidding ice with all my strength.

In five seconds, I was stopped. We were stopped. Ripping off the oxygen mask with my free hand, I shouted the names of my companions.

The porter answered.

He was forty meters beneath me. Another hundred meters beyond, the ice slope we were on ended in a brink that left no doubt as to the fate of the Italian. And the porter was not moving, not front-pointing back up the slope toward me. So, taking up rope as I moved, I crept backward, toward him.

In a few feet, I saw why he was not climbing. His cramponed right boot was pointed backward. Moving down just above him, short-roping him, I traversed over to easier ground, humming to block out his cries of pain as I moved him.

I also blocked out his cries as I pulled his leg, turned it right-way around, and splinted it with his ice axe. Then, remembering the morphine that we each carried in our first-aid kits, I emptied an ampoule into his hip, right through his wind pants and down under-suit. His cries ceased almost immediately, and his voice returned to him.

"You had better give me the rest of it, Patrick, sahib," he said, his voice just loud enough to carry above the wind, his accent musi-cal, even through his pain.

"The rest of it?"

"The rest of the morphine in your kit, sir. Yes, sahib. And all of the morphine in mine."

Grasping what he was getting at, I shook my head.

"Patrick, sahib, I beg you to think about this. We are at better than 27,500 feet. Our camp is fifteen hundred feet below us. The nearest help is a mile and a half down. And the weather . . . There is no way we will get me down. Please, sahib. Sir, please. Give me the rest of the morphine."

I turned my back on him, fished the radio out of the inside of my down suit, where I carried it to keep the batteries from freezing, and informed Base Camp of our status. I told them that I was mov-ing the injured porter back to our tent at the high camp, and they said that they would have four people—two expedition climbers and two porters—moving up the mountain immediately. Because the weather was turning, the team would have to stop and camp partway up, but they would be moving again before first light, and would be with us by morning.

I got the porter down to our high camp. And yes, I realize that it seems as if I am skipping something by saying it like that, but the truth of the matter is that I cannot remember how I got him there. In some endeavors, the concentration required to succeed is so great that it subsumes the secondary functions of the mind, even memory. And that, I believe, is how our descent went—all fifteen hundred feet of it.

I do remember carefully removing the porter's crampons and his left boot in the threshold of our tent. I remember that we had a better medical kit there, with air splints, so I put one of those on his fractured leg, and then zipped him into his thick, expedition-weight sleeping bag. We repeated the morphine dose, and this time there was no more talk such as what we had shared up top.

I reached outside, scooped snow, melted it on our little white-gas stove, and made several cups of beef bouillon, which we both drank, and then used more snowmelt to reconstitute a freeze-dried turkey Stroganoff, of which the porter could not handle even a fork-ful. So I ate my share and then, to keep it from wasting, I ate the porter's, as well.

That night, my sleep was nearly nonexistent. I had put the porter on oxygen, but used none myself, wanting to conserve that for the trip down the mountain. So I would drift, but just as I was about to fall into a resting sleep, the lack of oxygen would bring me back awake, gasping. At about three in the morning, I was still awake when the porter began to moan in his slumber, so I administered another dose of morphine, and a few minutes later he was quiet again.

At five in the morning, I brewed tea, but the porter could drink only a little of it, a fact that greatly concerned me, because the Baltis, like all Pakistanis, are great tea drinkers. He looked pale, the sclera of his eyes gone yellow, and I began to suspect that the icefall had done more than break his leg. But I had already rendered to him every bit of medical care for which I had been trained. He did not need first aid. He needed a hospital, and to get him to a hospital, he needed a helicopter, and to use a helicopter, he needed to be gotten down the mountain, because our camp was thousands and thousands of feet higher than any helicopter in the world could fly.

Base Camp had scheduled a radio call for six, so I heated the radio batteries in a billy on the stove, made the call, and learned that no word had been heard from the rescue party that morning. Every climber in that team had carried a radio, so communications failure could all but certainly be ruled out. That left only one possibility.

The sky was blue where I was camped, but just a few hundred feet below me, the fluffy tops of clouds rolled like a sluggish sea. There had been fresh snow during the night, and the lower part of the mountain was especially prone to avalanche.

My porter was unconscious by this time, and had long since ceased to moan. By ten in the morning, his pulse was barely detectable. I used a little oxygen to get a couple of hours of sleep, and when next I checked him, at noon, there was no pulse at all, and a hand mirror held to his lips and nose stayed clean and shiny.

I remember arranging his sleeping-bagged body so it was as straight as possible, thinking that, when—if—we came back to retrieve it, we would want to wrap it in a nylon tarp and lower it ahead of us, like a sled, and I knew that he would freeze solid in a matter of hours. I started the stove, melted snow, and forced myself to drink some bouillon and eat a whole package of stew. As I did that, I reflected on the fact that, because I had called for rescue, it was six people who were now missing and almost certainly dead. Six people, rather than two. Pulling the sleeping bag hood snugly over the dead porter's face, I tidied the tent, put on my boots and my crampons and my pack and my mitts, zipped the weather fly shut behind me, and started down the mountain.

Practically the whole of my journey was in cloud. I'd slung the oxygen cylinder on my chest, where I could get to the valve more easily, and only used it on the difficult bits. When I rested, which was often, I flexed my toes and fingers constantly, encouraging blood flow, mindful of the dangers of frostbite. In long sections of the route, the rope anchors had come free, but I refixed them and continued. For a stretch of nearly a hundred yards, the fixed rope was gone entirely, carried away by avalanche. Amazingly, I found the next section below, and continued.

We had established three lower camps on the mountain, and of the two that remained, none were occupied, all personnel having been summoned to Base at the first announcement of incoming weather. Tempting as it was to stay at one of these snug little tents, I did not, because there was continuous wind now, a low howl that flung stinging snow horizontally at blurring speeds. I did stop at each one to change oxygen cylinders, though.

When I got to Camp Two, the sun had long since set, the twilight fading. I went inside the tent, brewed tea, cooked and ate some sort of pasta dish that I only vaguely remember, set the camp back in order, and continued my downward journey in the night. Of that leg of the journey, I remember only six things: darkness, snow, wind, cold, pain—and being thankful for the pain, because it meant that I still had blood moving to my limbs.

At five the next morning, I came to the base of the fixed rope. I knew that this was within five hundred meters of the Base Camp, but everything around me was blackness; when I switched on my headlamp, all I could see was a fuzzy, gray ball of whizzing snow. Then, over the howl of the wind, I could hear voices—the voices of our Baltis, trudging to the kitchen tent to begin breakfast.

I trotted toward the voices, lost them, stopped, regained them, and trotted that way again. Doing this six times, I at length almost collided with a man carrying two jugs of water. He cried out, people surrounded us, and I was carried to the medical tent, where I promptly passed out.

Our expedition remained stranded at Base Camp for better than the next two months, kept there first by the storm, which socked us in for three straight weeks, and then by the flooded rivers on our retreat route, which prevented the camel teams from coming in to fetch our gear, and kept us from walking out.

It was August, then, by the time we got to the first village with a telephone. A week later we were in Islamabad, where a seemingly endless stream of government officials waited to take our statements, and conduct tedious and repetitive interviews through barely understandable interpreters. Part of this was to be expected; of the six men killed on the mountain, three had been Pakistani nationals.

But when the interviews began to repeat themselves, we began to make inquiries, and discovered that certain village headmen from the northern part of the country—people who had nothing to do with our Baltis—were claiming damages because of the losses. So we cabled our sponsors, got the three thousand dollars necessary to silence our blackmailers, and arranged for flights to take us home.

Through all of this, I had done considerable soul-searching. Six men had died, and I had come off of the mountain thirty pounds lighter, but with not a scratch on me, not so much as a single square centimeter of frostbite. It hardly seemed right.

I wanted nothing more to do with ice axes and crampons. But I also knew what I did want.

An adage that older climbers share with newer ones (but oftentimes forget when it comes to themselves) is that one should think twice before climbing anything that one cannot down-climb. Failing to do so may lead to a commitment for which one had never bargained.

Rock Climbing Holds and Basics

THIRTY-FIVE

From the American embassy in Islamabad's Diplomatic Enclave, I placed a call to Preacher and asked him if he could recommend, and smooth a way into, a Bible college that could prepare me to be a pastor. I spoke almost nonstop about all that I had been thinking about on the mountain, about how my selfishness had died with the men I left up there, about my transcripts from WVU—which were exemplary, as all I had done there was play football and study. I assured him of my willingness to make up any classes expected of undergraduate students in theology.

Preacher listened to all of this, and then he was silent, silent for so long that I called, "Hello?"—thinking that the line had gone dead.

"I'm still here," he told me. "And yes, sure. I can do all of that, Patrick. Happy to do it. I know people at several schools where you could start in the fall; you'd have your choice. But, Patrick, there's something you need to know . . . something about Rachel."

Visions of car accidents, of house fires, of plane crashes, of disasters of every sort and magnitude raced through my mind.

"Is she all right?" I asked him.

"She's fine," he assured me. "But, Patrick . . . well, she met someone. They were married last month."

It is a mistake to believe, even for an instant, that any climb concludes at the summit. It does not; there is still the descent. To think of the summit as an ending point is to bring things to a conclusion when one is really only halfway through.

Rock Climbing Holds and Basics

THIRTY-SIX

Looking back, I suppose it was denial that took me to Lynchburg, to Liberty University. Somewhere, somehow, I think I believed that, if I stayed the course and did the right thing, it would all come out okay and Rachel would come back to me.

Of course, I knew that could not be. If Rachel had entered into a covenant to be someone else's forever, then to someone else she would forever belong. She did not make promises blithely and she never, ever broke them. Realizing this, I was, for a month, a very angry undergraduate, challenging my professors' assertions, and throwing myself into research that could refute them. My passion was mistaken for intelligence, and certain of the faculty began to notice me, and to offer me extra studies, extra credit, extra attention.

My anger was, however, too hot a flame to burn for very long. And I did not really know who it was that I was angry *with*, anyhow.

It could not be with Rachel; I had told her not to wait. It could not be with her new husband, for how could I blame any man for falling in love with her? The question in my mind, really, was how any man could meet Rachel and *not* fall in love with her.

And I could not be angry with God, because all God had done was stand aside and let me exercise my will—allow me to follow my own vanity.

Still, at night, as I got into my bed and realized that somewhere, Rachel was slipping into bed with some other man—Rachel, with whom I had shared only that single, haunting kiss—I seethed. That was when I realized I was angry with myself, furious over what I had let go. And self-anger cannot sustain itself. It ends in suicide or it goes away. But I was too much of a survivor to even entertain the idea of suicide.

Having taken the matter into my own hands and thoroughly screwed it up, I took the broken pieces and put them into God's hands. I prayed as the apostle Paul had admonished the church at Thessalonica to pray—without ceasing. I was virtually a resident in the campus chapel.

Then, one morning, I found myself praying that Rachel's husband would die, and that woke me up. Here Rachel had never, ever, wished me anything but well, and I was selfishly praying for tragedy to enter into her life. I ceased my prayers. I ceased my hopes. I studied. I ate—not much. I slept—a lot.

When, by mid-December, I had not called home or made arrangements to go back to West Virginia for Christmas, my father called, and I told him that I would not be coming home. To do that, to go to Christmas Eve services at Weeping Oak Community Church's new assembly hall, and risk seeing Rachel on the arm of her new husband? That was more than I could contemplate, and more than I could bear.

Two days later, then, my father was knocking at the door of my dorm room.

"Grab a quick shower," he'd told me. "The van's waiting downstairs."

"Van? Dad, I can't go anywhere. I'm not packed."

"You're packed. I brought you a bag of things from home. Looks as if you're back to your regular weight." I was, and then some. "They'll fit."

I looked at him, rubbed my stubbly chin.

"Dad . . . I don't want to go climbing. I can't."

"We're not going climbing. Now get showered and get dressed. We've got to get to Richmond. Our plane leaves in six hours."

"Richmond? Plane? What do you have in mind?"

He tapped his watch. "Let's go, pilgrim. We're burning daylight."

I did what he said, and we were all the way to the airport, checking our things at the ticket counter, before I realized that my father was taking me to Hawaii. Or actually he was taking me to Atlanta, and then Los Angeles for an overnight stay, and then Honolulu—just long enough for a day-trip around Oahu—followed by an island-hopper to Kauai.

Kauai is home to the cliff-guarded Na Pali Coast, and Waimea Canyon, fully 3,000 feet deep, but most of the rock there is heavily vegetated, lush with tropical foliage. That which is exposed is mostly deteriorated lava stone that crumbles at a touch. So climbing was, even if I'd had a change of heart, quite happily out of the question.

I ran instead, running along the beach at Poipu, alternately sprinting and jogging the tide line, and then finishing the run with a plunge into the amazingly blue waters of Kewaloa Bay. I would swim out into the current until my arms ached for a reprieve and only then would I turn over and lazily backstroke in to shore, letting the Pacific push me home.

I did this every morning, and after a week, I was coming out of my funk, the endorphins from the exercise lifting me out of my depression as surely as any drug—better than any drug ever could have. I began taking lazy kayak trips down the Hanalei River with my father and looking at fog-dotted green cliffs and silver ribbons of waterfalls that appeared for all the world to be a Japanese painting brought magically to life.

It was at the end of one of those long swims, just after I had tousled my hair semidry and pulled on my shirt, as I was beginning the walk back to the hotel, that I crossed paths with a young woman dressed in a gauze skirt and a swimsuit top, her dark hair pulled back off her neck. She was reading a paperback book as she walked and she looked up from it as I passed and we said hello to each other.

Something pulled at me.

She was very pretty. Actually, she was beyond pretty; she was downright beautiful, and the modesty of the skirt did nothing to hide the firm, lithe lines of her body.

But it wasn't her beauty that stopped me in my tracks. There was something haunting about her. Haunting and—familiar.

I turned around to get another look and discovered that she, too, had turned and was looking at me. Her book was in her hand, at her side. I was getting all of her attention.

Finally, after a second's awkward pause, she said, "Liberty. Right?"

I nodded, found my voice and said, "Right."

She nodded, walked back and extended her hand. "Sarah Alexander, Psychology."

"Patrick Nolan, Theology."

We shook hands, and even though she was not going my way, I walked her back to her hotel.

You know where this is going now. We had breakfast together that first day, and then lunch. By the next day, Sarah and her parents had accepted an invitation from my father and me to come dine with us at our hotel. They reciprocated with an invitation for dinner at theirs the following night. My father suddenly developed this penchant for reading novels on the beach, leaving me ample time to see the island with Sarah. Our families spent Christmas Eve together, exchanging Hawaiian gifts, and the next morning we all went to a Christmas sunrise service on the beach, even my father, who came along willingly, although he did not sing any of the hymns. He just stood there and smiled.

After the holiday break, Sarah and I returned to school and discovered that ours was not merely an island infatuation. Our love warmed, and then simmered. By Easter, it was well along toward a bubbling roll and we became engaged at brunch, after church.

The wedding was in June, in the chapel at Liberty, a logistical nightmare for poor Mrs. Alexander, and a date that elicited gentle questions from all three of our parents—we both had, after all, a year left of school. But *passion* had become a poor word for what we were feeling for each other, and we could not—would not—wait. So I married the second girl I had ever kissed, and a year later, in July, one month after we had received our respective degrees, Sarah gave birth to our daughter, and my father melted in tears when we told him that we had decided to name her "Laurie."

Was it happily ever after? Of course it was not. It was life, and life is, at best, a serpentine chain of emotions. But from what I have gathered, ours is better than most. My father made a big to-do out of setting up a trust to pay me the maximum possible tax-free annuity. "For your share of the climbing shop," he told me, which was silly, as I was his only heir, and he was paying me, in effect, for something that was destined to come back to me anyhow, if life followed the natural order of things.

But he insisted it was something that his tax attorney had advised him to do, so between that, and my pastoring income, and what Sarah brought in from the counseling service that she operated from her office in the rectory, we were comfortable, and never had any of the money problems that seem to prove the wedge in most marriages.

Laurie was followed after a year by little Michael, and we bought better furniture, and went to Disney World, and did all the things that families do, and loved one another very much—*love* one another very much—all four of us.

But sometimes, when I am alone in my study, or early in the morning, when I get up to shave and Sarah is still warm and asleep in our bed, my mind wanders back to Rachel, and to what might have been, if I had been as selfless as she . . . if I had chosen two other words in that Christmas Eve conversation. Words like, "I'm sorry."

Or, "Forgive me."

Or even, "Marry me."

And when I think of Rachel, or rather of Rachel-long-ago, I remember that faint taste of peppermint when she kissed me, of the scent of her hair as it closed around our faces, of the touch of her hands to the small of my back. And I wonder if it is a sin to think of things like that: a sin, or human nature, or—as so very many things are—both. And I ask for forgiveness, because I believe it probably is, and I place that memory under the blood of my Savior, and I go to find my Sarah and I kiss her.

And life?

Life goes on.

*A kernmantle rope can be trimmed of damage at its end, but should be retired as soon
as possible after sustaining a significant fall or suffering damage to its center. It is a
false economy to expect more from the rope than its due.*
Rock Climbing Holds and Basics

THIRTY-SEVEN

On October 22, 1987, the Gendarme broke away from the Gunsight Notch ridge of Seneca Rocks and tumbled down the West Face and its scree field—the side facing Judd Horton's general store and the climbing shop—taking down enough timber to construct a large house before coming to rest well above the lower cliffs. Its sling-festooned rappel ring was pointed at an angle downhill, aimed almost exactly at the summit crack of Thunderbolt and Lightfoot.

No climber was on the Gendarme at the time, and no one knows exactly why it fell. Perhaps a crucial pebble had eroded a critical final millionth of a millimeter by the insistent pressure of wind funneling through the gap. Perhaps one of the Rocks' resident pigeons had landed in just the right place as that critical erosion happened.

Or perhaps it was just time for it to fall.

The exact time of the collapse—three minutes shy of 3:30 in the afternoon—*is* known, because Tony Barnes, a local guide and the last person to summit the pinnacle just a few days earlier, was with a client on Conn's East and heard it when it happened. He described it as sounding "like a prolonged plane crash." Finding the fallen pinnacle later had proven easy. All he'd had to do was follow the trail of downed trees.

I heard this all in the past tense. I was no longer living in West Virginia. And I was not there to tell my father, "I told you so," because my father was no longer living there, either.

Almost two years earlier, in November of 1985, the remnants of an East Coast hurricane dumped rain on West Virginia in such quantities as to put the North Fork over its banks in a hundred-year flood. That inundation not only took out the swing bridge leading

up to the Rocks—an occurrence that had been repeated with frus-
trating regularity over the years—it swept away a newly constructed
National Forest Service visitors' center (the construction of which
had been opposed by my father on the grounds that it would
encourage the incompetent to venture onto the Rocks), scoured
away all traces of a Forest Service campground, and uprooted and
washed away both Judd's picnic pavilion and the grandiose scrap-
wood entrance to his campground. It had also seriously undermined
the foundations of both the climbing shop and Judd's general store.

The rising waters had made the national news, and I'd spoken
with my father by phone from the rectory at the small Michigan
church I'd just joined as pastor—now the much larger church that I
still pastor today. He'd told me that, because so many area residents
lived in homes accessible to the main highways only by private spans
and swing bridges across up-hollow creeks and even the North Fork
itself, the state had called for evacuation to school and college gym-
nasiums and the National Guard armory in Elkins.

We'd both known well ahead of time that this would not work.
Mountain people are an independent folk, wary of the government
and suspicious of authority, and many of them, including several
well up in years, would stay put in homes that would soon be cut
off by floodwaters and threatened by rockslide. Neither the weather
nor the terrain was going to be conducive to the use of helicopters,
so rescue teams were already being formed among local police, fire-
fighters, rangers and volunteers, and my father was, of course, one
of the first people who had been called.

My church had provided me with a four-wheel-drive Ford
Bronco, the better to reach our rural shut-ins in the event of snow-
storms, and I had offered to make the drive down and help, but my
father had vetoed the idea.

"Sport, I'm not even sure you'd be able to make it in," he'd told
me. "Some of Route 122 is under water. They're already closing sections of Route 33 because of the rockslide danger, and we're expecting at least some of the road to wash out. Besides, that Bronco of

yours gets what—eleven, maybe twelve miles to the gallon? It'll cost you a fortune to drive all the way here, with gas prices what they are. I'll need you after Thanksgiving, to help me clean out and shore up the shop. But there's no use in making two trips down, one right after the other. Just stay where you are, and I'll call you when it's over."

It had crossed my mind to talk to him then about God, about heaven, about getting things right—to try again with him the conversation that had gone nowhere so very many times before. But that was all the thought did: cross my mind. It never made it to my lips because, while my father had never objected to my vocation, he had objected strenuously and repeatedly to being its object, and such conversations had invariably been a source of strain between us for days afterward. So I'd let it go, and told him we'd talk again soon.

Of course, we never did.

Here's what I know: Rachel's brother, Jimmy, was in Elkins along with several of the people from the church, helping care for the evacuees. He'd just gotten back to the gymnasium at Davis Elkins College with a vanload of bottled water. It was getting late, almost nine at night, and the Weeping Oak ladies were cleaning up after having served hot chocolate and cookies to the more than four hundred people there. The support people were down to a few. Most of the folks seeking shelter were bedding down for the night on cots on the floor of the gym.

The church ladies told Jimmy that his father and mine had left the gym just minutes before. Preacher Ransom had been there with his church, my father had come in with one of the rescue teams, and Preacher had convinced him to stick around for a late dinner: chili—my father had always been a sucker for a good homemade chili.

That had been around six-thirty, maybe seven o'clock, and my father had lingered, after the chili and after the cookies, passing on the hot chocolate, and then accepting a mug of coffee when Mrs. Ransom put on a pot before she left for the night. Preacher and my father had been speaking—speaking in earnest, the ladies of the church said, with lots of head nodding and lots of gestures over the cafeteria table between them.

"I cain't say for surely, but it looked to me powerfully like Preacher was witnessing to your daddy" was the way one of the women had explained it to me later.

That's when the call had come, the call on the big, military walkie-talkie that the Forest Service had issued to my father for the duration of the evacuation. A woman at the Franklin evacuation center had thought her elderly mother had been picked up by her brother, and her brother—who'd sought shelter at the Petersburg ranger station, had been under the impression that his mother was with his sister.

The old lady's house was in a remote hollow, up a two-track and across a feeder stream running into the North Fork, the house accessed by a wooden bridge that had no doubt disintegrated in the first twenty-four hours of the flood. The hillsides were steep there; some slides had already been reported.

The crew my father had been with had already left to go home. It was raining, it was dark, and the consensus had been that they had accomplished all they could until morning. But the woman's daughter was frantic, and my father had agreed to go have a look. Preacher Ransom had told him he'd go with him, so the two of them had left, still talking as they walked out into the rain and the wind and the night.

The old lady was not missing. She had gotten out with a neighbor from up-hollow; that much was learned the next morning. She turned up on the roster among those waiting out the storm at the high school down in Davis.

For the rest we have only the evidence. My father's truck, a Toyota Land Cruiser that he had picked up after the VW had worn out its third engine, was found the next morning. It was parked on the side of the road and across the stream from the old lady's cabin. The stream had climbed its steep banks and claimed a third of the road as well as the bridge to the cabin, and the hatch was up on the Land

Cruiser. One of my father's ropes, still coiled and tightly wrapped, was lying on the ground behind it.

It would be a week before they found Preacher's body, seven miles downstream and snagged on a jam of logs, brush and pieces of what were once houses. For nearly a month after that, the state worked the North Fork and its tributaries, searching all the way down to the Potomac River proper, skidding logs out of streams and busting up logjams with bulldozers, carefully searching the under-cuts of the banks. The number of people still missing was consider-able, so they kept looking long after the news of the flood had left the headlines. But they never did find dozens of the lost, and they never found my father.

That's the hardest part: the uncertainty. Sometimes, late at night, lying awake in my bed with Sarah sleeping silently beside me, I think of him being borne down the river on those floodwaters, the roar and the dirty foam of the North Fork giving way to the swollen Potomac. I think of him drifting in the night down, downstream, past the early morning lights of Washington, and then out into Chesapeake Bay, being pulled by the outgoing tide into the great Atlantic proper. I think of him being swept up into the great, glacial circle of the broad Gulf Stream, being pulled in that slow, eternal journey, under stars so bright they appear to be jagged points of ice, under skies where the horizon is always a flat and featureless blue.

Adrift.

Apart.

Alone.

And I wonder what he was talking about with Preacher Ransom on that last night: what views were exchanged, what points were conceded, what decisions, possibly, were made.

Because I believe what Preacher told me long ago in the cold, swift waters of Seneca Creek. I believe that when I close my eyes on this life and open them in the next, the first face I see will be that of my Savior, and the second will be that of my mother. But I wonder—and this is the thing that keeps me awake in the small, dark hours—I wonder if, after that second face, I will turn and see, perhaps, a third.

On that, I haven't a shred of certainty.

But I have hope. And on those long nights, when finally I rest and yield to slumber, it is always because I have remembered another time—the evening of the very last day that I was alone with the first girl I loved. And I remember and I cling to the other thing that her father told me . . .

That sometimes, hope is all we have.

And sometimes, hope is enough.

AFTERWORD

Thank you for reading this book. Time is a precious commodity, and I am humbled and thrilled that you chose to spend such a considerable quantity of it with this, my work. I hope the finished project was worthy of your effort.

This novel began when I received a Bicentennial quarter in my change eight years ago—a quarter whose reverse side bore the image of the Revolutionary War drummer, exactly like the quarter with which Patrick pays his campground fee in Chapter Eight. I wrote the first draft off and on over the next several years without a publishing contract for the project, riding simply on the faith that it would find a home once it was completed. That it did so is due to the grace of God . . . and also to Dave Long and the other editors at Bethany House, and to Don Pape, Lee Hough, and the rest of the good people at Alive! Communications. Some have entertained angels unawares, and some of those angels have publishing connections.

Several elements of this novel are grounded in fact. Seneca Rocks is an actual rock formation in West Virginia, and the Gendarme was a feature of that formation—a feature that toppled off the rock at the date noted and in the manner described in the final chapter. The village at the base of the rocks was once known as "Mouth of Seneca," although it has since been changed to the more logical "Seneca Rocks" (a decision that probably bears the fingerprints of a marketing committee). There actually was a great flood that struck the valley of the North Fork in 1985, causing considerable loss of both life and property. And heaven, of course, is real, as is God and the fact that his Son remains heaven's sole key.

As for the rest of this, I made most of it up. For that I particularly owe a word of apology to John Markwell, whose climbing shop—the Gendarme—was already standing at Seneca in 1976, on the spot in which I fictitiously placed The First Ascent. Rather than banish him entirely from the world of this novel, I gave John a cameo-appearance-once-removed in Chapter Two, and trust he will not hold any of this against me—my meddling with the facts in this fashion.

Thanks once again for reading, and if this work has touched you—or rubbed against you—I would love it if you dropped me a line. It helps to dispel the notion that I am doing nothing here but mumbling to myself in the dark.

Tom Morrisey

Orlando, 2007

www.tommorrisey.com

TOM MORRISEY, the author of four previous novels and numerous short stories, is a world-renowned adventure-travel writer whose work has appeared in *Outside, Sport Diver* (where he serves as Executive Editor), and other leading magazines. He holds an MA in English Language and Literature from the University of Toledo and an MFA in Creative Writing from Bowling Green State University. He lives in Orlando, Florida.

More Superb Storytelling From Tom Morrisey

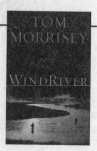

A backcountry fly-fishing trip turns into a journey to the past when Soren Anderton confesses to a deadly crime committed decades back. Before Ty Sawyer, his fellow traveler, can believe the ugly truth, nature wreaks her revenge. Trapped in a frantic race to safety, each man must own up to his own past or risk being consumed.
Wind River by Tom Morrisey

More Exciting Fiction From Master Storytellers

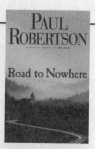

When a controversial road project tears a peaceful town in two, everyone starts looking to their own interests. But things take a deadly turn when somebody is willing to commit murder to make sure things go his way.
Road to Nowhere by Paul Robertson

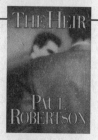

When given the throne to his father's corrupt business empire, Jason Boyer only wants to walk away—he saw how it ruined his father. Yet despite his efforts, the power intoxicates him, and he soon finds himself battling for his life…and his soul.
The Heir by Paul Robertson

Her brother's mysterious death brings Vera Gamble to the tiny island town of Winter Haven, Maine. Determined to find the truth, her search reveals other secrets haunting the island. Will her desperate questions find answers, or will Winter Haven claim yet one more dark legend?
Winter Haven by Athol Dickson